THE
GRANDEST
GARDEN

A NOVEL

THE GRANDEST GARDEN

GINA L. CARROLL

SPARKPRESS

Published by SparkPress, a BookSparks imprint,
A division of SparkPoint Studio, LLC
Phoenix, Arizona, USA, 85007
www.gosparkpress.com

Published 2024
Printed in the United States of America

Print ISBN: 978-1-68463-236-7
E-ISBN: 978-1-68463-237-4
Library of Congress Control Number: 2023919031

Interior design and typeset by Katherine Lloyd, The DESK

For Nanny, Granny, and Mama T

AN ANCIENT GIRL

In the garden, I am ancient. When my feet return to soil, every fiber of my being knows I am home. I am a piece of the inter-woven yarn of forever. I am the river that flows backward and forward, downstream and up, all the way back to Eve.

I know things.

In the garden, I am ancient. Sewn into my soul is what my grandmothers know and their grandmothers and theirs. This antiquity is me, through and through. But also, them and me, my own and also, never my own.

And I know things.

The garden is the one place where I stand firm, my legs solid like tree trunks, because in my grandmothers' gardens, I was root and sprout, stem and blossom.

And I know some things.

In the garden, I am ancient. And it is here that I am whole.

And every inch of me,

every millimeter of my flesh and bone,

my entire soul,

belongs.

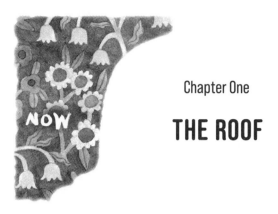

Chapter One

THE ROOF

NEW YEAR'S EVE

The door to the roof is battered, a heavy metal relic, rusted. The top and bottom corners curl inward like calla lily folds, preventing the door from closing properly. Bella gives the door a gentle push. It opens easily. The frigid night air assaults her face and every other tiny break in her cold weather armor. She had changed the clock face on her Fitbit yesterday to show the time, date, and temperature, her grand gesture to signal her transition from a ne'er-concerned-about-the-weather Californian to an always-prepared New Yorker. Tonight, the clock face reads zero degrees. *Zero degrees.* She has never been out in zero degrees. She knows it's much too cold for Eddi, her mother, and her to be outdoors, but it's New Year's Eve, and Eddi has arrived from Los Angeles just this morning to help Bella move in and transform her tiny new bedroom into a cozy home in the sixth-floor walk-up she will share with a stranger.

New York decided to welcome them with an unexpected cold snap, so they are wearing most of the clothes Bella packed just to spend a moment on the roof in celebration of the New Year. They thought their layers of T-shirts, hoodies, leggings, and jeans would do the job a proper winter coat might, since neither of them have one. But they are wrong. It's five minutes until midnight when they climb the one flight of stairs up from the apartment and face this pathetic door. Bella shudders as she walks over the threshold, thoroughly cold within seconds. She decides that this New Year's celebration is going to have to be quick.

"I don't understand why we couldn't just stay indoors and have a civilized glass of champagne," Eddi protests.

"Because the view from the roof is spectacular," Bella says. "You can see the Empire State Building. And because this is not *just any* New Year, Mom. We have so much to celebrate."

"You are so right, sweetie."

Eddi takes one look at the door and scoffs.

"How in the world do they keep this building warm with the door open like this? Can it even close?" she asks.

Bella moves toward the front of the building, turning to coax her mother with a wave. Her Converse All Stars slide along the icy tar until they hit upon a gritty patch. Bella regains her balance. Her mother is still standing in the doorway.

"C'mon, Mom," she urges, "just be careful."

A deafening boom sounds off nearby. Soon they are surrounded—crackles, pops, and explosions from every direction. Bella hurries over to the edge of the building to locate the source of that last big boom. On the street side, the building face extends up to her chest to create a wall that keeps her from falling over the edge. On her tiptoes, she can look down and see the front door and stoop of the tiny sushi restaurant on the first floor of her building, where she took her mother for her first dinner in the city. It only holds about fifteen people, but tonight it is over capacity with New Year's Eve partiers. She looks across at the rooftop on the other side of the street and sees the outline of a man lighting a small firework cannon. Another *boom* sounds off. Eddi, still in the doorway, ducks down and covers her head. But then the

4

sky above them is alight with a shower of flaming red, green, and white sparkles that shimmer briefly and then, like falling stars, are gone. They both laugh, delighted. This promise of coming wonders seems to convince Eddi to venture past the threshold.

"You know, we really aren't supposed to be on this roof," Eddi says. Her face is turned up and her eyes reflect another shower of white sparkles. "Did you or your dad read the lease? I read the entire agreement, every word, and it explicitly says that if you are caught on the roof, your landlord can fine you twenty-four hundred dollars! Imagine your dad's reaction when that surprise shows up on your next rent bill!" Bella wonders how her mother got a copy of the lease agreement, but she doesn't ask. She stays out of her parents' dealings.

"Don't worry," Bella says, "since my apartment is the closest to the roof, the super said we can come out here any time we want. If he says it's okay, I'm sure it is! And I have big plans for this space. It's going to be amazing!" Bella spreads her arms out like a game show host, as if she were showcasing the garden wonderland she envisions and not the current dirty, desolate landscape of rusted metal, moldy brick, and ice-covered tar.

Eddi has moved out toward the center of the roof now, releasing the door at the last possible moment. She is staring at the top of the Empire State Building.

"Look. It's all lit up. Christmas colors! Beautiful," she says.

"Come on, Mom." Bella coaxes her mother to meet her at the edge. "Let's take a selfie in front of the skyline." Bella looks down at her phone and sees that the battery is at five percent. "Quickly, Mama, before my phone dies. I can't believe my battery is so low!"

Eddi scurries over to Bella and grabs her daughter's arms to steady herself. "This freezing weather is probably zapping your battery," she says.

They turn their backs to the Empire State Building, positioning themselves for the photo. A gust of frigid wind catches the free ends of Eddi's scarf, lifting it over her shoulder, and Bella catches it before it is airborne. Bella is helping Eddi rewrap the scarf when they hear the door slam shut behind them. For the first time since Bella's arrival two days ago, the roof door is completely closed.

"Oh, shit. It actually closed." Eddi whispers, "Please, God. Don't let it be locked."

"It can't lock, Mom. There is no doorknob. Now, smile!" Bella says and snaps a series of selfies.

Bella slip-slides her way across the ice to beat her mother to the door and pulls. When the door doesn't budge, she sticks her fingers in the doorknob hole and pulls again.

"Don't play around, Bella," her mother says.

"I am not playing around, Mom. The door is stuck. I don't know how, but it is."

"Okay, okay. Not to worry. Call your roommate."

"Camille is all the way downtown," Bella says, "too far away. And I don't think we have that kind of time."

Bella has barely laid eyes on her new roommate, a senior engineering student at NYU. She is the daughter of Bella's father's best customer, another father who resents paying his daughter's New York rent. Yesterday, she met Camille for the first time. Bella came straight from the airport and when she arrived, Camille let her in, gave her keys, and then left with her boyfriend, Charlie, a Columbia University student. On the way out, he'd said: "We tend to hang out on my side of town. You won't see much of Camille. But if you haven't been to Columbia, we'd be happy to show you around." Camille did not endorse or reject her boyfriend's offer. She simply said, "Everything here is basic, easy to figure out." Camille was not rude or dismissive, but she was not friendly either. It was clear to Bella that she does not want a roommate and she is not going to be much of one. So even if Bella reached her by phone right now, she is not sure Camille would come.

She doesn't want her mother to panic, but at zero degrees Bella doesn't think it takes long to freeze to death, at least it doesn't feel like it takes long at all. She looks down at her watch. Now, it says negative one degree.

"Call the restaurant downstairs," Eddi says. "Ask them to send someone up."

Bella takes her phone out of her pocket and finds the number she used earlier to make a reservation. Just as she presses the button to call, her phone dies.

"Mom, my phone is dead. Give me yours!"

"I didn't bring it," Eddi says. She is alternating between pounding on the roof door and peering through the doorknob hole.

Bella takes a deep breath to quell her own panic. The freezing air hurts her lungs and makes her cough. She already can't feel her face, and her feet are rock-hard hammers. She runs back to the edge of the roof and looks down again at the sushi restaurant. People are spilling out of its front door to see the fireworks. Bella sees the waitress who served them last night bring out a small boom box and set it down on the stoop. She turns up the volume so that the speakers are blasting techno music. Bella yells down, trying to break through the music and their drunken outbursts, but the explosions and whistles drown her out. Eddi makes her way over to the ledge of the building where Bella is standing. Eddi is not even wearing socks, just soft black leather flats, jeans, a cotton turtleneck shirt under a sweater, and a wool scarf that is covering the bottom half of her face. She comes up next to Bella, pulls the scarf down under her chin as she peers over the edge.

"Help!" Eddi yells.

"They can't hear us, Mom," Bella says.

"But they are right there!" Eddi says about the sushi crowd six floors down.

"*Help!*" she screams louder. "*Please*, help us."

Eddi continues like this, her yells heightening into full screams. Bella looks at her Fitbit. They have been on the roof for twenty minutes. Explosions are firing off nonstop in every direction—it appears to be a convergence of several celebrations across the city. The sky is bright with color and light. Everywhere they look, missiles and flames are shooting heavenward, exploding out like dandelion stars and then raining down in a slow descent. One after another, then two and three at a time, and then an endless cycle, *pop, pop, popping* to a wondrous climax. Eddi and Bella stop in their tracks and watch in silence for what feels like a long time, because it is the most spectacular sky they have ever seen, and because there is nothing else they can do. They are frozen in place and their bodies numb. A slow ache is rising from Bella's ankles toward her creaky knees. Her hands hang heavy from her dead arms. Finally, the noise begins to die down. Bella's Fitbit says they've been on the roof for nearly an hour.

The crowd starts to go back into the restaurant. The waitress has taken the music indoors. Eddi sees this, and as her last desperate effort, in one swift movement she pulls off her wool scarf, gathers it into a ball, and throws it down toward the group. "Hey, up here!" Now, her screams are raspy barks. The air catches the scarf. It unfolds fully and begins to float in languid, undulating waves, like a magic carpet. Finally, it lands on the sidewalk just left of the sushi restaurant steps, but the last person in the crowd, a young woman, has already turned toward the entrance. She ascends the stairs and disappears into the restaurant, closing the door behind her. She never sees the scarf.

"Oh my God," Eddi wails. She has begun to rub her hands with a rolling motion. Bella sees that Eddi's hands have turned a bright red with gray blotches, and this brings her attention to her own hands. Her fingers feel like sausages, the tips throbbing with a pain that cannot be assuaged with movement.

"We are going to die here and it's all my fault," Eddi says.

"How is this your fault, Mom?"

"I had a feeling, didn't I? I didn't want to come up here, did I?" she says.

"So, it's my fault. That's what you are really saying," Bella says.

"No, no, baby. It's no one's fault. I just, I just . . . I just should have brought my phone and made us bundle up better. I should have. . . ." Eddi trails off. Her shoulders are hunched, and her hand motions are picking up speed. She is rubbing them together in a circular motion, faster and faster. Her eyes are wide owl circles, her face ashen.

Bella is sorry she lashed out. She blames her throbbing hands and her helplessness. She wants to hug her mother to calm her, but Eddi is too agitated to be contained, and Bella thinks her mother's movements might be keeping her warm.

Bella follows Eddi back to the door and they both pound on it despite the excruciating pain this exacts on their arms and hands. They yell through the doorknob hole hoping maybe someone has made their way home. Only silence. Bella runs to the back wall opposite the street and looks over the edge.

"There's a fire escape one floor down. I can shimmy over the wall and jump down," Bella says, calculating how far she would have to hang from the ledge to drop to the small metal cage protruding from the sixth floor.

Eddi comes over and looks. "No way, Bella! It's too far and the landing is too narrow. If you miss it, you will die," she says. "Look at the ledge. It's covered with ice. No way, baby."

Eddi slinks down against the wall to a squatting position and wraps her arms around her legs. She starts to rock. Bella stoops down beside her.

"We should get up and keep moving, Mom."

Now Eddi is still. She is no longer rocking or fidgeting or rolling her hands. She's parked both hands between her thighs. She is staring forward. The only movement now is the steam clouds coming from her nose. Bella is so worried about her mother that she forgets about her own frozen body, until she reaches down to the gritty floor to sit, and her wrists don't seem capable of supporting her weight. Like her knees and elbows, they are frozen hinges.

Eddi's head is at an odd angle, tilting to one side. She is staring straight forward and doesn't seem to blink. Her mouth hangs in a frown. Her jaw is slack.

Bella knows that her mother is gone.

Bella knows because this is what her mother does. She checks out. She envies this ability. Bella wants to leave her frozen, aching body, too, but she does not have this skill.

"What about me, Mom? What about me?" Bella says in a whisper. Does her mother ever think about her when she leaves?

"Mom?" Bella says in a whisper. Bella needs her to come back and help her figure this out. She tries to remember what she is supposed to do. How did her father deal with her mother when their family was still together? Didn't he have a trigger word? What would it have been? It's been too long; Bella can't remember. Fitbit says another fifteen minutes has passed. It's minus ten degrees.

"Mother," she says louder in her full adult voice, dropping the question from her tone.

"Mommy?" Bella pleads. The adult is gone, and the question is back.

Eddi does not answer, so Bella waits, she and Fitbit counting the minutes.

Then Eddi takes in a long breath. She coughs out the frigid air and wipes her nose with her forearm.

"I am so sorry you got stuck with me as your mother," Eddi says, her voice low, a raspy whisper.

"Mom, don't say that. I had a great childhood," Bella says aloud, but she is thinking, *Oh, shit, here we go.*

"I know you did, sweetie. *I know* you did. That's just it. I was just a bystander. Mothers are supposed to *give* their children wonderful childhoods. That is their job. But all I could manage to do was to stay out of the way and allow your childhood to happen." Eddi's chin is shivering now, and her shoulders are shaking. Bella wonders if this is what hyperthermia looks like. Bella is certain her mother is losing her grip on her hard-wrought mental stability.

"Please, let's get up and move around," Bella says and tries to keep them in the present. But Eddi doesn't move.

"My greatest accomplishment as your mother was not jumping in and fucking it all up. You know that, right?" Both Eddi and Bella laugh at this truth. But Eddi's laugh is a sad one. Her expression is one Bella knows well—despair, vulnerability, hopelessness.

"Thank you for that, Mom," Bella says. "I always felt so helpless. I could never do anything to make you feel better."

"That was not supposed to be your job, Bella."

"I know, I know," Bella says. That phrase, *that's not your job*, was the chorus of her childhood. "But it *felt* like my job," she adds.

"Well, it wasn't. Your job was to be a little girl, an awesome teenager, and a beautiful woman—and you have excelled at all three."

"Mom, we have to do something. My hands hurt, and I can't feel my feet. I think we are seriously in danger."

11

"But if we die, Bella, when we part ways in the hallway between heaven and hell, know that you are the best thing I have ever done. You and Bernard are all I have that I didn't fuck up. And no matter what I've ever said or done, no matter what I say or do henceforth, that will always be true."

"So, Mom?" Bella grabs her mother's face with both of her frozen nub-hands, "you and I, we, right now, are at the beginning of our lives. We are just starting something new for ourselves. We are not going to die here on the roof of my new goddamned apartment!"

"Okay, okay, yes, all right," Eddi rallies herself, "let's find a way then. People will begin to come home, right? It's quiet now. Let's wait until we see someone and let's throw our shoes."

"We don't have time to wait. I'm going to climb down to the fire escape."

"*No!*" Eddi says. She stands up and stagger-runs back to the edge of the roof over the street. She leans over the wall and begins her pleas again. Several minutes pass. The streets are empty. The restaurant is dark. The sushi crowd and Eddi's scarf are gone.

Eddi turns in one direction and then the other in frenzied circles, searching. She runs to the wall next to an adjacent building. There is a seven-foot barrier in front of the wall on that side, a kind of silver metal grate supported by a grid of long metal poles. Eddi presses her face against the grate to peer through. She jumps back as if something has startled her.

"Bella! The other building is right there."

"I know, Mom, but that is just their roof too and no one is over there."

"But I think their roof door is open. I think I see, yes, it's ajar. Light coming through."

"What are you going to do? Jump across to the other side?"

12

"I don't have to jump. The buildings are connected. I just
have to climb over this metal thing."

"What? Are you sure?" Bella asks, approaching. "Oh my
God, we just have to climb!"

Eddi finds a foothold and then another. Every few inches there
are small holes that allow solid steps upward. Bella follows. The
poles across the barrier allow them a firm grip. And even though
their hands stick to the ice with every grab, they endure the pain
of dislodging them and climb quickly to the top of the barrier.

"Be careful, sweetie," Eddi says, straddling the top.

"This is a piece of cake," Bella says, lifting one leg over the
top of the barrier and then the other. "This is just like Granny's
holy wall," Bella says, referring to a wall in her grandmother's
garden where Bella and her older brother, Bernard, used to climb
with regularity. They both laugh at this comparison. They jump
down on the other side.

"Yes, it is!" Eddi says as she lands. They grab each other. But
the movement is too quick. Their feet slip from under them,
and they land hard on the icy surface. Eddi's soft shoulder saves
Bella's head from colliding with the ice. Now they are laughing
harder. They are frozen in a heap and their uncontrolled laughter produces its own cloud of steamy smoke. They scramble to
their feet, slipping and sliding their way to the open door.

The heat from inside the building pulls them in and holds
them in its merciful embrace. They take the stairs slowly as their
legs thaw—one, two, three floors down. They descend into a
dark hallway jam-packed with party revelers who are trying to
crowd into an open apartment door. But the apartment appears
to be already stuffed with people. Loud rap music is blasting from
inside, and everyone is in the middle of a call and response with
a deejay who is not visible from the hallway.

"When I say *happy*, you say *New Year!*" the deejay shouts,

"Happy!"

"*New Year!*"

"Happy!"

"*New Year!*"

Eddi and Bella are wedged between people. For a moment they are trapped—there is no clear way to proceed forward or backward. Bella can feel the heat their captors are generating through their clothes. She is grateful to be thawed by them. In this moment, the exchange of warmth feels like love and world peace, enlightenment and nirvana. They are being moved this way and that, purely by the force of the crowd, and they surrender to it. All they can do is smile at each other as the blood returns to their hands and toes, their cheeks and ears. The music is so loud that it replaces Bella's own thoughts. Eddi reaches out to her and wipes a line of snot from the top of Bella's lip. Bella hugs her mother. Now her face is hot, and her eyes fill with tears.

"You saved me," Bella says near her mother's ear.

"What?" Eddi yells back, trying to hear over the music. Now Eddi and Bella are face-to-face and Eddi sees her daughter's tears.

"You saved us," Bella says again.

"Happy New Year," Eddi says.

"Happy New Year, Mom."

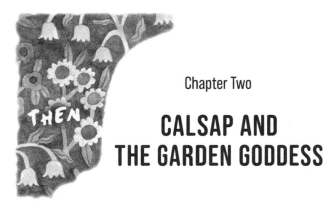

Chapter Two

CALSAP AND
THE GARDEN GODDESS

The day of my Grandad's funeral the rhododendrons were resplendent. All my childhood memories are like this—moments defined by what was in bloom, punctuated by one scent of my grandmother's garden and then another. Granddad died three days after my tenth birthday, and we buried him only three days after that. In my despair over how someone could be gone and buried so quickly, I sought comfort among the rhododendrons. September is the end of their peak blooming season, so the soft pink buds had mostly all opened to full bloom, presenting clusters of white blossoms with deep red throats. I loved these flowers with the irrational affection you feel for things whose uncommon beauty never disappoints. They have always been here for me. Gran called them her Calsaps, the name of this particular variety. They were a full-grown shrub, ten years old just like me. She'd planted them near the holy wall along the northern side of the garden on the day I was born. I am not sure if she also called me Calsap, because the Calsaps joined the family when I did, or because in my grandmother's garden of many splendors, she knew they were my favorite. The Calsaps and I grew up together, and like the reaching branches of this ever-searching plant, I loved to climb the holy wall too.

The holy wall was a six-foot-tall structure erected by Grand-dad between the garden and the asphalt driveway. It was made of rectangular cement blocks, with flat stone pavers lining the top. Most of the blocks had solid faces, but some had diamond-shaped cutouts clear through to the other side of the brick. The cutouts served as footholds, which made the wall easy to climb, so my older brother, Bernard, and I called it the holy wall, not because it was sacred, but because it had holes. The holy wall separated the universe of the garden from the outside world. Granddad built the wall himself. He was a mason. The walls, the bean tee-pee, and the raised beds—they were his contribution and his attempt to interject some order into my Gran's garden chaos.

Once we returned from the funeral, I didn't follow the sol-emn crowd into the house. Instead, I walked up the driveway and through the gate. As I approached, the Calsaps winked at me through the holes in the wall, and I began to cry again. The sight of them made my heart swell, and I didn't know how to reconcile these feelings of contentment and belonging in the midst of my grief.

I placed Gran's garden stool deep into the rhododendron bush and sat among my sisters. I let their gentle fragrance fill my head and their blossoms kiss my cheeks. I looked out at the garden. The intruders were taking over (Gran never called them weeds). And some of the perennials were waning. Gran could not tend the garden in those last weeks. She was caring for Granddad until the very end, when pneumonia would finally take him, brought on by a fatal mix of emphysema and silicosis.

I could hear a rising murmur coming from the house, visi-tors arriving with platters and Pyrex dishes full of casseroles and desserts. I looked up to see my mother standing at the open door. The screen door remained closed, but I could see her silhouette in the doorway. She seemed to be looking out at me. She didn't call me in, though. She just stood for a moment, and I didn't have to see her expression to know it would be vacant—her lovely features waiting patiently for her return. She slowly moved away from the screen door, allowing me to see through the kitchen and into the living room.

I could make out my grandmother's tiny frame sitting in her favorite chair, her head in her hands. She looked up and turned toward the screen door. She seemed to see me, so I leaned back into the Calsaps. I grabbed a cluster of blossoms at the place on the stem where a single branch shoots out into many, and I pulled the blossoms in front of my face to hide. I'd done this many times with my Gran when she was pulling intruders or deadheading. I'd stand right in front of the bush and only cover my face with one cluster of blossoms, pretending to hide to avoid the work. It was one of our many private jokes. I knew right then that she saw me because she laughed, and the unexpected sound cut through the murmurs and reached my trained ear. I peeked around the blossom and saw Granny get up from her chair. Just then someone hugged her, and then someone else. She made her way slowly toward the back door, through well-wishers and condolence-givers. They flowed around her like spirits, and for a moment, she disappeared from sight. They'd swallowed her whole. I closed my eyes, ran my palms along the stems, and held the leaves between my fingers. The tops of the leaves were smooth. The under leaves were coarse and fuzzy. I focused all my attention on these sensations until I felt a cool breeze rustle the blossoms and pass over my face.

"Can I hide with you, Calsap?" my grandmother whispered. I opened my eyes, and there she was, leaning heavily on the folded café chair in her hand. I smiled and said yes. Her eyes were red and swollen, weary and sad. Her black dress hung from her frame like a ship's loose sail in a still sea. Her cheekbones were sharp and jutted like the edges of cliffs, and the hollows in her cheeks were shallow caves. Her gray-streaked hair was combed around her face. I rarely saw her hair like this, coiffed with bangs and side tendrils. She wore her church pearls, of course. I was so relieved that she was close that I started to cry again. She had tears in her eyes too.

She opened her chair, carefully parted the bush, and pushed the chair deep into the shrub right next to me. Her chair was slightly higher than my stool, which made it easy to lay my head in her lap.

"Your grandfather loved you very much," she said, stroking my hair, putting the wildest strands behind my ear. "You were as dear to him as your brother. You know that, don't you?"

"Yes," I said, believing her, even though we both knew of my brother's special bond with Granddad. I buried my face in the folds of her dress and sobbed. The realization that my grandfather was gone for good washed over me again like a tidal wave. I remember thinking, *Granddad isn't here to serve whiskey to the men crowding his study right now. I am never going to help him change the oil in the old truck or fix the tomato trellis in the garden. And I am never going to watch him construct his fragile model military ships.* I wondered where his monocle magnifying glass was right then. I wondered what would become of it.

When my crying shudders subsided, I turned to look up at Gran. She beamed down at me, the sun streaming through our green canopy, casting strips of light and shadows across her face. For all the difficult times in my life, my grandmother's smile had been the lifeline that kept me safely moored. I reached up to wipe the tear that was traversing her nose. She took my hand in hers and kissed it.

"We'll plant a tree," she said, "for Addison." She never called my grandfather by his name when speaking to me. She always said, "your granddad." But it seemed right in this moment because I knew he would be the new tree's namesake.

"It will be. . . ."

". . . a magnolia tree," I finished my grandmother's thought. Granddad loved magnolias, and he often talked about the demise of the last magnolia to grace the garden, many years ago, before I was born. Scale killed the tree, and Granny never replaced it. She said the disease spread almost everywhere and killed off her garden, which had been modest back then. This was not exactly true, of course. She just didn't want a big tree in her garden. Granddad protested this often.

"Look at that. The rhododendrons have sprouted legs," my father said through the screen door.

I sat up, and Gran and I giggled at the thought of only our black-stockinged legs showing through the bush. My father's arms crossed his chest.

"Maybe we should go back in," Gran said. "Are you hungry?"

"No, ma'am," I said.

"Dessert, maybe?" she asked.

"Maybe later?"

"Yes, later," Gran said. "Let's go visit the Goddess."

"We'll be in in a minute, David," Gran told my father. He smiled, turned, and became a shadow among the other spirits haunting the house. Of course, we could do whatever we wanted. No one would begrudge a mourning widow this moment with her granddaughter.

My grandparents' small house sat on a large lot in the middle of south-central Los Angeles. They'd bought it in the 1960s when the housing track was new. Theirs was a rare property located right at the curve where the street bends west. Their front yard was small like everyone else's. But because it spanned the curve of the street, the backyard was an expansive space, the largest in the neighborhood. Over the years, my grandmother had filled every corner of the backyard with her garden. The property backed up against an alley and beyond it, a state-supported housing project took up three blocks. The alley was almost wide enough to qualify as a bona fide street, and it served as a throughway, mostly pedestrian, between the projects and my grandparents' neighborhood. Over the years, the alley had become a hotbed of petty crime and gang activity. It was a conspicuous dividing line between the haves and the have-nots (more like the have-a-littles and the have-nothing-at-alls). My grandfather built a ten-foot wall along the back of the yard to keep out the unwelcome. When he built the wall, he used the few leftover diamond-shaped cutout bricks, providing just three places where passersby in the alley could peek in and glimpse the secret garden within.

To the untrained eye, my grandmother's garden was wild and unrestrained. She always said, and I came to learn the truth of it, that natural gardens require extra care and planning to make them look effortlessly wild and beautiful all the time. Gran's garden was beautiful year-round. This meant the winter grasses had to be planted and maintained so that they were green when the fall grasses were dying out. And the perennials had to be maintained just so, so that once the annuals faded into their winter sleep, the perennials could take center stage and perform their solos for the season.

The edges of the garden held low, unstructured beds of different blossoms and shrubs—the big bush of rhododendrons near the holy wall, the ancient camellias with their generous red blossoms along the house. Pink and white tree peonies grew against the east side, and fragrant star-shaped white jasmine along the west. The tomato trellis held down the only shady corner of the garden, near the garage. At the feet of the perennials, Gran often planted flowering annuals—impatiens, geraniums, primroses, and cyclamen, depending on the time of year. She had a particular love for grasses, so she devoted the center of the garden to her show of tall ornamentals. She created a circular patterned walkway lined with river rocks and narrow beds on each side for the grasses. The walkway began with grass varieties that grew close to the ground—Blue Fescue and Carex, then taller and taller varieties in a circular swirl that graduated to the middle, with the tallest Indiangrass and feather reed that grew well over our heads. The center grasses made the garden look even more expansive than it was, and Gran planted them deliberately to hide the garden's secret treasure.

The swirl of the walkway drew you into a tight circle of river rocks surrounding a six-foot plaster statue of the Garden Goddess. She wore a long shroud and a veil over her head. Her arms were outstretched, palms open but barely visible under the draping sleeves of the shroud. Her toes, too, only peeked out from under her skirt tail, which draped generously on the ground. Her face, hands, and feet were dark brown. When you stood before her, her gentle smile welcomed you, as if to say, "You found me, good for you." When you knelt at her feet, her downcast eyes were looking right at you as if to say, "I've called you here for a reason."

We walked the circle among the grasses, the short path that Gran called the Circle of Remembering. As we made our way to the Goddess, Gran, as was her custom, picked up three stones along the way. Sometimes they were the river stones along the flower beds. Sometimes they were dirt rocks in the path. When we reached the Goddess, Gran laid the rocks in a line before her. This had been performed so many times over the years that there were three indentations in the soft dirt in front of the Goddess's feet where the stones were always placed.

Garden Goddess was not the statue's permanent name, meaning that Gran called her many things depending on her mood or the time of year or what was happening in the world. Sometimes she called her the Queen Mother, who reigned over all of nature and the forces that nurtured Gran's garden. Sometimes she called her Ngame, the African triple goddess of Akan, mother-goddess, and creatress. Sometimes she called her Isis and sometimes, simply Mary. But whoever she decided the statue embodied on a particular day, Gran would offer the three-stone ritual. She'd set the stones down one by one and say:

"One for the sun, one for the moon, and one for the rain," or

"One for health, one for wealth, and one for wisdom," or

"One for the mother, one for the daughter, and one for the spirit," or

"One for peace, one for love, and one for Bobby Sherman."

She said this last prayer meant that every person, known or unknown, could benefit from a blessing. Once our prayers were completed with a long moment of silence and contemplation, we'd return the stones to their places in the garden exactly where we'd found them.

On the day of Granddad's funeral, clothed in our funeral black, our approach to the Goddess took on an extra solemnity. We walked in silence. Gran's hands were pressed together and held to her lips, as if she was already in prayer. She chose two of the biggest rocks on the path and pointed out another large stone. "Pick up that one, Calsap."

It was heavy and I had to use both hands. I rushed the remaining steps to the Goddess, and I dropped it down in the first spot.

"One for Addison's soul." Gran said, coming up behind me. She knelt down on both knees and placed a stone in the second spot. "One for the gifts Addison left to us." Then she dropped the last heavy rock into the final spot. "And one for our memories of Addison." Her voice lowered, jagged with emotion, she said, "May the best part of him continue to reside in us."

We knelt in silence for a full minute. But then, I heard the voice of the Goddess, loud and clear in my head. She said, *Addison came to me and wanted to stay in the garden. His spirit has spread itself like a blanket over this place.*

I closed my eyes and bowed my head. My tears fell from my cheeks and became a part of the garden floor. Gran turned her face up to the Goddess and said, "Thank you."

And that was when I knew that Gran heard the voice of the Goddess too.

A Handful of Hydrangeas

As Gran and I came into the kitchen through the back door, visitors were beginning to leave out of the front. I noticed the small handful of hydrangeas in a petite gold-trimmed vase at the center of the kitchen table and knew immediately how they got there. Gran didn't love hydrangeas then. But I did and so did Nan. Before I saw her, Nan, my other grandmother, my mother's mother, hugged me from behind.

"Hello, my sweetheart," Nan said, burying her face in my neck. She was dressed in her funeral best, a black suit with a satin collar and a lace camisole underneath her jacket, and her signature patent leather high-heeled pumps, topped with little matching patent leather bows. Her double-stranded church pearls draped her neck, of course. As always, she was drenched in her favorite Estée Lauder perfume. She pulled away from our embrace and kissed me on my forehead. I would proudly carry her scent for the rest of the day.

"You brought your hydrangeas," I said as I turned around and hugged Nan at the waist.

"Of course, I did." Nan said. "How are you holding up, sweetie? Have you eaten?"

"We're about to eat now," I said and turned, pointing to the apple pie on the table. Nan looked on as Gran retrieved ice cream from the freezer. I watched the disapproval move across Nan's face like the beginning of a thunderstorm.

"Apple pie was Granddad's favorite," I offered, feeling that an explanation could improve the weather. Nan crossed the table to hug Bernard. He moved away from her hug, so she gave him a peck on the cheek and an affectionate pat on both shoulders. She understood Bernard's unique sorrow, and she left him to it.

"Let me do that for you, Mom." My father tried to intercede, reaching to take the ice cream carton from Gran.

"No, no, dear," Gran said, turning to the table and toward Nan, "I see you've brought these lovely hydrangeas, Miriam, thank you." Gran set the ice cream down, and Dad brought three bowls and the ice cream scoop.

"The hydrangeas are from my garden, and they are simply glorious this time of year," Nan said, "but I am sure yours are just as lovely in your yard."

"Gran doesn't grow hydrangeas," I said, "she doesn't love them."

"I love all of God's creations, Calsap," Gran said.

"I know they are not easy to grow," Nan said. "One must know her soils, her nitrogen, and her PH levels if she wants the vibrant blue hues. Those are my specialty."

"Actually, they are quite easy to grow in these parts," said Gran, "And they'll take over if you let them. So much fuss for such an unnatural color."

24

"Well, Bella likes them, don't you, sweetheart," Nan retorted.

"Yes," I said, feeling both defensive of Nan and disloyal to Gran. This was not the first face-off between my two green-thumbed grandmothers. Neither seemed to remember having played out this very same hydrangea discussion at least twice before.

"Your rhododendrons are exquisite," Nan said, pointing her chin toward the back door. She had softened her tone and moved to embrace Gran. "How are you holding up, dear?" she asked. "My, my, my, Addison certainly had many friends. They'll drink up all the liquor if you let them."

Nan was referring to the crowd of Granddad's friends who had come straight from the funeral site—fellow masons, old navy buddies, and neighborhood pals who were crowding his study around his private stash of drink.

"Let them," Gran said, "that liquor was a big part of their brotherhood."

"Well, you'll want to make sure you have some left for when you need to entice them back here. You never know when you'll need a handyman," said Nan, the experienced widow.

"Leave it to you to think of that," Gran said. They shared a laugh. Gran dished up the pie and ice cream. Nan handed Bernard and me our bowls.

"Well, we must, if nothing else, be practical women," Nan said, distributing spoons.

Chapter Three

NO SHOW I: TOO EARLY, TOO EAGER

FEBRUARY

Bella arrives at the gallery too early, even though she did a trial run the day before her appointment—plotting out the two-train trip and ten-minute walk from her East Village apartment to Midtown. She was confident with her travel plan but left extra early anyway to allow time to stop at her favorite coffee spot a block from her apartment. By the time she walked up to the entrance, the line was coming out the door and into the cold. She had expected to stand in line, but not in the cold, so she skipped the coffee, landing her at the gallery with twenty minutes to spare. Nan used to say, "Life is better when you leave early," and nothing in Bella's life so far has proven this wrong. But perfect timing is hard to achieve—too early, too eager; too late, disrespectful. Slightly early says you are in control.

Today, Bella knows that she is too early and too eager. She turns in the opposite direction and takes a slow stroll around the block. As she walks, she rehearses what she will say about herself and her work. She is confident, partly because Dorian has already told her he is interested in representing her and show-ing her work, and partly because she likes Dorian. She thinks he is charming and attractive. She believes he might be a little attracted to her too, and not in a lurid kind of way. A girl can sense these things, even one who has had as little experience with the opposite sex as Bella. She's never had a serious boy-friend, but she has had plenty of interest. She knows flirting when she sees it. She could tell by Dorian's tone, how he tilted his head and lowered his lids when he spoke to her the first time they met. She could sense it by how readily he laughed at her jokes and how he went on and on about her photographs.

She feels sure she can handle Dorian, but she wants to show that she is professional and prepared. She runs through the facts about the gallery she learned from her online reconnais-sance. Though she has already walked by the gallery three times since she moved to New York, she has never ventured inside its doors. Just the quick walk-bys were almost too exciting to bear. She knows that the gallery is family run. She may have to meet other family members today. She tries to remember their names—Davis and Ellen Herman. They are the owners and Dorian's parents. Davis is no longer living. Bella found his obit-uary online, dated five years back. Dorian has a brother, Frank, the lawyer of the family.

When she rounds the corner to the gallery's glass doors, the receptionist is already unlocking them with a jangle of keys. She is a tall, slender young woman with such a flawless cocoa-brown complexion Bella wonders how she achieves this look. How early would Bella have to rise in the morning to apply the layers of foundation, precise eye shadow, and pristinely outlined lipstick to arrive so perfectly put together as this aspiring cover girl receptionist? Bella has to assume she is an aspiring cover girl because who else would take all that time and effort? The receptionist even had time to pick up coffee along the way. She is holding the steaming cup of what looks to be the latte Bella should have waited in line for.

"You must be Bella Fontaine," she says, holding the door open. She is looking at the calendar on her phone. She takes off her heavy navy peacoat and gray-and-white knit beanie. "Yes," Bella says as she follows her inside, swirls of coffee aroma beckoning Bella's regret.

"Ellen has not quite made it in yet." The woman stores her coat and hat somewhere behind the high reception desk, fixes her hair.

"Ellen?" Bella says, "I was expecting to meet with Dorian."

"Oh, shoot. Yes, that's right," the receptionist says. She has opened her laptop and is looking intently at its screen now.

"Dorian was called out of town at the last minute. You'll meet instead with Ellen, his mother and the owner."

"Okay," Bella says, because there isn't much else she can say.

"Dorian didn't tell you," the receptionist says, more as a statement than a question. She is shaking her head like a disappointed parent. "I'm so sorry about that."

"No worries." Bella shrugs, trying to relay confidence, nonchalance. But she is nervous now. She needs to walk. "Can I look around?"

"Yes, of course," the receptionist says, then adds, "I'm Stephanie. I'm pretty much the only person who keeps time around here. You should know that." She laughs.

"Okay, got it."

"I recommend starting in the first room to the left, that's Gallery One, then work your way around," Stephanie suggests. "We have three galleries. I would take you on a tour, but I gotta set up for the day. Some things were oddly left undone last night."

"To the left. Okay, will do," Bella says, appreciative for the direction.

She knows from her research that Davis and Ellen Herman inherited the gallery from the Herman side of the family. It has been in their family for three generations. Dorian and Frank are the only children and Bella is pretty certain, part owners too. She is hoping Dorian has as much authority as he implied when they met. Maybe he has more than his mother, who is taking the appointment in his place.

She strolls through the first gallery. The walls are covered with mixed media canvases—part collage, part oil landscapes. Bella reads the poster at the entrance of the gallery introducing the artist. She is Haitian. In her picture, she looks to be in her mid-forties. Bella has never heard of her.

The next room has sculptures—a series of orbs, clear with swirling colors inside, mostly blue-and-purple oceans. The accent lights hit them just right and they glow. Bella stands in the middle of the room and takes in the view of all the sculptures. She counts twelve. The room is quiet, and she decides to accept the peaceful vibe of the orbs and the ocean. She takes three deep breaths. Her heartbeat seems to slow. She feels calmer.

"*You can do this, Bella*," she assures herself. Three more breaths.

The last room holds miniature portraits. Paintings in black and white, some in silhouette and some with the subject facing forward. The eyes are painted a one-dimensional white with no pupils. They look ghoulish, haunting. Bella tries to imagine who would want something so disturbing in their home. She wishes she could ask Stephanie what they mean, why their eyes are white blanks. She is betting it's some brilliant explanation about race and gentrification or some such. She resolves to come back when she can find out.

She is concerned now that there are no photographs anywhere.

She is not sure her pieces will fit in here. She doesn't know enough to know if this matters.

The last gallery leads her to a back hallway. She passes an office. The door is open.

"Ms. Fontaine?" says the woman behind a desk. "Please come in."

Bella enters the office and the seventy-something Jewish woman stands up from her chair. Bella recognizes Ellen from the gallery's social media feeds, short and thin with shoulder-length salt-and-pepper hair so curly, it's almost an afro. Stephanie enters the office right behind Bella.

"This is the photographer Dorian is so excited about," Stephanie says.

"And I see why," the older woman says. "Aren't you lovely? I am so sorry to keep you waiting, dear." She extends her hand, "Ellen Herman."

"So nice to meet you, Mrs. Herman," Bella says in her most formal voice.

"I was not aware you were coming in today," Ellen says. "Did you bring some prints, a contact sheet, anything to show me?"

Bella is surprised and befuddled by this request. In all her planning, she didn't think to bring anything to show. Dorian asked her last week to email more examples of her earlier work. That was the second batch of photos she'd sent. He's had her CV for weeks. She figured they had what they needed.

"I can pull up my website," Bella says. She hears the uncertainty in her own voice. She knows she sounds weak and unprepared. But then Stephanie steps in to save her.

"I forwarded the email of her photographs as soon as Dorian asked you to cover for him, Ellen. I also printed out some contact sheets. They are in that green folder on your credenza, as you requested." Stephanie does not hide her annoyance.

"Ah, well, why didn't you say so," Ellen says. She makes an

30

exaggerated scowl at Stephanie and then smiles and winks at Bella. Stephanie walks out of the room, not bothering to respond. Bella hears Stephanie's loud exhalation as she moves down the hall. Ellen swivels her chair around toward the credenza behind her desk. She picks up something, the folder, Bella presumes. She cannot know for sure because Ellen's chair has a high back that obscures her movements once she has turned away. She stays this way, her back to Bella, for several minutes, leafing through papers.

"I don't see on your résumé where you have shown before."

Bella is relieved to be staring at the back of Ellen's chair. "I placed first in the Kleinberg Photofest in Toronto. I've participated in several student art shows at UCLA and several local shows and festivals in Los Angeles. The list of those is on the last page of my CV," Bella offers.

After several minutes, Ellen turns back to face Bella, who can already tell that Ellen is not impressed with what she has seen.

"Yes, I see. The Kleinberg is your only exposure outside of Los Angeles?" she asks.

"Well, I was featured on emergingart.com, which is a website that has an international audience," Bella says with confidence, though she is not at all certain the website, which included some of her photos for a Black History Month online show, actually has followers outside of the U.S. Since it is a website, she figured this can't be much of a stretch.

Ellen asks, "To which competitions have you submitted recently? Are you showing anywhere currently? Do you have any reviews to share with me?"

"I do not have any current submissions or exhibitions," Bella says, "I have the judges' notes from the Kleinberg and the write-up in the *Toronto Sun*."

Ellen Herman goes through Bella's three-page CV, lifting page after page as if something suitable might magically appear if she continues to shuffle through. Bella wants to shout, "This is it. It's all I've got. No magical missing page." But she just sits up straighter and awaits Ellen's next question. Ellen finally sets the CV down on her desk and picks up a contact sheet from the folder.

"You," she draws out the word, "have a very sensitive eye, my dear. But I am not sure your work is a good fit for us." Ellen pauses, pulls her chair in closer, and squares her shoulders. "In fact, I am sure it is not."

Even though she was telegraphing her displeasure from the moment Bella sat down in her office, Bella is not prepared for Ellen's proclamation. Dorian had indicated that she was in, that her series was already on their exhibition calendar. This show was the reason she convinced herself and her father that she was ready to make the move to New York. She thought she was coming in today to sign a contract.

"What is your day job?" Ellen interrupts Bella's panic attack, effectively cutting it short.

"I do weddings," Bella says, swallowing hard, "and events. I photograph events."

"Oh," Ellen says, "well, splendid. Perhaps we can add you to our go-to list of event photographers." This is Ellen's consolation offering. "As I said, you have a sensitive eye and a gift with light. And I imagine you are affordable."

Bella is too stunned to say thank you. She tries to smile to acknowledge the compliment, even though it is packaged in a but-you-are-not-quite-good-enough wrapping. Ellen stands, extends her hand again, and says, "Thank you so much. We have your contact info."

Bella stands up, but her legs are shaking, her knees actually knocking together, and she feels light-headed. She drops back down into the chair.

"Are you all right, Belinda?" Ellen asks.

"It's Bella," she says as a wave of nausea washes over her.

"You don't look so good, honey," Ellen says. She screams for Stephanie, who runs into the room.

"Get Belinda some water, please."

"I think it's Bella," Stephanie says and turns to face her. "It's Bella, right?"

"Yes," Bella says. "I'm fine. Thank you, again." She takes three deep breaths, stands up, and follows Stephanie out.

Only when she gets out onto the street does she get angry. *What just happened?* This morning she had her first solo art show in hand and now, she has nothing. Should she have stood up for herself? How do you even defend yourself when the person who dismisses your work is complimentary while doing so? Bella is walking fast down the street. She decides to walk all the way home. And like so many people she's encountered since she moved to New York, she is talking to herself out loud.

"Who is this Dorian that he would draw me in and not even bother to let me down in person but send his mother in to do it?" Bella crosses the street against the light, maintaining her pace.

"Is this how business is done here? Set people up, just to destroy their freaking dreams?"

By the time she is three blocks from home, a walk that has taken a little over an hour, the buzz in her head has subsided and her breathing is rhythmic from exertion and no longer from panic. Her frontal lobe has switched back on, and she is able to reason with herself. She realizes what she did wrong.

"I should have calmly asked Ellen why my work is not a good fit," she says, still talking aloud. "I should have been calm and mature enough to ask her advice about other places that might better show my work." Two teenaged girls passing by give Bella a sympathetic stare. She realizes they think she is mentally ill. And she thinks that maybe they are right. Maybe she *is* having a mental breakdown in this moment. She's just suffered a profound disappointment when she was reasonably expecting something wonderful. Rejection is a bitch, especially when you thought you'd already passed muster.

Bella rounds the corner to her coffee spot, and the line has moved indoors. It's still cold, but the sun has made its way through the clouds to deliver slightly warmer temperatures. Maybe this morning went so badly because she bypassed what has become her morning coffee ritual. She pledges that next time she will stand in line like everybody else and start the day out right. Perhaps it's not too late to redeem this one. She will email Dorian this afternoon and ask the mature questions about his change of mind and other possible opportunities. And she will send Ellen some pictures from her portfolio of event coverage so that perhaps she will indeed add Bella to her go-to list of event photographers.

"We can do this, Bella," she says to herself. "We can make it happen." She opens the door to the coffee shop where the heater is blasting an inviting warmth infused with the smell of freshly brewed coffee.

When she gets home, she puts away all the alternative interview outfits she left strewn across her bed earlier this morning. She cleans last night's dinner bowl and scrubs the sink. She puts her dirty clothes in the laundry hamper, save her T-shirt, which she uses to wipe down the kitchen countertop of leftover toast crumbs and dust. She steps into the bathroom, grabs the whisk broom from its hook above the clothes hamper, and sweeps the floor of hair—hers and Camille's, but mostly hers.

Now that it's clean, the apartment feels roomier, able to accommodate her outsized energy. She decides it's time to email Dorian. She plops down in the middle of her bed and opens her laptop. As she contemplates how she will address Dorian, her anger wells up and she unloads her first try at an email message:

What the fuck, Dorian?

You call me out of the blue. Tell me you "love my work." Think that I am a visionary. You invite me to exhibit. Tell me you will feature my series in your most important gallery space and introduce me to the art world. "Our show is going to make your career, Bella Fontaine," you said. "You've worked hard, and you deserve to be known," you claimed. Was this just a bunch of bullshit? Do you even have the power to make those kinds of decisions? Or are you just a little boy pretending to be a gallery owner when Mommy's not looking?

I picked up and moved from my home, from a place that I could afford, to make it in New York City based on your assurances and representations—only to have your mother, who didn't even bother to remember my name, brush me off as some kind of wannabe, some pretty face you were only flirting with, some fucking aspiring event photographer. I AM NOT aspiring to be an event photographer! I am an artist with a day job. And you are a motherfucking asshole! So, fuck you, Dorian Herman.

Sincerely, Bella, NOT fucking Belinda, Bitches!

She slams the top of her laptop down. She takes a deep breath, lies back, and closes her eyes. Her grandmothers are standing over her now, together. They are in the habit of doing this lately, popping in on her, unsummoned and uninvited. She doesn't mind so much now because when they appear, it is as if they are transported from her childhood. But right now, they are not impressed. Both shaking their heads, Gran is laughing and Nan is looking at Bella over her reader glasses.

"Ah! I know that felt good," Gran says, "calling that young man a motherfucker."

"You sure told him," Nan chimes in.

And then Gran again, "Now erase that poetry of profanity and start again."

Poetry of profanity makes Bella laugh, but she is not happy that they are here to witness this moment of failure. Still, she knows they are right. She breathes in deeply through her nose and pushes the air out of her mouth with a loud *whoosh*. Then she opens up her laptop, deletes the first email and begins a new one.

Dear Dorian,

I had the pleasure of meeting Mrs. Herman this morning. She let me know that she has considered my work for exhibition and decided that it is not a good fit for your gallery. Needless to say, I am disappointed. I strolled through your gallery rooms as I waited and was impressed and inspired by the current exhibitions. I did notice that you were not currently showing any photography, but I'd hoped that this would soon change with the showing of my From the Soil Series.

Frankly, when Mrs. Herman delivered her decision, I was taken by surprise and unprepared to respond. So, I thought I would take this opportunity, for my own edification, to further inquire about the basis of her decision. And since you expressed such positive impressions of my work, I am hoping that you might let me know if there are perhaps other galleries that might be a better fit.

Thank you so much for your time and consideration.

Sincerely, Bella Fontaine

"Perfect," Nan says.

"That'll work," says Gran.

Bella presses Send.

Chapter Four

A SERIOUS GIRL AND A SERIOUS GARDEN

At Nan's house, by the time I am ten, I'm in charge of bringing the silver tray out to the veranda for Sunday tea. Already adept at arranging tea service—three starched white linen napkins, one to line the tray; two of Nan's Lenox china cups and saucers; two small silver teaspoons; an Earl Grey tea bag for Nan and English Breakfast for myself; and usually, scones—I carry out the tray slowly, carefully, because today it is extra heavy. Earlier, Nan baked snickerdoodle cookies, my favorite, so the tray contains our usual scones, the cookies, *and* a new gardening book Nan purchased from the used bookstore.

The wide expanse of Nan's veranda is an infinite universe. It holds a whole houseful of white wicker furniture and a family of huge hanging Boston ferns. These ferns remain full and vibrant through every season, if you can even call what we have in Southern California seasons. Gran used to say that Nan's ferns defy logic. She'd bought them from the grocery store years ago, and everybody knows that once you bring home grocery store ferns, they rarely survive the week. But years later, here they are—abundant and thriving, almost too big to hang from their rafter hooks.

Though Nan's home is perfectly appointed, filled with pristine post-modern furniture and reproductions of important Harlem Renaissance art, she entertains guests almost exclusively on this veranda. The roof of the house extends over the space, overhanging the deck all the way across to the wooden stairs down to the garden. This provides cover so that even during a rare Southern California rain, Nan can serve lunch or tea outdoors. And rain or shine, everyone, including the women of the Church Guild, who are especially attentive to how the humidity affects their hair, loves to come over to Nan's veranda, partake in her exceptional hospitality, and behold her spectacular garden.

When my family visits Nan on Sundays for dinner, my mother spends the entire time alone in the kitchen tending to the meal. This is her preference, that we leave her to her preparations. My father and Bernard stay glued to one televised sporting event or another, so I have Nan and the veranda all to myself. Nan and I start our visit with a stroll around the garden, noting what is in bloom. We usually take cuttings for the dinner table. At the end of our walk, I take the freshly cut flowers in and bring tea service out. Then we read through Nan's garden design books and magazines. After tea, we sit on the porch swing. This is when Nan tells me stories, often about my grandpa Jeff, my mother's father, whom I never had the opportunity to know, and about other important people and plants. The best view of the entire garden is from the veranda swing.

Nan's garden is a colorful tapestry, all geometry, clean lines and brilliant hues. The veranda is a few feet above ground level. From the deck, you have to walk down four steps to meet the garden path, so from our place on the swing, if you squint as you take in the entire view, Nan's garden becomes the street map to wonderland—a grid of beautiful blocks and intersections.

Because it is constant and reliable, purposeful and deliberate, it comforts my young self. It is my oasis of predictability.

Nan is a bona fide green thumb, but she doesn't really garden. That is to say, she doesn't work the garden herself. She is a master at management, never really getting her hands dirty. Mr. Blackshear does all the actual work. He was a longtime friend of my grandfather's and an ardent admirer of Nan's once Grandpa Jeff died. Mr. Blackshear seems to have transferred his devotion from my grandmother to her garden, fully deferring to her expertise in design and her love of traditional French and English gardens. Nan likens her garden to the Orangery Parterre of Versailles—fruit trees and topiaries, geometrical cutout squares of lawn. Only she has added beds of roses in sunny spots and hydrangeas in the partial shade. She is most ambitious with her roses, aspiring to amass as many varieties as the great gardens of England—determined to accomplish greatness in effect what she does not possess in scale.

But the garden did not begin this way. Before the garden was Nan's, it belonged to my grandpa Jeff. He planted it to relieve the stress of being a detective for the Los Angeles Police Department. He'd come home from the police station early in the morning after the graveyard shift, sleep only a few hours, and then tend his garden. His were modest aspirations. At first, he grew mostly vegetables and wildflowers. But to please Nan, he built raised beds in front of the veranda, just a foot or two from the bottom step. And he filled the beds with her favorite flowers—mostly hydrangeas. She rewarded him by sitting out on the veranda whenever he worked the garden. His constant requests for her planting desires motivated her to buy gardening books so that she could direct him. When he asked what she wanted, she, very soon, had answers. And this is how they rekindled something that time had worn away. Nan once said, "Marriages have seasons too, you know?" She was speaking in that far away tone that crept into her voice when she spoke of my grandfather. Theirs was a kind of December courtship, a marriage revival that intensified when he turned his garden plans over to her.

"Your grandfather would exhaust himself out in the sun for hours," she'd told me. "If he was out in the late afternoon, when he finished, we would sit in this very swing and watch the sunset. I would provide a cold beer, and he would put a small cluster of hydrangeas behind my ear." Nan shared this memory more than once, and each time nostalgia painted a wistful smile across her entire face—her eyes smiled, her cheeks and chin too. She'd gently push off, setting the swing in a gentle, soothing rock, and I would close my eyes and try to place the handsome man I'd only seen in photographs in the swing next to Nan.

Once Nan expressed her desire for a more formal, dignified garden, my grandfather was determined to deliver. He had been in the middle of transforming it to her specifications when he died. His heart failed him while he was planting irises along the center path. Nan was on the veranda, sitting at the wicker table, looking down at the book in her lap when he fell. My mother, Nan and Grandpa Jeff's only child, saw him first and ran out to him from the house. She was sixteen when she knelt next to her dying father and watched him take his last breath. She has not, to my knowledge, been in the garden since.

Gran thinks Nan obsesses over the garden since my grandfather's death as a form of penance. She says Catholics believe deeply in contrition. I never understood this conversation until I was much older. But I believe Gran was right, as always. At ten, all I knew was that Nan's garden was the perfect happy place for me, and I strove to be perfect company for her.

I set the tea tray down on the table and hand Nan a napkin. I pour the hot water into our cups. I open the individually wrapped tea bags, hand Nan her Earl Grey, and drop my English Breakfast into my cup. This is before we knew that real traditional tea service involves loose teas and long periods of steeping. (But later this knowledge does not change our ritual.) I dunk my tea bags a couple of times. Nan has already sweetened her tea and has opened the new book. I take my cup and saucer over to Nan's side of the table and set them down near hers. And then I climb onto her lap. We leaf silently through the book. I turn the page when Nan lifts her cup to her lips, and she turns the page when I take a drink. We are synchronized and efficient. I set my cup down.

"Nan?"

"Yes, sweet."

"When I grow up, I am going to write a gardening book."

"Oh, that is a splendid idea."

"I'm gonna take all the pictures and do all the writing. I'm gonna call it, 'Gardens Are Not Built in a Day.'"

"Ah, and why have you chosen that title, clever one?"

"Because it is true, and lots of people don't seem to understand that you cannot rush a garden," I say with conviction.

"You are, of course, so right."

"We are planting a garden at my school, and we get to work on it at recess."

"Oh, that is wonderful news."

"Yes, my class planted seeds last week—snapdragons and sunflowers."

"Those are good choices, don't you think?"

"Yes, ma'am. They are fast to sprout and bloom, and they are hardy."

"Exactly."

"But even so, the kids are already frustrated that their seeds are not full-grown plants in just one week. It's maddening."

Nan laughs. She hugs my shoulders and snuggles her head next to mine.

"Children are like sprouts too, you know," she says, "You must also be patient with them. You have an expertise and a gift that most of your classmates do not. Your hands have been in the soil all your life, so be patient and teach them what you know."

"Kids have such short attention spans," I say in my most adult voice as I pick up my tea and sip. Nan giggles at this and I smile at her over my cup.

"Well, you'll let them know that successful gardening takes lots of planning and a little luck."

"If I take beautiful pictures and show how a seed becomes a plant, I think everyone will fall in love with how cool it is. Don't you think?"

"Yes," Nan says. "I guess you'll be needing a camera, then."

"Yes, ma'am, a thirty-five millimeter," I say. "I've put it on my Christmas list."

"But Christmas is a ways away," she says. "You know, your grandfather loved photography. I think he had a thirty-five-millimeter camera, a Nikon that he absolutely loved."

"Do you still have it? Can I use it?" I ask.

"I am betting that these cameras have changed considerably in the many years since your grandfather's day. One thing he always said, in photography you must keep up with the technology. He always had the latest thing. I am thinking that you may want an easier kind of camera to start with, no?"

"No, ma'am, I looked it up and a thirty-five millimeter is the right camera for a serious photographer," I say, having only skimmed through the photography magazines in the public library.

"All right, then, no time to wait," Nan says, "a serious camera for a serious girl."

Chapter Five

FINALLY

MARCH

When Bella moved to Manhattan's East Village, it was just a place in New York where a young college student needed a roommate. She didn't know that tucked into the nooks and crannies of its avenues is the highest concentration of community gardens in the nation. Her discovery of this fact—that her new apartment is surrounded by community gardens and the people who love them—is how Bella came to decide that she was exactly where she was supposed to be, despite her Herman Gallery disappointment.

With a brand-new Green Map, the key to every garden location in the city, Bella is determined to visit the community gardens in her neighborhood. She unfolds the stiff accordion of paper and plots her morning. Not every garden will be welcoming to new members. But she feels sure that the one she chooses will choose her back. Winter is waning, and spring is New York-aggressive. When Bella arrived at the New Year, the landscape in the East Village along its orderly blocks was in a deep winter sleep. The small plots of dirt along the street were as hard and unyielding as the concrete, and the tree branches hung low like the arms of naked maidens.

Just last week when Bella took the long way home through Tompkins Square Park after picking up dumplings for dinner on Ninth Street, it was dusk and a frigid wind was blowing, but she noticed that green sprouts were muscling their way through the cold, hard dirt. She was so impressed at the resolve of these tiny seedlings that she stopped in her tracks, took out her mobile phone, and captured their breakthrough. She took pictures of every sign of life along her path—abstract patterns of snow and grass, green shoots reaching out from what was just a day ago barren dark gray bark, the dappling light of a fresh, new green canopy against the last of the sunlight and the purple sky. In the interest of arriving home with still-warm dumplings, she stopped with the pictures and resolved to return the next day to take more. But then she had a photo gig the next day and forgot. By the time she returned two days later, the park had exploded with color and life. Bare beds had sprouted daffodils, and brown mole hills had transformed into grassy knolls. The trees had full green afros. She was reminded that nature waits for no one, and the thought renewed her too.

Now that her art show has fallen through, she needs to somehow get in touch with the rightness of her move to New York. It is time, Bella resolves, to find her people among the community garden set. She leaves her apartment at eight this morning. This early hour on a Saturday feels as if she has the whole neighborhood to herself. The normally bustling streets are virtually empty. The bodega fronts are freshly hosed down and crates of produce begin to appear on the curb, but only the coffee shops are open for business. Bella's coffee spot doesn't have a line at this early weekend hour, so she breezes in and out.

The map tells her she has a lot of ground to cover. The gardens are spread out among thirteen blocks between Houston Street to Fourteenth. Bella will start at Petit Versailles Garden on West Houston Street on the easterly edge of the East Village and work her way west, back toward her apartment, located on the opposite westerly point. Petit Versailles is also a great starting point because on her map this garden has every feature icon, meaning it offers everything a community garden should. It is run by a diverse community and has been remediated and repurposed on land that was once a vacant lot. The bonus is that it offers performances and art exhibit space.

Buttressed between two brick buildings, the garden spans the full lot between West Houston and Second Street. The front looks like the entrance to a green cavern. Fresh new ivy covers the chain-linked fence like a veil, and the mix of towering trees creates a canopy over the entry. Bella is too early to get in, but she can see through the gate that the garden space is a puzzle of narrow beds of shrubs, vines, and perennials just revving up for spring and asymmetrical community plots, some newly planted. The annual beds along the building walls are still empty. The center of the garden is dominated by a large wooden platform, the stage where the cultural and artistic endeavors happen. Bella is thrilled with the idea that this garden might be a community of artist-gardeners like herself.

She knew when she set out this morning that most of the gardens would not be open to the public until early afternoon. But she thought she might find some early risers working their plots. She is harboring the hope that she will find the perfect garden and that some friendly gardener will see her at the gate and invite her in to help. Gran used to say committed gardeners are up with the sun and the morning dew. Bella is really wanting to work in the dirt today. She misses it.

But no one appears at Petit Versailles. She supposes this is best since she cannot both work in the gardens and visit them all in one day. Traveling down Second Street, she reaches the Peach

Tree Garden. There are no gardeners here either, but through the fence Bella can see that it is a small classic neighborhood garden with a handful of community plots—some raised, some decorated with small statues. A mature peach tree, the garden's namesake, is rooted near the entrance and looks to be still in its winter slumber. Bella turns south on Avenue B, walks the block to East Third, and crosses the street at the Miracle Garden. She sees immediately that the garden got its name from the towering weeping willow that dominates the site. Already, the willow's leaves cascade down like a flowing green waterfall. This garden is a larger, more upscale oasis, carefully planned and well-kept. The path has precise red brick pavers. Snugly squeezed between two mid-rise apartment buildings with a few other mature trees in communion with the weeping willow, the space is mostly a shade garden.

Bella sits on the bench outside of the Miracle Garden gates to contemplate where she will go next. She decides that even though she is enchanted by both the eclectic, art-focused gardens like Petit Versailles and the promising structure of this small, well-kept Miracle Garden, she will search out a larger garden with a bigger community. She reviews her map to find the biggest gardens closest to her apartment when she hears the sound of trickling water. It takes her several seconds to remember that this is her mobile phone's ring tone. Her phone rings so rarely that it surprises her every time. Bella clears her throat and answers.

"Hello. Bella Fontaine," she says.

"Bella? It's Dorian Herman."

Shit.

"Hello, Mr. Herman."

There is a pause, a silent moment on his end as if Dorian does not know what to do with Bella's formality. This is the first she has heard Dorian's voice since her visit to the gallery a month ago. An eternity.

From the moment, over eight months ago, when Bella's college photography professor introduced them on a virtual chat, she and Dorian had established a casual and friendly rapport, even a little flirtatious. But right now, she feels she must take a formal tone to let Dorian know that she will not be toyed with. Formality is essentially all she has in this balance of power between them.

"I am still just Dorian," he finally says.

Bella doesn't respond. She lets the tension build. She wants this tension. It feels like protection.

"I was wondering if you might have a free moment today."

"Today?" Bella says. She wants to say, I have been waiting weeks, asshole, where have you been? But all that comes out is, "Today?"

"If you have a moment, I'd love to talk. I know I owe you an explanation and a statement of the gallery's intentions. I promise I won't take too much of your day. Are you home? Can I come to you?"

"Actually, I am out and about already."

"Then let's grab coffee. How about nine thirty at the Starbucks on Avenue A?"

"I'm heading to the community garden. I am dressed for gardening," she says. Under her coat, she is dressed in what she slept in and her work boots. Her hair is in a fuzzy bun, not a fashionably messy bun but a ball of fuzz gathered above a crown of frizz.

"No worries," Dorian says, "I've just rolled out of bed myself. My calendar opened up this morning and I hoped you could fit me in. We are long overdue." Bella pictures Dorian sitting on the edge of some designer bed in some fancy trust fund loft, with no shirt, his curly black hair uncombed. Her mind has endowed him with a deeply muscular chest, though she has only really seen him in person once and he was covered in layers of winter clothes.

When Bella first met Dorian in person, her first week in New York, it was at this same proposed Avenue A Starbucks. Dorian made an impression on Bella that first meeting. His confident, slick business persona was overlaid with sincerity and kindness. He took his time with her. He told her about his family's gallery—its seventy-five-year history and its reputation for launching the careers of young artists, many of whom are now famous. He dropped a few names, and she pretended to recognize them. He mentioned that his family had a particular track record with African American artists and with women. He named two Black women artists whom Bella recognized—Alicia Boatwright, the legendary painter of Black historical figures, and Tanesha Jones, the multimedia artist who became the go-to for album covers among successful rappers and musicians in the 1990s. Now he had her attention. Well, he'd always had her attention, but now he had fanned the fires of her hope.

"This show will put you on the map," he'd said. "With the right handling, you can become a household name. The art world needs to know about more young Black woman photographers," he claimed, "and I think you are unique among them." He said this as if he knew something about Black women photographers, and Bella did not feel on solid enough ground to challenge him. He explained that he would represent her personally. He only represented one other artist so far, so they could grow together. It felt not just a little bit like he was proposing marriage, and by the end of the meeting, Bella was ready to say, "I do."

Bella finally agrees to meet Dorian at nine thirty. She no longer trusts him. Since she cannot make it home in time to clean up, she stops at the corner pharmacy to buy cheap lip gloss, eyeliner, and a knit beanie on sale to cover her unkempt hair. She pulls herself together while she walks and arrives right on the half hour. But she does not beat Dorian, who is already seated at a tiny square table. He is wedged in the corner of a long bench. He is holding two grande-sized Starbucks cups, drinking from one and handing her the other.

"Hello," he says. "I took the liberty of ordering you a latte to avoid the line." He points to the long line snaking out of the door, "It was short when I got here." Now he is standing and extending his hand. "You still like lattes, right?"

"Yes, thank you," Bella says. She smiles as she shakes his hand and sits in the café chair opposite him. She is impressed that he remembered how she likes her coffee. *This is how he wins people*, Bella thinks, *with a good memory and good teeth.*

"First, I want to apologize again. This was not how I wanted things to start out."

"Thank you," Bella interrupts him, "but first, could you start out by telling me why Ms. Herman does not believe my work is a good fit for your gallery?"

Dorian stops. Takes a sip of his coffee. And then another. Bella has thrown him off his spiel.

"At some point, I would like to have a more detailed discussion, between you and Ellen, of her observations," he says. "But as I mentioned, she did not have the benefit of a full presentation of your work or your story. For now, I hope you can accept that I believe your photographs are a good fit and would like to continue to discuss the possibility of representation and a first show." He drinks more coffee. Dancing eyes. Confident smile.

Bella takes a drink of her latte, trying to hold his eyes with hers.

"Do you always call your mother by her first name?" Bella asks.

Dorian laughs.

"Only in the business context," he says.

"You know, the email I sent you on the day your mother turned me away was the second one that I composed. The first one I wrote was . . . what would you even call it? An angry rebuke!" Bella says. She is only partially smiling. Her eyes are direct and unflinching. "The entire experience was deeply upsetting. I just wanted to tell you that."

"I understand, and I am really sorry. I know that I probably deserved that first email. Going forward, if you choose to go forward, you will be represented by me, and I will do a better job of protecting you. Okay?"

"Okay," Bella says, "I appreciate your faith in my work."

"I hope to earn your trust." Dorian extends his hand again. Bella takes it and gives it a firm shake, the way Nan taught her when she was young and meeting people at church. Dorian and Bella sip in silence. But then Dorian looks at his phone, and this breaks the magic of the moment. Bella wonders if he is looking at the time to see how quickly he was able to reel her back in. Does he have another appointment with another desperate artist?

"So, what's next?" she asks, pushing her paranoia aside.

"I will have you back at the gallery for a real tour and to discuss the formalities of our relationship going forward. My brother, Frank, handles the legalities. We'll get with him and tie things up, set a date for the show and get it on the calendar."

"I guess there is more to it than I realized," Bella says, understanding how naive she had been to move to New York with so little certainty.

Dorian seems to read her mind. "I am glad you are here, Bella. It's going to be great. Don't worry."

"Thank you, Dorian."

"So, you were out early on your morning walk?" he asks.

"Something like that. I was on a self-guided walking tour of the gardens in the area. I am hoping to join one soon, but there are so many. I really love my new neighborhood."

"*Nice,*" Dorian says. "What other gardens have you seen in the area? People don't realize that New York is like a garden city. I was just at a buddy's new condo for a birthday get-together, and his building has an incredible roof garden."

"Really? I love roof gardens. I aspire to have my own one day." Bella sips her coffee. "I really haven't gotten around to see much outside of my neighborhood. I'm pacing myself."

They both laugh. Then Bella remembers she is here to take care of business.

"You know, one thing Ms. Herman did mention when we met was that I could maybe do some event photography work for the gallery. Do you think that is possible? Event photography is my day job. I am trying to break in. . . ." She trails off as she hears herself asking Dorian for more when he has already promised a career.

"Oh, for sure. That's easy." Dorian picks up his phone and begins to text. "I am sending Stephanie a text to put you on the photographers' list. And it's not a very long list. We have our usual go-tos. But now that you will be one of ours, you will get priority."

"Wonderful! Thank you."

"So, I just had an idea. Can I take you somewhere?" Dorian asks.

"What do you mean?"

"I am asking you to trust me and come with me to a surprise location. If you wouldn't mind putting off your community garden search, I think this adventure will be worth it."

"You are full of promises," Bella says. She remembers in this moment that she has not showered, and her hair is a bird's nest under her beanie, but she decides to play along. "Okay, I'm in."

Dorian is back on his phone, punching directions into a car service app.

"We have three minutes until pickup. Drink up!" he says.

A black Prius pulls up to the curb. Dorian opens the rear door for Bella and slides in next to her. They sit as close to their respective doors as they can in the tight quarters of the back seat, Bella's shoulder pressed against the window ledge and Dorian's legs wedged under the door handle. Bella senses that Dorian is uneasy. The creases on his forehead are dotted with sweat, and he is shaking his left leg up and down with rapid, nervous quivers. Bella remembers his words from earlier, that he only represents one other client. Maybe his confidence is not as rock solid as it appears. Bella wants to put her hand on his knee to stop it. His shaking knee is making her nervous too.

"South Bronx, right, folks?" the driver breaks the silence. He is young, early twenties, but his voice is of a much older man, like a forty-year smoker. The car smells like an ashtray, as if he has already smoked forty years' worth.

"That's right," Dorian says. "Are you taking two seventy-eight to the Bronx River Parkway? That's the best route."

"Yeah, that's what my navigation is telling me," the driver responds.

"Okay, don't say any more about our destination," Dorian tells the driver. "It's a surprise. She doesn't know." The driver nods his head. He and Bella make eye contact in the rearview mirror.

"This gentleman is not kidnapping you, is he, ma'am?" The driver smiles a wide grin that showcases a spectacular space where at least two teeth should be.

"No, sir," Bella says, laughing, as does Dorian.

She moves her backpack from her lap to the space between them.

"Are your cameras in there?" Dorian asks.

"Yes," Bella says. Though she only has one professional camera, she always counts her phone as a photography tool.

"Good," Dorian says. He seems particularly pleased with himself. At first, Bella assumed that they were going to his friend's roof garden. She has not been outside of her neighborhood except her treks to the Herman Gallery. She welcomes exposure to something new.

"I actually love surprises. Good ones."

"Well, I am pretty certain this will be a good one. So, what made you pick up a camera?" Dorian asks.

"I wanted to show people about the miracle of the plant world. I was a precocious child, but only with regard to gardens."

For the nearly forty-five-minute drive Dorian asks Bella about photography—how long she has been taking pictures, how she chose her subjects, what is it about gardens that appeals to her. She tells him about growing up in her grandmother's gardens and that she learned about the natural world and the nature of people at her grandmothers' elbows. She describes how different her two grandmothers' personalities had been and how this was reflected in their two very different gardens. She tells him that she is most at home in a garden and already has plans to create her own here in New York. In the midst of her revealing the details of her life, Dorian shifts in his seat so that he is turned completely toward Bella, his knees almost touching hers. She has his full attention, and he seems to be hanging on her every word. This shift comforts Bella and loosens her restraint.

Before he can ask, Bella tells Dorian that she recently lost both her grandmothers and that his interest in her work came just at the right time because she was in a very dark place. She surprises herself by telling Dorian Herman that he is responsible for her move to New York, and that her move to New York saved her.

"I would prefer not to talk about what happened with my grandmothers," she carefully keeps control of the conversation, "but I just want to thank you for showing up when you did."

"Oh, I had no idea," Dorian says, "I am sorry for your loss."

"Thank you. And how about you? You grew up surrounded by art and artistic types. How interesting your childhood must have been."

Dorian sighs. "Yes, I was just thinking how different our worldview must be. I grew up at the elbow of two very vanguard parents, who viewed our gallery as a mirror into New York's ever-evolving culture. My parents took over the gallery when I was five. It was the middle of the eighties, which was a pretty wild time for art in New York. They wanted to change things up, shake the gallery's reputation for being conservative. To my grandfather's credit, he saw the art world changing and didn't feel he could shepherd in that change, so he let my parents. I was with them when they were hot on the heels of the already big-named artist rock stars—Keith Haring and Basquiat. Their timing was off, you know, late, and they could not compete for them, so they pulled out all the stops to get this scrappy white kid from Gloucester, New Jersey, who was leaving his graffiti all over the city, just beginning to be noticed. He was distinct because his messages were about racial harmony and economic equality. The art was beautiful—color, unique pattern, and the message was a slap in the face of the uber-capitalism of the time."

Dorian continues, "My parents came very close to signing him before he became *the* Chester Harris. I think that was their biggest loss at that time, not signing Harris. I remember how much time they invested, trying to turn the gallery into the kind of place the Chester Harrises of the world would want to associate with. They considered becoming a gallery-nightclub type space, like the Mudd Club. But they weren't sure they could pull it off. My grandfather thought the idea went too far, of course. Back then, the art world was a hard-partying, drug culture. A lot of the artists my parents took interest in flamed out early and didn't make it to the nineties. My dad got caught up in it all—out all night, hungover and strung out during the day. My mother was the one to take things over and keep the business running—including while my dad was in and out of rehab. He was charming as fuck when he was high and a motherfucker when he was coming down. Excuse my French." Dorian pauses and looks at Bella. "Well, my dad became the cautionary tale my mother read to us at bedtime."

"Oh, man," Bella says, "I'm sorry."

"It all worked out. My dad finally pulled himself out of it. He got interested in photographers who were using photos, film, and graphics to create social commentary—themes like consumerism, female stereotypes, and sexism. Have you heard of the Neo-conceptualist Pictures Generation?"

"Not really, no."

"Barbara Kruger, Cindy Sherman, and Sherrie Levin?" Dorian asks. Bella shakes her head.

"Well, my dad became obsessed with this form of art, Barbara Kruger's in particular. At that time, he cultivated a lot of photographers doing this kind of work. Some of the work involved the use of other people's art and images—appropriation was a big part of the art form. But some of the young artists got into hot water over using other artist's work without permission. They, and we, had considerable legal troubles from some work we exhibited. This kind of thing, using the art of others as a basis or critique or comparison, was new at the time. We had to back away from it after the lawsuits. But as a kid, I loved it as much as my dad. It's how film and photographic art became a mainstay of the gallery for a period. I tell you this so that you can know that your work, your photographs, most definitely fit who we are."

Bella smiles and nods. She sees that art is in Dorian's blood as much as the garden is in hers, in a similar way. She loves his description of his childhood so much that she wants to kiss him. Their eyes meet and for a moment Bella knows hers betray this thought. His eyes soften in recognition. He turns and looks out of his side window, so Bella looks out of hers. They exit the expressway and pull up to the curb.

"Arrived," the driver's navigation app announces.

"Welcome to the New York Botanical Gardens," Dorian says.

Chapter Six

GRAN AND THE CHURCH LADY

"Here are the clippings we need, Calsap; be quick," Gran says.

"I will," I say, taking the scrap of paper on which she has scribbled the list of herbs.

I dash from Gran's front window where we were watching Ms. Jefferson approach the house from the street.

Ms. Jefferson is one of Gran's friends from Central Avenue Baptist Church. She used to be housebound due to arthritis but now can get up and about. She is slow and a little unstable, relying heavily on her cane. But she swears that Gran's herbs are the only reason she can walk at all.

I am out the back door, determined to get the herbs Gran wants before Ms. Jefferson reaches the living room and settles herself onto the sofa. Once she settles in, she is not moving for some time. Ms. Jefferson does not believe in short visits. And any minute, Nan is due to pick up Gran and me for the Annual St. Martin's Church Chili Cook-off. Nan's Church Guild puts on this event every year, and the three of us always go. I am the only chili eater among us, but Gran enjoys the choir performances, and Nan just loves to run things. And since she is in charge of the entire event, we must arrive earlier than everyone else.

I race around the garden in my most efficient manner. I want to be quick, but I don't want to soil my church ensemble. I am wearing a new cream satin blouse, a pink floral pleated skirt, matching pink stockings, and black Mary Jane shoes. My outfit is as mature and current as my eighth-grade status requires. Nan and I shopped for this ensemble just for today's occasion.

Gran does not plant her herbs in one place in the garden. She "puts her herbs to work," so the rosemary is a border hedge on the west side of the garden near the house. Once I snip three twigs, I race over to comb through the grasses along the Path of Remembrance to find a turmeric root; then I go to the other end of the garden to gather some chamomile blossoms near the tomato trellis. Gran says tomatoes and chamomile are best friends because chamomile protects tomatoes from fungus. I spot a perfect tomato near the top of the trellis. I snap it off the vine to save for later.

I open the back screen door, and because I am distracted by my perfect tomato and my perfect church outfit, I have forgotten the mint. I turn back to the garden, run toward the rear wall to the raised beds, and reach under the rectangular boxes where the winter mint is protected from the sun and growing wild. I snatch a handful, careful not to kneel on the ground and soil my pink tights. When I get back to the kitchen, I can see that Ms. Jefferson is seated comfortably on the sofa, and Gran is shaking her head up and down, her eyes already glazed over. Ms. Jefferson reminds me of Loretta Devine's character in *The Preacher's Wife*, only older. Her high-pitched, singsong voice is the same as Ms. Devine's, and because it's nonstop, it has a hypnotic quality.

"Yes, I see," is Gran's refrain to whatever Ms. Jefferson is saying. Gran looks over her shoulder at me and sees the ripe tomato in my hand. One singular eyebrow raises to an arch. I set the tomato down on the kitchen table and go straight to the drawer by the sink. I get the right number of zip-top sandwich bags and the black permanent marker. I separate the herbs into the bags, press the air out, and seal them. I write the names of each herb on its bag. I know the routine, and I am trying to make up for the extra time I took in the garden, hoping to make my grandmother's one disapproving eyebrow go back down.

Nan announces her arrival with two quick toots of her horn. The sound travels from the driveway where she has pulled up in her champagne Cadillac Coupe de Ville. Ms. Jefferson is in the middle of an explanation of her ailments. I hand the herb bags to Gran, and she begins to remind Ms. Jefferson what to do with them. Nan honks the horn again. I run out to the car.

"Hi, Nan," I say, breathing heavily from all the running.

"Hello, sweet. Don't you look beautiful today?"

"Thank you."

"Where is your Gran?"

"She is coming. But Ms. Jefferson, the church lady, is here to pick up some herbs. And we tried to take care of things before she sat down, but. . . ." I pause, trying to be tactful, "Ms. Jefferson has a lot to say."

Nan puts the car in park, opens her door, and gets out. She is wearing a peach polyester pantsuit with a matching floral scarf and the most beautiful shoes I have ever seen. They are peach-and-burgundy brocade. They have high, thick heels. The peach on the shoes is the exact color of the pantsuit. The burgundy picks up the exact shade in the scarf. My grandmother looks magnificent. My eyes grow big with admiration and pride. But Nan does not notice this because she is headed to the house, taking big, self-assured strides. I follow her up the porch stairs and into the living room where Ms. Jefferson has not stopped to take a breath. I believed until this moment that nothing could stop Ms. Jefferson once she got going. But she takes in the vision that is my nan and stops cold—mid-sentence. Nan takes advantage of the silence.

"Hello," Nan says as she extends her hand, "I'm Miriam."

"Hello," Ms. Jefferson says, taking Nan's hand with one hand and grasping her cane with the other. She slowly rises to her feet. "You are simply beautiful!"

"You are too kind," says Nan.

"This is Sister Hattie Jefferson," Gran says, "and this is Miriam James, my son's wife's mother and my dear friend."

"I am so sorry to interrupt your visit," Nan says, "I know you must think me so rude to be honking my horn outside like a mad woman. It's just that I am picking up Olivette and Bella, who are accompanying me to church this afternoon."

"Oh, Heavens, Sister Olivette, why didn't you tell me? I have certainly taken up enough of your time." Ms. Jefferson sounds flustered, self-conscious. "Sister Olivette has been so kind to give me these healing herbs and her wonderful advices. I simply do not know what I would do if she hadn't cured so many of my ailments. She is truly a gift, and I. . . ."

"Yes, she is." Nan cuts her off, puts a hand on the back of her shoulder, and leads her toward the door. Nan walks the woman all the way to her car, setting a pace that is quite a bit quicker than Ms. Jefferson is accustomed to walking.

Gran takes a quick look in the mirror. She is wearing one of her favorite church dresses, a navy-blue shift with a sailor collar and gold military buttons down the front. She has matching stockings and leather ballet flats.

"You look nice," I say.

"Well, one must not look shabby next to your Nan," she says, grabbing her purse and my hand. She locks the front door, and we make our way to the Coup de Ville.

On our way to St. Martin's, Gran scolds Nan for manhandling Ms. Jefferson.

"Well," Nan says, "Ms. Jefferson is a lovely woman, but I suspect she can hold her own."

"No doubt," says Gran. "Still, Miriam, she is ailing."

Nan shrugs, offering no remorse. "She says you cured her? Cure is a mighty strong word. What did you do?" she asks.

"Cure is not the word I would use," Gran says, "she has terrible arthritis, terribly crippling, so I gave her some plants from the garden—I showed her how to make some teas and tinctures. And evidently, we hit upon some helpful things for her."

"Before Gran's herbs, Ms. Jefferson couldn't even walk," I say.

"I don't believe it," says Nan.

"Neither did her rheumatologist," says Gran, "but she swears by them, and who am I to argue? She'd been unable to leave the house, and I went to visit her with the other members of the Usher Board. I knew she was a tea drinker, so I brought her some chamomile blossoms and sweet marjoram tea for the inflammation and pain. She called me a few days after that visit and asked for more. So, I started to give her some other things."

"Well, she was moving pretty well today," Nan said.

"Yes, it's been . . . how long now, Bella? At least nine months or so," Gran says, not waiting for my help. "I think the chamomile and marjoram mostly help her sleep, which is a blessing. The rosemary tincture helps with just about everything else because it helps you function better—head and heart. Yes, it fortifies the head and heart."

"I did not know you were such an herb evangelist," Nan says.

"Well. . . ." Gran sounds hesitant. "I am not so much an herb evangelist as I am just an old woman who knows the properties of the garden, Miriam. And I don't at all mind sharing, but I told Sister Hattie that her next steps should be to start her own garden. Herb seeds and plants are the cheapest pharmaceuticals on the planet. The fresh air and the exercise in the garden are the best for the body and soul," Gran continues, "but word has spread about Sister Hattie, and I do not plan to continue being the herb pusher for my church folk. It's getting to be too much."

"Indeed," Nan says, "that could take over your life. You need to start charging folks for your efforts, Olivette. That'll get them gardening on their own."

"How is your herb garden, Miriam?" Gran asks.

"Oh, you know, I have a little of this and that."

"There's basil and parsley," I report, "the oregano is struggling a bit, though. Nan does not love growing herbs so much."

"They can look so unkempt no matter how you tend them," Nan says.

"All of your gorgeous roses, Miriam," Gran says, "roses need thyme."

"Of course, they do," Nan says. "patience is a virtue when it comes to roses."

"No, no, I mean the herb thyme," Gran says.

"Ah." Nan is amused at this new comprehension. "Bella is always saying that to me. And I always thought she was meaning, wisely, that roses need *time,* that they require patience." Nan looks up at me through the reflection in the rearview mirror. Our eyes lock and I smile because I never really understood what the saying meant either, until right now. Gran always said it, and I often repeated it. But I thought she meant time too.

"No, dear, thyme, T-H-Y-M-E. Thyme helps keep the aphids away from your roses."

"Yes, aphids are horrid. But thyme is so unruly," Nan says as she pulls into the St. Martin's Church parking lot.

"Not as unruly as aphids, Miriam, not as unruly as aphids," Gran says.

Nan's roses got aphids once, and I helped Mr. Blackshear spray each stem with soap and water. We wiped the translucent bugs from the larger stems, and then we finished them off with a bag full of ladybugs purchased by mail order. In the gardening world, aphid-eating ladybugs are superheroes, even the ladybugs that come in the mail.

There are only two other cars in the church parking lot, and Nan appears pleased with her timing. "Let's get this show on the road," she says, grabbing her peach purse from under her seat.

Nan retrieves the keys from the pastor in the rectory and unlocks the auditorium. Rows of chairs are set in place, and tables are arranged on the periphery of the room with tablecloths and easels. Soon trucks pull up with chili cook-off crews and all manner of cooking apparatuses. Mr. Sullivan, St. Martin's choir director, rolls the piano from backstage to its proper position down stage left. He asks a few young men in choir robes to help him with the welcome sign. When it is hung, he stands near the back door to greet the choir groups arriving early for a run-of-show.

Gran has just finished helping to set up the ticket table and makes her way to a seat in the center of the front row. This is her favorite part of arriving early. She can listen as each choir takes the stage to do their voice exercises, warm-ups, and run-throughs. I busy myself helping chili competitors set up their displays. This way, I can get a little whiff of the chili lineup. When the chili booth setup is nearly complete, and I am no longer useful, I follow Nan around and act as her assistant.

"Bella, would you kindly please run to the car and fetch my purse?" Nan says.

"But I remember you bringing it with you," I say. I look around in the places I believe Nan has been and quickly find her purse on a chair in the auditorium kitchen. I bring it to her.

"Thank you, sweet." Now she rummages through the purse. "I cannot seem to find my note cards for the program. Would you please grab a printed program from the welcome table, dear one?"

People are filing in now and filling the seats, congregation families and a bus full of seniors. I see a few kids from my middle school, who also attend St. Martin's church. Gran has invited a few of her acquaintances to sit with her in the front row. Soon the choir practice is finished, and the chili tables are ready to serve. It's showtime.

"Ms. James, it's time to do the welcome and benediction," one of the organizers tells Nan.

"Bella, won't you come up with me? I need a wingman today," Nan says. So, I follow her onstage. She approaches the microphone stand.

"Good afternoon," Nan starts. "Welcome to the Fifteenth Annual St. Martin's Chili Cook-Off." The audience claps. "I would like to thank a few people before Pastor. . . ." Nan pauses, looking down at the printed program in her hand. "Pastor. . . ." Pause. Uncomfortable pause. I look up at Nan and realize she has forgotten the pastor's name.

"Father Benedict," I whisper.

"Pastor Benedict. Before Father Benedict comes up to bless us and our food, I would like to thank a few people." Nan places the reading glasses she is holding in her hand onto the tip of her nose. I look up at the printed program and see it is covered with her beautiful cursive. I wonder when she had time to do all that writing.

"Firstly, thanking God for his grace," she says. "Would the Church Guild members please stand?" As the crowd claps, Nan reads the names of her longtime Guild friends from her notes. They stand as their names are called. She finishes reading, and the standing members start looking around at each other. Some point to Sister Jones, who seems to be uncertain. She is half standing and half sitting.

"You forgot Sister Jones," I whisper.

"Oh, Heavens," Nan says, then turns back to the microphone, "and last but certainly not least, our beloved Sister Jones."

Sister Jones pops to a full standing position and pulls her skirt down over her hips so that it lengthens and covers her chubby knees. She is all smiles and waves now.

"This is your Church Guild, Ladies and Gentlemen, and the planning committee for this event," Nan says. "Please give them a hearty round of applause." Nan beams down at me from atop her beautiful brocade high-heeled shoes.

"And now please help me convince your pastor, Father Benedict, to come up and say a few words and blessings." Nan tucks the program under her arm and claps her hands. The crowd joins in with thunderous applause.

When all the blessings and announcements are delivered, Nan and I leave the stage and proceed to the back of the auditorium. "Thank you, wingman," Nan says as we are walking. She holds up her hand and I high-five it. "And as compensation for your service, you may be the first to fix your plate."

Ms. Daniels, the youngest member of the Church Guild, runs up to us just as I am getting my bowl and says, "Pardon me, Sister James, would you please point me to the trophies? I cannot seem to find them."

"I believe I put them in the kitchen, as always," Nan says.

"No, ma'am, they are not in the kitchen. I looked there and backstage," says Ms. Daniels.

Nan turns to me. "Bella, did you see where I set the trophies?"

"No, ma'am. Are they still in your trunk?" I ask.

"Ah, perhaps. Grab my keys and check, would you, wingman?"

I set down my bowl and take off in a run because I am trying to get back to the business of the chili. But when I open the trunk, it is empty. Ms. Daniels catches up and, seeing the empty trunk, turns to Nan who is standing in the auditorium door. Ms. Daniels shakes her head no. I run back with the keys.

"Bella, come with me. I am afraid I will have to send you and your granny on a mission."

While the chili cook-off is in full swing—people eating, comparing, and judging, Gran and I head to Nan's house to find and retrieve the championship trophies that Nan now believes she left out on her veranda.

"Why do you suppose she had them on the back porch?" Gran asks me when we are stopped at a red light.

"That's probably where she displayed them in the days leading up to today," I say. Gran doesn't understand that everything of importance in Nan's house happens on the veranda. She somehow just thinks the veranda is any ole back porch. Once we pass through the porte cochere and reach the back of Nan's driveway, I bypass the house and go straight through the gate to the backyard. I take the veranda steps two at a time, but I can already see that the trophies are not there. I get Nan's extra key from under the fake rock near the gate and unlock the sliding glass door to the house. The house is silent, except for the *tic-tic-tocking* of the wall clock in the kitchen. I look all over the family room. I do not see any trophies. I exit the side door and motion to Gran that I cannot find them. She gets out of the car and comes inside.

"I don't see them anywhere," I say.

"Let's spread out," Gran says.

She points me in the direction of the kitchen, and she goes

down the hallway to the bedrooms. I search the kitchen including the pantry. I join Gran in Nan's bedroom. She is standing transfixed in front of Nan's dresser, staring into the dresser mirror.

"What the holy hell?" Gran says. I turn and understand why she has paused. The mirror is covered with a sea of yellow, blue, and pink sticky notes. They appear to be organized in clumps, in a grid pattern, much like Nan's garden. We both move in closer and see that the notes have names of old friends and family members on them. One clump has the names of Nan's vitamins and medications, another has various names and phone numbers of people I do not recognize.

"Did you know that your nan did this?" Gran turns to me. "This must be how she plans her days."

"No, ma'am," I say. I see there are a small group of Post-its with church member names on them, but there are also many more groups represented in this mass of notes. I am feeling like I have failed Nan in some way that I cannot yet explain. I am so accustomed to providing translation services between my two grandmothers, but I am at a loss about this. The sticky-note display looks like some sort of long-term project. Nan always shares her projects with me. I am always her helper. It's why I can finish her sentences and anticipate her next move. This project also looks fun and interesting. Maybe it's a puzzle or strategic plan. I cannot fathom why she would keep it from me.

"Well, this is not any of our business." Gran is suddenly whispering as if she thinks the walls will tell Nan about our intrusion. She leads me out of the room even though I do not want to go. I want to figure it out. On our way back down the hallway, we see the tops of the trophies sticking out of a cardboard box sitting on the floor.

"There," I say and point to the trophies.

Gran grabs the box, and we head for the car.

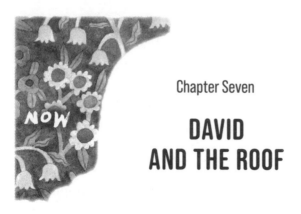

Chapter Seven

DAVID
AND THE ROOF

APRIL

"Dad, if I show you a secret, do you promise not to freak out?" Bella asks her father, who is standing in the middle of her living room, assessing her apartment for the first time.

"I can promise to *try* not to freak out. . . ." David Fontaine says, shifting from one foot to the other because he is too big for this tiny space and there is no place for him to sit. His new girlfriend, Amy, is sitting on Bella's miniature sofa, the only seating available.

"Amy, would you excuse us for a moment?" Bella says. Amy looks relieved to be excluded. Bella suspects Amy already knows that the Fontaine family has a whole slew of baggage of which she wants no part. David and Amy are visiting from Portland. Before Bella moved in, she and her father had only seen pictures of the apartment and taken a short virtual tour online. David trusted his friend and oldest customer's representation of the space when the two fathers agreed on this roommate arrangement for their daughters. Now, David has arrived to inspect Bella's situation for himself.

The new girlfriend he has in tow, a thirty-something blonde white woman, is her father's first official girlfriend since the divorce, at least to Bella's knowledge. Amy is youthful, pretty, and pleasant enough.

"We'll be right back," David assures Amy. "This better be good," he whispers as he and Bella leave the apartment.

"I'm not excluding Amy, Dad, I am sparing her," Bella says when they are in the hallway. She laughs but David doesn't. He follows his daughter down the hall and up the stairs. The raggedy roof door is wide open. Bella has not asked the superintendent to fix the door because she thinks it's too risky—she doesn't want to alert him to her plans. He might not approve. He might address the door's glitch, but then install a lock. So instead of a formal repair, Bella has fashioned a loop of thick twine through the doorknob hole and tied it to a hook screwed into the wall right outside of the door. As an additional safeguard against it getting stuck again, she glued a doorstop to the bottom edge and now when the door closes, the door jamb is already in place to prevent it from slamming shut. David steps out onto the roof and takes in the view.

"This is the beginning of my new garden," Bella says.

She shows her father the few pots that hold newly planted seeds and seedlings. The seedlings have barely broken through the thick blanket of mulch, and her three sapling dwarf fruit trees have just begun to spread their roots in their new pots. Right now, they just look like sticks in dirt.

"Oh, you tricky little minx," he says, "this is why you love this apartment, isn't it."

"Yes," Bella says, "the building owner's mother used to live on the sixth floor, and this used to be her garden."

"But tenants aren't allowed out here," he says. "There's a hefty fine."

"As it turns out, the building has three different roofs. The other roof surfaces are unsafe, and the super keeps those doors locked. But this one is begging to be a garden again."

"Don't tell me, Olivette-Junior," David says, hugging Bella by her shoulders, "you believe that the old phantom garden has called to you and begged you for a revival. Have I got it right?"

"I am *not* Olivette-Junior. I am my own self," Bella says, rejecting her father's comparison to his mother, "but you are absolutely right, this was meant to be."

David is shaking his head. "Whatever you say, but that is some craziness your Gran would say, and you are her mini-me."

""I am *not* her mini-me," Bella says, "and it's not craziness. It's true. Garden spirits are a real thing."

"Jesus, Bella. I am not financing a roof garden. And you cannot afford it with your spotty photo gigs."

"That's funny. One minute you think I am Olivette-Junior and the next minute you don't. I'm starting out super slow and I've spent pennies so far. I know how to build a garden for next to nothing. Gran *did* teach me that."

"Well, you don't have *next* to nothing. You have nothing. But the point is, the time you are spending building this garden, you should be working a job."

Bella takes in a breath. "Of course, you're right," she says. She realizes that her father's reaction is the one she expected, the one she deserves. He agreed to pay for her apartment. He arranged this ideal setup with his client's daughter, Camille, who, as it turns out, is never home. So, it feels to Bella almost like she lives alone, which is her preference. In return, Bella promised to support herself and work hard to relieve her father of the rent obligation. She just hoped he would see how perfect the roof is for a garden. She knows he has no love for gardens or gardening, having resented his mother's passion. All his childhood, he felt imposed upon by the time she spent in her garden and the work she required of him. He always felt like his mother's second priority. So, he is not likely ever going to come around to endorsing this same fixation in his daughter, even though he is at least partially responsible by leaving Bella under the care of her grandmothers. Still, Bella knows she was foolish to expect him to understand or support her roof garden aspirations. She has no right to show her disappointment.

"We'd better get back to Amy," she says. She will accept that at least he has not forbidden it.

"Bella, I know this is important to you," David says, "and I know you are going to do it regardless of how I feel about it. But try not to let it take over your life. You have professional goals and now is not the time to. . . ." He trails off and looks around. "This place really is set up well already, isn't it?"

"Yes, pretty much; it already has drainage and water spigots in four places. I found them under a pile of insulation and tape!" Bella tries to contain her excitement lest she show that she is already obsessed. The look on David's face tells her that he already knows this is true.

"It's who I am, Dad."

"I know, sweetheart, but promise me this will be a garden you alone can afford. This means that it does not take precedent over your paid work. Promise me."

"I promise."

"Where did you get those galvanized tubs?" He is trying to be open, and she loves him for it.

"From the community garden. I volunteer at the Plaza de Cultural Community Garden on Mondays," Bella says. "One of the other gardeners is moving to the suburbs and was planning to discard them."

"Bella." David is annoyed again and Bella regrets mentioning the community garden.

71

"I never get jobs on Mondays, Dad. Never any weddings, rarely any events happen on Mondays. Plus, I already got a wedding and a birthday gig from people I met at the community garden."

He looks unconvinced.

"That's how it works, Dad. In this line of work, you gotta put yourself out in the community to get gigs."

Bella grabs his arm and pulls him over to the front of the building. "That's the Empire State Building right there, you know?"

"I didn't even notice it," David says.

"So, this Amy, how did you two meet?" This is a big shift in the conversation, and it is unchartered territory. She and her father have never discussed their love lives.

"In yoga class," he says.

"Wait! *You* do yoga?"

"Yes, ever since I ran into Amy in the grocery store with a yoga mat. She was in front of me in line at the checkout. She crossed the street and went into the studio. So, I joined."

"That's gross, Dad."

He laughs, shakes his head, and shrugs in agreement.

"What about you? Have you put yourself out there yet?"

"If you mean, am I dating someone, the answer is yes, sort of."

"Who is he? Does he make you laugh and never make you cry?"

"Well, it started out kind of rough," Bella says, "I blamed him for ruining my artistic future, but he has redeemed himself."

"Don't tell me you're dating the clown who bait-and-switched you into moving here? Not the gallery guy."

"Yes, the gallery guy," Bella says, trying to hide her embarrassment.

"Jesus, Bella."

"He didn't know his mother was going to crush my dreams."

"Your art show is back on, then?"

"Well, it's going to be. The gallery is going through a bit of a management transition right now."

"Oh, boy! Does the mother know about this transition, or is it all in your boyfriend's head?" David asks. Bella is amazed and annoyed at how her father has rightly surmised the generational tensions at the Herman Gallery, even with the limited information she has provided him in their short phone calls. Now that her father has agreed to help with her move, he has been reaching out more and checking in on her. This visit, she knows, is his way of extending himself in the absence of her grandmothers.

"And you're dating Jewish guys now?" David asks.

"No, I am dating *a* Jewish guy. And isn't that the pot calling the kettle black?" Bella says. David laughs so hard, a whoop and holler that Bella had not heard in a very long time. His laugh makes her laugh hard too. After a full minute, they get a hold of themselves. David is nodding his head yes. He has to concede this point.

"Bella, the young man has to prove himself." The mirth of the moment is gone. "I don't trust him. He sold you a bill of goods that he had no title to. He brought you here under false pretenses. Now that he has you, what do you have?"

"It's not like that, Dad."

"Well, only you know. Don't sell yourself short, Bella."

"How about I don't sell myself at all," Bella says. How can she get her father to understand that something truly special happened between her and Dorian among the still barren rose bushes in the New York Botanical Gardens.

Dorian had said, "I guess this is not the best time to visit. It's too early yet?"

And Bella said, "Oh, no, no. This is a perfect time. I love this time of year, when spring is having its way with winter, like it's saying, 'Okay, Winter, you have had your last hurrah. Now, it's my turn.'" She had taken Dorian's arm and led him down the path, near the edge of one of the rose beds. "Look. See the leaf buds forming on the stems? There are a million different miracles happening all around us right now," she'd said, but then she'd felt self-conscious about how gleeful she was to be there—surrounded by exotic varieties of roses on one side and ancient trees on the other. She was so thankful to Dorian for bringing her.

"Honestly, these bushes look like they are dead, dry sticks to me," Dorian said, "but I like seeing this place through your eyes. You're like an awestruck kid and an ancient sage all rolled up into one person." This is when their eyes met, and Bella saw something different in Dorian's.

"I *am* an ancient girl," Bella said.

"I did say ancient, didn't I? That is your word."

"Yes, it is."

Bella knows her father would never comprehend what it's like when someone knows so much about your work that they have adopted your language. How could she explain to him how Dorian's wild and crazy childhood and her own complicated one have somehow intersected. Like two circles in a Venn Diagram, they overlap at an essential place, where childhood trauma and wonder become the same thing in the same way. David knows that Dorian appeared in Bella's life at the exact right moment. But he doesn't know that she did the same for Dorian. She knows that David will never understand this, so she decides that she will keep her feelings for Dorian to herself.

"I'm just going to see how it goes, Dad," she says, pushing her father toward the roof door. "We should go make sure Amy's not trying on my clothes."

"Be nice. She likes gardens, too, you know," David says as they descend the stairs.

"Amy? Really? You connected yourself up with a gardener?"

"Yes, she grows vegetables and herbs. Nothing serious, radishes and onions. And mint, all over the place. Easy stuff."

"What do you know about easy?" Bella teases.

"Don't you forget, your grandmother forced me to be her farmhand when I was little. I know more than I care to."

"Well, I should have taken Amy up to the roof instead of you, then."

"Yeah, you should have."

"Next time I will. I took Mom up to the roof when she came for New Year's, and we almost died."

David stops in his tracks. His sudden, unexpected halt just as he steps from the last stair into the hallway of Bella's floor causes her to plow into him from behind.

"Your mother came here?"

"Yep, she came to help me move in and set up."

"She got on a plane and flew across the country? By herself?"

"Yes, Dad. I thought you knew. We had a great time . . . other than our dicey roof experience."

"You know your mother doesn't fly, right? She has always been too afraid, anxiety attacks, the whole bit."

"Yeah, well, I picked her up from the airport. She was happy and relaxed . . . well, as relaxed as she ever is."

"That's wild. You know, she asked all these questions about your move. Wanted to see the lease. Kept after me about your move-in dates. She was planning to come all along. She didn't tell me." David, talking in a near whisper, is thinking things through, trying to wrap his head around it. "So, what happened on the roof?"

Bella relays the story of how she and her mother narrowly escaped death by hypothermia. Bella has cultivated this version of the story so that it is both harrowing and funny. She tells it whenever she meets someone new, as her first and best that's-so-New-York story. But David doesn't laugh. It's as if he thinks Bella made it all up.

"Your mother didn't freak out?" he asks.

"Yes, we both freaked out. Mom had a moment when she did her disappearing act. But then she snapped out of it and got very philosophical—told me that she loved me and that we were the best thing that ever happened to her. She was all last confessions and 'if we die.' And I was like, 'we ain't dying today, missy.'"

"We? *We* were the best thing that ever happened to her?"

Bella sees a hopeful spark in her father's eyes. She knows what that hope feels like from the inside.

"Yes," she stretches the truth, "she said our family is the best thing she has ever done."

"Huh," he scoffs, "how long was she here?"

"Three short days. We shopped and bought winter clothes and groceries. We explored the main library and cooked for each other."

"Sounds like normal mother–daughter stuff," he says.

"Yep, it was pretty wonderful. Mom really is a different person, Dad."

"I know. I'm happy for you. You finally get a mother."

"But you don't trust it, right? You don't believe she is back for good."

David stops in the hallway before they enter the apartment. He turns to his daughter, his eyes finding hers.

"There is no real 'back for good,' Bella. Your mother is back until she is not."

He starts walking to the apartment again. Bella wants to ask him if he still loves her mother, but she cannot get up the nerve. It would be too tragic to know for sure, even though she thinks she already does.

Amy is standing at the window in Bella's bedroom when they return, looking at her phone. She says she's hungry and is searching for a place to eat. Bella suggests they walk to a popular Italian restaurant a few blocks away. When they descend the six sets of stairs to the street, the weather that greets them is glorious—the sky is indigo, and the sun is setting behind the skyline, reflecting a whole spectrum of orange hues across New York's glass towers. The wind is gentle but insistent.

"When there's wind like this, I feel like I am Mary Tyler Moore," Bella says as they reach the end of the block. She spreads her arms and does a half twirl.

"Who is Mary Tyler Moore?" asks Amy.

"Old TV show? The seventies? Mary Tyler Moore as Mary Richards, cult hero of every single-girl-in-the-city." Bella says.

"You mean Carrie Bradshaw?" Amy says.

"No, no, not the same," Bella says.

"Mary Tyler Moore could have been Sarah Jessica Parker's grandmother," David says. "How do you even know about Mary Tyler Moore? That's way before your time."

"Hulu," Bella says. "When I first moved here, I read a satirical article about adjusting to the city as a single woman, and it provided a TV watch list. *Sex in the City* was, of course, on the list. *Living Single*, which I also love, set in Brooklyn. Also, *Mary Tyler Moore*. She is supposed to be in Minneapolis, but I love Mary. I marathoned that show for days. I guess I am more of a Mary than a Carrie."

"I can appreciate that," says David.

"Thank you," Bella says.

"I'll have to check it out," says Amy. She walks a little ahead of David and Bella. She is tiny, yoga-tight-bodied. After her mother's visit, Bella called Bernard to tell him about her new experience with their mother. She rarely talks to her brother, but the visit was so monumental, Bella felt the need to tell someone, and Bernard was the only person she felt could fully understand. Bernard, in turn, informed Bella that their father was dating Amy, only he didn't call Amy by her name or even "new girlfriend." With typical Bernard sarcasm, he'd said, "So you know about your father and the teenager?" Amy is nowhere near a teenager, but since she does not know Mary Tyler Moore, Bella decides that, yes—Amy is more adolescent than adult. David found Amy just one month after he relocated himself and his business to Portland.

"So why Portland, Dad?" Bella asks.

"It's beautiful. It's cheap compared to LA. People love the outdoors in Portland, but they don't like mosquitoes. The city had a little West Nile disease problem a few years back. So, I saw an opportunity to grow the business there." David owns and operates a mosquito systems business. He installs and maintains them in homes and businesses. His impeccable business timing and intense work ethic have made his business successful, even during the recession. West Nile disease has been his best friend.

"But don't you run into a lot of naturalists and environmentalists in Portland?" Bella asks. "How do they feel about a mosquito system that emits poison into their air?"

"It's not poison, Bella. Right now, the environmentalists don't love the idea of our mosquito system, but you know what they hate even more?"

"West Nile Disease," Amy and Bella say in unison.

"That's right. They hate the possibility of their children getting sick and dying." He sounds like the masterful salesman that he is. "Because it's invisible, people forget the system is there until they let it run out of juice and the mosquitoes show up. It's my job to never let them run out of juice. People are funny about their commitment to environmental causes once the enemy starts to affect their own lives."

"I guess I can see that," Bella concedes.

"Did you know that Portland is called the City of Roses?" David asks Bella.

"No, Dad. Pasadena, California, is the City of Roses."

"No," David says, "Pasadena has the Tournament of Roses. But before Pasadena was even a city, Portland became the official City of Roses. Back in the late 1800s, someone planted roses along the roadsides for two hundred miles."

"Wow. That's impressive. It's the reason you moved there, right?" Bella asks, knowing better.

"Definitely not, but it's a good reason for you to come visit at some point."

"Honestly, I've had a little falling out with West Coast roses. I don't love them so much anymore." David knows his daughter enough to know the impossibility of this statement and how it relates to her Nan.

"You don't like roses? Says nobody ever!" Amy chimes in. "Who doesn't love roses?" Amy, incredulous, looks at Bella and then at David. To her credit, she takes the silence between them as a sign to leave it alone. Bella suspects she's been coached.

The restaurant is two blocks farther than Bella remembered. David complains about the walk and the long wait for a table. He pledges that once they are seated, he is going to take his time and enjoy the meal he has earned. True to his promise, he orders extra appetizers, big entrées, and three bottles of wine.

"Oh, look at that adorable dog," Amy says about a Pomeranian whose head is sticking out of the lady's purse in the next booth.

"So many people have those purse dogs here," Bella says. "It was in the news recently. At first, they were the hottest accessory. But establishments started banning them and not letting people bring them inside. That's when they became comfort animals. Now all you need is a note from your shrink and your little Boo gets to eat dinner next to you everywhere."

"Well, *I* think they're comforting," Amy says, trying to mount a defense for the dog world.

"Yep, until they take a shit in your purse!" David says. He and Bella think this is hilarious. Amy doesn't. Bella wonders how long Amy will be able to endure her father's dark humor and hard-earned cynicism.

After dinner, David wants to hire a car back to the apartment. Amy tells him, "Oh, come on, David, let's walk. When in New York, do like New Yorkers. And what kind of Portlander are you, anyway." Then she says to Bella, "Everybody walks in Portland too."

So, David relents. On the trek back to the apartment, Bella sees that someone has discarded an old iron patio table out by the curb. One leg is bent, and the paint is chipped, showing many layers of colors—black, green, and some brown that might actually be rust. As they pass by, Bella sees that there are two matching chairs lying on their sides near the gutter.

"I *love* this about New York!" Bella almost yells. "Dad, help me take these back to the apartment."

"No," he says, keeping a steady pace, determined to keep moving. But Amy and Bella have stopped.

"Please, Dad. These are perfect for the roof, and they are free."

"Jesus H, Bella," David says. He walks back to the discards because he knows he is caught in his own cost-free mandate.

"This is what we in New York call freegan furniture," Bella says, repeating a phrase she has only overheard once, when her roommate and her boyfriend were discussing how to live cheaply in New York.

"Oh, I know what freegans are, people who eat out of the trash. You don't pick out of the trash for food, do you, Bella?" Amy says as she picks up one of the chairs.

"No, ma'am. I just pick up these perfectly useful discarded household items," Bella says. At this, David starts to walk away again.

"David." Amy raises her voice, establishing a new authority, "Get the table! Jesus, don't be such a buzzkill. One man's trash is another man's treasure."

He stops walking and turns. Amy cocks her head and widens her eyes. She stares David down until he returns and picks up the table. Right then Bella changes her mind about her father's girlfriend. From now on, Bella is Team Amy.

Chapter Eight

NAN
AND THE FALL

We pause to survey the blossoms, seeking just the right candidates for the Sunday dinner table bouquet. It's warm, but the late morning sky is overcast. I take a deep breath in. The air is humid, still, and thick with the smell of soil and Estée Lauder perfume. I am holding Nan's hand when we cross the patches of lawn to the garden path. The dew on the grass makes the tips of our shoes wet, and the damp pebbles on the path clump together to form slippery mounds around our steps.

"We'll cut some Dutch iris," Nan says, stopping in front of the cluster of tall, mature flowers. Nan looks them over, assessing them.

"Do you see the Dutch iris, Bella?" Nan asks.

"Yes, ma'am," I answer, confused by the question. Of course I see the irises right in front of us. These are the clusters I helped Mr. Blackshear prune last spring when the bulk of the older plants threatened to spill over onto the path. We were following Nan's orders. She could not abide, she'd said, this kind of disorder—leggy stems and spent blossoms bending beyond their borders. I don't say *of course I see them* out loud. But perhaps my expression does.

"No," Nan says, "I mean have you *really* looked at the Dutch iris? To truly see them, dear one, first you must close your eyes." Nan closes her eyes and turns her face up to the sky just as the clouds clear and the garden is bathed in the sun's commanding light. She smiles into the warmth and holds her breath.

"Do you feel a breeze of any kind?" she asks.

"No, ma'am," I say. Now my eyes are closed, my face turned skyward too. I only see bright orange through my eyelids. I am concentrating, but the air in the garden is stock-still.

"So then," Nan says, "look at the irises now."

I open my eyes and focus them on the patch of blossoms. I see that they are swaying ever so slightly and haphazardly, some leaning north and then south, some west and then east, like a crowd of teenagers moving to their own beat.

"Are they doing that on their own?" I ask.

"Yes, they are speaking to us, Bella, letting us know that they see us too. Perhaps this late in their season, it's their last dance."

It is late fall, and the blooms are sparse, but this variety is a colorful mix of blue, lavender, and purple.

"Thank you, beautiful ladies, for allowing us this gift," Nan says. She does a short curtsy, her arms outstretched. The dancing irises seem to sway a touch more, this way and that, in acknowledgment of Nan's gesture. She turns and reaches for the step stool she uses when she is ready to take cuttings.

"Who else will we cut today, Nanny? *I* want to thank someone," I say, enjoying this ritual of honoring the flowers before they become our table dressing.

"Just the irises," Nan says, "they alone will go well with your mother's dinner."

My mother is making smothered pork chops with purple cabbage coleslaw, a family favorite.

"Yes, but can we put them in your yellow vase, the one you

usually save for the Midas Touch tulips?" At twelve, I've developed an interest in the dinner table flower arrangements, usually Nan's only Sunday dinner task.

"Well, now, dear, you know that very special vase is only for my very special tulips," Nan pauses, reconsiders, "but, yes, we can. That will be a beautiful combination."

The Midas Touch, so bright yellow they look like shiny gold coins, are Nan's favorite tulip variety. But the bulbs aren't even planted yet. Nan lets them stay extra long in the refrigerator since the Southern California cold is not always cold enough to result in a hearty springtime display. I decide the iridescent yellow vase is too pretty to ignore for an entire season.

I run to the west side of the garden behind the garage to the potting shed to grab the shears. I race back. Nan turns and catches me mid-sprint.

"Do not run with those shears, Bella! You know better!" she says, with a sharpness to her tone that stops me in my tracks. I stand on the path and hold up the shears to show that I am at least holding them properly, blades down, handles up. Nan sees that I have grabbed the wrong ones.

"No, no, dear. Get the pruners with the red handle," she calls out.

I return to the shed and just as I exchange one tool for the other, Nan yells out.

"Bella!"

I turn but I do not see her. She is not where she was.

She calls out to me again. "Bella?" This time it is a question and then a moan that barely escapes her throat. I drop the pruners and run to the path. She is down, lying on her side and holding her left thigh with both hands. I run to her, screaming for my father. When I look up to the house, I see that my mother is already through the sliding glass doors and standing on the veranda. Her eyes are big, round circles, and her face is even more ashen than my grandmother's. She is not moving. Nan screams in pain. With every scream, I yell out for my father, who finally pushes past the statue that is my mother and runs to us.

"Eddi, call nine one one," my father says, "*Eddi!*" He is trying to break through to my mother, who finally runs into the house. Dad and I are listening to hear if she picks up the phone in the family room. But we do not hear the sounds that we should—the lifting of the receiver or her voice—and she does not return. After what feels like an eternity, Bernard appears at the door.

"Bern, go see if your mother is calling nine one one," Dad says as he sits down behind Nan and eases her back onto his thighs. She is still gripping her leg.

"There now, Miriam, try not to move. Let's just sit tight."

I am sitting on my haunches beside her. I touch her shoulder. But every time she cries out, I draw my hand back.

"Did you see what happened, Bella?" Dad asks me.

"No, I was at the potting shed."

"I tripped, David, over the blasted stool," Nan says. Her voice is a mixture of disgust and anguish, her breathing labored, like she's been running laps.

"I am feeling a little queasy, David," Nan says between gasps.

"Breathe, Miriam," Dad says, "deep breaths in and out. In through your nose. Out through your mouth. Slow. Slow."

Nan closes her eyes and follows Dad's instructions. She seems calmer for a moment. But with the slightest move, she shrieks in pain. Now, I'm feeling queasy too. I take in gulps of air. We hear sirens in the distance. Bernard appears on the veranda.

"They are coming," he says.

"Go out front and show them back," my father says, "and get your mother."

"Leave Eddi be," Nan says, "just leave her be."

We follow the ambulance to the hospital. In the car, my mother is frantic, inconsolable, her chest heaving as if she cannot catch her breath. Her face is red and blotchy, wet with her tears. Between the siren and my mother's sobs, we barely hear her say, "I feel like I'm being swallowed whole."

My father, focusing on the ambulance that is pulling away at a much faster speed than he dares to drive, does not ask my mother what she means. But Bernard and I hear her say, "swallowed whole" from the back seat, and we look at each other in fear and bewilderment. Swallowed by what?

After an endless Sunday night under the too-bright lights of the emergency waiting room, it's Monday morning. Dad wakes us early. We get ready for school, but instead of heading to drop-off, we go in the opposite direction. We are going to Nan's. Bernard and I look at each other, our eyes asking the questions we don't voice. We never miss school unless we have a fever. Dad looks so tired. He is wearing what he wore yesterday, his untacked, wrinkled shirt and dirt-stained pants from kneeling with Nan on the garden path. His face is unshaven with an uneven beard already asserting itself.

When we arrive at Nan's, he tells us to wait in the car. Soon he comes out with a suitcase. He sets it down on the porch and waves in our direction to come and get it. I beat Bernard to it and bring it to the trunk. Bernard opens the driver's side door and unlatches the hatch. As I am getting back into the car, my mother and father appear at Nan's front door. I freeze at the sight of my mother. Dad has his arm around her shoulders. She is holding his other hand. They pause as he readjusts his hold so that he can close the door behind them. He is supporting her as if she cannot propel herself even though she is trying.

"I will drive you, Eddi," he is saying, hushed, gentle but insistent.

"I think it's better if I drive myself. I want to do this, David. You stay with the children. I can get myself there." Her voice sounds thin and fragile, and I wonder why my father is not pointing out the obvious. She can barely stand.

Mom is going back in. The first time my mother checked herself into Summer House, the place she goes to get well, it was after that final argument with my father about her refusal to seek help for her illness. She was not herself almost ever, he'd said. She wasn't doing her part, he insisted. We all needed her to check in *all of the time*, he pleaded. She had refused to commit to help. This is just who she is, she'd said. My father did not accept this. Get help or get out, he'd said. Well, those were not his exact words. But they are what Bernard and I heard, and they are exactly what she did. More precisely, she did both. She was gone for weeks. When she resurfaced, she was moving in with Nan. She had met my father's conditions, but she did not return home. I remember understanding why she would want to live with Nan. I wanted that for myself. I never considered then the effect this must have had on my father. I am sure it broke his heart. But he never expressed any outward emotion to Bernard or me, ever. He was stoic and utilitarian. He delivered me to my grandmothers and Bernard to the baseball field.

On the first Sunday after Mom moved in with Nan, the three of us—Dad, Bernard, and I—arrived, as usual, in time for afternoon tea. As before, Mom stayed in the kitchen and prepared dinner. On our way back home after dinner, we asked my father why Mom was not coming home with us.

"She is still getting better; we want to give her all the time she needs, right?"

"But why does she have to be *here?*" Bernard pressed.

"This is where she thinks she is best, for now," my father said vaguely. "It's not for forever."

"Maybe she needs to be with her mom," I whispered to Bernard in the back seat of the car. I was sure Nan would know what to do for her, and I wanted to clear up Bernard's confusion. He did not know Nan like I did.

For six months of Sundays, we went home after dinner without our mother. And then, on a Sunday of no particular significance, when routine and managed expectations bore a comfortable normalcy, Nan fell, and all my mother could do was stand on the veranda like a statue.

"I understand you would like to go on your own, Eddi," my father says, "but there is no reason to have the car sitting at Summer House, in the parking lot. First, we'll drop the children at my mother's. Then I will take you. Okay?"

They arrive at the car and me. I realize in this moment that my face is wet, and my nose is running. I have been so focused on trying to hear their exchange that I ignored my own tears. My mother looks at me for a long moment, taking in my wet and snotty face. She smiles a small smile. Her eyes are sad, perhaps embarrassed.

"Okay." She nods and turns to my father. "Okay. You drive."

"You two have everything you need for school, yes?" my father asks.

"Yes," Bernard and I say.

"But I don't have school clothes at Gran's," I say.

"I will bring them by later today, okay?" He is being gentle with me, too, so I don't tell him that I never like his choice of school clothes when he picks them out. Instead, I keep my mouth shut and take my seat.

We stay with Gran for an entire week. My father comes over for dinner. And after dinner, before he leaves without us, he sends Bernard and me to my grandfather's study to do our homework. Then he and Gran confer about what to do about Nan, my mother, and us. Bernard and I position ourselves on the floor as close to the door as we can to eavesdrop.

"Eddi is not accepting visitors," my father says.

"I see," says Gran. "Well, I suspect space is what she needs, time and attention, opportunity to focus only on her wellness."

"I suppose," Dad says.

Gran asks, "What about Miriam?"

"She is doing as well as can be expected. The doctors say she may not walk again, given her age and that there are two breaks in her leg."

"I am not the least bit worried about Miriam walking again. She is too stubborn and too . . . can I say it? Vain," Gran says with such certainty that I, too, am now certain Nan will be okay. Gran is never wrong.

"But her bones have deteriorated, and she also has some form of dementia. Not too advanced. They are doing more tests. They don't advise that she live alone."

"Oh dear," Gran says. "Yes, well, Bella and I saw some signs that she was not as sharp as she had been. None of us are, you know? But . . . what's to be done? She has lived on her own terms for some time."

"I am hoping that maybe Eddi will pull herself together enough when she returns to be there for her mother."

"But what do you mean, David? Why wouldn't she come home to you and the children?"

"I don't think she will want to," my father says, "I don't think she wants this marriage anymore, Mom."

"Why do you say such a thing?" Gran stands now, moves over to the chair closest to her son.

"When I dropped her off at Summer House, she said as much. She does not think she will ever be able to . . . to. . . ." My father pauses but not soon enough to avoid the change in his voice, the cotton filling his throat and the soprano cracks in his baritone. "She does not think she can handle being a wife and mother."

"Oh, David. I am so sorry," Gran says, "but maybe this will change after her stay?"

Bernard sits upright, pushes his books to the side.

"Mom is not coming home!" he says in a loud whisper.

"Ever?" I ask.

"Ever," Bernard says, "and honestly, it's not like she did anything anyway. She was already good as gone."

We hear our father pushing his chair away from the kitchen table and coming down the hallway. We scurry away from the door and reposition our books on the floor farther in the room. Dad peeks in.

"You two all right? Have you finished your work?"

"Not yet," Bernard says.

"Almost," I say.

"When you finish you can turn on the TV. But no junk, okay?"

"Okay," Bernard and I say in unison.

Dad closes the door completely, and now no matter how close we sidle up to it, we cannot make out what they are saying when their talk resumes.

"If Mom is not coming home, does that mean we don't get to go home?" Bernard asks. "Why is Dad not bringing us home?"

"If Nan can't live by herself, does that mean she has to go to an old folks' home and never see her garden again?" I ask.

"I don't want to live with Gran," Bernard says.

"I don't want to live without Nan," I say.

We stare at each other, our two separate worlds crashing and burning at the same time, our mother the least of our concern.

Chapter Nine

HIS ONLY CLIENT

MAY

Bella approaches the lobby of the most beautiful building she has ever seen. It looks to be the newest edition to Downtown Brooklyn's historic district. The ordinary brick facade is like so many in Brooklyn, but it is pristine and fresh, like a newborn surrounded by family elders. It's broad arched glass entry showcases a dark and moody interior. The building's impossibly high ceilings and gleaming surfaces, in a spectrum of grays and rust, denote a no-nonsense but serene tone. The message is—serious people live here, and the things they are serious about are beauty, comfort, and the exclusion of mediocrity.

Bella's job has taken her to a fair number of large and opulent homes throughout Los Angeles, around UCLA and other affluent neighborhoods, where she photographed private parties and music industry gatherings. But the interior of this Brooklyn apartment building is beyond her imagining. The space is not lavish or grandiose, but minimal and open, filled with texture and color, shadow and light. It is the kind of space she would choose, she believes, if she had the means to choose it, even though she has never seen the use of concrete and wood, stone and honed marble, or the rounded, sculptured way the walls turn and open out to one room and then another.

She has arrived early, so before she approaches the front desk, she just stands in the middle of the entry and takes it all in. She wants to take photos, but she doesn't dare. Instead, she tries to commit to memory all the exquisite detail.

"Can I help you?" the man standing behind the reception desk asks Bella, who is still making circles around herself in that one spot. The receptionist is a young Black man in a dark gray suit so well-fitted it looks like it was sculpted onto his body with a steel chisel. His name tag says he's Kenneth. She approaches the desk and looks at her phone for the apartment number.

"I am going to apartment PH one," she says.

"Ms. Fontaine?

"Yes," Bella says.

"Mr. McAffrey is expecting you," Kenneth replies. He escorts her around the corner to the elevators. One set of doors is already open. He reaches in, uses a key card to press the top button, and holds the doors as she enters. She says thank you.

Alone in the elevator, Bella checks herself using the reflective brown tinted mirrors on the walls and overhead spotlights inset in a ceiling of gold luster tiles. The tiles give off their own glow. She refreshes her lipstick and wipes her pants to clear any lint. She is wearing her usual all-black work ensemble. She's added large silver hoop earrings and has swept her hair back into a single braid because she knows she will be under the male gaze today, and that her subject is accustomed to the groupie culture—women who work hard to look pleasing for him. She also wants to look her best for Dorian. She is trying to balance looking well put together but not like she was trying hard.

Dorian hired Bella to take photos of his only other client, basketball phenomenon Kyrone "Drip" McAffrey. This is the first time she will be working in front of Dorian. And she doesn't know how he will be with her. Does Drip McAffrey know about their relationship? Is their relationship even something to know about? She looks again at her reflection to check her eyeliner and slick down her hair at the crown of her head. She pops a mint from her purse into her mouth.

When the doors open, she is looking into the living room of a penthouse apartment right through to a view of the Brooklyn Bridge. Dorian is waiting for her. He kisses her on the cheek and smiles his gleaming smile.

"I am excited for you to meet Drip," he says. "You look great!"

"Thank you." Bella adds in a whisper, "This place!" Dorian nods his head.

"I know, right? It's crazy," he says. His eyes are wide, and he raises his hands out to the side in an exaggerated sign of surrender. "Just wait."

Bella is happy to know that he is just as impressed with their surroundings as she.

"Remember, we don't have a lot of time," Dorian says.

"Right. He's leaving for Europe, Milan, right?" Bella says.

"Yes, new team, new life."

"But who leaves *this* life?" she asks, looking around the spacious penthouse apartment in search of their host.

"Someone who doesn't have much choice if they want to keep playing basketball. Olimpia Milano is his second chance."

"He got cut from the Nets, right? I looked it up. Promise I won't mention it," Bella says, lowering her volume.

"Thank you, but he's fine. Italy loves him. But we gotta make this quick, okay? He has some last-minute stuff to do."

"I am an artist. But I will do my best," Bella says.

As they cross the living room, Bella comments on the art covering every wall. A series of miniature ink-on-white-paper drawings are hung in a grouping on one wall. There are at least twenty of these framed works. The drawings themselves are simple—only a few strokes, but the frames that hold them are in an ornate baroque style, all lacquered black. On the other wall are large colorful, complicated drawings—some of them are cartoonish with musical themes—caricatures of shapely women, men with microphones to their mouths, dancing figures and what looks to be rap lyrics scrawled in cursive. The shapes are swirling and surrounded by color strokes and symbols.

"This art is really something!" Bella says. "These would make amazing tattoos."

Dorian stops and turns, follows Bella's gaze.

"They are tattoos," Dorian says. "All this art is Drip's. He started out as a tattoo artist in high school. Got famous for it in college. Learned the art from his uncle. When he hurt his shoulder and couldn't play, he got serious about the other expressions," Dorian says and points to the swarm of ink-on-papers, "but the tattoos are his roots."

"Amazing," Bella says.

"Drip is who I was chasing when I stood you up for our first meeting," Dorian says. "When he got his offer to play overseas, I had just signed him. An art dealer in Milan caught wind that he was coming and put on a hard press. I had to get there to represent him and protect our interests."

"Ah," Bella stops, "so this is the famous person who stole your heart and my show date?"

"Yes and no," Dorian says, embarrassed at how this must be sounding to her. "It doesn't quite work like that, Bella. There is no competition here."

"Okay, if you say so," Bella says, unconvinced but good-natured.

Dorian puts his left arm around her shoulders and squeezes. He leads her across the living room through double doors and out onto an enormous rooftop deck. She wonders what Dorian had to do to secure this new high-profile artist, but before she can ask, the view from the deck demands her attention.

She is awestruck at the sight of the Brooklyn Bridge from this vantage point. From the street, the bridge did not seem so near, but from this roof, it is enormous and looming over the buildings like a sleeping dragon.

"Man! This view! Could you ever get used to this view?" Bella asks Dorian, but he does not respond because he has advanced out of earshot to greet their host.

Bella hesitates to follow as she takes in one wonder after another. The roof deck is a large expanse. It is fully furnished like another living room—high-end wood and iron furniture, complete with a full bar and barbecue stove and grill. The space is three times the size of Bella's entire apartment, and she notices immediately that the only greenery is in large planters on its periphery. The planters are filled with monkey grass. This makes her sad. The garden she could create in a space like this would be wondrous. But she quickly realizes that monkey grass is the perfect choice—the low maintenance, hard to kill ground cover is just right for a bachelor pad.

Drip is sitting in a high stool at the bar, holding in one hand what looks like a tall glass of orange juice, and he is anchoring his phone to his ear with the other. He is deep in conversation and doesn't notice Dorian and Bella until they are right upon him. He stands to greet them, while still maintaining his phone conversation. He is dressed, all six foot ten inches of him, top to bottom, in art. His shoulder-length dreads stick out from under his black porkpie hat. He is wearing a fitted deconstructed orange shirt that is part button-down and part wraparound. The collar only partially circles his neck and runs down the front of the shirt. He is sporting tight-fitting tattered jeans, but the holes are not at the knee. There are vertical rips and small frayed openings on the front of each thigh, as if he has busted through the fabric, Incredible Hulk-like. He has on sneakers Bella has never seen before, high-tops in orange, green, and yellow.

This is where he gets his nickname. Drip McAffrey takes his fashion very seriously. He is known for his forward-thinking and daring fashion sense. In the world of basketball, distinguishing yourself as a fashion icon among fashion icons is no small feat. Bella notes that under all that color is a handsome young man, probably around her and Dorian's age.

Drip puts down his orange juice and holds his free hand high for Dorian to slap. They give each other a simple dap, ending with a knuckle grab to the chest. Dorian seems pleased with himself; his face is alight with a smile that Bella is certain is a pure form of satisfaction. It is almost childlike. Bella wonders why men immediately become children in the presence of their sports heroes.

"Drip, this is Bella," Dorian says, "Bella, Drip."

Drip tells the person on the phone that he has to go and will see them later. He assures them that he will be on time. He stands, apologizes, and shakes Bella's hand. Then he looks from Dorian to Bella and back again with the kind of smile that tells Bella these two men have been talking about her.

"So, Bella, the magic picture-maker, you are the person Dorian has been jumping through hoops for." Drip says sitting partially back down in the chair, negating the height difference between them so that he can look Bella eye-to-eye.

"And you, the globe-trotting tattoo genius who Dorian stood me up for," Bella says. She gives him a side-eye and moves in closer as if to share a secret. "Have you met Ellen Herman yet, Drip?" she asks in an almost whisper.

"You know what? I haven't."

"Then, in such case as that, I win," Bella says. She steps back, tilts her head to the side, and crosses her arms in front of her, announcing the end of the discussion. All three of them laugh. Dorian casts his eyes down and shakes his head as he takes the hit to himself and his mother. His disapproval seems feigned and his amusement sincere.

"Bella is competitive. I like that," Drip says. "Don't worry, sis, I can already see I cannot compete with you." He says this looking at Dorian with a subtle nod of approval that is not subtle enough for Bella to miss. She shifts into work mode and asks, "So what do we want to do here? What kind of photos are you looking for? I see the subject is dressed and ready for the shoot."

"Always," Drip says, standing up, adjusting his pants legs, and moving toward the door.

"Let's take some shots with Drip and the skyline while we are out here," Dorian says. He is all business now too. Drip changes direction and moves to the other side of the deck where the dragon is looming.

"Yes, we gotta get that bridge in, this view is amazing," Bella says as she raises the camera to her eye. Now, Drip's confidence wanes a bit, he shuffles from one foot to the other.

"How do you want me to stand?" he asks her.

"Just do you," Bella says. She asks him to move two steps to the right to isolate him from the corner of the building, so the frame captures only Drip and the bridge. She takes several shots, and then she kneels on one knee to shoot an angle that makes him look even taller. He takes his place among the skyscrapers. The sky is cloudless and the sun, relentlessly bright, is not quite directly overhead. Before it gets there, she wants to capture Drip's endless shadow. She has to remind Drip not to squint.

She directs him to face the bridge and look to the side, so she can get his profile. She is talking nonstop. When she tells him to turn and face the bridge, she says she wants to take a picture of his butt for the fans and asks him if he can twerk. She captures his look of surprise, his questioning eyes and laughter.

She is telling joke after joke to keep him laughing. She has decided that his smile is his best feature, his laugh infectious. He refuses to twerk, but he shows his favorite dance moves. He tells her he can't keep dancing unless she sings or raps. She attempts freestyle but cannot come up with words that rhyme with the directions she is trying to relay. Drip thinks the failure is hilarious—more laughter, finger pointing. He signals with his hands for her to stop. She ceases her freestyle attempt, but her camera keeps clicking. She has captured it all.

"Okay, then, if I'm so bad, you try it," she teases, "let's hear what you got."

Drip, without hesitation, starts in:

"Yeah, Hunnid thousand for the cheapest ring on a nigga finger, lil' bitch, woo. I done flew one out to Spain to be in my domain, and Audemar'd the bitch, woo."

With this offering, Drip concedes that he can't freestyle either. Bella laughs. She knows the song "Life is Good" by Drake and Future. She joins in as the hype man, adding in her own "woo" at the end of every phrase.

"Dropped three dollars on a ring. Call it Bentley truck, lil' bitch."

"Woo!"

"I was in the trap serving cocaine. I ain't been the same since."

"Woo!"

"Hunnid thousand for the cheapest ring on a nigga finger, lil' bitch.

"Woo!"

Drip is keeping his own beat. When he raps about the ring, he shows his own sapphire pinky ring to the camera and then moves against the skyline as if he's in a music video doing his best Future imitation. Bella never stops taking pictures or misses a "woo."

Dorian breaks in, "Okay, let's do some shots inside with the art." His words feel abrupt and ill-timed, killing the vibe and creating an awkward moment. Drip turns to Bella, as if for permission to move inside.

"Yep," is all she says. She picks up her backpack and follows Dorian to the living room.

Drip looks at his watch. "Shit, I gotta get going. I got a meet-up with the dude storing my car. I'm sorry, Dorian, we need to wrap up."

Bella registers this shift in Drip's demeanor. She is annoyed with Dorian for killing the rapport. She knows she won't get it back.

"How much time do we have, Drip?" Bella asks. She keeps her voice neutral. She can see from Dorian's body language that he knows what he's done. His posture is almost too erect, his shoulders high, nearly touching his ears, and both hands are in his pants pockets.

"I've got a solid ten minutes," Drip says, "let's go!"

"Okay," Bella says, taking in the room again, "let me get you over in front of your two opposing galleries. And then next to your favorite pieces on each wall."

"No sweat," Drip says.

Bella spends the remaining time taking pictures that are more formally posed. After she has captured him in front of the large canvases, she asks him which tattoo he is most proud of. She is expecting him to choose one of the canvases currently on the wall. But Drip starts unbuttoning his shirt. Bella suppresses her surprise by preparing to take the picture. She brings the camera to her eye. But when he turns his back to show her, she gasps. She brings the camera down and walks up to Drip. His entire back is covered with the Black Madonna. She moves in closer and zeroes in on the Madonna's face. It's the same face as Gran's Garden Goddess. The same knowing smile, gentle eyes, shrouded arms, and brown hands in a posture of acceptance and compassion. The sight is so familiar and so comforting that tears fill her eyes. She wants to close her eyes to fight them back, but she fears they will spill over.

"So, do you like it?" Drip asks over his shoulder. Bella is struggling.

"I . . . I honestly don't have words, Drip," Bella says in such a hushed and reverent tone that Drip turns around to look at her.

"I'm sorry," Bella looks up at Drip, "she's the most beautiful tattoo I have ever seen. You drew this? I mean, this is your creation?" She holds his gaze so that he knows just how moved and appreciative she is. He sees her wide, waterlogged eyes and he is touched by her reaction—Bella can see that he's appreciative too.

"Yeah, my business partner did the work. He's the only other tattoo artist I trust."

"Can I?" She says as she turns him back around for another look. He smiles and relents.

"I'm sorry, can I take the picture?"

"Of course," Drip says. His energy has shifted again. Now, he is in no hurry. He seems to be basking in Bella's admiration. No, it's more than admiration. He takes hers as an artist's understanding of the significance of his work.

Dorian is looking on and watching this moment unfold between Bella and Drip. He clears his throat. He seems hesitant to break the spell again, but he can't help himself. Under the guise of respecting Drip's time, he tells Bella to finish up so that Drip can get on with his day.

Bella does not want to be rushed. She wants to look at every detail of this tattoo, take in every color choice, every swirl and line. She knows that the only way to do this is to take the pictures. She backs away, raises the camera, and carefully captures this Madonna, Drip's Madonna. Her Madonna.

How in the world has the Garden Goddess found her? And why on the back of Dorian's only other artist?

Chapter Ten

NO SHOW II: DORIAN'S MOTHER

MAY

The bar is like a tight dress Bella would never choose for herself—confined, overly adorned, and pretentious. It has oversized chandeliers and an '80s vibe with so much film and fashion memorabilia on the walls and hanging from the ceiling as to make the room feel even more crowded than it is. It's only six o'clock, but a happy hour crowd is taking up the seats at the bar and in booths. Bella, occupying the smallest booth, senses people looking at her and judging her claim on it. Everyone seems to have come straight from work, rewarding themselves with cheap happy hour drinks. It is her first time here and now she wishes she'd sat up at the bar. She is about to leave the booth when she hears her name.

"Bella?"

She turns toward the bar and the voice. "Stephanie?" She is surprised to see the Herman Gallery receptionist. It's been weeks since they met again on her second, more successful visit with Dorian and Ellen at the gallery.

"Hey, girl. What are you doing here all by yourself?" Stephanie says, "I'm so impressed you remembered my name."

"And thank God, because you remembered mine first," Bella says. They both laugh.

"Well, sister, I am good with names. It helps with my job. Plus, I love 'Bella.' It's . . . *molta bella*," Stephanie says, "and that right there is my best Italian accent."

"Thank you," Bella says, "I am actually waiting for Dorian Herman."

"Oh, shit, so you're the *chica* he changed his shirt for."

"Did he?"

"I'm excited about your show. I hear your photos are kick-ass. Contract signing time, yeah?" Stephanie says.

"I hope so. What do you know?" Bella asks Stephanie, hoping for some intel on where she stands in the process.

When Dorian asked Bella to meet him tonight, he said he had good news. He'd said that the presentation he'd put forth to Ellen was well-received. Ellen had also warmed up to Bella. At least, she seemed to view Bella as an artist, not a flirtation.

"Dammit," Stephanie says, "I hope I didn't ruin anything. Look, girl, I'm gonna make myself scarce before the boss gets here."

"It's good seeing you, Stephanie, and thanks for the heads-up."

"Listen," Stephanie says, sitting down opposite Bella in the booth. "Dorian is all about it. But the person you gotta totally win over is Ellen. And she is going through some shit right now. Your show is not secure until you get solid with Ellen."

"How do I do that?" Bella asks.

"You gotta get your name on a sticky note. Until your name is on one of her sticky notes, you don't exist," Stephanie says. Bella looks up and sees Dorian walk through the front door and up to the hostess podium. "That's our secret, girl, but it's the truth." Stephanie slides out of the booth and back into the crowd, rejoining her group of girlfriends at the bar.

Bella likes Stephanie. She feels like an ally. She is about Bella's age, probably a little older. She is a cultivated pretty—long curly weave and eyelashes so long Bella can't imagine they are her own. Her makeup is flawless tonight, just as it was when Bella first met her at the gallery. She is thin but shapely and dressed impeccably in a fitted cobalt-blue shift with matching stilettos. All her friends have a similar comportment—all put together and professional. They look friendly—all smiles and laughs. They direct all their attention toward each other, and they hug a lot. They look like the cast of an Ava DuVernay movie, all gloss and polish, like some idealized, camera-ready version of Black girl besties. They are the group of girlfriends Bella has never seen in real life. Real or fiction, she has never felt the need for a group dynamic like this, until now.

Stephanie's departure leaves a void, and Bella feels she needs some clarity before Dorian fills it. Stephanie's mention of sticky notes makes Bella uneasy. She wants to ask Dorian, but since Stephanie invoked the sister code with her inside information, Bella knows she cannot. She may have never had a group of besties, but she still knows to adhere to the sister code, especially with the Herman Gallery receptionist.

Bella stands up so that Dorian can see her, and he does. In the weeks since the botanical garden, Dorian just gets more beautiful. He is not Bella's usual type of heartthrob—which has always been tall, dark (as in Black man dark), and handsome. Dorian is a five-foot-eight-inch, light-olive-skinned man who struck her at first as more adorable than handsome. He wears his curly black hair short. His face is round. His kind eyes and gorgeous smile do his bidding for him, and he knows it. He flashes those perfect teeth, handiwork of years in braces, easily and often. He also has nice hands, heavy and more solid than his thin frame requires. He has long, elegant fingers . . . the hands of an artist.

"So sorry I'm late. Have you been waiting long?" Dorian draws Bella to him and kisses her left cheek at the jawline.

"No, this must be your office hangout." Bella points her chin toward Stephanie.

"I guess, yeah," Dorian says. He looks over at Stephanie. "Stephanie is good people."

"Yes, I really like her," Bella says, "so what's the good news?"

Dorian is holding Bella by her arms at the triceps. He looks down at the floor and takes a long, deep breath.

"I was planning to bring the contract drafts for the show, for you to take and review, but we have a problem."

"What kind of problem?"

"Ellen. I'm not even sure how to explain. Let's sit down." They sit on opposite sides of the booth.

"What's up, Dorian?"

"This kind of thing just does not happen at our gallery. We pride ourselves on our transparency and our respect for our artists." He is talking into his hands, as if to himself, which is beginning to make Bella angry.

"What kind of thing?" Bella asks. Her heart rate feels like it's at two hundred bpm and rising.

"Ellen has put another artist in your slot. We had you slotted for the winter, and she thinks your work is better for the summer. We have to push your show two years down the road."

"You're saying that your mother has changed her mind *again*? Is this because we are seeing each other?"

"I am saying that we just don't change our minds at this point when the contracts are drawn. It's been our policy for years."

"Dorian," Bella says, but he interrupts her.

"This has nothing to do with us and everything to do with Ellen. She is not herself. She hasn't been herself for some time. Today, she was totally—I don't even know, someone else. And I don't know what to do about it."

"But we can fix this, right? I mean, can't you work it out?"

"Here's the thing, Bella, I don't think so. Ellen has a signed contract with the other artist and has committed the gallery. He is a big name, big draw. I just found out about it when I went in to get your contract drafts. There *were* no drafts."

"You had no idea that she was pursuing this person?"

"No. Well, yes. But not for your spot."

"There is no other time slot this year *or* next year?"

"We are all scheduled, committed, for the next two years. Originally, your slot opened up because someone dropped out. That is rare and the likelihood of that happening again is slim to none."

"So, Ellen beat you out for my slot? I am trying to understand."

"No, I didn't know I was in a race. You met with her. You know she was all in. But today, she, again, acted like she'd never heard of you. It was like the Twilight Zone."

"No, it sounds more like I just lost out to a well-known artist. Ellen made a business decision."

"But we don't do that."

"Evidently, you do," Bella says, trying not to raise her voice. All Dorian's talk of his family's ethics and moral reputation sounds like meaningless dribble to Bella now. It sounds to her like he didn't fight for her show. His mother changed her mind about her for the second time, and he didn't step up on her behalf.

"You know what, Dorian? This is bullshit. Your precious gallery policy is for shit. Call me when you have it sorted out." Before she really gets ahold of her thoughts, Bella is up and heading out of the bar. Once she navigates through the crowd at the door, she almost runs down the street into the dark. She hears Dorian calling from the door. Somehow this makes her even angrier. She speeds up to her subway stop and descends the stairs two at a time.

When she reaches her apartment building, she is out of breath because she ran all the way from the train station. She climbs the six floors to her apartment. It's a slow slog up, but once she reaches her floor, she decides to go up one more to the roof. She sits down in one of the iron chairs. The only light is the hallway light shining dimly through the doorway. She welcomes the darkness. Bella is trying to focus her breathing, and this has a calming effect. She sits deeper into the chair. And now that she is calmer, she takes in the smell of all that is growing around her. The rich, damp soil gives off its own perfume. The azaleas call out to her with their sweet, soft scent. She drags her chair over to them and sits close enough for the petals to touch her face. These are not her grandmother's rhododendrons, but they are close. The azalea varieties found in New York have bigger blossoms and are much easier to grow than the varieties at home, so she loves and appreciates them almost as much as their California cousins. They are newly in bloom this time of year, and because they are her own children and she is meticulous about pruning, they will last for months, until the hottest part of the summer. She is so appreciative that they are here tonight to receive her. They are, Bella decides, her besties, and she is not sad about this truth.

"You will never let me down, will you, girls?" Bella says out loud.

She decides to visit everyone tonight. This is just what she needs to sort out this new development in her career. She won't even think about what this all means to her relationship with Dorian. She traverses the roof to the electrical outlet, unwraps the end of a string of lights, and plugs it in. A golden canopy illuminates the darkness. It is made of crisscrossed lights that Bella strung from the door all the way to the metal grate on the other side, the one she and her mother climbed to freedom months ago. Bella has discovered that she loves planting at night. She bought some pumpkin seeds from the everything-but-the-kitchen-sink hardware store down the street. The idea of growing pumpkins on the roof is so intriguing, Bella decides that this is what she is going to do tonight. It's already May, a good time to plant pumpkins so they will be ready for Halloween.

Bella unlocks the storage bin where she keeps her supplies and retrieves her gloves, tools, soil, and peat moss. She pulls on her gloves as she approaches her makeshift planting bench. Someday, she will purchase a proper planting table, but for now, she has propped an old door on stacks of cement blocks, which works just fine. She tears open the new bag of soil and fills two plastic starter flats, which she takes to the water hose to wet the already damp soil. Back at the table, she uses her pinky to make holes for the seeds.

"Bella?"

She turns around to Dorian who is standing in the roof doorway.

"Don't take another step," she says. She immediately feels violated. In her mind right now, he is the enemy, and he has invaded her sacred space. "How did you get up here?" Her voice sounds even harder than she intends.

"Bella," Dorian says again. His voice is pleading and contrite. "Your roommate let me in. I'm sorry. I'm going to fix it. I promise."

"Don't make promises you can't keep, Dorian. That's how we got here in the first place."

"Bella."

"Stop saying my name," Bella demands, now more annoyed that he has interrupted her peace and her place. "Can you just leave?"

"Do you really think I wouldn't fight for you?"

"All that's left for you to do is fight, then, Dorian. And you can't do that here."

Dorian looks up at the canopy of lights and then around at the garden. He is taking deep breaths. "Did you do all of this? This is . . . amazing."

"Please leave, Dorian."

"Okay, I'm leaving." He takes two steps backward into the hallway and stops. He is leaning on the rope in the door and only his head sticks out of the doorway. "But can I just share something with you by way of an explanation?"

Bella turns fully toward him and crosses her arms over her chest.

Dorian pauses, looks around again, and says, "I have an idea."

Bella remains in her stance.

"When I was little, my mother used to keep this garden of potted plants on the balcony of our apartment. The balcony was just a narrow strip of cement, and her garden was pretty pitiful. But she would make me help her plant and water. And I would help her replace one dead plant with a new one fairly often. I liked playing in the dirt and getting my hands dirty."

Bella tries to imagine growing up in New York, with only a few dying houseplants and so little connection to natural settings. She can't really wrap her head around it. Dorian takes advantage of this momentary distraction to step one foot back onto the roof.

"While we were planting or watering, my mother talked about her own mother, who was evidently a serious gardener with a big garden. My mother grew up in Westchester with a big backyard. I never met my grandmother." Now he brings his other foot out of the hallway and stands upright. "She used to help her mother garden and she would talk about that while we tended our balcony. She always said she missed it."

"Okay, Dorian. What's the idea?"

"Let's bring her here."

"She won't come here. Why would she?"

"Because she likes your work, and I can encourage her to investigate you on her own," he explains. "She often does the due diligence on an artist. If she were invited to your apartment to see your work in person, which is also customary, you could bring her up here and show her your source of inspiration. Tell her about your grandmothers' gardens. I think she will make a connection that would be meaningful."

"But what's the point, if she doesn't want the show to happen?"

"She has more resources than I do to make something happen for you. It's definitely worth a try. Her mind used to be a steel trap. And now it's just not."

In this very moment, Bella remembers Stephanie and the Post-it notes. She remembers Nan and her sticky notes—how they helped her keep her secret, how hard it was for her to acknowledge what was happening even when it became undeniable. Ellen is suffering from dementia. She might have Alzheimer's.

"Has your mom seen a doctor? Don't you want to be sure there is no medical reason for her change in behavior?" Bella asks, gently. Now is not the time to announce her suspicions to Dorian. This would be a devastating blow, and it is not her place.

"Her doctor is an old friend. She is always seeing him for the slightest thing. She's a bit of a hypochondriac, to tell you the truth. And I think this is about her struggle to hand things over to us, her sons, even though she has raised us for this very purpose."

Though Bella has only a suspicion, she is heartbroken for Dorian. She knows what may be ahead for him and his family, that bewildering no-man's-land between diagnosis and confirmation, that door they will enter where there is no turning back, only a vague memory of a blissful "before" to their frightful after. Bella walks over to Dorian and hugs him.

"Thank you for trying to make this happen." She wants to say more, but she can't come up with words that are quite right for this moment. And now that she understands what is likely going on with Ellen, she knows that bringing her to the garden is the right thing to do.

Chapter Eleven

NAN AND
THE BIG MOVE

On the day Nan is discharged from the hospital, Gran accompanies us to pick her up. When we arrive, Nan is fully dressed. Her clothes, spare leg brace, and discharge papers are bagged and arranged at the foot of her bed. She is sitting in the wheelchair with her red coat buttoned up to the neck. Her hair is styled in a bun, topped with a red matching beret. After greetings and kisses, my father pulls a chair up to Nan's wheelchair and takes her hand.

"Miriam, the doctors are recommending that you not live alone," he says, "we have an idea we would like for you to consider."

Gran steps forward. "You look fabulous, Miriam. Much better than I expected."

"I suppose I should say thank you, Olivette," Nan says with raised eyebrows, "but what exactly were you expecting?"

"Oh, that came out all wrong," Gran says and laughs, not apologetically but as if she forgot what her assignment was supposed to be. "Of course, you look as splendid as always. Is there ever time when you don't look splendid, Miriam?"

Nan ignores Gran's question and turns toward Dad. She smells a conspiracy.

"What is your idea, David? I can tell you right now, it better have something to do with how I will manage at home, because that is precisely where I plan to be going on this day!"

"I would like to invite you to convalesce at my home, Miriam," Gran says, "I have an extra room and we can keep each other company."

"Oh, Olivette, that is more than generous and kind of you," Nan says, the words cordial but not her tone, "but I have become a solitary animal. You have no idea how unpleasant I can be, and frankly, I don't want to have to *not* be unpleasant when I so desire. You know what I mean, don't you, dear?"

"Oh, I certainly do, even with your use of double negatives," says Gran, "but do you know that you have been given a thirty percent chance of regaining the full use of that leg? And are you aware that the doctors believe that a large part of your diminished odds have everything to do with continuing to live alone? I cannot imagine you are completely done with wearing those expensive heeled shoes that you so favor. And I cannot fathom that you are resigned to leading the Church Guild with a pronounced limp. So, though I cannot guarantee *anything*—I do not presume to be masterful at the healing arts—I do believe your chances are better with me than in that big ole house by yourself."

Nan seems unprepared for Gran's offensive shift. She sits up in her wheelchair fully erect, her chin pointing accusatorially at Gran.

"Eddi is there. I will not be *completely* alone," Nan says.

"Eddi is back at Summer House. And we do not know when she will be out," Dad chimes in to deliver the difficult news. Nan only looks up at David and then turns to me. She takes my hand as if I am hearing this news for the first time too.

"We are not talking about forever, Miriam," Gran says, softening her jaw and folding her hands at her waist. "If I am willing to open up my peaceful abode to you and your moods, surely you are willing to give yourself a chance at full recovery."

Now, we have all circled Nan's wheelchair—the full appeal—Dad, Gran, Bernard, and me. She looks at each of us with her most disagreeable frown—the corners of her mouth turned down as if she has eaten something rancid. Then her eyes rest on me again. I give her my best smile.

"I want you to get *all* well, Nanny. I think there is healing in Gran's garden. I've seen Gran's church friends get better, you know, Ms. Jefferson? It will be good. You will have your own room." I am pleading now. I take hold of her other hand. It's a tight fist.

Wordless moments pass. Everyone knows to remain silent. If she refuses me, she will surely refuse everyone else. I bravely hold her eyes with mine, so I see the very moment the light turns on inside of them.

"I had almost forgotten about your church friends and that healing garden, Olivette. However unruly it is, your people are quite convinced. Well, all right, I will give it a try." Nan releases my hands, closes her eyes, and smooths the sides of her hair with her fingers. She is bringing herself to her new reality. She takes a quick breath, opens her eyes, and delivers a smile I know well. It is the smile she reserves for business transactions.

"Thank you, kind friend, for the offer. I will stay only as long as it takes me to get out of this contraption, which I am determined to do in record time."

"You are welcome, and I have no doubt whatsoever!" Gran says.

My father claps his hands together exuberantly to mark the deal done.

"We'll stop off at my place to grab a few things and inform Mr. Blackshear," Nan says as she reaches for the bags on the bed.

"I have already let Mr. Blackshear know that he will continue to be in charge of the garden on his own," Dad says.

Nan stops her gathering and grabs my father's arm. It is a quick move that surprises him. She is holding onto his sleeve.

"You'll give me a moment at home, won't you, David?" she asks.

"Yes, ma'am, of course," he relents.

"Very well," Nan says, "I'm appreciative of this devious plot . . . and your care and concern, all of you. Now, please get me out of this dreadful place. I am lucky to have survived as it is."

The gravel path in Gran's garden is not kind to Nan's wheelchair. When she arrives with all her luggage in tow, she leaves Dad at the car to deal with her belongings because she wants to go straight to the garden. This request surprises everyone, but especially Dad, who days before had constructed a wheelchair ramp alongside Gran's front stairs in hope and anticipation of Nan's arrival.

The Sterling Silver roses along Gran's front walk have just sprouted a proliferation of lavender-colored buds. These bushes are old and established. Granddad Addison long ago shaped them into topiary trees that now stand uniformly four feet tall. They are by far the most orderly arrangement at Gran's, which is why I was certain Nan would consider them an inviting welcome to the household. She has a few Sterling Silver bushes in her garden, but she has often marveled at the robustness of Granddad Addison's. She likes this heirloom variety because lavender is her favorite color, and Sterling Silvers are easy to cut and arrange into drop-dead gorgeous arrangements, as their stems are almost thorn-free.

Today Nan doesn't even notice the Sterlings or the beautiful ramp fashioned just for her. She is preoccupied with getting to Gran's garden in the back.

"Bella was all set to give you a garden tour once you got settled, Miriam," Gran says, "but it looks like you'd prefer to do that now?"

"Yes, yes, I would love that, thank you," Nan says as she turns to find me over her shoulder. She reaches for my hand.

Once I push the wheelchair past the asphalt driveway and the holy wall, the going is hard. I use all my strength against the gravel stones that feel more like quicksand. The chair is a new lightweight model with dirt bike wheels. It's supposed to be all terrain, but I am not finding it so. I am determined to stick to my planned tour route. I push Nan past the rhododendrons and turn at the path by the flower beds along the house. I take her all the way around the outer periphery of the garden and then to the spiral path among the grasses. I want to save the Garden Goddess for last.

"Bella, sweetie, take me to the herbs," Nan says. "Where are the plants that Gran uses to help her church friends?"

"They are all over the garden, Nanny. Gran doesn't have an herb garden. She puts her herbs all over the place, where their services are needed," I repeat Gran's oft-spoken words verbatim.

Nan seems to be contemplating this.

"I could show you the raised beds in the back. There are some herbs over there," I offer.

"Good," Nan says.

I push the chair along my planned route but try to pick up the pace toward the desired location. The raised beds along the alley wall are waist high. This allows a whole bed of shade-lovers, like the winter mint, to grow underneath, I tell Nan.

"Gran changes these beds often. This is her test kitchen." Again, Gran's own words to describe these vegetable boxes, dwarf fruits saplings, and edible flowers. Currently chives, leeks, garlic, calendula, and borage blossoms are in one raised box. Marigolds, honeysuckle, violets and anise are in the other.

116

"What are these beauties? They look like something from the tropical rainforest!" Nan reaches for small blossoms hanging their drooping heads over the side of the first raised box.

"Star flowers," I say. I love this plant because the blossom is bright blue. Their prickly purple star-shaped spines make the flower look a little dangerous. But in fact, they are safe to eat—the leaves and blossoms have a clean, uncomplicated flavor.

"Star flowers are borage blossoms," Gran says, walking up behind us. "They are a delightful substitution for cucumber when you are making a salad and you want to show off. The leaves make a powerful tea used to break a fever."

"Ah, so this is your medicine cabinet, Olivette," Nan says. "What do you have here for me?"

"Well, Miriam, you will find answers in this entire garden," Gran says, "but for now, I have dinner for you on the table. It looks like you have come to the end of your tour."

"No, we actually are just beginning," I say. "We haven't even visited with. . . ." Gran cuts me off before I ruin my own surprise.

"We have plenty of time for your Nan to get familiar with *everything*." Gran gives me a wide-eyed look, meaning I should follow her lead on this. And so, I do. Gran helps me push Nan all the way to the front of the house so we can use the new ramp.

"I promise you, I will be out of this godawful wheelchair as soon as I am able," Nan says, trying to help by pushing the wheels forward.

"Oh, I am certain of it, Miriam," Gran says.

"Perhaps you have some magic to help me heal," Nan says, looking over her shoulder as Gran takes over the maneuvering of the wheelchair through the door and into the living room.

"I know no magic, Miriam," Gran says, "but science is on our side."

"I like science too," Nan says, and she and Gran both laugh

their most agreeable laughs. "I hope I can see your herb garden soon, Olivette. Bella can show me around."

Gran looks over at me. I don't know how to respond. Gran helps me figure it out. "I don't really have an herb garden, Miriam."

"Gran puts her herbs to work all over the garden," I repeat as if for the first time because for Nan, it is the first time. "I will give you the full tour," I say, and Gran smiles at me.

My father has left the three of us to ourselves. We sit around the kitchen table, making room for Nan's wheelchair. Gran serves my favorite meal, baked chicken, brown rice with curry and raisins, and a gigantic bowl of green salad. There are several kinds of flowers and herbs in the salad. As Gran tosses it, Nan spots the star flowers.

"There they are. Borage blossoms in the salad," Nan beams up at Gran, "you are showing off."

And she's back. I smile at Gran. She rubs my back.

"Yes," Gran says, "I am showing off just for you."

I am happy in this moment that my grandmothers are together. I believe that having one place to come and be with my two favorite people is my good fortune.

After dinner, Gran and I help Nan unpack her necessities and get ready for bed. She is able to stand and with the help of a walker, she makes it to the bed. We help her into her gown and Gran lifts her legs onto the bed and under the covers.

Now that I am a freshman in high school, I have begun to sleep on Gran's sofa when I stay over. The only television in the house is in the living room, and now Gran allows me to watch once she goes to bed. But tonight, I want to sleep with her. She has two twin beds in her room, hers near the window and my grandfather's bed near the door. Tonight, I crowd my grandmother's bed with her.

"Are you troubled, Calsap?" Gran asks.

"Yes. I am worried about Nan. She forgot that we were just in the garden."

"I know," Gran says, "we will just be patient. We will help her heal her leg, and we will help her mind regain its snap. We will never say, 'But I just told you' or 'You have already asked that.' We will always just repeat ourselves. We will be helpful, without judgment. You understand what I mean, don't you, Calsap?"

"Yes, ma'am, but what if she forgets me? What if she forgets who I am?"

"Oh, my dear, you are her one great love. She is beginning to forget, yes. But you are the very last person she will hold onto. And we will help her hold on for so long that she will not likely get to forgetting you."

"Well, good, because I think she believes you have a magic cure for her in your garden. I kind of told her that to get her here."

"So, you did. I do have a cure, but it's not magic."

"What is it?"

"Do you know that your Nan has never seen the Garden Goddess?" Gran says.

"Never?" I am surprised. I realize just now that Nan and I have never discussed the Goddess. On the rare occasion that she visits Gran, she never ventures very far into her garden. But I thought surely she had been to the center of the grasses.

"No, she doesn't even know the Goddess is there," Gran says. "Imagine her surprise."

I giggle because I am encouraged. Of course, the Goddess will tell Nan what she needs to know and do to get better.

"Is the Goddess calling Nan to the garden, do you think? Is that why she is so anxious to be out there?"

"Maybe," Gran says, "but you stop your worrying for your Nan. The Goddess and I have a plan."

"You rhymed. Nan, plan!" We both laugh.

"I did," Gran says, "I'm a poet and I don't even know it."

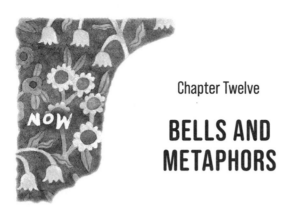

Chapter Twelve

BELLS AND METAPHORS

JUNE

Bella is still in bed. She wants to sleep in. It's Saturday and she has the entire first half of the day free. But she cannot sleep. She has a gig to shoot tonight, and it's not just any shoot. Ellen Herman has hired her to photograph a book signing, her first engagement with the Herman Gallery.

She looks at her Fitbit and it's only 5:45 a.m. Even though she has nothing left to prepare for the gig, she can't shake the anxiety. She slips back under her covers and closes her eyes. She does not have curtains on her apartment windows, which extend almost the full length of the wall. To her delight, the windows face east and welcome the morning sun. The building behind her apartment is under construction with no current residents, and the normally active and noisy construction site is silent on the weekends. There is nothing to keep her from slumbering in the warmth of early daylight, if only she could.

She brings her phone under the covers with her and goes onto the Herman Gallery's website. She searches for the gallery's photo feed and scrolls for the fifth time through all their event pictures. She sees that the posts use only formally arranged photos—all posed group shots and staged pictures of art and books. No candids, no video. Ellen Herman is in almost every picture. She loves the camera, and it loves her. Bella makes a note to try a little video with her and to take some pictures with her and Dorian. There are very few pictures of him. She suspects that if she includes Ellen in all the pictures of Dorian, those shots might survive Ellen's editing for the website. Dorian could use the exposure to raise his profile.

She notices that most of the pictures are a little on the dark side, underexposed. That means the gallery's main studio eats light. She decides to take her light meter just to be safe. Now, she is certain she is ready for this gig, and with this knowledge, she closes her eyes. Even if she can't sleep, she is determined to stay in bed to rest for a few more hours. She is determined to show up ready to do her best. She used a third of her earnings to hire an assistant, Geri, a friend from the community garden. The book signing is Bella and Geri's second gig together.

Geri calls a few minutes before five o'clock. Bella has just come down from the roof, where she spent the early afternoon watering and pruning, and then combing through some regional gardening books she'd picked up from the secondhand bookstore. She is already packed up to go and dressed in her work clothes, black slacks and a black embroidered button-down shirt—dressy and flattering but comfortable and invisible.

She is so thankful that Geri is reliable and always on time. Geri, short for Geraldine, looks like she is fifteen years old, but she is nineteen. Though she is young, she helps manage the garden and has established herself as a respected authority within the garden community. Her family moved to New York from the Dominican Republic when she was a baby. Though her face

looks freshly adolescent, she is taller than Bella and more substantial. Her body is full and ample. It's hard to know how ample
because she wears her clothes big and loose. She has worked
the La Plaza Cultural Community Garden ever since her mother
signed her up when she was seven years old for its summer youth
program to keep her out of trouble. It was free and two blocks
from her home. No one else in her family cares about gardening
or the plant world. But for Geri, the garden is her calling. This
gig with Bella is a godsend, the income allowing her to avoid
full-time grown-up work a bit longer.

Today, at Bella's request, she has traded in her usual flannel
shirt and khakis for an all-black ensemble—black denims and
a long-sleeved T-shirt. Bella is accustomed to doing for herself
all the functions she will delegate to Geri. But since she is new
to the New York art and literary scene, she finds it much easier
for a young assistant to ask the names of the important people
Bella suspects she is supposed to know but doesn't. She's learned
in her short time as a professional in Los Angeles that famous
people get annoyed when you recognize them but offended
when you don't. So, she assigns this task to Geri, whose youthful
appearance and outsized personality will be her cover. Geri is a
charmer—she maintains the Dominican accent in a way that is
both commanding and endearing. This arrangement helps Bella
avoid embarrassment and judgment. She needs to impress Ellen
in every way possible.

"Hey, Mama! You ready for the big show?" Geri asks.

"Yes, I am. Are you?"

"I am two blocks away."

"Most excellent. Just buzz when you get here."

Geri makes good time and arrives out of breath. "Geez, those
six floors are a bitch!" Geri says, walking down the apartment's
narrow hallway, made even more narrow by Bella's framed photos

stacked vertically along the wall. "Ooh, is this your stuff?" Geri stops to look through the stacks.

"Yes."

"These are beee-uuu-tiful," Geri says. Then she sits down right in front of the third stack. "Who is this?"

"My grandmother," Bella says.

"Wow! She looks . . . otherworldly. Is she how you got into the plant world?"

"Otherworldly is right, and yes, both of my grandmothers. I grew up in their gardens."

"You are lucky you had your grandmothers growing up. I didn't."

"Yes," is all Bella says. She can't bring herself to talk about her childhood right now.

"Well, these are amazing, and I am glad I get to know you before you blow up, Mama!"

"All right then, grab that bag and let's go impress the gatekeeper."

Bella and Geri arrive at the Herman Gallery only minutes before the author, Martha J. Jackson, a famous trans woman and drag queen. When Bella first got the call from Stephanie about this gig, she did her research and learned that Martha, now in her late seventies, became famous as a brave and committed pioneer of the gay and trans liberation movement. She was made even more famous as the survivor of a mob kidnapping that made the news and mobilized the entire Greenwich Village community to free her and prosecute her abductors. Her new book is a tell-all about her early days, her activism, and her famous disappearance. Many books have been written about Martha. But this memoir is her first.

As Bella and Geri enter the Herman Gallery doors, Martha's

entourage pulls up in two black SUVs. Bella and Geri wait inside, Bella preparing her camera to shoot the grand arrival. They look on through the gallery's glass entry as the car doors open and women spill out. They are all glitter and shine—big hair, high heels. and all manner of color, sequin, and couture.

The driver of the first SUV opens the passenger doors and helps Martha exit. She is very tall and very thin, her posture only slightly bent with age, her shoulders still square and her chin skyward. She is dressed impeccably in a long silver frock made of thick, undulating jersey fabric. She and the dress shimmer in the early evening light. The large red and yellow silk flowers along the neckline of the dress adorn the jutting cliffs of Martha's collar bones. A thin shiny purple patent leather belt cinches her tiny waist, a single red flower in place of a buckle. Martha wears impossibly high metallic red platform shoes and flawless makeup, her lips generously painted with her trademark high-gloss red lipstick. Bella wonders how Martha can see past her thick, long, jet-black eyelashes and how she manages to strut under the weight of all that hair, enough loose flat-ironed curls falling down her back to make two wigs. Martha looks just like the pictures Bella has seen of her on Wikipedia, only somehow younger than her image taken decades ago. And expensive, the only word that fits. Martha has resources that she did not have in her youth when she was living on the streets and helping other trans women who had even less than she.

More people emerge from her car. The women who accompany her are all trans and gorgeous. She waits as they fan out in front of her and prepare the way. It's choreographed pageantry how they strut and fuss over Martha, a beehive around their queen. Once inside the main gallery, they help her get situated. Ellen Herman and the gallery staff join the swarm. They show Martha to her setup, already staged in the main gallery.

She sits in a chair that is more like a throne—heavy old wood, high back, thick arms, chartreuse velvet upholstery. Stephanie provides bottles of water. One worker bee touches up Martha's makeup.

Bella captures everything on camera. She is excited to have such a larger-than-life subject. In moments like this, she knows she is becoming a part of history with her pictures, and she wants to do it right, to catch every detail. After she circles the group with a set of snaps, Martha notices her and begins to pose. She shoos the fussing members of her entourage with a few swipes of her precisely manicured hand to clear the way for Bella.

The doors to the gallery open at seven o'clock. Already, a crowd has gathered outside. Stephanie and a representative from the book seller have organized the crowd into a queue. Books are piled high on a long table in the foyer, ready for purchase. Bella makes a mental note to buy a signed copy.

"Do you usually start working right when you walk in the door? The event has not even started yet," Dorian says to Bella in a rare moment when she is standing still.

"Yes, when it's Martha J. Jackson," Bella says. "Is there something else you'd like for me to be doing?"

"Yes, I want us to meet with Ellen before the doors open."

"Will we talk gardens?" Bella asks. She is anxious to put their plan in place.

"No, not yet, but I want the three of us to connect and reset, you know?"

"Of course," Bella says, shaking her head to relay enthusiasm. "Honestly, Dorian, this job is a reset. I am so grateful. Thank you."

"Well, this was all Ellen," Dorian says.

"Well then, lead the way. I can thank her myself."

Bella calls for Geri, who is standing with Stephanie, going

over the guest list. Bella introduces Geri to Dorian, and the three of them walk to Ellen's office.

"Ellen, you remember Bella Fontaine," Dorian says, approaching Ellen's desk. She is sitting back in her chair and drinking from a water bottle, which she puts down and stands.

"Hello, Bella," Ellen says with a wide smile, "where have we met again?"

Geri is standing a step behind Bella. "Is she the one who . . .?" Geri whispers in Bella's ear.

"Yes," Bella answers. Her voice and head movement are quick and sharp, pruning Geri's question at the bud. Bella takes a breath, giving herself time to answer Ellen's question free of resentment and indictment. But Dorian seizes the moment.

"Mother, Bella is photographing the event for us tonight."

"Well, where is Hank? He couldn't come?" Ellen asks.

"We didn't ask Hank," Dorian says "Bella, our upcoming art-ist, is now at the top of our event photographer list."

Bella is feeling weak at the knees and a little dizzy, recognizing this sensation as her body's reaction to disappointment. But she reminds herself to be patient and empathetic with Ellen. These are what her lapses look like. She notices Dorian's stiff posture, the way he is holding his head is as if his neck is in a whiplash brace, like he wants to face Bella to apologize but cannot make the turn. He is staring at his mother wide-eyed. Is he trying to send her a signal, or is he just mortified that Ellen has forgotten?

"Oh, oh, yes, yes. I am so sorry, dear," Ellen says and makes her way around her desk. She puts on her glasses and approaches Bella with her hand extended. "I don't know what to say, except thank you for being here to get those wonderful moments of Martha's arrival. Is she not fabulous?"

"She is a photographer's dream," Bella recovers. She recognizes that Ellen has just returned to herself. She knows what this looks like. "I truly appreciate this opportunity to work this event. Thank you, Mrs. Herman."

"You're welcome. And call me Ellen."

"Okay, Ellen, this is Geri. She is here to assist me. As this is my first time working with you, please let me know if you have a preferred way with photographs. I noticed that you mostly post posed shots on your social media and website gallery. Because Ms. Jackson is so expressive and colorful, I think her entire entourage will provide some magical candid shots."

"Well, do your thing," Ellen says, "show me what you got. I believe they are unrolling the red carpet out front, as we speak. We had not planned to use it. We only thought of it tonight because we saw you taking pictures as Martha arrived. It is particularly fitting for Martha's energy and her book's message. So, good for you. And keep up the good work."

"Thank you, Ellen," Bella says, meeting Dorian's approving eyes. He looks relieved.

"You're welcome," Ellen says. "And Ms. Geri! Welcome to you. You girls seem like a mighty good team."

"Yes, ma'am," Geri says, "if you see someone we have not paid the proper attention to, please let me know and I will inform Bella."

"Ah, yes, will do," Ellen says. Her smile is warm now. She rubs Geri's arm and nods to Bella as she walks out the door and toward the gallery. "Chop, chop," she says over her shoulder, "it's showtime!"

The main gallery, filled with as many rows of folding chairs as can fit, is wall-to-wall people. The book buyers' queue in the foyer has folded on itself many times, filling the entire space and continuing out the front doors and down the street. Dorian and Frank are managing the gallery seating, helping people fill in the few remaining empty seats. Stephanie and the bookstore representative are selling books and providing slips of paper for the buyers to write the name they want Martha to use when she signs their books. Martha has stopped signing and is in place to begin her talk with her audience.

Ellen introduces Martha with very short remarks. She knows this crowd wants as much time as they can get with Martha, and she knows the room is over capacity and will be uncomfortable in a very short time. When she hands over the microphone to Martha, who is now nestled comfortably on her throne, Martha is delayed by the deafening applause—whoops and hollers, bravos and yas queens. She makes several false starts as the noise does not diminish. Finally, she rolls her eyes and says, "Darlings, enough, already! I haven't even said anything brilliant yet."

The volume of the noise increases in response. Martha is impatient and begins amid the cheers. "I wrote *If You Ain't Got Soul* only because Raymond told me to. He had been nagging me about it for some time, and every time he brought it up, I'd say, oh, muffin, I am too busy living to be writing about my life. But then he showed me a whole book somebody else wrote about me. It was, oh, gee, four-hundred-some pages, loves! He brought it home, and we cracked it open somewhere in the middle. And on the very page that we began to read, there was a mighty untruth. A bold-faced lie. It wasn't harmful, you understand, but it was not the truth. And Raymond said, 'You see, Martha? Do you see why you must write your own book? You are the only one who can set the record straight.' And you know, darlings, he was right."

Martha stops, smiles her trademark smile, broad and toothy. She holds up her book. "And so . . . here it is! Friends, *here . . . it . . . is!*" The audience erupts again.

Bella is standing in the archway between Gallery One and Two. Gallery Two is decorated for a post-signing private reception sponsored by Sparkle and Shine, the cosmetic company that owns Martha's endorsement. There is a dark blue velvet rope across the archway. Because Gallery One is so packed with people, Bella finds it too difficult to maneuver for pictures, so she is posted in this corner. When Dorian finds her, she is so captivated by Martha's storytelling that she has stopped taking pictures altogether and holds her camera at her waist.

"I am so glad there is an after reception. Will Martha be up to a party after she signs all these books?" Bella asks. "I went outside to take a picture of the line, and it goes all the way around the corner."

"Martha is a legendary party animal," Dorian says, "but we will move her chair when the time comes, and she can sit it out if she wants to."

"She looks pretty comfortable right now," Bella says.

"Yes, she is in her true element and can probably do this talking part all night. Ellen will have to break through when the time comes to wrap it up, and she will not win any popularity for it."

"No doubt," Bella says. She moves in closer to him and whispers another thank-you in his ear. They turn to face each other. It is the first moment since Bella arrived that they allow themselves to drop their professional personas and see each other. Dorian smiles down at her. His mouth is a small lopsided smirk, but his eyes relay tenderness and admiration as they hold Bella's for a long minute. She returns the emotion with an acknowledging smile, tilting her head and lifting her chin toward Dorian. She blinks slowly, a long flirtatious gesture, and nudges him with her shoulder. He lets out a low whisper of a laugh.

The audience erupts in applause and cheers again in response to Martha's words. "Honeys, the book focuses on the kidnapping. It is a trauma that I continue to suffer from, has changed the way I move in the world, my level of trust. But it did not defeat me, no, ma'am! I do discuss how the community came to my rescue, how they rallied the police department to *do* something. I honor Detective Stacy Smith, who was closeted at the time, but who took my disappearance seriously and pushed her department to find me. To apply the pressure that brought about my release. I owe her my life, friends. My very life!"

"Hey, I almost forgot," Dorian says to Bella, snapping back to business, "I hope you are taking some special pictures. Like, not just for publicity, but to grow your portfolio. Martha Jackson is a rare opportunity to create pictures to build a future show around."

Bella nods. Of course she knows this, but she lets Dorian do his job.

"Also, the people speaking with the videographer over there are Martha's handlers—her publicist, her assistant, and the Sparkle and Shine Cosmetics marketing people. Do you have business cards?"

"Yes," Bella says, reaching in the front pocket of her backpack and pulling out one of her brand-new business cards that she designed and ordered online. She hands it to Dorian. He looks at it. "Okay, so we'll get you some suitable business cards."

"Hey!" Bella says, offended.

"Sorry. If you are married to these, then fine. But I think we can do better."

"These are what I could afford," Bella admits, still defensive.

"Understood. We'll connect you with Martha's people once we see your pictures. We'll send them all some special ones with your *new* card."

"Okay," Bella says. She likes the feeling of being managed by a pro.

"I need you to connect with Martha tonight. Get her to remember you. Do your Black Girl Magic thing. Do with her what you did with Drip."

"But this is not a photo shoot," Bella says.

"The hell it isn't!"

The private reception very quickly becomes an after party. Martha has signed nearly two hundred books, and the effort seems to have fueled her. She is tireless.

Ellen asks Martha if she needs a break between signing and the reception.

"We have a quiet room prepared for you upstairs if you'd like to take a rest. There are some light snacks and beverages for you. A chaise lounge," Ellen offers.

"Oh, yas, honey, let's take a breather," one of her protégées says, reaching out a hand to help Martha stand. Martha accepts the assistance. Once she is on her feet, she interlaces her hands and loudly cracks her knuckles.

"No, no, dear loves. I will rest when I'm dead," Martha says. "Let's go."

"Is this bitch the Diva or is she not?" the protégée responds, snapping her fingers and wrapping Martha's arm around her own.

"Let's make a pit stop to the bathroom, pee and powder our noses," Martha says.

"Pit stop, pee, powder. Got it," the protégée repeats and leads Martha to the restroom. They bypass Gallery Two, where the crowd is already noisy and dancing to music with a strong bass beat.

While Martha is in the bathroom, Bella uses the time to duck into the back hallway to look through her pictures. She scrolls through the shots on her camera screen to see if she has anything "special," as Dorian put it, looking to see if there is a particular angle, mood, or theme she can riff off or duplicate.

Geri sees Bella crouched down and hovering over her camera. "What's up? Everything okay?"

"Yeah, yeah, I'm just looking through my shots. Dorian put the pressure on to do something special, translation— artful. I'm always going for that, of course. But he got me feeling like I need to step it up."

"Well, this whole scene is just, like, walking art, right?" Geri says. "I mean, I ain't never been around the trans community. They are just like all drama and theater. In the room, you got the cheerleader-groupies up front. You got the haters whispering and sayin' rude shit about each other in the corner in the back. And Martha! Holy shit! Martha is like some kind of magical being. She is *so* real, so street, but she's got that 'it' thing that just draws you in." Geri pauses to take a breath, shakes her head. "I'm just sayin', the subject matter don't get any better than this, mama."

"Absolutely right, Ger. But it comes with a pressure to not miss anything. I could fail to capture it all. Fail to make sure all this energy comes through. Which means we need to think through our strategy for the reception."

Geri joins Bella in a crouch. She shakes her head and leans in, eager to be in this new and exciting environment.

"Let's get back in before Martha. Here, take my phone and get some video of Martha's entrance," Bella instructs Geri so that she will have video to review later once she is at home. She'll pull stills from the footage.

"Dorian wants me to make an impression on Martha tonight so that she remembers me," Bella says as she stands up and puts the camera strap around her neck.

"Well, shit! Does he want you to serve drinks and juggle too?"

After the Herman Gallery gig, Bella and Geri celebrate another successful job together. They choose a neighborhood hangout, The Mole, near Bella's apartment. The Mole is a tiny hidden spot around the corner that feels more like a cave than an establishment and located down a flight of stairs from the street. Its subterranean dark and dankness feel like the basement that it is. Bella buys Geri a drink, and they debrief by sharing the memorable moments of the gig—the funny and unexpected; the harrowing and risky; the things they've learned and tips they want to remember for next time.

"Bells, I gotta just thank you for letting me do this job," Geri says.

"Ger, you are the best assistant I have never had!" Bella says, convinced more than ever that Geri's help is the insurance policy she affords herself because Geri allows Bella to focus only on taking pictures. "Plus, Ellen was right. We are a mighty good team."

"Yeah, speaking of Ellen," Geri says, "what is her deal? She doesn't remember you. Then you are her best friend. Then you are a stranger? Wtf!"

"Yes, at least we got to see the real Ellen today. I've now met her on three different occasions, and I think this is the first time I've seen the Ellen everybody else knows. And *that* Ellen is pretty cool." Bella does not share her suspicion that Ellen is suffering early signs of dementia, or her and Dorian's plan to win her over. She simply tells Geri, "Rumor has it, she's into gardening."

"Oh, yeah?"

"So, she can't be all bad, right?" Bella says.

"Fo' sho', no way," Geri says, holding up her drink in a toast. "She should love your stuff, then, right?"

"You would think. We'll see." Bella clinks Geri's glass of beer with her own.

Over Geri's shoulder Bella catches a glimpse of a familiar body at the other end of the bar. His back is to her, but even in the dim light, she knows from his height and the way he moves;

the colorful, expensive clothes, and the dreadlocks. Just three nights ago, she'd been preparing the Drip McAffrey photographs for final submission to Dorian—over two hundred shots. She feels like she'd know Drip's profile and silhouette anywhere.

In one motion, Drip reaches for his drink and turns in her direction. When their eyes meet, it feels to Bella as if he'd already spotted her before she'd seen him. He does a reverse nod of his head and makes his way over.

"Who is that?" Geri asks with a trace of whisper in her voice that makes her question sound more like a gasp.

"Drip McAffrey," Bella says, "pro basketball player."

"No, shit. He's a neck-breaker."

"Neck-breaker?"

"You know, super tall."

"Hello, Drip McAffrey," Bella says in her most formal voice.

"Yo," Drip responds. He does not match Bella's formality. Instead, his voice is casual and familiar with an unmistakable flirtatious lilt to it.

"What are you doing so far west of home?" Bella asks.

"This is not so far west," Drip says, laughing at Bella's attempt to cover her New York rookie status. "If you want me to be honest, I came to ask you about the pictures from the shoot." He sits down on the bar stool next to Bella. "I am leaving for Milan in a week and a half, and I'm eager to see how they came out."

"No, way," Bella says, "how'd you know I was here?"

"Dorian. I showed up for the book event. He told me I missed you. That you took the photos for the event. I guess he was supposed to join you-all here, but he got tied up. I'm sure he told you that."

"So, you showed up so late for Martha J. Jackson that you missed the book signing *and* the after party?" Bella teases Drip about his reputation for tardiness.

"Wait, you had a photo shoot with a pro ball player, and you didn't think to ask me to help?" Geri breaks in. "Hi, I'm Geri Baez, Bella's assistant." She holds out her hand to Drip, who takes and daps it. Geri returns the gesture with a broad smile of appreciation. Bella is impressed with Drip's astuteness.

"Well, it was only a one-person photo shoot, Geri. Otherwise, I would have." Bella turns to Drip. "You should have gotten to the gallery earlier so that you could see how they treat you when you are the artist and the honored guest. They go all out. I mean, Martha J. Jackson is a special case, but still, I think you would have been impressed."

"Oh, yeah?" Drip says, "so I'm not a special case?"

Geri picks up on the flirtatious way Drip is coming at Bella and she decides that three is a crowd.

"So, Bells, can we settle up? I need to get to my mom's before it gets too late."

"Of course," Bella says. She pulls out her phone and sends the payment virtually. She was not expecting Geri to abandon her with Drip. She wonders if there was some cue between them that she missed.

"Thanks, sis, and thanks for the beer. Always a pleasure. You really did miss a spectacle," Geri says to Drip. "It was an experience I will never forget!" She offers up her hand to Drip, who grabs it again.

"Good to meet you, Geri. I am sure I will be seeing you around."

"Yeah, for sure," Geri says. "See you at the garden, Bells."

"Okay, thanks again, Ger."

"So, Bells," Drip says.

"You have to earn the right to call me by a nickname," Bella says, playing along.

"Oh, oh, is that right?"

"Yes, and you have to do more than just be cute and wear expensive clothes."

"Hmm, I see," Drip laughs his hearty, unrestrained laugh. "So, you think I'm cute?"

"I think I managed to make you look cute on camera."

"So, you're saying," he pauses and waves down the bartender, "I'm only cute with the help of your camera magic."

"That's pretty much what I'm saying. You'll see. I make you look pretty damn good." They are both laughing now.

"Hey, I didn't mean to break up your party," Drip says.

"I know, but you want to know about your pictures."

"Well, no, if you want me to be totally honest, I came to see you."

"What's the deal with you and being honest," Bella says. She is not ready to address the move that Drip has just made. "Don't you expect that everyone will always want you to be totally honest?"

"Honestly? No, I don't believe they do," Drip says, only partially serious. "But I get the feeling that you are a no-nonsense kind of person. So, I guess I just want you to know when I am being straight with you. No games."

"Wait, no games?" Bella says. "Didn't you come here knowing that you were taking Dorian's place?"

"I said no games. That doesn't mean I won't grab an opportunity if it arises."

"And what opportunity is that?" Bella says.

"Look, I'm sorry. It's just that I thought we had a moment the other day at my place, and you know. . . ."

"Know what? I know you and Dorian talked about me, and not just about my professional credentials. I know you know there is a relationship between him and me. So, what *is* this?"

"Maybe I'm trying to save you both," Drip says. His smile

says he's being coy. "You and Dorian will be working together. Do you think it's a good idea to be involved like that?"

Bella does not respond. She just searches his eyes to see if he is joking. She is sure he must be, and she does not want to be taken in.

"Anyway, I know when I've had a moment with someone," he says, "and I am not one to leave a page unturned."

"You are not joking, are you?" Bella allows her incredulity to show. "Aren't you leaving for Milan any day now? To use your book metaphor, you are about to start a new chapter in your life. Dorian is a part of that chapter, not me."

"But we did have a moment, right?" Drip says in a way that acknowledges Bella's position, while still remaining playful. *This is how confident people deal with rejection*, Bella thinks.

"I had a moment with my delicious latte this morning. That does not mean I should date it." Bella tries to muster as much mirth as she can to match Drip's.

"See? I knew you thought I was delicious."

"Okay, I'm going to head on home now," Bella says as she leaves her chair and gathers her backpack and jacket. "We never had this conversation, right?" Drip finishes his drink and doesn't answer.

"Right," Bella answers for him. "I'm going to give your proofs to Dorian no later than the end of this week. I think you are going to be really happy with them."

"See you later, Bells," is all he says.

Bella decides to leave because she does not trust herself. If she stays, even though she does not enjoy this superficial kind of banter, she is afraid that she may show herself. She refuses to admit that for the last week she has been poring over Drip's photographs for hours at a time. She will never tell him that she has tacked the pictures of his Madonna tattoo on her vision board over her bed. Or that he is exactly the type of man Bella is attracted to, historically speaking. She loves tall men, his broad-featured handsome. She loves athletic. But she has an aversion to his kind of fame and privilege, the kind she found in most of the athletes she encountered at UCLA. When she met Drip in his penthouse apartment, he was too polished, with too much affectation to even raise her interest past the professional. She has developed an armor against this type of guy. But the Madonna tattoo broke through it. Once she saw that tattoo, she felt like she had somehow seen into Drip's soul. She felt like they were connected in a way that might take a journey to discover. At night, when she is no longer preoccupied with pleasing Dorian, winning Ellen, and earning her keep, when fatigue melts away the concerns of her life, she thinks of Drip, and she wonders, *Who is the artist behind the hype?* Who permanently cloaks himself with the Black Madonna? A tattoo of that size and scale is a life commitment—like a marriage. Who is the guy who does that?

But tonight, Drip's approach was all wrong. The way he sought her out was flattering and reaffirming, but his manner felt forced and practiced. She is not interested in this Drip. She wonders what it would take to get to know the hidden one.

Bella turns and heads out the door and up the steps to the street. She is praying Drip does not follow her. And he doesn't.

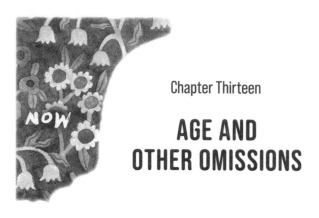

Chapter Thirteen

AGE AND OTHER OMISSIONS

JUNE

On days like today, Bella marvels at her own gift. It is the very first time she has created a garden all on her own, mostly from seed, and she loves every single feature—every pot, plant choice, tool, and piece of furniture, new or used, freegan or saved-for—precisely because she and only she chose it. On the day of Ellen Herman's first visit, she sees her garden the way Ellen might, through a visitor's eyes, and she is pleased, proud, and confident. But before she entices Ellen to see the garden, they have tea in Bella's apartment.

"You present an impressive tea service, Bella," Ellen says in starts and stops. She is still out of breath from her slow slog up the stairs. She sits at Bella's tiny round table holding her cup of Earl Grey tea in one hand and the saucer in the other. She takes a sip, bowing her head to meet the cup. Her pinky points up as best it can with its defiant arthritic knuckle.

"Thank you, Ellen." They are sitting opposite each other in Bella's only two dining chairs, the flimsy metal café chairs she found on the street. She brought them and the table down from the roof and cleaned them off for this occasion. She bought a white tablecloth and new floral seat cushions to make them more comfortable. The tea service tray, also a bargain find from her favorite neighborhood thrift store, barely fits on the table, and even though she and Ellen are on opposite sides of the table, their knees are touching.

Ellen agreed to review Bella's work and assess its value for the gallery, and Dorian delivered her to Bella's apartment at the appointed time. He called Bella once he pulled up to the curb and then made a hasty exit. Bella ran down to help Ellen up the stairs, encouraging her to take it slow. She is not sure what Dorian had to do to get Ellen here, but Ellen seems to think it was her idea.

Bella takes a big gulp of her English Breakfast tea, places her cup in its saucer, and stands. "Okay, I thought I would take you through the series while you enjoy your tea." She walks over to the stack of framed photos at the end of her entry hall near the table. Earlier, she put them in the order that she felt best shows her theme and creative process.

"Ah, yes, it's why I am here, isn't it? But that is not how this will work, dear."

"No?"

"No. Dorian has already briefed me. You will leave me alone with the work." She looks around. "This tiny place of yours . . . is there someplace you can go?"

"Yes," Bella says, realizing this could play right into her plans. "You know what? I have a rooftop deck. It's just one floor up . . . not even a full flight of stairs. Do you maybe want to come and get me when you are finished?"

"Yes, perfect. I will do just that," Ellen says, "I won't be long."

"Okay, great."

"So now, how many photos in this series?"

"Twenty-one,"

"Splendid," Ellen says, "plenty to choose from."

"Yes, ma'am." Bella shows Ellen her ordered stack of photos in the hallway, and she takes her leave.

While Bella is waiting on the roof, she cleans things up a bit more. But really, the garden is in full bloom and showing off. The late afternoon sun is low, hovering just over the Empire State Building, providing a burnt-orange glow and gentle shadows. The sky is clear and cloudless. A soft warm breeze circulates through the garden. She opens a fresh bag of potting soil and takes out one of her small hand shovels. She turns the soil in the bag and shovels a thin layer along the edges of the pots and planters in hopes of releasing the soil's fresh, rich scent. She wants Ellen's introduction to this garden to be multisensory.

She sits near the azaleas and waits. And she waits and she waits. After an hour and a half, she is afraid it will get too dark to dazzle Ellen. Just in case, she plugs in her stringed lights. It occurs to her that Ellen may have forgotten where she is supposed to come. Right when Bella decides she will go down and check on her, Ellen steps over the threshold and out onto the roof.

"Belinda, your work is quite extraordinary, quite extraordinary. I wish I'd seen it earlier. I would have loved to get it in the gallery this year. We have not shown photography in some time."

"Yes, ma'am, thank you," is all that Bella says. She wants to shake Ellen and tell her that she *did* see her work early enough to show this year. She wants to remind her that she gave her spot away. She wants to scream that her work might be in her gallery right now if she'd just allowed her son a real decision or two. But Bella doesn't express these things. She remembers Gran's directives and reminds herself that Ellen's lapses are not her fault. She doesn't even remind Ellen that her name is Bella; she will gently slide that correction somewhere in their conversation.

Ellen looks around her and breathes in deeply.

"Oh, my word. This is what heaven must surely smell like," Ellen says. "Is this a common space for the building? How lucky you are to have such a lovely retreat."

"Well, not really a common space. This is my garden. I planted it myself."

"You didn't!"

"Yes, ma'am, I did."

"Do you mean to tell me that you are responsible for this entire glorious place?"

"Yes, may I show you around?"

Bella gives Ellen the tour. They visit every planter and pot. Ellen has questions at every stop—how different is a roof garden from the ground? What is the scientific name for this? Is this an annual or perennial? How often do you have to water this, fertilize that? Did you grow this from seed and if not, where did you buy it?

Bella shows her the potting table, seed jars, and storage bin full of supplies. Ellen wants to know everything.

She walks over to the front of the building and looks up toward the Empire State Building for several minutes. When she turns around, something has changed, something in her eyes and her carriage. She seems nervous, like she is struggling to compose herself.

"This is simply beautiful," Ellen says with a more formal tone now, "is this a common space for the building?"

"Well, not really a common space," Bella repeats. "This is my garden. I built and planted it myself."

"And you are?" Ellen asks.

"I'm Bella. You've come to review my photographs for the gallery."

"Yes, I know that. I know who you are, Bella, dear," Ellen says, her smile missing its usual confidence.

"This is one of my favorite flowers," Bella says, ushering Ellen over to her hibiscus shrub. "My *Hibiscus moscheutos* is so happy right now. Have you ever seen such gigantic blossoms?" The green of the plant is barely visible under the broad white flowers, which look like large umbrellas in flight.

"My mother used to grow hibiscus in her garden," Ellen says. "Her blossoms were not so big as these, but I always loved them. I grew up in Westchester, you know?"

Bella smiles and pretends she doesn't know, but Dorian has told her a lot about Ellen's upbringing.

"We had quite a lot of land, and my mother was a master gardener. She had two gardens, a kitchen garden of vegetables and fruit trees, and a rose garden, mostly roses but other favorites too. My mother lived in those gardens. And if I was to spend any time with her, it would have been there." Ellen seems to find comfort in this solid and crystal-clear memory of her mother. She gently cups a hibiscus blossom in her hands and bends slightly to smell it. The hibiscus has no fragrance, but neither of them comment on this.

"The same for me and my grandmothers," Bella says. She walks Ellen over to the hydrangeas. "I grew up in their gardens. They taught me everything I know."

"Oh, well, I learned a little from my mother, as well. I could never pull off all of this, though." Ellen waves her hand in a sweeping motion then turns to the hydrangeas. "Hydrangeas! These were one of my mother's favorites. Mine too. My wedding bouquet was mostly my mother's white hydrangeas."

"That must have been beautiful," Bella says, "Hydrangeas were my Nan's favorite flower, as well."

"The women in the photos, they are your grandmothers, aren't they?"

Now Bella knows why Ellen took so long to make it to the

roof. She would have had to go through her apartment to find the photos of Bella's grandmothers put away in her bedroom.

"Tell me about those."

"The photos?" Bella asks.

Ellen nods her head yes.

"Well, I took them for a school assignment at UCLA. My teacher liked them enough to submit to the Klineberg, which is a photo competition in Toronto. That's why they are framed. One of the photos of both grandmothers won first place."

"Yes, of course," Ellen says, "those are the photos I want, dear." She walks over to a garden bench and sits down heavily.

"I didn't see many of the pictures of your grandmothers. Do you have any others in that series?

"No," Bella says. She is trying to keep her composure. This was not how she saw this playing out. "And to think I almost left those at home in LA."

"They are painful for you, then?" Ellen asks.

Bella nods yes.

"You no longer have your grandmothers, I presume?" Ellen asks.

"No," Bella says.

"Shame. I understand," Ellen pauses, "but why did you *not* leave the photos behind?"

"They are my only awarding-winning photos. I guess I thought I should bring my full portfolio when I moved here."

"Exactly," Ellen says, "so we will intersperse them with the other series. I believe the show will be quite stirring."

"Yes, ma'am."

"Welcome to the Herman Gallery. Congratulations. We will do a one-night exhibition next summer to start. One day is all we've got. You will be next year's Herman Gallery featured emerging artist." She stands, looks around at the garden once more and moves to the roof door. "You know, you have more furniture out here than in your entire apartment." Ellen turns toward the stairs. "Call me a car, will you, dear?"

To Bella, Dorian's apartment feels palatial. It's loft-like with few walls and lots of open space. He lives on the tenth floor of an older condominium on the Upper Westside, which is one of the high-rent districts of the city, where the crevices of the buildings do not smell like urine and all the windows are clean.

When he opens the door, delicious aromas of dinner waft out to greet Bella. He draws her into a hug.

"Hey!" he says.

"Hey."

"Well, congratulations are in order! Congratulations!" He is in high spirits. He picks her up and does a half twirl. "My mother is making arrangements for your show as we speak."

"Really?" Bella says, happy that Ellen made it back home with her memory of their visit intact. "We'll see if it sticks, I guess." Bella says this reflexively to protect her own fragile ego and to keep her expectations in check. But it has an immediate dampening effect on Dorian.

"I'm sorry," she says.

"No, no, I understand. Dinner is almost ready."

"I am so excited for your cooking. What are we having? It smells delicious."

"You'll just have to wait and see," he says, making his way to the kitchen. Bella stops him. They are face-to-face. She unbuttons the top button of his shirt and kisses his neck.

"I am not feeling very patient tonight," Bella says. He wraps his arms around her, and they kiss.

"Maybe we can put off dinner," he says, moving her to his sofa.

"Maybe for a minute," she says, "cuz I am starving!" They both laugh as he pulls her onto the sofa. She returns to unbuttoning his shirt. Bella likes Dorian's chest. It's muscular and covered with curly black hair. He has nice shoulders too, broad and angular. She kisses his left nipple, and he laughs a breathy, muffled laugh that lets her know he likes this. She finds his mouth. His hands are caressing her ass over her dress, then he wraps his fingers through her thong and moves it out of the way as one finger moves downward.

The oven begins to cry out—the buzz of the timer stops and starts twice, getting louder and longer each time.

"I guess I better not burn dinner," he says.

"No, please, don't," Bella says, disappointed that they are interrupted, but she lets him up and they both go to the kitchen. "How can I help?"

"You can open the wine and take it to the table. I'll be right behind you."

Bella grabs the sauvignon blanc and the corkscrew and sets about opening the bottle. She sees that Dorian is very organized, all the serving platters and utensils for dinner set out. With one fluid motion, she twists the corkscrew and pulls.

"You look like a pro," Dorian says.

"Yes, one of my many skills from my waitressing days."

He is arranging asparagus on a platter. "You were a waitress?"

"No," she says, "it just felt like it sometimes. My parents were big wine drinkers. My brother and I were in charge of uncorking. We had a little competition. He always won, but let's just say, we both got lots of practice." She gathers up the cork housing and finds the cabinet where the trash can is hiding. She tosses the trash in and closes the door, but not before she sees Italian restaurant bags in the trash. Dorian's meal is not homemade. She is disappointed. He invited her to a "home-cooked" meal,

147

and she'd made a big deal out of his professed ability to cook. That had all apparently been a lie. Still, he has gone to a lot of trouble, and Bella is happy that the food will certainly be delicious. She rounds the corner to his dining room with wine bottle in hand. His dining room has a full-sized dining table made of all glass with six black chenille upholstered chairs pulled up to it. It is set with a vase of tulips and a sea of tea lights already ablaze.

"Ahh, the table is beautiful," Bella says.

"I am glad you like it," Dorian says.

"You are too much," she says, forgiving his restaurant charade.

She sets the wine bottle in the center of the table. She sits down in the chair facing the door, a habit she picked up from her father, having something to do with being the first to know "when conditions change."

Dorian sets two platters down—one with pasta, the other with asparagus, bright green with tips slightly singed—then returns to the kitchen.

"Is that shrimp scampi?" Bella asks, the room filling with the aroma of garlic and butter. She grabs the wine and pours the two glasses. "I'm gonna pour the wine, okay?" she yells as an afterthought since she'd already done it.

Dorian shows up with a big salad bowl full of delicious-looking restaurant salad.

"So Dorian, do you do a lot of cooking?" Bella asks, "Like, how do you have all these plates and serving platters and stuff?"

"Well, I've been on my own for a long time, Bella. I've been meaning to broach this subject for a while." He says this as he is standing over her, filling their plates with salad.

"What subject?" Bella asks.

"I know you think you and I are the same age," he says, "but we're not. I'm a lot older."

"How much older?"

"I turn forty next year."

"Dorian Herman, you are *thirty-nine*? You . . . are thirty-nine years old?" she asks again because she is trying to let her brain catch up.

"Yes," Dorian says, "I know I look younger than that. . . ."

"Way younger," she says before he can finish. "But when we met, you gave me all these reasons why representation by a younger person was advantageous. You said we were contemporaries!"

"I know. I *think* of myself as your contemporary. . . ." Dorian trails off.

"Why would you do that? Why wouldn't you sell me on your years of experience at the gallery instead of being deceiving?"

"Well, I haven't actually been working at the gallery that long. . . ."

"What do you mean? You grew up at the gallery."

"Yes, but I've only actually been working in my current capacity for two years. I didn't initially want to do the family business. I did sales for a bit."

"What's a bit?"

"For twelve years, right out of college."

"What did you sell, cars?"

"No. Hospital equipment."

"So, you are as new to this as I am!"

"No, not really. I *was* groomed by my parents all my life, I just. . . ."

"All except for those twelve years. Basically, your adult years."

"I guess so, yes."

"You know, you are way closer to my dad's age than you are to mine. He's forty-eight."

"Wow, then, yeah," is all Dorian has to offer. He has finished serving salad and taken his seat. "Are you going to eat?"

Bella is frozen in her seat, staring at him. She is desperately trying to adjust Dorian's dishonesty and the sudden shift in her perception of where he is in life. She'd thought he was ahead of the curve, an early bloomer, endeavoring to take his place in his family business early. And now, she is realizing that he is behind. She knows she should be saying, "Oh, honey, age is just a number," or "What we have transcends age," or "Good, I prefer older people." Which is true, she does prefer to spend her time with older people. But she can't muster the sincerity to say any of these things. His lies about his age, his inexperience, and the restaurant dinner combine to make Bella feel anxious and uneasy, so she says nothing. She just picks up her fork, spears her salad, puts the leaves in her mouth, and chews.

They eat in silence. When they finish the salad, Dorian serves up pasta and asparagus. Bella swirls her linguini around her fork. Before she takes a mouthful, because she can no longer take the tension, she says, "The plan with your mother worked perfectly. She really seemed to love the garden. She told me all about her mother and her upbringing in Westchester. Next, I would like to take her to my community garden. See if she takes to it. The people are really friendly. She's a people person. I suspect she will love it."

"Okay, how can I help?" The conversation now feels like a business transaction.

"I go to the garden on Mondays. I have already asked my friend to try and get your mom a plot of her own. Do you think she can come next week?"

"I think she will if you ask her. You are her new favorite person."

Bella decides in this moment that Ellen is her new favorite Herman. She feels bad about it. But she can't help how she feels. She is hoping this disdain for Dorian will pass, so much is at stake, but she doesn't think it will.

Chapter Fourteen

NAN AND HER GLAMOUR GLOVES

I am hiding in the shadows of the driveway gate, shielded from the blazing California sun and safely out of view. From here, I can see that Nan has gotten much stronger. I am usually so busy when I visit that I rarely just take a quiet moment to watch.

The last three months have been a long, tough road to recovery for my Nan. Doctors initially told her she would likely never walk again with the multiple fractures in her left leg, because of the nature of the breaks and the shock they caused to her aging body. She took the prognosis as an unlikely suggestion, so certain that Gran and the garden would bring her total healing. But she thought it would be magic and not her own hard work. She thought it would be instantaneous instead of months of slow progress and setbacks.

Gran, of course, rejected the doctor's pronouncements outright and assured Nan that she would be up and about in good time. Gran helped her gain her strength and resolve in those moments when she was ready to give up. She accompanied her to every physical therapy session. She fed Nan foods to help her heal, and she massaged her legs to relieve the pain and improve circulation. I helped with the massages. By now, at fifteen, I am as tall as my grandmothers, and my hands are as strong. Nan seemed to love the massages the most, and I wanted to be in on the few parts of the healing process that she enjoyed.

"Healing is in the work," Gran told Nan to get her out in the garden to help with the tending. When Nan insisted, "I am too old to be out in this merciless sun, working this hard," Gran shared stories with her about the old farmers of her Arkansas people, who toiled every day and lived to be one hundred years old. Nan scoffed, "Those are your people, Olivette, not mine." But Nan always relented and did the garden tasks Gran assigned her.

Now, from my hidden spot, Nan looks like a new person. She is a paradox—somehow different *and* more herself. She is standing her full height, her spine ramrod straight, clutching her walker with gloved hands. She is wearing Glamour Gloves, a brand of gardening gloves designed for the fashion-forward green thumb. They are bright green and reach her elbows, where they are secured by pink ribbed satin bows and rhinestone-studded buttons. The fingers and hands of the gloves have clumps of dirt on them. This is the new part: Nan's gloves are dirty. In her home garden, her gloves rarely touched the dirt.

Today, she is dressed in fitted, side-zipped denim pants that are cropped at the shin and a crisp light blue gingham blouse with the quarter-length sleeves folded into cuffs. Her hair is perfectly coiffed in its trademark helmet shape with side bangs, and she is wearing her church pearls. Her brown apron has two pockets. The blue rubber handle of a small hand shovel sticks out of one pocket. Nan looks like a 1950s magazine model, the lady-gardener, except for the walker and the clumps of dirt on her Glamour Gloves.

She is making ground with her walker, deftly maneuvering through the grasses. I look around and I don't see Gran. Nan is in the garden by herself. She has now moved through the reeds and has arrived at the Garden Goddess. A thinning section of the reeds allows me to see to the middle of the spiral. She turns her walker around to face the opposite direction so that when she sits on the walker's small saddle seat, she is facing the figure that she calls Mary. She steadies herself and then bends down to tackle the intruders around Mary's feet, pulling at the crab-grass and digging below the soil to uproot the stubborn sedge tubers. She is singing her favorite hymn in a soft, high-pitched falsetto—

Be joyful, Mary, heavenly Queen,
Be joyful, Mary! Your grief is changed to joy serene. . . .

I wonder in this moment if her song is for the Madonna or for herself. I watch in amazement as she puts the pulled plants in her other apron pocket, then turns her face up to meet the blessed face above her. She closes her eyes and is very still for several minutes. The walker seat makes me think of a church pew. Nan is smiling when she makes the sign of the cross and stands.

Alleluia! Rejoice, rejoice, O Mary!

She sings louder as she grabs hold of the walker and moves from the circle of grasses to the raised beds. I can no longer see her, so I walk quietly along the house to the other side of the garden for a better view. In front of one of the wooden boxes that make up the set of four raised beds, she moves the walker to the side and leans against the box brimming over with flowers and herb plants. As she rifles through the herbs, pulling out the small intruders, she nips off the tops of some of the herb sprouts, puts them in her mouth, and chews. I have seen my Gran do this many times, nip and taste the edibles when she is tending the raised beds. This is my first time seeing this practice repeated by Nan. It makes me laugh. It is so unlike her character. But watching her work gladdens my heart, and I decide to leave her to it. Gran has always used her early mornings in the garden as a meditation, preferring to be left alone for an hour or so. I won-der if Nan has established this practice for herself, claiming the garden in the afternoon.

I go inside the house from the back door. When I call for Gran, she comes out of the bathroom with a plunger in one hand and a bottle of Drano in the other.

"Hello, loveliest," she says.

"Hi, Gran," I say, "the bathroom drain giving you troubles again?" The bathroom sink is an old porcelain antique whose tiny drain often backs up. Gran has had to employ Granddad Addison's tricks now in his absence. The plumbing in their aging house was his domain all the years before he died.

"Yes, dear," she says with a big exhalation, "but all is well again." She puts the plunger and Drano under the kitchen sink, and we join each other at the table. My car keys fall out of my pocket, and I retrieve them from the floor.

"Did you drive here by yourself?" Gran asks.

"No, ma'am, I drove with Dad. He dropped me. I have my own keys. Six more months until I can get my license."

"So exciting, Calsap! When you have your license and your freedom, you can go anywhere. If I were you, I would drive straight to the beach."

"No, you wouldn't," I say, knowing better.

"Yes, when I was your age, I had no access to a beach. When Addison and I got to Los Angeles as newlyweds, one of the first things we did was go to Long Beach. I couldn't believe how won-drous it was. A body of water so big and wide. I loved it so much that I took a job in housekeeping at a resort near the shore. It was my first job in my new life here. For a long time, after every shift, I would go to the beach and put my aching feet in the warm sand to sooth them," Gran says.

"Why do you never go to the beach now?"

"Unfortunately, it reminds me of that terrible job. I had a cruel boss who could not be pleased." Gran shrugs and laughs a sad laugh.

"Well, my favorite place is right here. And that will be true always and forever," I say.

"Ah, well, we'll see about that," Gran says, "the world is big and full of amazing places, Calsap."

"I wish I could have come sooner today to help you with the sink."

"I've told your grandmother that I can easily call Mr. Blackshear to come and fix that ancient sink once and for all," Nan chimes in through the screen door. She is laboring up the back stairs, struggling with the door and her walker. I run to help.

"That's a good idea," I say to Nan, "I bet it's been a minute since you've seen Mr. Blackshear."

Nan does not respond, but Gran says, "Well, it's handled for now."

"When did you get here, Bella baby?" Nan asks.

"Just now. I was hoping to catch teatime."

"Well, you have." Nan makes her way to the china cupboard.

"Let me," I say. I intercept her progress by stepping in front of her walker and pulling out a chair so that she can sit. Gran sits across the table from Nan and says, "There are cookies in the cabinet."

I open the cabinet and spot them. "In their usual place," I say as I grab the Tupperware containers that store the sweets. I open the top.

"Oh, I love Fig Newtons," I say and open the second container, "and what are these? Oatmeal cookies?"

"Yes," Gran says, "they are a new no-bake recipe I am trying. Full of goodness."

"They are delicious," Nan says, "not too sweet, nice and chewy."

"Do you want to have tea in the garden?" I ask, placing the healthier desserts on a plate.

"No, dear," Nan says, "I have just come in."

"You sound tired," I say. I know that her time in the garden is her workout for the day—fighting the grass with the walker, bending and pulling intruders, reaching and lifting the watering cans. These make for a pretty effective exercise regimen.

"Tired? No, not so much," Nan says, "I've got some afternoon plans with an old garden book I've rediscovered."

"Oh, which one?" I ask.

"Do you remember *Ten Thousand Garden Questions?*"

"Yes, yes!" I say, "That one is a real throwback."

"That old book?" Gran says. I can't tell if she really knows the book or if she is just faking it to be a part of this conversation. She has never been big on gardening books.

"You know it?" Nan asks her.

"Well, you showed it to me last night." Gran leaves her chair and turns to the stove where the water kettle siren saves her from her own sarcasm.

"Well," Nan says, not catching Gran's humor, "Bella, there is an entire section on herbs. All these years, we've all but ignored it."

Gran commits to her contrarian stance. "I thought you two favored picture books. That book barely has a decent picture in the entire volume, and it's over a thousand pages long!"

"Well, you can't answer ten thousand questions in less than a thousand pages, Olivette, not good answers anyway," Nan says.

"I suppose you are right about that, Miriam. You are surely right about that," Gran says, deciding to be agreeable.

I take the kettle from Gran and fill the three teapots I've placed on the tray. They are tiny one-serving pots that allow us to properly steep according to our own individual tea preferences. I move a large ceramic bowl of walnuts that takes up the center of the table.

"Who's the big walnut eater?" I ask.

"We are," Gran says with a rare overzealousness.

"We are trying to be," Nan says with much less gusto.

"Walnuts are so good for us," Gran says, "so we are working on our walnut habit."

"I like walnuts," I say. "They are tasty, and they look like little brains."

"Exactly," Gran says. She takes a walnut and the nutcracker from the bowl and cracks it open. "Left hemisphere, right hemisphere," she says, digging out the meat and popping both sides of the nut into her mouth.

"There," she says, "my mood is better already."

Nan and I follow suit. We crack open one walnut each and pop the meaty halves in our mouths. We wait for our tea to steep.

"So, Nan, have you visited your garden lately?" I ask. "I miss it. I thought maybe, since I have my permit, I could drive us over and check on it one day soon."

"Honestly, dear, I have not been home in some weeks," Nan says. She seems to mull over my proposition. "We tried, didn't we, to make it a happy place. But beautiful is not the same as happy, is it? I am happier in this garden. The best part of that garden, baby Bella, was you, and I have you here, don't I?"

"But don't you miss your hydrangeas?" I ask. I feel the blood drain from my face. My stomach closes in around the walnuts and cookies I have just consumed.

"Funny you should ask that today, Bella," Gran says, noting my distress.

"Yes, we have cleared the tomatoes to grow hydrangeas here," Nan says.

Both of my grandmothers are smiling at me; they have worked out a compromise and seem to be waiting for me to join in their excitement. But I am overwhelmed by all this change. Nan's dismissal of her garden, where she and I had so much invested, and Gran succumbing to hydrangeas in her garden, the flowers she loves to hate. It's all too much for me. My chest tightens like its corset strings are being pulled, and my heart starts to beat fast. Now, I feel like my face is on fire. I have to work to catch my breath.

"Bella?" says one grandmother.

"Are you all right?" asks the other.

I nod my head yes and close my eyes. I take in several deep breaths.

"That's it, dear, b-r-e-a-t-h-e," Gran says.

There are several moments of silence while I do this. Nan breaks in.

"Have some of your tea," she says.

"I'm fine," I say. "I just. . . ."

"I know, sweetheart," Gran says, "change is hard. You've never been very good at it, have you, love?"

"But none of the important things have changed, Bella," Nan says. "We are here, we are drinking tea. And in a moment, we will return to one of our favorite books, right?"

"Yes, ma'am," I say. My breathing is back to normal, and my heart's drumbeat no longer sounds off in my ears. I smile at my two grandmothers and sip my tea. I let the aromatic steam from my cup fill my head and the sweet liquid calm me. I finish the cup and get a refill. "Maybe things are even better." This is my effort to turn my own sad tide. "Your leg is healing. You are happy," I say to Nan.

Gran moves around the table and hugs me from behind.

"And I am happy too," she says.

Gran encourages us to get to our reading of *10,000 Garden Questions*. I follow Nan into her crowded bedroom. When she moved in, Gran allowed Nan her favorite, familiar things, those parts of her life that made up some of her routines. And so, Nan chose a few of her prized furnishings—her chestnut vanity table and silver-painted chair, the sterling silver cross that hangs over her bed, and almost all her gardening books. Gran cleared out the bookshelf in the spare bedroom so that Nan could have a place for her collection. I helped Nan organize most of her books into stacks so that she could take her time and place them in the bookshelves. She decided to arrange her gardening books from top to bottom by age. This is how she came across *10,000 Garden Questions*.

Nan and I settle on her bed and she opens the book at her sticky-note marker. She points to the section where she left off and asks me to read. The book is organized as a question-and-answer exchange on a wide and unpredictable array of gardening topics.

"'What is a knot garden? A garden of low-growing plants or hedges planted in a formal, intricate design. They are now used in parks, herb gardens, and formal gardens.'" I pause. "You never really know in what direction the questions in this book will take, do you?"

"I do miss my garden sometimes, Bella." Nan hugs me closer. "I miss my roses and my blue hydrangeas."

"I miss the veranda the most," I say.

"I miss the veranda too," Nan agrees, "but there are things about that garden that I do not miss."

"I know," I say. "The nasturtiums that keep popping up even though we did everything to eradicate them."

"Yes, dear, the nasturtiums and the ghosts."

"Ghosts?" I repeat. I think she is kidding, and I want to properly respond to set up the punchline.

"Yes, there are any number of unhappy ghosts in that garden." There is no punchline. "I tried to appease them. I desperately wanted to make them happy ghosts." She pauses. "I really think the most important part of that garden was you," Nan's tone brightens as she hugs me closer still. "The ghosts were always happy with you."

"Do you think Gran's garden has ghosts?" I am testing her ability to detect spirits because I already know the garden has at least one.

"Yes, many, I suspect. But they are your Gran's ghosts and not mine."

"Grandpa Addison is in the garden," I say.

"Oh, good," she says, "I was afraid he was in the study, but now that I know he is not, I will spend a little more time in there, maybe add my books to that wonderful collection in those shelves."

"Well, if Grandpa is in there, that is where he is the happiest, I suspect. I am not so sure he would be a happy ghost in the garden."

"Well, he's not my ghost," Nan concludes with a giggle. She takes *10,000 Questions* from my lap and turns the pages. "Let's read." She leafs through until she reaches the herb section. It is organized alphabetically. She keeps turning until she gets to L, lavender.

"Lavender!" I say and put my hand on the page. "Let's read about lavender. I love lavender. When I grow up, I am going to live in a house surrounded by lavender fields."

"Then you'll have to live in Provence, France, where, I understand, lavender is grown this way—rows and rows for acres and acres," Nan says.

"Well, I suppose I will have to be rich, and then we can have a summer home in France," I say, and Nan nods her head in agreement.

"Yes, France is one of my bucket list favorite places to dream about," she says. "You know, I love the grand gardens in France. But I think Provence is the countryside. Every picture I've seen of the French countryside looks beautiful."

I take the book and read aloud about lavender—how to care for and propagate, how to harvest and use, where and when to plant from seed. When I finish with lavender, I pass through the L section until I reach M. I look for a discussion of mint.

"How weird is it that they spend two pages on lavender and one short paragraph on mints? Nobody has questions about such an important herb family?" I ask. Nan doesn't respond, except I hear her heavy breath, almost a snore. She is asleep. I close the book and leave it on the bed. I climb over her carefully and rejoin Gran in the kitchen. She has cleared away the tea service and is sweeping dust out the back door.

"The garden wears her out, doesn't it?" I ask.

"Yes, she is getting stronger, though. She has taken over the care of the Goddess. She seems to have a particular gift, a keen efficiency for ridding the garden of intruders. And she has learned about almost every single plant in the beds."

"Those walnuts must be really working their magic," I say. We both laugh.

"It takes more than walnuts, Calsap," Gran says. "What is marvelous is how your Nan has embraced a new way of being."

"She gets her hands dirty."

"Yes, indeed, she gets her hands dirty," Gran says, "well, her Glamour Gloves, anyway!"

"She really seems happy, Granny. Thank you for that."

"She is quite something, that Miriam," Gran says. "She has a powerful will. I love having her here." She looks over her reader glasses at me. "Quite surprisingly!" She laughs out loud, and I do too.

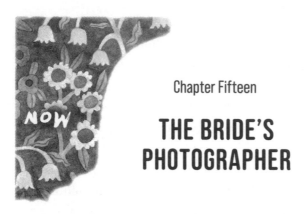

Chapter Fifteen

THE BRIDE'S PHOTOGRAPHER

SEPTEMBER

Geri pauses as she is loading up her backpack for the trip Uptown. "It's weird to only have to worry about the bride," she says to Bella, who is already packed and putting on her jacket.

"Honestly," Bella says, "it's always only about the bride. Any good wedding photographer knows that her job is always all about her. The bride is the center of the universe. You've got to make sure you photograph every wedding detail, but the bride's entire experience had better be your top priority."

She and Geri are on their way to the Thompson-Green wedding. Bella has been hired with a group of seven photographers. Of the group, Bella has been assigned to the bride. Bella has never had a gig like this—where she is a part of a team, all hired to photograph one event. She is the youngest, least established among them, yet she snagged the most important job! The photographers had to go through an involved interview process, first with the wedding planner, then the bride and the bride's mother. Bella would have been pleased to be chosen as an assistant to some of the other well-known professionals on the team. She is pretty pleased with herself for landing the job.

"Well, who gets to be the groom's photographer?" Geri is laughing. "I want that job."

"Right?" Bella agrees. "Damian Sanders is shooting the groom. He does freelance for GQ. He was, of course, the groom's choice. He's shooting the bachelor party too."

"I'm just happy we didn't get the in-laws," Geri says. They both laugh and so does their Uber driver. "So, what is our strategy?"

"We are going to take a gazillion pictures. Every angle. Every person the bride touches. We are going to do an eighty-twenty split. Eighty percent candid, twenty percent posed."

"Do you still want me to take down subject names?" Geri asks. This has become her primary job on gigs.

"Yes, only on the posed pictures, of course. It's going to be a huge crowd so, yeah," Bella says. "I've got a list of the wedding party, and the bride and groom know their people, so you don't need to worry about wedding party names."

"Got it," says Geri.

"I am going to give you my iPhone at certain times so that you can take some candid shots and maybe some video with it. You know the drill."

"I'm no pro, girl, but I'll do my best."

"Everybody is a pro with an iPhone," Bella says. "You did great with Martha. I just want you to go at it, okay?"

"O-kay," Geri says, unsure. In addition to the formal wedding pictures, Bella likes to use iPhone photos and video to give the bride and groom a taste of what it was like to be a guest. She uses a series of shots that focus on movement and mode—candid shots where the subjects are in motion, and they get progressively less active and slightly less focused toward the end. She added these pictures to the traditional package for one of her clients in Los Angeles and they loved it.

"Once we leave the bridal suite, it's going to be competitive with the other photographers. We have to stand our ground when it comes to the bride." Bella knows this because all the photographers had a conference call. Since they have never worked together, they won't have a set protocol. It's every man and woman for themselves. And this, at least in part, is what the bride intended when she hired a corps of photographers. She wants the feel of paparazzi throughout the event.

Bella and Geri are sailing up FDR in the back seat of a black Honda Civic. "You girls sound like you're ready," says the driver. "I never realized taking pictures required so much planning." The driver is a tall, thin man in his fifties. He favors Abraham Lincoln—long scraggly beard, huge ears, and pronounced cheekbones. He is sporting a newsboy cap that almost touches the ceiling of the car. He wears a dingy buttoned-down shirt that used to be white.

"Yes, sir," Bella says, "I have been preparing for a week. Weddings are a lot of pressure. Brides are notorious."

"And we get to spend all our time with Bridezilla today," Geri says.

"How do you know she's a bridezilla?" Bella asks.

"Seriously, Bella?" Geri looks at her, incredulous. "This is New York, momma."

"Oh, and a rich bridezilla," says their driver. "Seven different photographers? Wedding at the Pierre? The rich ones are the worst."

"We'll see," Bella says, "Geri, here, is going to use her charm and wit, and we are going to be so thorough that she'll have nothing to complain about."

"Until her next wedding!" Geri says.

"That's terrible!" Bella says. "No bad karma today."

"You're right. I take it back!"

The driver takes the 61st Street exit, and they descend into traffic. Bella is not worried; they should still arrive two hours earlier than expected. They will have enough time to survey the wedding venue, the reception ballroom, and hopefully, the hotel suite. Bella's adrenaline is already pumping. She is excited, determined to do her best. She wonders if this is how Drip McAffrey feels before a big game . . . if he gets nervous or just pumped up and eager like she is now. Drip McAffrey. He keeps popping up in her thoughts at the oddest moments. She attributes this to the time she has expended on the pictures from his photo shoot. She'd presented them to Dorian a few days earlier than promised because once she started working on them, knowing that Drip was eager to get them, she worked overtime, carefully choosing the best shots and adding some features—filters and special crops—to make them unique. Dorian had loved them. But she was surprised she hadn't yet heard any feedback from Drip himself. It's been weeks since she turned them over.

Bella turns her attention back to the wedding, another fortunate opportunity provided by the Herman Gallery. She got the interview because Stephanie put her name forward to Allysia Thompson-Green, the bride, a budding socialite and daughter of a media mogul. Her mother is a loyal patron of the gallery. Bella has met with Allysia twice so far—once for the interview and a second time for the walk-through.

They are creeping toward Central Park. Bella sees it up ahead. The Pierre Hotel is right across from the southeast tip of the park.

"You're late," Allysia says, when she answers Bella's knock on her bridal suite door.

"Actually, we've been here for over two hours," Bella says, careful not to return Allysia's attitude.

"Then where have you been?"

"Checking the venue, to be sure I get your every move."

"Well, you missed me getting out of the car at valet," Allysia says, though they never discussed any arrival pictures when they did the walk-through.

"I was there, right behind the doorman," Bella says.

"I thought that was you," says Allysia's fifteen-year-old sister, Margaret. "I called you paparazzi. I said the paparazzi is already here." She says to Allysia, "Remember I said that?"

"Then let me see the pictures," Allysia says. She wants proof.

Bella shows Allysia her camera screen. She scrolls through the shots she took of the Thompson-Green family and bridesmaids getting out of their cars. Geri steps up and shows her the shots she took on the iPhone.

"You are so awesome!" Allysia says, shifting moods with dizzying speed. She is smiling now as she plops down on the gold damask sofa.

The sofa is among a close grouping of furniture in her spacious suite. There are two rooms off this main one. Bells surveys the layout, notes that there is one room dedicated to the bride, the wedding dress hanging from the ensuite bathroom door, and all seven noisy bridesmaids are setting up in the second room. Their Tiffany blue bridesmaid dresses are draped on doors to the bathroom, closet, and TV armoire. Their flat irons and other hair appliances are parked side by side on the bathroom counter. Bella takes a picture of the wedding dress, with the one-foot train carefully draped over the carpet. Then she takes some shots of the bridesmaids bustling around their room. They dart around each other like tropical fish in a Tiffany blue ocean.

Once she feels like she has captured the most important pictures for this moment, Bella sets her camera down on the coffee table and stands before Allysia, who is still sitting on the sofa. A woman wearing a black smock with brushes and combs in the pockets is finalizing Allysia's hair. The bride is looking fretful, frowning and rubbing her hands together as if she is applying lotion.

"So, Allysia," Bella says and waits until she has Allysia's full attention. "Today is your special, once-in-a-lifetime day. Me and the other photographers are going to capture every moment. I am going to take awesome pictures of you. But even with your gorgeous dress and your perfect hair and makeup, your pictures are not going to come out beautifully if you are not happy."

"Tell me about it!" Allysia says.

Bella continues, "And happiness is a decision. No one is going to make you happy today but you."

"Darryl *better* make me happy today," Allysia says about her groom, and her seven bridesmaids all chime in in agreement.

"I am sure Darryl is going to do his part," Bella says, "but *you* have to decide that today is going to be magical, no matter what. And it will be."

Allysia stands up and grabs Bella's face between her French-manicured fingers.

"You are right, photographer girl," she says, "where'd you get that speech from anyway, Jennifer Lopez?" Her bridesmaids love her *Wedding Planner* movie reference, and they all laugh. Even their laughs have an accent that Bella, relatively new to New York, is unfamiliar with—loud, harsh, mean around the edges. Already they sound like a gaggle of cackling geese to Bella, and the day is young.

Bella smiles a broad smile, nods to show her good nature.

"Yes, well, my name is Bella," she says.

"Bella, you are the most beautiful Black girl I have ever seen," Allysia says, "isn't she, Sandy?"

Sandy is in the bridesmaid room getting her dress and accessories together.

"Sandy!" Allysia screams.

"What!" Sandy yells back.

"Isn't Bella the most beautiful Black girl you've ever seen."

"Who's Bella?" Sandy has come forth out of the room, and even at close range, she is still yelling, "Who is Bella?"

"Photographer girl," Allysia answers, pointing.

"Oh, yeah. You're gorgeous, Bella. Pretty name too."

"That's why I hired you, you know . . . Bella," says Allysia. "Everything about this wedding has to be beautiful, even the photographers." More cackling.

"Well, thank you, Allysia, for the compliment, and the job. I am going to disappear now. You-all do what you do." Bella and Geri commandeer a corner of the room opposite the sofa. Geri sets the camera backpack down. Bella pulls up two chairs.

"Told you," Geri says as she sits.

"Yep, you called the bridezilla thing," Bella whispers.

The mayhem of the bridal suite ensues. Even though the videographer and his crew are capturing the scene, Bella tells Geri to take some video. They cover the room among the chatter and the swishing sound of satin and crinoline.

When Allysia begins to whine or complain, which is practically every five minutes, Mrs. Thompson-Green, Allysia's mother, repeats Bella's admonition, "A happy bride is a beautiful bride!" A short, stocky woman with brassy hair, she winks at Bella every time, thankful for the check Bella put on her daughter, however ineffective.

"Who taught you how to be a bridezilla whisperer?" Geri asks when she and Bella come back together in their corner of the room.

"Jennifer Lopez," Bella whispers back.

For all the preparation and production, weddings are remarkably brief. Allysia's photography team ends up fighting for positions at every turn. Not surprisingly, they choose the same locations and angles to shoot. So, Bella decides that she will not jockey for a place. She is the bride's photographer, she reminds herself. She does not have the size or the experience to pull rank, but she can easily squeeze between the others and get out in front. She can wedge herself in key places and hide so that she does not interfere with the ceremony.

By the time they make it to the reception, Bella is loving this assignment. The thrill of competition surprises her. She tells Geri to stop taking video of the bride and take photos of her in some of her locations. Bella wants proof of her clever creativity to use later for her promotional materials. She is everywhere the bride is. She is behind the wedding party dais and on the second-floor balcony. She is nearly under the tables and following behind waiters. This is her new trick—following behind the waitstaff. People tend to give waiters the right-of-way, so she finds that if she walks closely behind them, she can move through a crowded room swiftly and invisibly.

As Allysia and her father step onto the dance floor for their dance, Bella finds a spot at the foot of one of the tables on the left side where the wooden dance floor meets the carpet. It's a table of young people who appear to be work colleagues of the groom, mostly men in suits. They look like second-string groomsmen, like the leftover crew who didn't get picked. Bella crouches down right in front of the table to take an upshot of the father–daughter dance. This is where she will start and then move to a center position in front of the dance floor. She is so preoccupied with the shot that she doesn't see one of the guests as he pushes his chair back from the table to stand up. Bella stoops down right as he pushes his chair into her. He knocks her forward and onto the dance floor. She lands on her elbows, right in the path of bride and father. They are doing some kind of sweeping waltz-like move and have to stop and redirect to avoid tripping over her. She rolls over on her back and takes a quick snapshot of the dancing couple. The bride gives her a wide-eyed, annoyed look as Bella scrambles up. The second-string grooms-man who knocked her over is standing over her with his hand extended.

"I am so sorry," he says.

"No worries," Bella says as she takes his hand, and he helps her to her feet. He is so handsome that Bella just stares. She thinks, *You look like Trevor Noah dipped in dark chocolate.* He is tall and slender. And his navy-blue suit fits him with a precision that a cheap suit never could. She suppresses the urge to snap his picture. She is so in picture-taking mode and his beauty so deserves to be captured.

"You played that off nicely, though," he says, "taking a picture from the floor. That was smooth." They both laugh and Bella notices his dimples.

"Always ready for the right shot," she says.

"I guess so; you have a lot of other photographers to compete with."

Bella initially thinks he is talking about the wedding photography team, but she follows his gaze and sees for the first time all the flashes going off from everyone's mobile phones. It looks like nearly every single person sitting at the tables surrounding the dance floor is taking pictures of the bride and her father.

"Geez, yeah," she says, "I better get back to it." She suddenly feels renewed pressure to deliver professionally.

"I'm Brad," he says, holding out his hand again.

"You are not!" she says, shaking his hand as they move off

the dance floor. She is thinking, *Black people don't name their sons Brad.* Brad knows what she is thinking.

"Yes, I am." Dimples again. "Short for Bradford. You can call me Bradford if your ethnic purity won't allow for Brad."

"I'm Bella." They both laugh again. "Short for Bella."

"There you go," Brad says, flashing those dimples. "Not short for Belinda? Bellisa? Basheba?"

"No, just Bella," she says, then conceding that her name is not exactly common among Black women, she adds, "I guess I can call you Brad."

Bella looks up to see Geri run across the dance floor. This is against her professional code. Geri knows she is supposed to make herself invisible. Bella gives her a look, shaking her head. Since she, herself, has just splattered herself across the dance floor at the feet of the bride and her father, she doesn't need Geri coming out of the background like this too. Geri makes her way to Brad and Bella. They've moved to the side of the dance floor, right in front of his table.

"Heads up, Bella," Geri says, "bride and father dance routine, choreography coming. Should I record it?"

"Oh, shit! Yes, please!" Bella says to Geri. "Nice meeting you, Brad," she says over her shoulder as she moves to the foot of another table in the center of the room where the bride and father are facing. The other photographers have already gathered in this spot.

"How fine is he?" Geri says, crouching down next to Bella.

"Right? Almost too much," Bella says as she points her camera in his direction, suddenly regretting not taking that picture earlier when she had the chance at a close-up.

"He has the most amazing dimples," Bella says to Geri from behind her camera. She zooms in and gets him in her frame. He is still standing in the same spot, and he is watching her take a picture of him. He smiles and then turns his head sideways in a dramatic profile pose. Bella takes the shots—holding the button down for a whole crop of pictures she will spend time with later at home. Then she takes the camera down from her face and smiles. He waves and returns to his seat.

Bella shifts her attention back to her job. She takes some shots of the bride and her father standing in position—feet apart, hands down to their sides, heads down. They are waiting for the music to cue, which, fortunately for Bella, is delayed due to some technical glitch. The bride holds her smile, but Bella knows Allysia will probably have someone's head for this later. Bella moves more to the right to get better centered, sits fully on the floor, and positions her camera on her subjects. Once she is set, she turns back to look at Brad one last time. He has his mobile phone pointed in her direction to take a picture, so Bella smiles. She turns her head sideways and lifts her shoulder—a dignified profile pose. Then she tilts her chin down over her shoulder and looks in Brad's direction. This is her best attempt at a sexy pose.

"What are you doing?" Geri asks her.

"Flirting hard," Bella says. Geri turns to look in the direction of Bella's attention.

"You go, Bels, I can't blame you there."

"Why are weddings so dangerous?" Bella says.

The bride and groom drive off in their Bentley limousine and Bella, standing in the street with the seven other photographers, takes pictures of the back of the car driving down the crowded street, the bride and groom waving in the back window as Bella instructed them to do. She holds her position, as the others return to the sidewalk, and turns to the crowd from her spot in the street to get shots of Mrs. Thompson-Green. She catches the mother-of-the-bride's wistful look, just in time. She is wiping tears from both cheeks. Her eye makeup is ruined. Allysia's father and Mrs. Thompson-Green, long divorced, have been on opposite sides of every room all day. Up to this point, they have begrudgingly taken pictures together, standing as far apart as they could, as if they cannot stomach even touching shoulders. But now Allysia's father sees his ex-wife's tears, and he wraps his arm around her shoulders. They don't look at each other, but they lean into each other ever so slightly. Bella snaps every detail of this unprecedented moment.

"You going to the after party?" Brad asks as Bella steps up on the curb. She looks up and takes in his beautiful features anew.

"No, Bradford," Bella says, "I am not a guest. I am at work." She sounds more indignant than she intends, especially since she thinks Brad just might be trying to hook up. She is not completely unwilling.

"Oh, right," he says, "you still have pictures to take."

"Actually, I am the bride's photographer, and the bride is gone. I am officially, as of this minute, off the clock."

Geri walks up and, seeing the flirtation between Brad and Bella, she says, "Okay, Bella, I am going to go do one last sweep of the suite and make sure we haven't left anything behind." Bella knows this is Geri's cue to give her a minute alone with Brad because they did a sweep earlier before they followed the bride out of the room.

"Geri, this is Bradford. Bradford, Geri."

"You can call me Brad."

"Hey, Brad, nice to meet you. You on the bride's side or the groom's?"

"Groom. We work together," Brad says.

As Bella thought, second-string groomsman. She is wondering why in the world the groom would not choose this gorgeous man to be in his wedding party. But then it comes to her. Brad is too good-looking. The groom was not trying to be overshadowed by those dimples.

"So, no to the after party then?" Brad asks Bella.

"Oh, no, but thank you," she says, "I'm wearing my work clothes . . . and I actually do still have some work to do at home." Bella wants to hang out with Brad, but she doesn't want to go to a party where everyone is looking their wedding best. *Plus, you have a boyfriend, Bella!* she says to herself, ashamed that it is the last consideration.

"You look great, and the party is right inside at the hotel bar," Brad pauses, "but I get it." Another pause. "Can I, at least, get your number? Maybe we can get a drink or something another time."

"No," Bella says. "You are too beautiful to be a friend, and I have a boyfriend." She surprises herself with this outburst of honesty, but she is glad for it. With this declaration, she has forestalled any further temptation to hook up with this perfect man. She is undeniably attracted to him and can easily envision the night ending in the bedroom of some spacious bachelor loft somewhere in this sleepless city. Brad steps back and bends over laughing. He thinks this is hilarious.

"You are something else," he says, straightening up some but still hunched over with his hands on his hips. He is shaking his head, giving off an unmistakable old-man vibe, reminding Bella of her grandfather. This old-soul-ness makes him even more attractive, which doesn't seem possible.

"Okay, I gotchu, Bella," he says. "I get it." He reaches into the breast pocket of his pristine suit jacket and pulls out a business card. "Just in case something changes, 'cuz I got a feeling about you, and I am rarely wrong." The old-man vibe hits Bella again like a strong waft of Old Spice cologne. She doesn't say another word because she is afraid she will say how she honestly feels, that she's got a feeling about him too.

Geri appears. "You ready?" Bella nods, turns on her heels, and walks away. Brad is watching her leave. She holds his card up over her head as if to acknowledge the gods who have brought them together. She doesn't look back and doesn't even look at the card. She puts it in her pocket.

"Momma!" Geri says. "Is that his number?"

"Yep."

"What you gon' do with it, because. . . ." Geri trails off as if to imply that she knows what to do with Brad's phone number if Bella doesn't.

Bella shakes her head. "I told him I have a boyfriend."

"Oh," Geri says.

"Why are weddings so dangerous?" Bella asks again.

"Let's go get our drink. Then you can pay me, and we can talk about *Bradford*," Geri says, using her best aristocratic impression.

Bella traverses the stairs to her apartment much more slowly than usual. The Thompson-Green wedding took more out of her than she is accustomed to. Usually, a successful gig revs her up, fills her with a kind of elation borne of completion and success. She felt that way at the bar with Geri, as they recounted the clever and wily ways Bella maneuvered through and around the other photographers to get the shots. She'd felt energized as they did their recap and laughed at how she ended up splayed out in the middle of the father–daughter dance. But now that the adrenaline has worn off and the two beers she'd guzzled at the bar have had their effect, her legs feel like redwood stumps, stiff and heavy. And her arms are sore and creaky at the elbows. She is reminded that she's had to hold her camera up to her face for hours, and this has taken its toll.

As she ascends from the fifth-floor landing, using the handrail to pull herself from one flight of stairs to the next, she encounters Camille and Charlie. They are on their way down.

"Hey, Bella. What's up?" Camille says with her usual muted affability.

"We left some Chinese in the fridge. You're welcome to it," Charlie says.

"Just don't finish it off though, okay? We are going to be back tonight," Camille says.

"My apartment is getting fumigated," Charlie provides the explanation for their return.

"Ah, I see. Thanks so much for the Chinese food offer. But I've eaten," Bella says.

"You out on a gig?" Charlie asks.

"Yes, a big wedding."

"Oh, nice," he says.

"Yeah, it was cool. But I'm wiped."

"We'll probably return around ten. We'll try to be quiet when we get back," says Charlie.

"No, worries," Bella says, "be safe."

It feels to Bella like Charlie is asking permission to return, as if the apartment belongs only to her, and Camille and Charlie are guests. Camille is so seldom home, and though Bella tried, at first, to minimize her footprint and keep her personal items within the confines of her bedroom, her life has begun to spill over. The apartment is small, and she loves the soft light in the living room, so in spending more time there, she has made it her own, adding furniture to the shared space and prints of her work on the wall. She believes she has improved it considerably.

Bella presses herself against the stairway wall to let Camille and Charlie pass. She watches them descend the stairs, Camille in front and Charlie behind. She has never seen Camille without

Charlie and wonders what that would be like, loving a man so much you don't want to be apart. She has never felt this way about anyone besides her grandmothers. Even in these early days of their relationship, she doesn't feel this way about Dorian, even though she likes him a lot and enjoys their time together. She and Dorian need each other in a way that feels like affection, but she cannot separate her affection for him from their business endeavors. And she does not fully trust him. Dorian is not her Charlie. She knows she is not Dorian's Camille. She can admit these truths to herself, and she is okay with both realities. And with this admission, Bella decides she will change her clothes, refresh her look, and go to that after party in search of Bradford. There is no harm in seeing if her Charlie is out there and if, by chance, Bradford is him.

Bella slips out of her flats and peels off her uniform black. She is in a hurry. By her watch, the Thompson-Green after party has been going on for a couple hours now. *How long*, she wonders, *do these things last once the bride and groom are long gone?* She rifles through her wardrobe hanging in the sliver of space that is her closet. She only has two choices of party attire—a white spaghetti-strap mini summer dress and a black-and-red floral silk blouse with matching black asymmetrical skirt. All three items she's had since high school. The blouse and skirt were among a few garments her mother left behind that Bella wore for dressy occasions. She didn't ask her father if she could take them. At that time, it was clear that her mother was not coming back, and since it pained her father to answer questions pertaining to her mother, she spared them both the awkward conversation and instead, took the liberty to make use of whatever she liked in her mother's closet.

Bella puts on the blouse and black skirt. In place of her flats, she chooses a pair of strappy high-heeled sandals. She washes her face and applies fresh makeup—heavier on the eyeliner and glossy wine lipstick. She wets her hair, sweeps it up into a high bun. She lets some curls stay loose and fall at the nape of her neck. She puts on a pair of silver candelabra earrings on her way out the door.

She arrives at the Pierre Hotel bar, where she finds a party in full swing. She is not sure that this is the right after party until she sees all of Allysia's bridesmaids and ushers still in their wedding attire. The bridesmaids have unpinned their updos and released their swirling ponytails so that their hair, fully liberated, is slinging and swinging while they dance. And they have taken their shoes off. Every single usher has abandoned his tie, unbuttoned the collar, some all the way down to the navel, and untucked their shirts. She looks around the room, and half the chairs have suit jackets draped on their backs. The dance floor is crowded, and a live band is playing nineties music. The crowd responds with a cheer when the three male singers start their rendition of Back Street Boys' "I Want It That Way."

Bella does not spot Bradford. In fact, there are no other Black people as far as Bella can see. She looks along the bar and scours the crowded dance floor. She moves around the periphery of the dancers to get a new angle, and that's when she sees him dancing with one of the bridesmaids, Sandy. Even though the song is sped up to a fast tempo, Bradford and Sandy are dancing very close together, as if they cannot part after the song changed from a slow number to this up-tempo. Bella moves in closer. Bradford may already be together with Sandy for the night. Since her only reason for traveling all the way Uptown is to see Bradford, Bella is decisive in this moment. She wants to sort out as soon as possible if he is no longer available. If he has committed to Sandy for the evening, she needs to know right now. She orders herself a beer from the bar so that she does not appear to have come straight in from the street.

"You just getting here?" the bartender asks, sliding Bella a glass of beer from the tap.

She nods.

"You sure I can't get you something stronger? You have some catching up to do."

"I'm going to go with a few beers, thanks," she says, before taking a big swig. Then another. She finishes her glass with the third gulp and asks for another. Bella has her eyes trained on Bradford as she downs the second drink. When the bartender delivers her third drink, he follows her gaze.

"There you go, tiger," the bartender says. Bella does not look his way.

She takes her drink onto the dance floor and approaches Bradford and Sandy. They do a spin together so that when Bella reaches them, Bradford's back is to her. But Sandy sees her right away.

"Hey, photographer girl!" Sandy says.

"Hey," Bella says, matching Sandy's enthusiasm, "It's Bella."

Bradford turns himself and his dance partner around so that he is facing her now.

"Bella!" His voice rings out over the music. "You came!"

"Yes!" Bella holds up her drink and leans her head and torso to the left and then the right, a swaying movement that relays a drunkenness that she has not yet achieved. "I am off duty and ready to rock and roll." She takes a drink of her beer.

"How long have you been here?" Bradford asks.

"Not long . . . you guys look like you are having a blast," Bella says. She turns to Sandy, "I thought maybe I could cut in. The Back Street Boys are my favorite."

"Hey, no, get your own dance partner. Plenty to choose from," Sandy says.

"Yes, but Brad, here, is the only person I know."

179

"Did Raymond send you over here?" Sandy asks.

"Raymond is her boyfriend . . . ex-boyfriend, we're making him jealous." Bradford signals with his head where Raymond is standing at the opposite end of the dance floor. His usher tuxedo is disheveled—his shirt wrinkled, his tie loose and hanging around his neck like a halfhearted noose. He is holding a bottle of beer down at his side. His cheeks are flush, and his red-rimmed eyes have the same unfocused glaze as everyone else's, but he is staring at the three of them, Bradford, Sandy, and now, Bella.

"Oh, *oh*, I see, I see! I suppose I should go ask poor Raymond to dance, then," Bella says, taking a drink and openly looking at Raymond over her glass.

"Don't you dare! Let him stew in his misery," Sandy says.

Bella turns back to Sandy and Bradford and takes a step closer to them. She puts her hand on Bradford's chest but looks at Sandy.

"Shame on you, using this beautiful person to make someone else miserable. Go sort out your man over there and let Bradford live his life!" Bella says. She takes Sandy by the arm and brings her in close to whisper in her ear, "Raymond is clearly suffering. Go handle your business."

Bella turns Sandy toward Raymond and releases her with a gentle push. Sandy looks back at Bella, then Bradford, and then at Raymond. She decides to obey Bella's order. Without a response, Sandy takes hesitant steps toward Raymond.

"You are something else, Bella Fontaine." Bradford laughs and takes her hand at the wrist, brings her closer to dance.

The lead singer in the band steps forward and launches into a Boyz II Men slow ballad, "I'll Make Love to You."

"When you are the least drunk person in the room, you have some advantages," Bella says. "I'm sorry. That was super presumptuous of me, Bradford. You really did look like you were having fun."

Bradford laughs again. This time it's short and sarcastic. He brings Bella closer in. He takes her drink and sits it on the nearest table, then wraps his arm around her waist and brings her hand up to his chest. He holds it there as they move in sync.

"I take my life of service seriously. Hippocratic oath and all. When I see human suffering, I answer the call. I guess Raymond's sin was that he paid Sandy's friend too much attention."

Bella puts her head on Bradford's chest right below his left shoulder. This shifts Bradford's energy. He bends his head down to her ear and says, "Something tells me Back Street Boys are not your favorite."

"No, you're right. That wasn't true. I just wanted . . . you know. But I *do* love me some Boyz II Men."

Bella and Bradford dance and dance until his coat jacket ends up on the back of a chair, and Bella has sweat through her mother's blouse. When the band begins to play a sped-up remix of "Macarena," they agree that this would be a good time to leave.

"You hungry?" he asks in a shout over the music.

"Actually, I am starving."

"I've got a good spot," Bradford says, "one of my patients owns a diner not far from here. Open twenty-four hours and they serve the best chili fries. Do you like chili fries?"

"I haven't had chili fries in years."

"These are not just any chili fries. You are going to love them."

And she does. In the almost-empty diner, over spicy, meaty chili fries, Bradford tells her his life story. He was an only child in a household of distracted parents. His father was a truck driver and seldom home. His mother was a nurse practitioner at a women's center in the Bronx that housed domestic violence victims and was always on the brink of closing. It was his mother's life work keeping the doors to the center open and helping women heal. His grandparents lived in the same building as his family, and this is where he spent all his time. His grandfather, a retired metro mechanic who was injured in an accident in one of the subway tunnels, was home on disability for many years. Bradford's grandmother ran a laundry business, cleaning and mending other people's clothes almost around the clock in their apartment. He and his grandfather were left to themselves. His grandfather was determined to lift Bradford out of their modest situation and into a real career. He wanted a prosperity for his grandson that had eluded him.

"So how did he go about raising a doctor?" Bella asks. She is doing all the asking, wanting to keep the conversation on Bradford's life, not her own.

"Books. We read nonstop. He believed that the answer to just about everything was in a book. It's all we did when we weren't fixing things."

"What did you read about?"

"Everything! But mostly we read a lot of how-to books. My grandfather liked learning about how things worked and how to fix them."

"Did he teach you how to fix stuff?"

"Yes, we fixed everything in my grandparents' apartment and my family's. Everything—every appliance, every light fixture. Anything mechanical. So, it was my plan to be a mechanical engineer. This was my grandfather's dream too."

"So, if something goes wrong in my apartment, like my microwave oven, could you fix it?"

"Microwave oven? That's a random choice, but yes, I could probably fix it. Depends, of course, on what is wrong. The most common problem with microwave ovens is the door interlocking system, right? Those wear out from people slamming the door.

If it does not close properly, it won't cook. Usually, a thermal or ceramic fuse is the issue. Yeah, I can fix that."

"Okay, I'm impressed!" Bella says, finishing off the last of the chili fries they are sharing. Bradford was right about the delicious dish. The fries are fat and fried crisp on the outside, soft on the inside. The chili is spicy with a fruity, tangy undertone—the perfect combination of sweet and savory. Bradford orders another round of fries and cokes.

"Well, because my grandfather could fix just about anything, my family was in the habit of buying cheap, used appliances or taking stuff that other people discarded. They would bring it home, and my grandfather and I would make it work and keep it working. It's what you do when you're too strapped to buy new stuff."

"When did you switch from fixing old stuff to fixing old people?" Bella asks as this connection dawns in her mind.

"When I lost my grandfather to a disease that nobody could fix. When he got sick, I started reading everything I could about memory loss. He was not interested in getting help. The medical system had failed him when he got injured, had rendered him immobile for life. So, he was done with doctors."

Bradford talks about the progression of his grandfather's dementia and how his disability, a broken leg that was never reset correctly, caused him to be stationary and a victim of type 2 diabetes, as well. He mentions how alone he was once his grandfather was gone . . . only fourteen, all the adults in his life too busy making ends meet and saving other lives to see the lonely boy who had lost his anchor to the world.

"So, what did you do?" Bella asks.

"Nothing, for a long time. Eventually, I wanted to honor my grandfather. And I heard him talking to me nonstop. There were just no other voices but his telling me anything. I know that sounds crazy."

"No, it doesn't." Bella knows all about voices.

"Well, early on, we, my grandfather and I, decided college was my way out. He'd always said that, but once he was gone, it took me a minute to remember. Once I did, I was on a mission to get the hell out of Dodge."

By the end of three orders of chili fries and five cokes between them, Bella feels like she knows Bradford. His story has a profound familiarity. She realizes that this is because much of his experience was like Bernard's, who had this same intense bond with their granddad, this same kind of isolated, on-an-island-by-themselves feel. Bradford's openness and comfort with his past, his genuine and kind smile—this alchemy pierces Bella's own reticence and makes her want more of him.

"You want to go back to my place?" Bella offers. She had straightened up her apartment before she left in anticipation of just this possibility.

Bradford looks up from the chili fries in surprise, then slowly shakes his head. "No, you have a boyfriend, right? I am not trying to get shot." Bradford laughs self-consciously.

"Really? Because I seem to remember you trying to get shot by Raymond at the wedding party!" Bella says. Bradford shakes his head.

"Yes, well, I was drunk then, and I know Raymond. He's harmless. Anyway, I'm not drunk now." His mood shifts as he wipes the chili from his hands with a soiled napkin. "Whenever I tell a woman my sad childhood story and they offer to take me home, it feels like pity. Like I am that hungry stray dog that needs saving."

"Well, I know you're not hungry. But you are so misguided. Your story—how you've gotten here—is extremely hot, not in any way pitiful. We women fall for that kind of thing." Bella eats another fry to fill in Bradford's silence. "I had a complicated upbringing too," she confesses, "and I cannot even talk about it with the clarity and openness that you can. I just think you are . . . you are something else, Dr. Bradford Ferguson." Their eyes meet. Bradford laughs first, recognizing that Bella has batted his own phrase back at him. He looks back down at the plate they are sharing.

"You know only old people say that, right? But yes, I am in a new relationship that I need to sort out. It's not going well."

"I'm sorry to hear that . . . I guess. Am I sorry to hear that?"

"I appreciate you, Dr. Ferguson. Everything—the chili fries, your awesome story, even your rejection. Let's do this again!"

"Absolutely," Bradford says, his dimples announcing that this is something he wants very much.

Chapter Sixteen

MR. BLACKSHEAR
AND AN
ABSENT MOTHER

The day after my sixteenth birthday, I am sitting in my family's driveway in my birthday present. I have finally received Nan's spare car, an old candy-apple-red Volkswagen convertible Beetle. I have always loved this car, and I claimed it as the car that should be mine when Bernard and I discussed whose extra cars we ought to receive once we secured our driver's licenses. This exercise of claiming our grandparents' cars was, at the time of our early adolescence, purely fanciful between us, as no one had promised us anything. But Bernard believed he should receive Granddad Addison's yellow 1970 Classic Corvette Stingray LT-1, which Granddad barely drove. When Bernard experienced how the roar of that V-8 engine made the walls of Granddad's garage vibrate and rattle, he felt that the rarity of those moments was a form of abuse, as if the car were a caged animal deserving its freedom. Bernard reasoned that he would do better by it. But by the time Bernard became its caretaker, on *his* sixteenth birthday, Granddad was long gone, and this beast was on the endangered list. Suddenly Bernard, too, became more a protector than a liberator, driving it sparingly and lavishing obsessive attention on it.

I believed that I should get Nan's dormant 1985 Volkswagen Convertible Beetle for much the same reason. This car deserved to be seen and experienced daily. It was already a mystery why a devotee of large luxury Cadillac models would even want a Volkswagen Beetle. How is it that my Nan, who liked to show up to her destinations with every hair in place, would choose a convertible? Bernard reasoned that our grandparents must have been planning to gift them to us all along. In our minds, this was the only scenario that made sense. We never expressed our theories or desires to our parents or grandparents directly. But a few well-placed questions and statements of adoration for the two mostly abandoned vehicles somehow communicated our wishes, so that Bernard received the Corvette the year before I got my convertible.

And here I am, sitting in my treasure, feeling like the luckiest sixteen-year-old on the planet. It must be this feeling of fulfilled fate and wholeness that brings out in me a certain invincibility. And it must be this invincibility that makes me decide that, as the first solo trip in my new-old car, I will drive to Nan's and visit my mother. When she returned to Nan's after her release from Summer House, she asked us to allow her time to transition. And so, at my father's direction, we were to give her the space she requested. I hold out hope that she will call for me on this auspicious birthday. This hope is not based on anything in our past as mother and daughter.

My mother has suffered from depression and crushing anxiety most of her life. My Gran hasn't named it. Nan hasn't named it. Neither has my father, even when my mother walked out of our lives three years ago in search of help. I have had to come upon the understanding on my own.

How Eddi Fontaine became a phantom who could be in the room but not *in* the room, is also a mystery. As far as I can piece together, she has had some years that were much better than others. Her college years must have been exceptional. She met my father when they were undergrads, and she was able to get a master's degree in urban studies. I have seen pictures of her smiling at professional cameras, Instamatics, and Polaroids, looking happy and productive with friends and colleagues at football games and parties. My parents' early marriage must have been mostly good. They both held down early-career jobs, my father realizing his gift in sales as a construction equipment salesman and my mother as a field worker for the Los Angeles County Public Administration Office. They did what young married couples did easily then—work, save for a home, have children. The pictures in our photo albums show that Bernard and I were born into a happy, striving family.

But for years, we have not had a fully participatory mother like everybody else. When I look at her old pictures, I wonder where that carefree girl went. What happened to turn her into my mother? When I was younger, I would approach her in the kitchen in the morning, never knowing if she would be fully there. If she, standing over a skillet of bacon, greeted me with, "Good morning to you," in her happy singsong voice, it was a good day. If she was silent, her face blank, with no acknowledgment of my being there at all, then not a good day.

Sunday mornings were the only reliable time I knew I'd find a happier version of my mother. We'd have Sunday Hair Day, and she was a miracle. She would get the temperature of the kitchen faucet just the right kind of warm, and she would have a pile of towels ready to wrap me up in. As she combed out my hair, I would sometimes read to her from our favorite book series, *Encyclopedia Brown,* and we would try to figure out the mystery before the young detective. Sometimes, we would just sing Michael Jackson songs acapella, laughing at some of the lyrics we would invent to fill in where we couldn't understand what Michael was singing. On Sundays, my mother was like Glinda the Good Witch. And even though Glinda almost always disappeared on Monday, Glinda was the vision I tried to hold onto for the rest of the week. Here is the thing: on Mondays, Mom did not turn into the Wicked Witch of the West. When Glinda's spirit exited my mother's body, no one came behind her to fill the void. At that point, it was like no one was home.

There is this cycle you get caught in with an absent mother. You know her mode of operation, her consistent inconsistency. You expect it as the norm—her distance and her neglect. In my young mind, her desire to mother ought to overcome her ailment. This is my judgment of her: she does not love me enough to overcome whatever it is that keeps her from wanting me, unfair as this may be. And yet, at the slightest sign of a change—of choice or priority, where she appears to choose me, I am willing to throw out all that I know about her and accept this hopeful change, no matter how many times she disappoints. I keep setting up these scenarios for her to step into and deliver on my hope, no matter how many times she fails.

This is what I am doing now as I head over in my new-old car with a plan to see her, to show her my achievement as a licensed driver. For the full drive over to Nan's, I am picturing myself at the front door. She opens it, and pure delight registers on her face as she sees that it's me. She welcomes me inside with an enthusiastic hug. I imagine Mom and me sitting on the veranda with tall glasses of lemonade, chatting about the weather and checking in on Nan's garden.

I pull into the driveway, and I don't see another car. Is Mom even able to drive anymore? I don't know. I know so little about her now. I get out of the car at the porte cochere just as Mr. Blackshear pulls up in his pickup truck. Mr. Blackshear must be in his seventies. He has lost all his hair, and the California sun has etched deep crevices around his mouth and across his forehead. His hands are like leather mitts—thick and heavy with callouses and a whole network of veins colliding across the landscape between his wrists and his knuckles. But his back is still ramrod straight and his shoulders square and strong. My grandpa Jeff's faithful friend, he is still caring for the garden in my grandparents' absence. I am comforted to see him. I know that, at least, the garden is okay.

"Is that Bella driving Ms. Miriam's old Bug?" he says.

"Yes, sir," I say, "my Nan gave it to me for my sixteenth birthday."

"Lucky you." He pats the roof of the car as he passes by, as if it is a good pet. I follow behind him.

"I am here to show my mother that I got my license."

"I imagine your mother is in there. I rarely see her. She doesn't visit out on the veranda like your grandmother did."

"No, she doesn't care for the garden, Mr. Blackshear. I have never seen her come out of the house past the veranda. Not ever." I follow Mr. Blackshear to the back gate.

"Well, there was a time when she helped her father out here. When I first saw this garden, it was very different. Your grandfather spent his free time here. Put in a lot of time. She was a simple garden back then. But she was pretty all the same."

I walk up to the locked gate and take in Nan's garden. I am so happy to be here. My yearning for this place overwhelms me, and my eyes fill with tears. I am embarrassed by this so when Mr. Blackshear holds the gate open for me, I run ahead, first up onto the deck and then down the steps through the center path.

He has maintained the garden perfectly. I am amazed at how beautiful and pristine it is, lush but orderly. Everything still in its place, just as Nan had intended. Something is set right inside of me. I feel the change not as a subtle shift but a monumental realignment of my bones and muscles. My head clears like when you are finally over a cold and the congestion dissipates.

"Oh, Mr. Blackshear." I hold my arms out and do a slow twirl, a full circle. "Can I help you today?" I ask, my tone already pleading.

"Miss Bella," Mr. Blackshear has come up behind me, "I don't think that is allowed. Miss Eddi has been very clear that she wants no one in this garden. I don't want to jeopardize my own license to be here."

"But where is she? I can ask her myself. She won't mind if I just stay long enough to help."

I go to the veranda and knock softly on the glass. Three raps. Then three more. I wait in silence. Mr. Blackshear climbs the steps, gently places his heavy hands on my shoulders, and leads me to the back gate. He says in a hushed voice, "I brought my grandson to help not too long ago, and she asked that I not." He says this to let me know that it's time to leave. Mom isn't coming to the door, whether she is here or not.

Just now I remember what my birthday excitement caused me to forget: Dad asked that Bernard and I not try to visit our mother. She had asked for space. I am not supposed to be here. I close my eyes against this realization, and the outline of who my mother actually is replaces the idealized version in my head. Mr. Blackshear is just trying to keep us both out of trouble.

I nod my head to let Mr. Blackshear know that I understand. I take a few steps forward to survey the hydrangeas, whose blossoms are so profuse that I can see Mr. Blackshear cannot keep up with the pruning.

"Will you see your grandmothers today?" he asks.

"Yes," I say, deciding just then that I will drive to see Gran and Nan, as a salve for my disappointment and to report on the wondrous state of Nan's garden.

"Then let's cut them some of Miss Miriam's favorite hydrangeas, okay?"

I nod again, run over to get the clippers on the planting table behind the garage.

"Things will get better, Miss Bella. I have a feeling. You be patient," Mr. Blackshear says when I return. I acknowledge this without words. I don't believe him, but I know he is offering all that he has. I help him choose the clippings for my grandmothers. Once I am back on the veranda, I turn to take in the garden one more time. It is a masterpiece. It is Nan's crowning achievement. And now the only person to enjoy it is Mr. Blackshear, who is caring for the garden so that it is as it should be for Nan's return. With this realization, I feel only loss and sorrow, because I know something he doesn't know. Nan has no intention of coming back to reclaim this garden for us. Those days are over forever.

Chapter Seventeen

ELLEN AND
THE GOOD DOCTOR

OCTOBER

Bella is waiting outside of the doctor's office to pick up Ellen. This is Ellen's first appointment with her new doctor, a geriatric neurologist who specializes in dementia and memory disorders. An old friend of Frank's who has known Ellen a long time and recognized her change in behavior suggested that she see a specialist. The soonest appointment is on the day Bella and Ellen have scheduled their first trip together to the community garden. Bella agrees to pick up Ellen and go directly from the doctor's office to the garden.

Bella planned her hired car ride so that Ellen would be at the curb, as arranged, by the time Bella reached the office. Since Ellen is not waiting, Bella is bargaining with the driver to stay when Ellen comes out on the arm of a tall Black man in a white physician's coat. Bella gets out of the car.

"Bella, I'd like you to meet my gorgeous new doctor," Ellen says, removing her arm from his and holding her hands out as if she is presenting a debutante. "Dr. Ferguson, meet my new artist friend, Bella Fontaine." Bella is so impressed that Ellen gets both her first and last name right that it takes her a minute to see who the doctor is.

"Bella?" Bradford Ferguson beats her to it.

"Brad?" Bella says.

There is a silence among the three of them as their brains race to reach the same point. Surprisingly, Ellen gets there first.

"Now, how is it you two know each other?"

"The wedding," Brad and Bella both say, almost in unison.

"What wedding?"

"The Thompson-Green wedding," Bella says. "I was one of the photographers. Dr. Ferguson, here, was. . . ."

"One of the guests," Brad finishes her sentence.

"Please tell me Celine and Henry *did not* get remarried!" Ellen says.

"No, ma'am," Bella says, "Allysia, their daughter."

"Ah, yes," Ellen says, "I knew that." Ellen turns to Bradford. "Celine Thompson is one of my very best customers. It only fits that she would hire one of the best photographers I know for her daughter's wedding. Only the best with that family." Ellen says as she turns back to Bella and reaches for her arm. "This young lady is a very talented artist. Did you know that?"

Brad looks at Bella and his entire face smiles. It is a smile that shifts from professional to intimate. It is a smile for Bella alone. Ellen turns to look at him, then Bella, and then back at Bradford again. She is assessing the situation between them. Bella is expecting Ellen to tell Bradford that Bella is her son's girlfriend, but she doesn't.

"Well, we'd better get a move on," Bella says. "I fear we are holding up our patient driver."

"I am going to the community garden," Ellen tells Dr. Ferguson. "Maybe I'll get my hands dirty."

"That is certainly our goal," Bella says, opening the door to the back seat of the waiting car. She helps Ellen in, and Ellen moves over to make room for her. While Ellen apologizes to the driver for making him wait, Bella looks up at Brad. He puts his hand up to his ear simulating a phone.

"Call me," he mouths in a silent, exaggerated gesture. Bella wonders if he irons his own doctor's coats. It is pristine as if he has just taken it out of brand-new packaging. His name is written over the pocket in red script. He continues to stand on the sidewalk with his hands in both pockets. His eyes hold onto Bella's. He tilts his head and smiles his perfect smile.

And there they are, Bella is thinking, *the dimples.* Where would Bradford be if those dimples didn't do the heavy lifting? Bella receives as a gift Bradford's open affection, his warm smile, and the time he is spending on the curb seeing them off. He likes her and wants to telegraph it. Ellen picks up the signal too.

They travel at the usual Manhattan snail's pace.

"He likes you," Ellen says, "as well he should. You two would make a lovely couple."

"Is that why you didn't tell him that I am Dorian's girlfriend?"

"Well," she pauses, "you clearly didn't either," Ellen says, looking over her tiny Benjamin Franklin reader glasses.

Bella tells Ellen that she met Bradford when he knocked her onto the dance floor in the middle of the father–daughter dance. Ellen finds this amusing. Bella refrains from letting Ellen know that she did, in fact, tell him she had a boyfriend, because in doing so, Bella would be confessing the flirtation between them.

"Well, I always say, these things happen for a reason," Ellen says.

"Is all of this your way of saying that Dr. Ferguson and I are a better match than Dorian and me?"

There is a long silence, so long that Bella is wondering if Ellen is pretending she didn't hear her question.

"You are an artist, dear. You need a stable professional with enormous earning potential. You need a doctor boyfriend. You two would make beautiful African American children together." Bella is rendered speechless. But Ellen is not finished. "Dorian, when it comes down to it, is an artist too," Ellen says.

"And he needs a nice, stable, high-earning Jewish doctor girlfriend?" Bella asks, adding some sauce to her sarcasm.

"No," Ellen responds quickly, "Dorian needs an accountant girlfriend with a strong personality and a lot of patience . . . and yes, Jewish would be nice."

"Well, people rarely choose what is best for them," Bella says as a concession, in hopes of moving past this conversation.

"And that is a shame," Ellen says. "You should go with the person who makes the birds, *and your loins*, sing. But most of us settle for either birds or loins, when we should hold out for both."

"And the person who has the right job and ethnic background gets you both?" Bella asks, still saucy. She can't help herself. Ellen chuckles a chuckle that feels condescending to Bella.

"No, dear," Ellen says, looking out of the opposite window facing away from Bella. "But I saw what was happening between you and the good doctor, and I just think we tend to hold onto good when we can have best. Do you know the word *smitten?* Dr. Bradford is smitten, and I don't know him well yet, but he seems like a kind and caring man. And he is gorgeous."

It feels to Bella that Ellen has somehow sensed her and Bradford's connection. Perhaps Ellen is reacting to what she witnessed between them—the body language and familiarity. Perhaps she wanted to claim as her idea something already underway. But then Bella wonders if Ellen has inside information about her relationship with Dorian that Bella does not. Maybe Dorian has told his mother about their last failed date at his apartment. Bella has not seen him since then, though they have communicated by text message. Still, Bella believes Ellen is being old-fashioned and ethnically elitist. She knows she should take this as a challenge . . . gather up her incredulity and recommit to her relationship with Dorian. But all she feels is ambivalence. Ellen's last statement about good and best might be right. There is something about Bradford that feels special. And with today's run-in, she got the feeling again that there was an inevitability about it. She, however, has no intention of conceding this truth to Ellen because, whatever Ellen's motivations, Bella believes Ellen has mixed it all up with her desire for a Jewish daughter-in-law. Bella decides not to fight for Dorian, as a boyfriend she may no longer have or want.

When they pull up to La Plaza Cultural Community Garden, Geri is unlocking the gate. "Whoa, your timing is perfect. Mrs. Herman, so happy to see you again, and welcome!" Geri is a senior member of La Plaza Cultural. Bella, as a newer member, has met most of her New York friends in this garden community. They supported her when she was setting up her roof garden, loaning her tools and donating their leftover materials. In return, she serves on the Plot Committee, mostly helping new owners get set up. This is how she and Geri became friends. Geri is the chairman of the Plot Committee. She has her own plot that is planted and blooming from early spring through the fall.

The community plots are small, five by four feet. Still, Geri's desire to keep hers beautiful and fruitful for the entire blooming season means that she replants frequently and tends constantly. She helps others with theirs too. She also serves on the Maintenance and Equipment Committees and helps with the Perimeter Committee that keeps the area on the outside of the fence clean and orderly—maintaining its curb appeal. Because she grew up in this garden and is one of the more active members of this community, Geri wields considerable power and influence. When a community plot became available recently, she offered to grab it for Ellen. It would officially be Geri's plot, of course, but she would allow Ellen to plan and maintain it. Today, they are going to clear it out and come up with a plan. Geri and Bella have already discussed some ideas in case Ellen needs some beginner's assistance.

They give Ellen a tour of the garden. Not wanting to wear her out, they take an efficient route by the communal plots of herbs and medicinal plants residing on a small incline and divided into six rectangular sections. Dense, well-established rosemary shrubs have taken over two of the sections. Leggy branches of basil and sage dominate the two sections in the middle. The last two are bare of plants, and it looks like someone has freshened the soil and prepared them for new planting.

The path bends around a tall pine tree. They lead Ellen to a bench overlooking the famous Prima Lingua fountain. The stone fountain is in the shape of a massive tongue, symbolizing the first language of earth and water. The water that spills over Prima Lingua flows into a pond that is bordered by jagged rocks and wild grasses.

Bella invites Ellen to sit on the bench and points out the family of red-eared slider turtles sunning together on a rock jutting out to the center of the pond.

"Ellen and Bella, this is Sima and Beth." Geri ushers two women over who look to be about Ellen's age. Sima is East Indian. Her hair looks like silver silk ribbon entwined in a long braid down her back. She is wearing a wide-brimmed straw hat, and her white T-shirt and loose brown linen shorts have dirt streaks on them. Clumps of damp soil stick to her knees. Beth is a white woman whose hair is cut in a short gray crop, and she is wearing all black—a long-sleeved T-shirt and ankle-length pants. Her nose is alarmingly pink even though her face is slathered with a thick white layer of sunscreen.

Ellen and Bella stand to greet Sima and Beth, who welcome Ellen with hugs and handshakes. They show her their adjoining plots where they are planting their autumn flowers and winter cabbage seeds.

"Sima and Beth are longtime members," Geri half whispers in Bella's ear. "We have a pretty sizable gay and lesbian contingent here at La Plaza. Sima and Beth celebrated their eighth wedding anniversary earlier this year in the garden amphitheater, but I am told they have been together way longer. The anniversary celebration was a huge party—beautiful."

"Ellen, we'd better get a move on," Bella shouts over to the three women, "we should finish our tour and get to your plot." Sima and Beth say their goodbyes, and Ellen rejoins Geri and Bella.

"Goodness, what did those lovely women ever do to you?" Ellen says to Bella.

"What do you mean?" Bella asks.

"Perhaps it was my imagination. But you did not appear to take to them very kindly," Ellen says.

"I don't know what you mean, they seem like very nice women." Bella hears the strain in her own voice. She looks over at Beth and Sima instead of facing Ellen. She is not ready to admit that she does not like them.

"Well, my mistake, dear. Sometimes I see what isn't there."

Geri leads Ellen through the old grove of willows. Bella trails behind. They circle through the amphitheater and then make their way to Geri's new plot. "Well, here we are," Geri says as they approach it.

"I'm ready to get dirty," Ellen says.

"You look a little dressed up to be getting dirty," Geri says to Ellen, who is wearing an ankle-length burgundy light-wool dress.

"No, no," Ellen says. She pats the large bag she has hanging from her shoulder.

"This is your little slice of heaven," Geri says, standing in front of a rectangle of dirt bordered by planks of wood. The plot is in the middle of a row of other plots that all look weedy and overgrown.

"Slice of heaven. Right," Ellen responds, much less enthusiastic than Geri.

Ellen walks over to a nearby bench and puts down her bag. She unbuttons her dress. Underneath she has on loose leggings and a long-sleeved T-shirt. She sits down on the bench and pulls her sneakers out of the bag, slips out of her sandals, and puts on the socks that were nestled inside the sneakers. When she places her sandals in the bag, she pulls out a flexible brimmed hat, shakes it out, and puts it on.

"Look at you," Geri says, "nice!"

Ellen returns to rummaging around in her bag, searching for something. She pulls out her phone and begins to press a phone number. She keeps pressing numbers, many more numbers than make up a phone number. She stops and tries again.

"Can I help, Ellen?" Bella offers.

"I think I have a doctor's appointment today," Ellen says, "but now I cannot remember my code to get into my phone."

"I don't know your code, but we have just come from Dr. Ferguson's," Bella says. "I just picked you up, remember?"

She is staring at the phone as if it has all the answers.

"You just picked me up from my new doctor's place? The gorgeous young Black doctor?"

"Yes, ma'am, Dr. Ferguson."

"Are you sure?"

"Yes, ma'am." Bella can tell that Ellen doesn't believe her. She is tempted to pull up the wedding picture of Bradford on her phone, but she knows this will create a whole set of questions she does not want to answer.

"I met Dr. Bradford Ferguson when he walked you out from your appointment and we got in the hired car." Bella shamelessly abbreviates history to exclude her and Bradford's connection. When Bella says Bradford Ferguson, she emphasizes the first name and looks over Ellen's head at Geri. Geri's eyes grow big, and Bella can't tell if her reaction is from comprehension or confusion.

"Okay, then," Ellen says, more resigned than convinced, "let's plant." She drops her phone in her bag.

"First, we weed and clear the plot," Geri says.

"And then we plan," Bella says, trying to shift to a lighter mood, the carefree optimism that Bella knows Ellen needs right now.

"The first thing you'll want to do, Ellen, is to moisten the soil so that weeding is a bit easier," Geri says. She hands Ellen the water hose and Bella a hand rake then walks over to a nearby shed and turns on the water.

Once the plot is moistened, they begin to hack and pull. It takes them a solid two hours to clear the plot of dead plant matter and weeds, and to mix in new soil with the existing dirt. The three of them are hot, sweaty, and euphoric. They sit on the bench letting the endorphins run their course, drink from their water bottles, and enjoy a moment with no words. The birds in the weeping willow seem to sing louder, and the trickle of the fountain sounds harmonically in sync with the buzz of a beehive two rows away. Bella takes a deep breath and enjoys the scent of dirt, greenery, and sweat. There is a faint smell of something sweet. She thinks it must be the honeysuckle that calls the bees to venture out of their hive.

"It has turned out to be a beautiful day," Geri says, breaking their silence.

"Yes," says Ellen, "what is your name again, dear?"

"Geri."

This is the fifth time Ellen has asked. Bella smiles at Geri to reward her patience.

"Thank you, Geri, for providing this plot," Ellen says. She pats Geri on the hand and then squeezes it.

"You are so welcome, Ellen, my total pleasure."

"So, Ellen, what are we planning for this garden?" Bella asks.

Ellen reaches behind them to her bag, lifts it to her lap, and dives in again. Bella is a little nervous that she is looking for her phone because she thinks she missed some appointment. After half a minute of rummaging, Ellen pulls out a folded piece of graph paper and unfolds it.

"Here is my plan for the plot. I sketched it out last night and I hope these plants will work. They are mostly flowers from my mother's garden in Westchester."

Geri and Bella look over Ellen's shoulder at the drawing.

"This is going to be beautiful," Bella says.

"You think?" Ellen says.

"I think," says Geri.

Dorian pulls up to the curb in front of La Plaza Cultural in his BMW sedan to retrieve his mother. Traffic is heavy and the street is crowded. He has to double-park. Bella opens the door quickly and helps Ellen into the front seat. Dorian remains in his seat behind the wheel.

"Hi, Dorian," Bella says, leaning into the window.

"Hey, thank you for picking up Mom from the doctor's office."

"My pleasure. It was on the way," Bella says to Dorian, and then to Ellen, "I will see you next week? Planting week!"

"Yes, I cannot wait," Ellen says. "Until then, my sweet Bella." She waves Bella near, and they exchange a cheek kiss. Dorian looks on with a smile that Bella cannot discern. He and his mother drive off, and Bella joins Geri for cleanup. There is not much left to do. Ellen insisted on doing her part to erase her footprint from the garden, a major tenet of the community commitment. Ellen gathered the remaining soil bags and replaced all the tools and buckets to their rightful places. Geri showed her where everything belonged and from whom they were borrowed. Now, Bella returns the water hose to the shed and closes the half empty bags of soil. She put them in Geri's storage spot in the shed.

Geri and Bella are the only ones remaining in the entire garden.

"Let's settle up, Geri," Bella says, "how much do I owe you?"

"Oh, thank you for reminding me," Geri pulls receipts out of her pocket, "my money is a little tight this week."

Bella pulls out her phone and sends her money through an app.

"You got plans tonight?" Geri asks.

"No, I'm turning in early. I'm doing a passport picture roundup for the senior center in the morning."

"What is a passport roundup?"

"I take passport pictures for all the seniors who are planning to take a group trip overseas in the spring," Bella says.

"Cool. I'll see you Saturday, then?"

"Yes. Thank you so much for setting this up, Geri, the Good Fairy."

"It's what I live for, Bella Donna."

"I'm going to hang out for another minute and lock up. You go on home." Bella needs a quiet moment in the garden to contemplate next steps with Ellen and how she feels about Dorian, so she strolls the plots. She finds her mind returning to Bradford. How does she get clarity on Dorian when Bradford keeps popping up? She makes her way to the place where Sima and Beth's plots are located. They rub her the wrong way, but it doesn't feel right to admit it. Though today was their first introduction, Bella had seen them in the garden before. They seem to be beloved by everyone. They have the confidence of seasoned master gardeners. In the few interactions that she witnessed, members came to them with questions, and they seemed to have all the answers. Is that it? Are they know-it-alls? Bella can't put a finger on the source of her annoyance with them.

She rounds the corner to their gardens to find the Goddess Kali reigning over Sima's plot. Every gardener knows the significance of Kali, the Hindu goddess of destruction. This plaster statue is unmistakably Kali. She stands fierce, weapons in all her ten hands except the one holding a severed head. Even in plaster, the Goddess's expression relays her rage—her eyes are wide, her teeth bared, and she is sticking out her tongue. Someone has painted her skin blue and her hair black. She wears a red-and-gold crown. The white garland around her neck is in the shape of small human skulls. The exaggerated tongue is a deep red. The paint looks new. Gardeners know that what the Goddess represents is important: There can be no life, no new beginnings, without death. Destruction is a part of renewal.

"Shit," Bella says out loud. Of course these women have a goddess in their garden. And of course, it's Kali, the raging destroyer. Bella is annoyed because now she is conflicted. Does this make Sima and Beth more endearing, or even more insufferable? Bella decides to give her confusion and uncertainty over to Kali. She sits down at the edge of Sima's plot, crosses her legs, and thinks about Kali. Then Ellen comes to mind, perhaps because in order to build this new life for herself, she must destroy the old one. Bella thinks about what they did in her new plot today. They had to destroy what was there in preparation for what they will create. With this thought, she jumps to her feet and begins to search the garden path for what she realizes she needs right now. She finds them easily.

As the sun hangs low in the sky and the garden is more shadow than light, Bella kneels before the Goddess to say a prayer for Ellen. It comes to her, and she carefully places the three stones she has just gathered—

One for death;

One for life;

And one for memory.

No, that is not right. She picks up the stones and tries again—

One for the past;

One for the present;

And one for the future.

No, wait, still not it . . . Again—

One for love;

One for hope;

And one for joy.

She picks up the stones again. But before another prayer comes, Bella hears the Goddess's voice.

Bella, Kali says, *I hear your words and I know your heart.*

"But how do you know my heart, when I don't?" she asks Kali, hoping this question is not disrespectful. She doesn't want to be on the wrong side of an angry goddess.

Bella, Kali answers, *you must forgive the destroyer.*

Bella doesn't know what she means. But then suddenly a prayer surfaces. She again lays her stones one by one:

One for death;
One for new life;
And one for forgiveness.

Yes, Kali says, *yes.*
"But I don't really understand," Bella says.
Oh, Bella, Kali says, *but you do.*

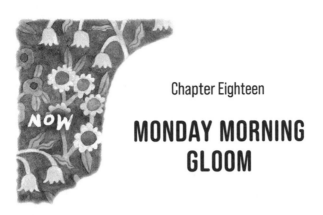

Chapter Eighteen

MONDAY MORNING GLOOM

OCTOBER

Sundays and Mondays are Bella's worst days in New York. On Sundays, she feels the kind of emptiness and grief you feel when your best thing becomes your worst. In her previous life, she loved Sundays. Sundays were family days. In her childhood, Sunday meant hair day with her mother and veranda days with her Nan. In her adolescence, Sundays were outdoor tea with both grandmothers that turned into casual open houses for their friends and neighbors. Now, Sunday is the day she grieves for all that she has lost.

Bella sometimes drinks too much on Sundays, finishing off a bottle of wine, or two, alone in her apartment, just to get through it. Camille is never home, so she doesn't have to hide from anyone her day drinking or self-pity. On Sunday, she knows she *should* clean her room and do her laundry for the week. She *should* update her work calendar and offload her camera. She *should* wash her hair. But she doesn't take these forward-thinking actions. She cannot bring herself to do them. She cannot think of them on Sunday, even if she expressed the intention on Saturday. Most Sundays, she cannot even make herself climb the stairs to the roof to seek comfort in her garden. Instead, Bella takes to her bed and stays there. She leans into the suffering until the wine smooths out the sharp corners and jagged edges. Most times, she passes out until morning.

And then Monday comes. On Monday mornings, she is either suffering from a hangover of depression or alcohol or both. After realizing that if she didn't do something construc-tive on Mondays, they, too, would be infected, and because she couldn't afford to squander two days out of her week, she decided that Monday would be her day to volunteer at the com-munity garden. She rarely has gigs at the top of the week, so she maintains purpose at the community garden, where work is the perfect combination of solitude and communal endeavor—this is the recipe she needs. The hard work is both curative and ther-apeutic. So, Mondays are better now, but she has not yet found a solution outside of the wine bottle to make Sundays bearable.

When she drinks enough wine on Sunday to make herself sick on Monday, like this morning, she leans into getting sick. The purging somehow clears her head as well as her stomach. Her frontal lobe is back on the job and working hard to erase the shame. She almost prefers to throw up on Monday. It's as if she is getting rid of Sunday, so that she can carry on. She never feels completely cleansed, but if she can throw up, shower, hydrate, take some aspirin, and then get to the garden as quickly as pos-sible, she can pretty well save the day.

Bella puts on gardening clothes, meaning whatever is in reach from the piles of not-work clothes on her floor—today she puts on layers for the cool weather. As she dresses, she looks out her bedroom windows. The sun is hiding behind a thick layer of clouds. It looks cold and damp outside; fall is not-so-slowly turn-ing to winter. She puts on thick socks and lace-up work boots.

She'll wear her heaviest coat until she gets to the garden, where she will begin to prep her plot for the coming cold.

She splashes her face with tepid water and brushes her teeth. She fills her canteen with water from the tap and puts an energy bar in her pocket. She plans to stop for her coffee fix before she heads to the La Plaza Cultural.

This morning, right when she locates her keys and retrieves her credit card from the pocket of her black blazer, which is also in a heap on the floor, she hears a knock at her door. There are only three likely unannounced visitors on a Monday morning—Camille without her key, the building super with an exterminator canister, or her next-door neighbor seeking to borrow toilet paper or sugar or, like that one desperate occasion, weed. There's another soft rapping on the door. Bella now knows from the knock that it is not one of the usual suspects. This is a gentle knocker, and they are not.

She gets to the peep hole and sees Bradford Ferguson standing in the hallway. *Shit.* Bella looks around at her apartment. She looks in the mirror near the front door. Both she and her apartment are a total mess. In case she was hallucinating, she looks again through the peephole. There he is—looking fresh and pristine, as a doctor should on a Monday morning. The sight of him makes her feel not-of-his-world, small and inconsequential. She wants to clean up the apartment and herself so that she can be worthy of Bradford. But she knows it is no use. Resigned, she opens the door.

"Hey," she says, part greeting, part question.

"Hey," Bradford says and flashes his radiant smile. Those goddamn dimples.

"How is it you've shown up on my almost worst day of the week?" Bella asks, smiling and glad she brushed her teeth. There is no possible scenario in which she should let him into her apartment this morning. She is not even sure she flushed the vomit down the toilet.

"If this is your almost worst day, what's your worst day?

"Yesterday," Bella says.

He laughs.

"So, it's a good thing that I showed up today and not yesterday?" Dimples.

"Maybe if you had shown up yesterday, you could have saved two days," Bella says, giving him her best side-eye flirt. "I'm heading out for coffee. Want to come?" Bella says, keeping control of the conversation and removing the possibility that he would gain admittance into the hell zone.

Bradford smiles again and looks at her until she meets his eyes. He is clean shaven. His complexion is without a single mark or hair bump. Bella wonders how this is possible. She smells his aftershave—a subtle, pleasant woodsy scent. He does not look so much like a GQ model today, though. He is wearing a tweed jacket with brown patches on the elbows. It hangs loosely with age and it's a little too long. His jeans are decidedly dad jeans. He is wearing brown suede Hush Puppies. Today, Brad's style is a little dated and makes him look, mercifully, a little less perfect, but all the more endearing.

"This is how you look right when you get up in the morning, isn't it?" he says.

Bella realizes that he is assessing her in the same way that she was assessing him. And she feels sad for herself. But somehow the expression on his face reads something in the neighborhood of admiration, maybe even desire. His voice is a low morning-voice whisper, as if Bella is the first person he has spoken to today. The whisper and the dimples are too much. She is embarrassed and flustered, completely off-balance.

"No, this is not how I look when I get up in the morning.

This look takes work. I mean, I've brushed my teeth." Bella smiles up at him. He smiles down upon her. "Coffee, then?"

"Don't you want to know why I am here?" he asks.

"Yes." Bella stops in her tracks. She has been so busy trying to keep him out of her apartment, she forgot to be curious.

"I've been thinking about you," he says and takes a step closer. "I don't know very much about you, and I'd like to know more." Bella opens her mouth to say something, but she closes it again because she doesn't know what to say.

"To be honest. I regret turning down your invitation the other night. And I got impatient for another chance to see you—you were not there last week to pick up Mrs. Herman from her appointment, so I thought about it for a few days and decided—"

"I want to invite you in," Bella interrupts, "but I really don't want to invite you in," and then she adds, "it's Monday, you know?" as an explanation.

"Oh, you are not alone. Right. I knew there was that possibility." He takes a step back.

"Oh, no, just me and my own mess," Bella says.

Bradford looks relieved. He turns toward the stairwell and offers his arm. "So, coffee it is, I'm good with coffee."

Bella puts her arm in his, but this doesn't work. She has to move ahead of him because the hallway outside of her apartment is too narrow to walk side by side.

"You showing up like this, you're willing to get shot now?"

"You know what? I must be willing to take a shot for you," Bradford says.

"You're not like forty-five years old, are you?" Bella asks.

"No, but I am a mature twenty-seven. People say I am an old soul."

"I love old souls," Bella says.

For the one-block walk to coffee, they talk about Ellen.

Bella is doing most of the talking. This time, Bradford asks all the questions—about the community garden, about the gallery and Ellen's sons. Bella avoids talking about Dorian, but by the time they join the queue at the coffee spot, Bradford asks how Bella and Ellen met.

She begins to tell him the entire saga. She talks about the show, Dorian, Ellen's health, even her plan with Dorian to help Ellen reclaim her mind.

"I totally agree that communal gardening is a great idea to keep her engaged with people and out in the fresh air . . . the exercise." Bradford takes on a tone that Bella imagines is part of his doctor's office persona.

"Maybe you and I can work together. Well, we are already working together, sort of, aren't we? But I have some ideas about how to stop her condition in its tracks. I know they work. I've seen it with my own eyes."

"Ideas, like what?" he asks.

"There are dietary measures and herbs, there are certain spiritual practices and mental exercises." Bella is excited to be sharing this with Bradford. "For someone who is willing, these things working together can be miraculous."

"How have you seen this in practice?" Bradford asks. He pauses, puts his interwoven fingers to his lips, and turns to her, taking the whole doctor's office persona to a new level. Before she can answer, Bradford continues, "There really are no easy answers or miracle cures, unfortunately. And every case presents differently. Sometimes, loved ones are so desperate to grab at easy answers because they feel helpless. But when you embrace some of those unproven *alternative* remedies, you allow the disease to wreak even more havoc on the entire family with failed hopes."

It feels to Bella like Bradford is closing a door, like you do when you first realize you are in the presence of a fanatic. He wants to remind her that he is the trained professional and she is the lay person. She takes a deep breath, remembering how Nan's doctors refused to consider her recovery as having anything to do with her changes in lifestyle. How quickly doctor after doctor attributed her improvement to a "spontaneous, unexplainable shift in her body's mechanism," and finally, to a misdiagnosis.

"I lost both my grandmothers to this disease. I know how complicated and treacherous it can be. How it destroys families," Bella says, "but I also know that you can slow it down, stave off the symptoms." Now, Bella is shutting down. She is disappointed in Dr. Bradford Ferguson.

It's their turn at the cash register. She orders a flat white and he orders a plain coffee. He gives his name, pays, and they move off to the side to wait.

"Listen, I do not mean to dismiss what you've experienced," he says.

"Have you not noticed that Ellen is better?" Bella realizes that, as her doctor, he probably can't answer that question.

He takes a deep breath and lowers his shoulders. "Listen, I would love to work together with you for Mrs. Herman's benefit." He is trying to be conciliatory. "The goal, after all, is to make sure she is as stress-free and as happy as possible. And yes, the community garden certainly seems to be improving her quality of life."

"How do you medical people learn to do that?" Bella asks him. "I sincerely want to know. Are there classes on how to be a pompous, condescending, close-minded prick, or is it just that the profession attracts them?"

Bella walks out of the coffee spot and into the Monday morning gloom. She can't decide whether to head to the community garden or back to bed. She chooses bed. It's her quickest escape. Bradford catches up with her at the intersection. He has their cups of coffee in his hands. He holds hers out and she takes it.

"Thank you. And have a nice day."

"Just so we are straight, you are not the first person to call me a pompous, condescending, close-minded prick," Bradford says.

"And you are not the first person to dismiss me as someone who doesn't know what the fuck she is talking about. But I know what I know." She shifts from one foot to the other, like someone waiting for a fist fight.

"My grandfather was the most important person in my young life. When I lost him, I had no one who cared about me." Bradford takes a sip of his coffee and looks down at his shoes. "I was the only person who knew early on that he was fading away. So, I got to experience his demise far longer than anyone else. His death is why I do what I do."

"You know what's interesting about losing someone to dementia? It always becomes about you and not so much about them."

Bradford takes a step back. He is trying to maintain that doctor-knows-all smile, but it requires too much effort, so he looks down at his coffee cup and then down the street, gathering himself.

"Your patients . . . Ellen. Her illness is not about you or your grandfather. It's only about her."

The street light changes. Bella looks down the street toward home. She changes her mind and decides to head to La Plaza Cultural. She won't let Bradford send her back to bed.

"Thanks again for the coffee," she says and crosses the street going north. Bradford puts his free hand in his coat pocket and watches her go. She doesn't turn back.

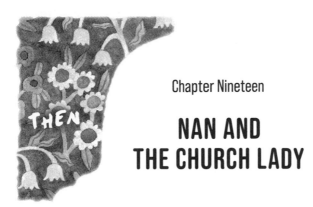

Chapter Nineteen

NAN AND
THE CHURCH LADY

When I pull up to the house, I see Ms. Jefferson's car. *Shit!* She is already here for her herb supply. I've arrived late to Gran's, straight from my last class of the week. I don't know how long Ms. Jefferson has been here, so I need to gather the herbs quickly before she takes a seat on the sofa and starts talking! I race straight to the garden because it's been weeks since my school schedule has allowed a real visit. I don't want Ms. Jefferson cutting into my time.

I grab some rosemary from the border hedge and then run over to the raised beds in the back. I reach under the box to pull some winter mint, but instead of mint, I get a handful of something else, a viny plant with small paddle-like leaves and white blossoms. I look under the box now and see that the winter mint is on the other side. I reach in deeper from where I am and gently take a handful of mint. I head over to the grasses for a turmeric root. As I turn into the grass spiral, I trip over Nan's foot and fall on the dirt path, dropping the herbs in my hand and skinning the palms. Nan is kneeling down in the path, with a shovel in one hand and turmeric root in the other.

"Bella! Are you okay, dear?"

"Yes, ma'am, I just didn't see you."

"My, my, my, it's so good to see you, honey!" she says as I brush the pebbles off my hands and hug her.

"What is your rush?"

"I am trying to get the herbs for Ms. Jefferson."

"Oh, well, yes, me too. I have them all right here, the turmeric root is the last." Nan sees my pile of herbs on the ground.

"Why did you pick the Brahmi herb? Has your Gran added it to the list?"

"No, I thought I was grabbing winter mint," I say.

"Oh, yes, dear. We have cleared some of the mint to make room for both types of Brahmi herb, *Bacopa monnieri* and gotu kola. We eat them every day. The winter mint is in the middle. You have picked the *Bacopa monnieri*."

She picks up the sprigs of Brahmi that I dropped on the path. "This Brahmi requires a lot of water. It's a thirsty little plant." She takes a piece of the herb, snips the sprig in half with her fingernail, and pops both pieces in her mouth.

I pick up the kitchen cloth full of herbs that she has lying by her side. I add mine to her pile and help Nan to her feet. She rises quickly. I take a step toward the house, but she stops me.

"Wait, dear. One last thing." Taking hold of my arm and leading me to the Goddess, Nan directs me to lay the bundle at her feet. When I do, Nan kneels.

"Come, Bella, let us pray." I want to tell her that we have to hurry, but I am obedient. I kneel down next to her. She makes the sign of the cross in front of her face and puts her hands together so that the tips of her fingers point up to heaven. This is one of the many characteristics that assures me that Nan is Nan. When she prays, no matter when or where—in church, at bedside, or at the dinner table, she never intertwines her fingers and folds them down into a prayer fist like most people. Instead, she presses her hands together palm-to-palm, finger-to-finger, like a child's prayer hands. They resemble the steeple of a church.

"Hail Mary, full of grace, the Lord is with thee," Nan says with her eyes closed. I close mine too. "We appeal to you right now on behalf of faithful servant Hattie Jefferson."

Did I know Ms. Jefferson's first name was Hattie? All these years, I don't think I did. Nan continues, "She is suffering, Holy Mother, and she has come for a few things from the earth that bring her comfort. Please bless these herbs and root so that she finds in them the relief that she seeks. In Jesus's name we pray, Amen."

I wonder when Nan started adding, "In Jesus's name we pray" to the end of her prayers. She usually says, "In the name of the Father, the Son, and the Holy Spirit," but apparently, not anymore. Has Gran turned her into a Baptist?

We rise to our feet together. I run and pick up three small rocks and return to the Goddess. I put them down before her feet and say, "In the name of the Father, the Son, and the Holy Spirit, Amen!"

Nan puts her steeple hands to her smiling lips. "Yes, amen!" She grabs my hand and says, "Let's go."

We make our way across the garden. Nan is moving with a swiftness that is new to me. The limp from her healed leg is almost imperceivable, her stride confident. When we get inside the kitchen, Gran is sitting across from Hattie on the living room sofa. They are drinking tea out of Gran's good china.

"You are so quick, Miriam, we haven't even finished our first cup," Gran says. With this, I realize that Gran and Nan have assumed the speedy-herb-relay game that was Gran's and mine. Gran is timing how fast Nan can retrieve Hattie's herbs. Only, they seem fully prepared to sit with Hattie *and* provide tea service. I have conflicting feelings about this. I am jealous and sad to be replaced.

But happy that Gran has used our old game to activate and motivate Nan. I place the bundle of herbs on the kitchen table, and I help Nan put the herbs in separate zip-top bags. Nan writes the names of the herbs across the bags in her beautiful cursive. Then she joins Gran and Hattie in the living room, herb bags in hand.

"Would you like more tea, Hattie?" Nan asks.

"Yes, please, Miriam, just a touch."

Gran rises from her seat to take Hattie's cup. "Let me get that for you. Are you still drinking chamomile?"

"Yes, please."

Nan hands the herb supply to Hattie, who gives Nan a wad of dollar bills. Nan drops the money into a large mason jar sitting atop the breakfront by the front door.

What is happening? Hattie is paying for her herbs now? The whole transaction between these three old women looks like some well-orchestrated drug deal. Gran brings Hattie more tea. Nan lands heavily in the easy chair opposite the sofa.

"Are you joining us for tea, Miriam?" Hattie asks.

"No, thank you," Nan says, a little breathless, "I will just rest a minute."

"How about you, Bella?" Gran asks.

"No, ma'am," I say, glad to be remembered. "I'm just having some water."

I bring glasses of water for Nan and myself and sit in the other easy chair. I am curious to see this new paradigm unfold. I have only been away a few weeks, but it feels like time has warped and I've missed an eternity.

"How have you been, miss?" Hattie asks me.

"Our sweet Bella is a college student now, Hattie," Nan says, "did you know that?"

"Why yes, I did. You well know that Olivette adds Bella to the list for prayer petitions every single Sunday."

"Yes, of course, I do," Nan says.

"How would you know that?" I ask Nan.

"Because your Nan accompanies me to Sunday service," Gran says, trying to sound matter of fact about this news.

"So, you *are* Baptist now," I say.

"No, dear, don't panic," Nan says. All three women laugh, and it feels like they are laughing at me. "Your Gran joins me at St. Martin's for Sunday mass, as well," Nan adds.

"Our Sundays are a double blessing," Gran says.

"Oh!" Hattie says. She is as surprised as I am. "My husband was raised Catholic, but you know what? I converted him. I can't take all the credit. It was really the Men's Auxiliary. Some of his best friends. But it all started when I brought him to Sunday service. So, watch out, Miriam, you might find yourself a Baptist yet," Hattie says, amusing herself.

I am tempted to declare that the conversion is already underway. She has already abandoned the Holy Trinity. But I keep that sentiment to myself.

At the end of the visit, Nan walks Hattie to her car. I barely allow them time to get out the front door before I turn to Gran and ask, "Why are you taking money from your church friend?"

"Your Nan convinced me that I should." Gran clears the teacups and saucers.

"But Ms. Jefferson has been offering to pay you for years. Why now?" I say, "What happened to 'this is God's work through the garden' and 'her wellness is payment enough'?"

"Yes, those things are still true," Gran says from the kitchen. "But your Nan makes a good point when she says that Sister Hattie wants to reciprocate. She is deeply grateful, but she clearly feels that her expressions of gratitude are not enough. She does not like feeling like a charity case. So, she gives a little when she comes, and we put it in the jar to donate to the YWCA. They provide meals-on-wheels to the elderly shut-ins of my church, you know?"

"She said that to you? That she feels like a charity case?" I ask, backing away from my judgment.

"Yes, she has, in so many ways over the years. Once Miriam pointed this out to me, I felt bad for ignoring Hattie's feelings in this way. I never wanted to accept money. I also didn't plan on being her herb supplier for so long. But here we are. She needs it. We cannot use all the herbs we grow. She is so pleased to hand over a few dollars. Everybody is happy." Gran returns to the living room and looks out of the front window. She waves me over to her side and points to Nan and Hattie, arm in arm, approaching Ms. Jefferson's car.

"Look at those two—Hattie is moving much better since the last time you saw her, isn't she? She is taking some kind of new supplement from India for her inflammation. She swears by it."

"They are both making good time," I say. Gran smiles.

"People want to feel useful and independent. We are old-school women, Calsap. We don't want to be somebody's charity case. You can understand that, can't you, dear?"

"Yes, ma'am, I suppose I can."

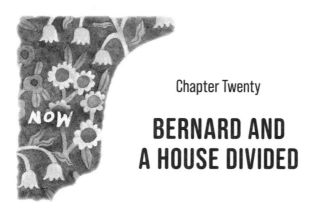

Chapter Twenty

BERNARD AND A HOUSE DIVIDED

NOVEMBER

Bella makes a committed effort to pull herself together because she is meeting up with Stephanie, and she knows that Stephanie will look effortlessly flawless, as usual. The truth is, Stephanie's beauty does not look effortless to Bella at all. Her perfectly matched and blended foundation, expertly applied eyeliner and shadow, the way her lip liner is just a touch darker than her glossy lipstick to accentuate her full lips—and how these elements all come together to create a blemish-free face that is glowing no matter what time of day or night—must take a great deal of time and effort. No, Bella doesn't think Stephanie's attention to herself is effortless. In this, Bella thinks Stephanie is a marvel.

Bella knows there must be secrets to Stephanie's look, but she does not know what they are, and it is not within her to find out. But she is willing to take more time with her own makeup tonight and she does her best—heavier eyeliner and red lipstick, light contouring under her cheeks, and blush. Instead of her usual utilitarian attire, she squeezes into a dressier black ensemble. She is going for sexy with this drape-necked, cap-sleeved

T-shirt, skinny jeans, and high-heeled strappy sandals. These are all new acquisitions from a big splurge in the garment district. She gathers her hair into a swirling beehive at the top of her head, takes extra time to smooth out the tight balls of kinky hair in back, and carefully combs her baby hairs in place at the crown of her forehead, gluing them down at the edge of her hairline with pomade. She pulls one of the iron café chairs into the bathroom and stands on it in order to see her whole reflection in the medicine cabinet mirror.

You clean up nicely, Bella thinks. This is one of Nan's sayings, used when she has come in from the garden and dressed herself for church. When Bella walks out the front door of her building, taller in her new sandals and shapely in her fitted ensemble, she feels like the Queen of the East Village. This only lasts the five-block walk down to Avenue A, where she encounters Stephanie on the street in front of their agreed-upon bar. Even straight from work, Stephanie looks like the star of a *Boomerang* remake. Her form-fitting fuchsia dress is business fierce with a strong undertow of sexy vixen vibe. She has truly mastered this look. Her hair is Robin Givens straight, her makeup Halle Berry perfect.

They hug and turn to the entrance. The bar is crowded, as expected for Friday.

"You look especially hot tonight," Stephanie says. "You have that fresh-faced, natural look we all wish we could pull off." Stephanie loops her arm through Bella's as they cross the threshold.

"Thank you." Bella laughs and shakes her head. "And you are perfection, as always." To this, Stephanie shows her appreciation by batting her impossibly long eyelashes.

"I am hoping the girls are already here with a table," Stephanie says, looking over the crowd of young, beautiful, mostly

Black people. Bella looks around to see if she knows anyone. She sees Lala and Teonna waving at them before Stephanie does.

"There they are," Bella shouts over the music. They make their way through the crowd. The two waiting women jump up from their seats, and dramatic hugging ensues, as if it has been months since they last saw each other and not just last Friday. The first time Stephanie invited Bella to join them, she explained that Lala and Teonna are her after-work crew, friends she met through her job. She will hang with them, get relaxed, unwind. Then she will go home, change her clothes, and meet up with her party crew. Bella is happy to be a part of this group. She is certain she could not keep up with Stephanie's party crew.

They slide into a crowded booth. Lala and Bella manage to be seated in the middle of the booth, Teonna and Stephanie opposite each other, capping each end. Bella loves this smashing together of gorgeous women, like all their good traits will rub off on each other. They touch shoulder to shoulder, reach over each other to grab hands when they agree with someone's declaration, and embrace each other in agreement over some point or another. Gratitude washes over her anew for this inclusion.

"We ordered your drinks, girls!" Teonna says, pushing a fresh vodka and tonic toward Stephanie and a beer toward Bella. Teonna Lawson works for Viacom, in marketing for MTV. She is tall and lanky, with caramel skin and thick wavy hair. She has a broad forehead and a long, slender nose. Bella thinks she looks Ethiopian. Tonight, Teonna's hair looks exactly like Bella's—an updo with baby hairs arranged with the same swirls crowning her forehead. Bella realizes in this moment that she subconsciously imitated Teonna's look from the last time they were together, and she feels embarrassed. Should she just own up to it and give Teonna her props for the perfect updo, or pretend that this twinning is a coincidence. But then Bella looks around and sees that half the Black girls in the bar are wearing their hair in the exact same way. She gets over herself and relaxes.

"So, Lala," Stephanie says, "tell us about this new man."

Lala, short for Lalisha Wilcoxson, is from Atlanta. Bella only knows this because her favorite pair of earrings are large hoops with ATL initials cut from gold plate attached to the inside of each hoop. Bella has never seen Lala without them. Lala is an inch shorter than Bella, but you would never know it because she has a four-inch heel height minimum for the stilettos that are a part of her daily uniform. She is shapely with an ample but even measure of bust and butt and an improbably tiny waist in between.

"Yeah, girl," Teonna chimes in, "This new brotha's name is not really Brad, is it?"

"Yes, girl. It's short for Bradford," Lala says. "You can judge if you want to, but this man is *The Package*."

It takes Bella a moment to focus on Lala's words. She hasn't heard the name recently, hasn't spoken it, even though Bradford has been on her mind often, as a regret and a counterpoint to Dorian. She was angry at Bradford for weeks. The day he showed up at her apartment, his condescension felt like rejection. He was not at all the same Bradford she encountered on the night of the Thompson-Green wedding. That Bradford was humble and down-to-earth. That Bradford felt like a kindred spirit. Lately, she's found herself thinking more about that Bradford and regretting not giving him a chance to resurface. She's also found herself comparing that Bradford to Dorian. Compared to Dorian, Bradford feels like a real person, not a fictional New York character . . . less like a striver and more like a settled soul, certain and solid. Bella regrets letting him get away. He didn't just get away, she pushed him away. Hard push. And now, can it be that Lala, beautiful, sexy Lala, has him?

"Wait, you are not talking about Bradford Ferguson, are you?" Bella needs to verify. "There can't be too many Black Bradfords in New York," she says to approving laughter.

"You know him?" Lala asks.

"Yes, Dr. Bradford Ferguson is Ellen Herman's doctor," Bella says, mostly for Stephanie's sake.

"Ellen Herman? Stephanie's boss?" Lala asks.

"Oh, crazy," says Stephanie. "How did you meet him, again, Lala?"

"He came to speak to my students on Career Day." Lala is an elementary teacher at PS.147 in Harlem.

"And you two are going out?" Bella asks Lala.

Lala gives Bella a sideways look. She seems to sense Bella's question is more than just curiosity. "No, I am just stalking him and trying to run into him," Lala admits. "We had a nice encounter at school, but he didn't get my number. So. . . ." She trails off.

"Lala is working on an app that locates professional Black people and businesses in Manhattan. You know, to make it easier to buy Black, support Black, be Black," Stephanie says. "This establishment is Black owned, you know?"

"No, I didn't know, but I should have. They've got something special going on in here," Bella says, referring to the mostly Black crowd of twenty-somethings, the music mix of new rap and old R&B, and the decor. There are black-and-white photographs crowding the walls, pictures of old Harlem neighborhoods. Bella recognizes some as reproductions of James Van Der Zee and James Latimer Allen, celebrated Harlem Renaissance photographers.

"Wait 'til you taste the food. I recommend the oxtails," Stephanie says.

"That's amazing," Bella says, refocusing on Lala and her app. "So, you want to add Dr. Ferguson to your app."

"Yes," says Lala, "*And* I want him for myself." Table laughter. High-fiving.

"Well, his practice is in Midtown." Bella pauses, as if she is considering ways Lala might find him. Lala gives Bella a look over her glass of beer. She is not buying Bella's helpful act. Neither is Stephanie, whose eyebrow is raised. Stephanie has a smirk that says, we will visit about this later.

"Oh, I already know where he works," Lala says, "I'm trying to run into him where he plays."

"Or you could just make an appointment," Teonna teases.

"Do you have a grandparent who needs a doctor?" Bella asks. This is her final offering. "He is a geriatric neurologist who specializes in dementia disorders."

"Yes!" Lala says, "that is what he told the kids. Something about his dead grandfather who raised him?"

"Yes, something like that," Bella says.

"Why does that story sound familiar?" Stephanie asks, looking at Bella. Her eyes are wide now. She has put things together and Bella suspects Stephanie feels she should represent Team Dorian.

Bella shakes her head to assure Stephanie and leans to her ear. "I met him at a wedding shoot and he's not my type," Bella whispers without much conviction. Stephanie holds Bella's eyes with a determined stare, but she doesn't press. She turns to Lala.

"We gotta find you an old person, Lala, girl," Stephanie says.

The waiter inquires if the group is ready for a new round of drinks. When he bends across the table to provide dinner menus, they see the person who has walked up behind him.

"Bernard?" Bella says. When the waiter moves on, Bella's brother is right behind, standing before the table. Bella's brain slows down to process this incongruous sight—Bernard in New York. She has not seen him in well over a year. And she is not accustomed to seeing him out in the world. "What are you doing here?" she finally asks.

"Hey, Bella, I thought that was you," Bernard says. He looks relieved yet self-conscious. "What are the odds?" he adds, taking in the table of beauties.

"My goodness," Bella says. The table is silent. "Everyone, this is my brother, Bernard." Bella introduces Bernard to each friend at the table. They say their own hellos, which feels to Bella a little like the beginning of a dating reality show.

"This is Stephanie. She runs an art gallery."

"Hi, Bernard." Stephanie bat-bat-bats her eyelashes.

"This is Teonna, she works for MTV." Bella holds out her hand, television hostess-style, in Teonna's direction.

"Hey, Bernard," Teonna sing-songs his name with a head tilt and a side glance.

"And this is Lala, she is a teacher and app designer." Bella adds Lala's aspirations because that is what dating shows do.

"What's up, Bernard?" Lala lifts her right shoulder and extends her hand. Bernard shakes it.

Bella asks to be released from the booth.

"I am in town to cover the World Series," Bernard says.

"Cover?" Bella says.

"Yeah, I work for CSports. It's an online sports media outlet," Bernard says, "I am one of the announcers."

"Ohhh," the table of women says as a chorus.

"I was going to call you later tonight," he says to Bella, "as soon as I check into my hotel."

Now that she is out of the booth, Bella hugs Bernard and punches him in the chest. "Yeah, you were," she says with the sarcasm they have cultivated throughout their childhood.

"Why don't you join us," Stephanie says. She bats her eyelashes again and flashes her gleaming white teeth.

"Yo, thanks. But I am meeting up with my camera man, EJ," Bernard says. He seems genuinely regretful, smiling his shy smile. In this moment he looks to Bella like little-boy-Bernard, whom she knows a bit better than grown-man-Bernard.

"I swear I was going to call you," he says to Bella. Now that they are face-to-face, she takes him in, his full-grown self. He looks so handsome. His hair is close cropped, with a pristine edge-up and carefully groomed stubble on his chin that is a little more than a shadow, but not quite a full beard. He is wearing a white buttoned-down shirt and crisply pressed khakis under a navy-blue sweater.

"Look at you," he is laughing a judgmental big brother laugh, "already in your New York black."

"And you look like a fucking LA Republican," Bella shoots back, "so fuck you!" Laughter from the table.

"Oh, shit, there's EJ," Bernard says.

"Okay, so call me and we will do dinner tomorrow, yes?" Bella says.

"Bet," he says, kisses his sister on the cheek, and waves to EJ. "Very nice meeting you all."

Bella turns to her friends who are all Cheshire cats.

"You didn't tell me you had a brother," Stephanie says.

"Well, it never came up. Bernard and I have been like passing ships all our lives." Bella turns and watches him settle in at the bar with his colleague, another Black man his same height. The unexpected encounter with her brother has left Bella feeling a new kind of homesick. It's a surprising and unfamiliar feeling she would not have guessed Bernard could evoke in her.

"Well, he's cute!" says Lala.

"Yes, but he's no doctor," says Teonna, sarcastic eyebrow up.

"No, but he is a soon-to-be famous sports announcer," says Lala. "He's got the look. He must have been an athlete, Bella?"

"Yes, baseball—high school All-Conference, college All-American. Cal Poly's Best-Thing-Since-Sliced-Bread," Bella says.

"I knew it," says Lala, "he looks like he's in good shape." The others laugh at how quickly Lala can shift her attention to a new prospect.

"Bernard lives in LA, Lala," Bella tells her.

"*I love LA*," Lala says.

"Then I will put in the good word, though I am certain I have no influence whatsoever." Bella sits at the edge of the booth right next to Lala, who wraps her arm through Bella's.

"Thank you, sister-in-law," Lala says.

For their dinner meet-up, Bernard chose a new hip and happening hotspot—hard to get a table and expensive. Bella is prepared to argue that he should pay. Just to be safe, and to avoid giving Bernard the wrong impression that she has any disposable income, Bella asks the driver of her hired car to let her off a block short of the restaurant right in front of the subway station. As expected, Bernard is already at the bar with a bottle of imported beer in his hand.

"Hey! Did you put our name in?" Bella asks.

"Fifteen minutes ago," he says.

"Cool." Bella takes in the crowd.

"You want a drink?"

"No, I'll wait."

"This is on me, Bella," Bernard says.

"Then yes! I'll have what you are having," Bella says, relieved.

Bernard's phone buzzes. "That's our table."

They are seated by the front window, where they are surrounded by the standing and waiting crowd. It's noisy and cramped, which Bernard mentions.

229

"Welcome to Manhattan! So how is your baseball coverage going?"

"Good. I don't officially start until tomorrow. It's my first time covering the World Series. I am here early to get the lay of the land."

"Is this your first time to New York for work?" Bella asks.

"No, I was here back in August to do a feature on an underdog team going to the Junior World Series."

"Uh, huh, which proves that you would not have called me this visit if I didn't run into you."

"Well, you didn't run into me. I found you," Bernard is quick to point out. "And last time I was only here for a day and then I went on to Pennsylvania for the series."

"Is Little League still fun to watch for you?" Bella asks.

"Actually, it's more fun as an adult," he says, laughing at the irony. "It's good baseball. Still pure. There's way more action than an MLB game, and there's this whole comical underpinning that makes it hilarious at times."

"I can imagine—the adults, right? I bet it's funny and sad how parents are so life-and-death about their little kids. Are parents still so overly invested like they were when we were little?" Bella asks, remembering even at the very few games she attended how obnoxious parents were a prominent feature.

"Exactly, yes, they are. Maybe more so. The kids are so about it, though. Their seriousness is cool. The adults, not so much. And how totally stratified everything is between the stars, superstars, and the truly gifted athletes." Bernard pauses, drinks his beer. "And then there is this whole racial undertone. I lived it as a kid and it's so intense to witness now as an adult."

"What kind of undertones?" Bella thinks she can imagine

but knows so very little about Bernard's baseball life firsthand. He was playing throughout the city and flying places while she was in her grandmothers' gardens.

"When I played Little League, I was the only one on every team," Bernard says, "I was expected to either be that superstar Black phenom or the welfare kid . . . or both."

"Really? You felt that way? I thought you loved it."

"Yeah, really. I loved it when I did well, met expectations. Hated it when I didn't." He takes another swig. "Weird how you missed my entire childhood."

"Well," Bella says, "not the hard parts."

"True. You know Nan took over Granddad's study when she moved in with Gran, right?"

"No, she didn't," Bella says.

"Yes, she did. She moved her fucking gardening books in and *Farmers' Almanac* charts and shit," he says.

"Well, that shouldn't surprise you, Bernard."

"No, I know. I guess."

"Anyway, those people are gone. Let's not talk about them," Bella says, hoping to end the subject.

"Whatever you say about your grandmothers, you definitely inherited their special brand of crazy."

"That's easy for you to say," Bella is trying to keep her tone light to match his, "Granddad died when we were young, when he was still perfect and flawless in your eyes."

"No, that's not exactly true. I was really mad at him right before he got sick. He let me down, and I cursed him. Then he died, and I thought it was my fault."

"How did he let you down?"

"Remember that big regional playoff game I got to go to? It was up in Santa Barbara, and it was a big deal. Granddad had been coming to almost all my games, and I believed he was my lucky charm. I had a whole superstitious thing about how lucky he was for me."

"Oh, yeah, I remember that. It used to piss off Dad a little bit," Bella says, "he kinda wanted to be the luck-giver."

"Well, I was going to pitch for that game, and I really needed Granddad to come. But also, when he came along, we always got there early. Otherwise, I was always late. You know Dad. Anyway, Granddad refused. He said I needed to believe in myself and not some superstitious notions, or some bullshit excuse like that. I was heartbroken and really mad, felt like he didn't give a shit. I told him to drop dead."

"It's not surprising that Granddad would not go far from home. That's who he was," Bella says. "He was as devoted to the indoors as Gran was to the outdoors. She called him her hopeless hermit, did you know that?"

"Yeah, there would be whole weeks when he would hole up in his study and not even come onto the front stoop. He would send me on his errands. I would even go to the corner store to buy his chewing tobacco," Bernard says.

"Gran would say, 'the stale air of this house is not good for you, Addison!'" Bella does her best imitation of her grandmother, "and he would say—"

"Stop trying to get me out in your dirt, woman!" Bernard takes the role of his grandfather.

"Yes!" They both laugh.

"I never understood his love of the indoors, but I do get why he loved his study. It was a wondrous place!" Bella says.

"While he lived there, yes, it was," Bernard says, shaking his head proudly, "most important room of the house. I could've lived there full-time. I miss it."

"Yes. The coolest stuff was in that study. Remember his

watches? I wanted to wind them so badly! And play with his model military ships."

"I know you did," Bernard says, "you were such a pain in the ass!"

"No, you were such an asshole about his shit. Like it was yours. I couldn't even read his books without asking you, like you were the fucking librarian!"

"Well, you always had dirt in your fingernails, tracking in mud from the backyard. No respect for the *grand salon!*" Bernard says, laughing through his beer.

"Well, that's probably true," Bella concedes. "You actually told Granddad to drop dead, though?" She is astonished that Bernard ever had a single bad thought about their grandfather, much less the bravery to express it. "But he was your person."

"I know, I was a little shit."

"Then he died," Bella finishes the story.

"Yep." Bernard avoids looking Bella's way.

"I remember after he died, you started acting like Mom. I feel like it was weeks of you not talking to anyone, hiding in the study, in the dark, curled up in Granddad's chair. But I thought it made sense that you were sad longer than the rest of us. How did you get yourself out of your hole?"

"I found his journal."

"Granddad kept a journal? It must be amazing!" The whole idea of a journal sets off fanciful notions in Bella's head of their grandfather's life adventures. "Does he tell all the mason's secrets? Did he have a wartime love child?"

"Bella, why are you so odd?" This is an old question that he has resurrected from their childhood. "It's not like a normal journal. He didn't write very much. Mostly just important dates, some names, appointments, shit like that. But on the day of my playoff game, he wrote pages and pages explaining why he didn't

233

come. He was already sick by then, emphysema from breathing in all that masonry shit. He didn't want to embarrass Dad and me with his coughing fits, and you know, his old-man shit. He talked about how talented and smart I was, how I was his favorite human, how he saw my promise and my future. He wrote it all in the pages of the book. Like a love letter to me, but he had no intention of giving it to me himself. Like he knew I'd find it after he was gone, like . . . right when I did."

"Yeah, well, you were his person," Bella says again. It's all she can manage to say. She is holding back tears for her brother's younger self. Bernard's eyes are also lined in red and full.

"He was my person, too," he says. Bella looks around and flags down the waiter. They both order another beer, even though Bernard isn't finished with the one in his hand. The waiter presses them to order food. They both choose gourmet hamburgers and fries.

"Who is your person now?" she asks.

"Granddad . . . Dude is still in my head, giving me advice, telling me what to do."

"Me too," Bella admits, "the Gran and Nan of before."

"Before they died?" Bernard asks, smiling as he drinks.

"Yes. Ghosts can't hurt you, Bernard. It's the living who will fuck you up."

"No shit," Bernard says and then holds up his beer as if in a toast before he finishes it off. "Speaking of Dad. . . ." Bernard says. They both laugh hard and long.

"Honestly, Dad has been great," Bella says in defense of Bernard's other person. "Amy seems to be making him happy."

"I'm not sure if it's Amy or yoga," Bernard says. "You know, his new favorite saying is, 'It must be the yoga.' He uses it for everything. Hey, Dad, you're looking pretty lean these days. 'It must be the yoga.' That was a good idea to rotate your tires. 'It must be the yoga.' It's annoying."

"And you don't think yoga is a metaphor for sex with Amy?" Bella suggests, Bernard ponders.

"Yeah, you're probably right," he finally says, "but honestly, I am just starting to think he likes yoga more than her. Now that she has a real job, making decent money, she seems to be sweating him a lot more about how he's living, including why he is still supporting us."

"Hey! Hey! What kind of real job puts her all in our business?" Suddenly Bella is no longer Team Amy.

"She's an accountant. She just passed the exam for her CPA certification. That shit is not easy, you know?"

Bella says, "No kidding! A yogi accountant. Who knew Ames had it in her?"

"Yeah, well, so Amy quits the yoga to take the real job and Dad starts teaching yoga."

Bella almost chokes on her beer. "Stop lying to me."

"It's true." Bernard is amused by Bella's reaction. "You gotta keep up, Bells! The fucking world is upside down. Where have you been?"

"Jesus!" Bella can't fathom this news. "How long has he been *teaching* yoga?"

"Not very long, and you know Mom is, like, famous, right?"

"What do you mean, famous?" Bella asks. "Dad told me she is working on some big secret project, something to do with urban land use. How is it a secret if she is famous for it?"

"It's one of those 'family is the last to know' things, I guess. There's a lot of buzz about it in LA," Bernard says.

"If family is the last to know, how does Dad know so much?"

"He keeps up with her. You know Dad is a glutton for

punishment. He takes a licking and keeps coming back for more. I think Mom is his one great love."

"Yep, and that just makes me sad," Bella says, "Mom just doesn't have the bandwidth to reciprocate."

"That's a generous way to put it. Or you can just say she doesn't give a shit about Dad."

"That's not fair, Bernard. Mom was sick. She was struggling just to put one foot in front of the other."

"And who had to take up the slack?" Bernard says, anger lacing every word. "Dad did."

"Well, he had a lot of help."

"The point is, he never gave up on her. But she left him in a lurch. She is the one who checked out."

"No doubt, she was checked out."

"Dad has been waiting on Mom for a long time. I don't blame him for partaking in some lightweight yoga life. He has earned the Zen and the opportunity to be taken care of by a young, hot accountant."

"Well, I am super happy for Mom, too, and I think she deserves to be famous and happy."

"Are you going to go out to see it, her project?" Bernard asks. "I hear it's pretty incredible."

"Yes, I guess, if she wants me to."

Bernard seems to register Bella's hesitance. "You can't avoid the ghosts forever."

"Forgive the destroyer, right?" Bella says.

"What?"

"Nothing."

The waiter arrives with their burgers. Bella starts on the fries. She is happy to be with Bernard. She decides that she likes this grown-up version . . . they have survived their upbringing and should be closer for it. He has earned his anger and his isn't any lesser or greater than hers, just pointed in a different direction.

"Hey, you think you might come to my show?" Bella blurts out with a mouthful of burger.

"I would love to. You think you might fix me up with your friend?"

"Which friend?"

"The sexy one with the crazy eyelashes and banging body."

"Stephanie. I don't know if you can handle Stephanie, Brother."

"You don't know my game, Little Sister," Bernard says.

"Baseball, you mean?" Bella says, certain it's the only game he's got.

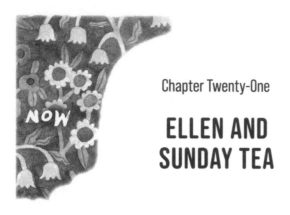

Chapter Twenty-One

ELLEN AND SUNDAY TEA

NOVEMBER

Bella is too ambitious with all the stuff she is trying to carry to the roof, performing a precarious balancing act as she climbs the stairs. She has two large and heavy gardening volumes under her left arm—*Mid-Atlantic Gardener's Handbook* and *New York/ Mid-Atlantic Gardener's Book of Lists*. Both have become Ellen's favorite go-to sources. In her right hand, she has a teapot full of hot water and two mismatched china teacups hooked on her pinky and middle finger. The tea tray's weight is unevenly distributed between her left and right hand. The teapot is too full and hot water is dripping down Bella's arm. When she comes through the roof door, Ellen sees her struggling and offers to help, but she is slow to stand and by the time Ellen is fully upright, Bella has already made it to the table.

This tea service on the roof is all a part of the Sunday ritual Bella and Ellen have established. Bella brings the tea and a gardening book or two. Ellen brings some kind of gift for Bella—a new gardening book, an envelope of exotic seeds, vintage postcards from the gallery. Bella has come to realize that Ellen's gift offerings are a kind of memory game she plays with herself. She chooses something in anticipation of the day, and then she has to engage all sorts of mnemonic devices in order to remember to bring it. Most of the gifts are small tokens, except for the last one: Ellen had a five-foot round patio table delivered to Bella's building last week, claiming to be tired of sitting at Bella's rickety curbside discard.

"I was very proud of that table," Bella told Ellen over their first tea service on the new one.

"Well, there was no reason to be. It's not like you saved up your money for it or made it with your own hands. It was someone else's trash," Ellen had said, and Bella saw her point. The new table's surface feels so luxuriously smooth and unblemished, made of iron with some kind of protective coating. It is sturdy and substantial like nothing else Bella owns in New York. When she runs her hands over its surface, it feels to her like commitment wrapped in stability. And in this way, the table represents what Ellen contributes to her life: commitment and stability just when she needs these most. Bella loves the table so much for what it is and what it means that she ate dinner on the roof for that entire first week she owned it.

Once she has arranged everything, Bella sits down across from Ellen. But just as she sits, Ellen stands up abruptly.

"Oh, dear! I have forgotten your gift."

"Ellen, this table is gift enough for *forever*," Bella says.

"No, no. You don't understand," Ellen looks frantically around the table and in her bag.

"I will have Dorian bring it. I must."

"Oh please, no," Bella says before she can stop herself.

"Please, Bella, let him," Ellen pleads, uncharacteristically. She is distraught because she has broken her chain of remembering. She calls Dorian on her mobile phone, instructs him on where to find the gift. When she ends her call, she has calmed down. She puts her phone in her bag and surveys the tea service.

"This is not the usual setup," Ellen says, not very happy about the change.

"Exactly. No. I would like to try something new."

Ellen looks a little miffed. Today may not be the best day to change things since she is already out of sorts about her forgotten gift. But Bella is already committed to this experiment.

"This is matcha tea," Bella says, holding up a small round tin.

"It's very green," says Ellen.

"Yes. This is an ancient green tea used for centuries in China and Japan."

"Green tea. I do believe I've tried green tea before, Bella. I don't think I liked it."

"I think matcha has a very unique taste and feel, and since it is very good for us, and since it is fun to prepare . . . I thought maybe you'd like to try it."

"Okay. I'm game." Her good mood returning, Ellen is willing to play along.

"You know what gave me this idea? The Chinese tea kettle you gave me last month."

"Ah, yes, and there it is," Ellen says of the cast iron kettle set in the center of the tray. It is the most beautiful and unique kettle Bella has ever seen— iridescent green, wide, and shaped like a flying saucer.

Around the kettle, Bella has arranged a tea tin, bowl, strainer, small scoop, and a bamboo whisk. She scoops the green matcha powder into the strainer, holding it over the bowl. Then she pours the hot water into the bowl and uses the whisk to whip the tea into a froth. This takes a full minute. But the tea is fragrant, and the green color seems to heighten. The top layer of foam makes it look more appetizing.

She pours some of the tea from the bowl into Ellen's cup and some into her own.

"Bon appétit," Bella says.

"Bottoms up," says Ellen.

Just as they lift their cups, Dorian walks out onto the roof. He approaches the table tentatively. Ellen takes a small tester sip of her tea. She sees Dorian and takes a full gulp.

"I like it," she says.

"Me too," Bella says.

"Good afternoon, ladies," Dorian says to both women, but he is looking at his mother.

"Oh, Dorian, what brings you here, sweetie?" Ellen's tone is surprise, with a little hint of disapproval.

"You asked me to bring you this." Dorian hands her a small brown rectangle.

"The gift, the gift. Yes, yes, the gift," Ellen says. She takes the brown-paper-wrapped package from Dorian and hands it over to Bella.

"Thank you," Bella says, blushing from Ellen's attention because it is, for the first time, under Dorian's gaze. He is witnessing their Sunday ritual for the first time. It feels to Bella like an intrusion. Three's a crowd.

Bella takes the gift and sets it down on her side of the table, right next to her tea saucer. Everyone seems to comprehend that she will open it when she and Ellen are alone again. Bella and Dorian have not been out on a date or in bed together for weeks. Ellen binds them together, though. They are regularly coordinating meetings at the community garden and at Bella's apartment. Bella is a part of Ellen's orbit, which has become very small. She has all but replaced Ellen's son as her companion about town, to view artists and other gallery showings. Ellen has slowed down her social engagements and largely

241

curtailed her work at the gallery to spend more time at La Plaza Cultural.

Bella does not know if Ellen is aware of the estrangement between her and Dorian . . . if she knows that she has all but replaced Dorian in Bella's life. Today is the first clue that she does.

"I think I drank my tea too fast," Ellen says, "I need to use the restroom."

Bella stands to accompany her down the stairs to her apartment.

"I know where it is, Bella dear," Ellen shoos her away.

"Are you sure?"

"Yes, yes, sit, sit." Ellen crosses the roof door threshold and is gone.

Bella turns her attention to Dorian. "So good to see you," she says and kisses him on the cheek. Dorian hugs her. It is a friendly hug, not a lover's hug.

"Thank you for bringing the gift. Your Mother was pretty upset about forgetting it."

"I work hard not to be 'punitive when she forgets or repeats herself,' something someone said to me early on. I am working very hard to remember those words." Dorian repeats the advice Bella gave him months ago.

"Yes, when you minimize the shame and stress of forgetting, her episodes will be less damaging," Bella repeats the rest of her speech, "and you should have seen how quickly she moved forward from that fretful moment when she discovered she forgot the gift. You made that easy for her."

"About us, Bella," Dorian puts his hands in his jean pockets. "I'm sorry I have not been very available lately."

"No, Dorian, it's fine. I've been crazy busy too. My gigs have really picked up and I am taking on more at the community garden."

"I guess now that you are helping with my mother and have her endorsement, you don't really have time for us."

Bella is confused with the switch in his tone, from apology to accusation. "Dorian, that's not fair. You just acknowledged that you have been too busy to get together. Can't I say the same about you? Now that I will be signed with your gallery and am spending my time helping with your mother, you are getting what you want without needing to date me, right? How is this any different? I am here, doing what I promised to do. What about you? What are you doing for me?"

"I got you here, right? I'm the one who found you. I am why you are here."

"Dorian, just admit that this is all you want—for us to be artist and agent. Just say that and I am fine with it. Don't pretend this distance is my choice."

"It just feels like you are dating my mother instead of me. Like you are happier in that relationship than ours."

"It's not like that. This is what it looks like to execute our plan—helping your mom slow the progression of her condition. It's working—she is happy and feeling well and experiencing less dysfunction, right?" Bella says this as if she is the older of the two of them. Dorian nods, conceding the point.

"In the process, your mother and I have just discovered that we are kindred spirits. I am deeply grateful to her and to you."

"I am grateful too," Dorian concedes. He holds Bella's eyes with his, "Like I said, I'm sorry."

"Let's catch up some time soon," Bella says, switching back to the transactional realm.

He exhales, frustrated that Bella doesn't offer more.

"Yep." He turns to leave.

"Thanks again," Bella says.

"Yep," he says again as he exits.

When Ellen returns, she is huffing and taking in big gulps of air. Bella is still standing and agitated from Dorian's departure. She knows he is not satisfied with her answer. She is disappointed that she has to be the adult between them.

"Is Dorian gone?" Did you two have a good visit?"

"Yes, it was nice to see him today. We've both been so busy, it's been a while."

"Aren't you going to open your gift?" Ellen asks as Bella returns to her seat. Bella smiles as if she has forgotten and takes up the package, unwraps the tightly taped paper, and uncovers a copy of *for colored girls who have considered suicide/ when the rainbow is enough* by Ntozake Shange. The book looks like new, except for the edges of the spine. She opens the front cover and sees that it has been signed by the author, it appears, ages ago.

"That is a first edition, and it was signed by Ntozake in the seventies, when the book was just gaining steam and we hosted her at the gallery for a reading. Have you ever read it?" Ellen asks.

"No, ma'am," Bella says, feeling like a cultural miscreant, "but my Gran took me to a local production when I was probably seven or eight."

Ellen smiles as if she knows something Bella doesn't.

"I loved the production because it was the first adult play I had ever attended outside of church, and I couldn't believe there was cursing and talk of sex! I felt very grown-up," Bella says. Both women laugh.

"I wanted you to have it because I want you to know that you have such power within you, Bella, and so much of it comes from your past and the strong women in your family, even maybe the damaged ones who came before you and have touched your life," Ellen says with a keen clarity that tells Bella she is fully herself in this moment. "I do not know your history, but I envy your pedigree as a Black woman. You are such a spiritual being and so tied to the earth. I hope that you are able to cherish the people who sowed that into you. I see them in you, even if you don't. Take it from an old woman—do not squander the gifts of your past and the people who reside there. Good and bad, easy and difficult—your people are all that you have."

"But I have you, don't I?" Bella says, struggling to figure out what has prompted this from Ellen. What does she think she knows about Bella's past? Bella wants to shift attention from herself to Ellen. "And I cannot tell you how grateful I am for you."

"Well, I am grateful too," Ellen says. "Read the book now that you are an adult and let's see what you find."

"Okay. And thank you so much again. Another treasure from you. I feel unworthy."

"Oh, Bella. *You* are the treasure. Dorian saw it first, didn't he? I will give him credit for that. And he still knows it, bless him. Yes, I must thank him again for you."

Bella smiles. Ellen's open affection is always unexpected. "Me too. You know you've saved me from Sunday. It's my hardest day of the week. And now, with you, it's not."

Ellen just smiles as if she knows Bella's life story, as if she knows about the Sunday teas of her past and how central they were to who she was and is no longer. Bella is all the more grateful to Ellen for sparing her any request for further explanation.

They finish a second round of matcha tea, then Bella shows Ellen her early pumpkin. It is planted in a big wooden barrel. The large leaves and long vines are covering up the fruit, which looks like a pale yellow ball.

"It's hard to believe that this will grow big and turn bright orange, but with luck, it will," Bella says. "I planted a few in this pot, and this is the only one that survived."

"I saw Beth's pumpkins at La Plaza," Ellen says, "and though her vines are huge, the fruit is tiny, just after blossom." She is impressed with Bella's.

"I know, I got an early start."

"I love the fall, don't you?" Ellen says.

"I do," says Bella.

Chapter Twenty-Two

INTRUDERS AND THE NATURAL WORLD

NOVEMBER

Bella sees the tree first. She is returning home down 9th Street with a bag of groceries in both hands when she passes PS 64, the phantom of the East Village. Sitting dormant between 9th and 10th Streets, it is a former school that takes up the lion's share of the block, looming in silence over the street.

Bella takes this route home often, but this is the first time she really notices the former school. It's so big, its outer walls so high that it almost hides in plain sight. She can see that it has been abandoned for decades by the degree to which plants have taken over—tall, dry groves of intruders—vines and grasses, unpruned trees and scrubs. What sticks out the most, though, is the full-grown tree growing out of a fifth-story window. *How did that tree get all the way up there? Did it self-seed, or was it an abandoned potted plant?* Bella wants to know. She needs to know. This is not the first implausible intruder she has spotted in New York, but it is the most audacious.

She crosses the street and walks along the front of the building, which is obscured by a barricade, an expanse of blue and

dark gray plywood, covered with posters and graffiti. She is looking for a way in. She knows the chances are not high, but she
tests the boards at the joints by pressing with her shoulder to
see if there is some give, a workable gap. The barricade is solid.
She walks around the block to 10th Street, to the backside of
the school. This side doesn't need a barricade. The building has
its own twenty-foot concrete wall. It is a fortress. Like the barricade on the other side, the wall is covered with dirt, algae, and
layers of graffiti. There are two doorways cut into the fortress
with orange plastic mesh across the front of wooden plywood
doors, which are chained. Since she is already invested, Bella
gives the first door a little tug to test it. It doesn't budge. She
walks over to the second door and pulls at the metal loop where
the chains feed through. This door gives some, surprisingly. She
looks around to see if anyone is looking. No one is on the street.
She gives it a harder tug. The entire door frame comes loose
around the edges as if someone has been kicking at it from the
inside. Now she is afraid the entire door is going to fall on top of
her. She pushes it back in place.

A woman and a small boy come out of an apartment building
across the street. Bella sets her bags down on the sidewalk, leans
over them, and pretends to adjust the groceries. The woman
does not seem to notice Bella. She is preoccupied with the boy's
scooter, setting it down and helping him mount it. They proceed
away from Bella down the street. Bella turns back to the door
and pulls open one side of the frame, careful not to tip the entire
thing. It relents again and she is able to climb over the orange
plastic. She squeezes through the door, lifting her two grocery
bags, one at a time, through the narrow opening.

Now she is in an open courtyard on the other side. She can
no longer be seen from the street. From where she stands at the
entry wall, the building surrounds her on three sides, the center

expanse where there are steps to the main entry and two side wings to the left and right. She looks up and remembers that her tree is on the other side of the building.

In every corner of the courtyard, someone has set up a home. There is a cardboard structure in one corner, a filthy mattress in another, but they are currently unoccupied. Bella realizes this pursuit is naïve and careless. Of course, this deserted building is going to draw folks who need shelter. She knows she should leave right this second. But she doesn't. She sets her groceries down on the side of the door and walks at a fast, no-nonsense pace up the cement stairs to the entry of the building. The glass in the front doors is broken out, but the doors are locked. She reaches through the glass and opens the door from the inside.

The center hallway inside is strewn with trash and debris. An overwhelming smell of urine hits her in the face like a warning punch. She is standing completely still, listening and trying to make sure she doesn't see any movement in the dark corners. Where would the stairs be in an old school building like this? She walks toward the other side of the building, where the fifth-floor tree is located. She passes through the door to the courtyard on this side. She is facing 9th Street now. She looks up at the side wing of the building to the left and sees the tree, its green leaves slightly waving in a breeze that must only register higher up. There is no breeze where she is standing. She takes her camera out of her backpack and snaps a few pictures. She has a good angle and from here, she can verify that the base of the tree is actually inside the building. The top of the tree has grown through the open window.

Now it occurs to her that someone may very well be living up there and caring for that tree. She wants to know, but she doesn't want to know. She wants to know. She walks back through the central hall and turns left hoping to find the stairwell. The school has large windows on both sides of the central hallway, but as she walks farther down a side hall of mostly classrooms, the light diminishes. She proceeds slowly, looking from side to side for the stairs. Midway down the hall, she finds a stairwell through a surprisingly small doorway. She turns to head upstairs, but the human smell intensifies, delivering another punch in the face—this punch is harder, more than just urine. Warning punch number two.

She runs up the stairs toward the light shining through the stairway door on the second floor. From the landing, she can see that this floor has been completely cleared down to the studs. It looks like a construction zone—just open space, beams, and windows. The light streams in from the unobstructed windows on all sides. There is no sign of any squatters on this floor. It smells less like human fluids and more like old cement and dust, as if this demolition happened just days before. This makes the second floor feel safer.

She runs to the 9th Street side and looks up at her tree. Now she has an even better angle. She takes pictures of the tree framed by the window. The fifth floor, where the tree lives, is the top floor. The windows on that floor are different. They are framed with architectural details, columns, and triangular-shaped valences. She had envisioned that the tree's window would be broken out, as if the tree had emancipated itself by breaking through the glass. But in fact, the window is open. She can see the lifted pane still intact. From where she is standing, she still cannot see the tree's base or any details of the room behind it. The ornate framing and the reflection of blue sky and white clouds in the glass around the tree create a surreal picture. She is happy with these photos, but still curious about how the tree is where it is.

Her curiosity trumps her fear. She is emboldened by the open space of the second floor and the beauty of the tree. She heads back to the stairs with the intention of ascending another floor, but she hears a shuffle, unmistakable movement, above her in the stairwell. Then the smell of fresh urine hits in a wave. Now the combination of her terror and the urine make her stomach lurch. Warning punch number three. She turns to leave.

"Get out while you can," she hears a voice say. The voice is clear and loud enough to produce an echo in the stairwell. She looks behind her up the stairs but sees no one.

She runs down the stairs, across the center hall, and out through the door. When she gets across the courtyard, Bella sees that her groceries are gone.

"Shit, someone has taken my bags," she says aloud. But then she looks out and sees an iron gate and wooden barricade. She looks up and there is her tree. She has exited on the wrong side of the building. She has to go back through the building to get to her bags waiting for her, she hopes, on the 10th Street side. She considers leaving her groceries. Instead, she will get out on 9th Street and circle the block for her bags. But there is no way to exit this side. She takes a deep breath to muster her courage, then takes the stairs two at a time up to the entry and runs back through the building. Once she is in the hallway, she races across. She doesn't even look to either side. She is focused on the door.

"*Get out!*" The voice is louder, angrier.

She gets to the fortress on the other side, grabs her groceries, and climbs through the door to the street. Now that she is back on 10th, she places the plywood back the way she found it and runs down to Avenue B.

As she crosses the intersection, someone's car horn makes her jump and lift her arms as a reflex just as she is clearing the curb. The sudden movement tears the handle of a grocery bag, spilling her groceries onto the sidewalk all while she is still in mid-step. When she lands, she trips on a glass bottle of sparkling water and falls to her knees. A car swerves to the curb behind her and stops. The driver gets out of the car and stands over her as she gathers her groceries.

"Are you all right?" Drip asks, holding out his hand. "I am so sorry. I didn't mean to make you fall."

"Drip? What are you doing here? *You* honked the horn? That was you?"

"Yes, I am really sorry. I'm in town for a few days. I saw you running, and you looked scared. I wanted you to know that I was here, in case you needed something."

"Geez, you have no idea," Bella says, standing erect and dusting off the front of her jeans and jacket.

"Let me give you a ride." Drip sounds like a concerned father. "You going home? You live nearby?"

"What are you doing in my neighborhood?" Bella asks, handing over the bags in each hand. "You came back to stalk me?"

"Looks like you need someone to watch over you, girl!" Who are you running from?"

"I just got chased out of someplace I should not have been," Bella admits, "I was taking pictures." She is still panting to catch her breath. "But I don't need you to save me."

This is the second time she has encountered Drip out in the world, and in each encounter, he posits himself as her savior.

"You live close by?" Drip asks again, ignoring her declaration of independence. "Let me take you home."

"Okay, thank you," Bella relents, "I'm just on the other side of the park. You can drop me off."

Drip puts Bella's bags in the trunk of a black Mercedes Benz as Bella settles into the front passenger seat. He gets in, shifts the still-running car into drive, and circles Thompkins Park.

"I thought you shipped your car," Bella says.

"I did. This is a rental."

"Huh, makes sense. It seems like you barely fit in it," Bella says, noticing that Drip's seat is set almost as far back as the back seat.

He turns left onto Bella's street, and she points to her building on the right. There is a parking spot right in front. This is a miracle for Drip, but not so much for Bella, who was hoping to jump out, grab her groceries, thank Drip for the ride, and be off.

Drips turns the engine off and settles back in his seat.

"So, what were you running from?" He asks again, "Was somebody chasing you?"

"Yes," Bella says, then reconsiders. "No. It felt like it. But I don't think so."

Drip says nothing. He is waiting for more.

"I ventured into an abandoned building to take a picture. I am working on a series, and I found my way into that old boarded up school."

"You *found* your way? You mean you broke in? Oh, shit, or worse, you found the back door, where the homeless get in, right?"

"I guess so."

"What happened?"

"A ghost told me to get out. Started yelling at me to get the eff out, so I ran."

"Who was 'the ghost'?"

"It was just a voice. I never saw the person."

"It was a spirit and it chased you all the way down the street?" Drip laughs, a soft chuckle that somehow feels to Bella like he is laughing with her and not at her.

"Well, the voice was very real, and so just to be sure, I kept running. I was going to run all the way home, or at least I was going to run until I'd run all the creepy chills away." Bella is laughing now too.

"You know what? You shouldn't take chances like that. This city is dangerous, and you up in a squatter's haven or worse, a drug den, is just not smart."

"I realized that as soon as the ghost told me to get out."

"So, you were lucky this time. Did you even get the picture?"

"I did," she says with an excited smile. "Some great shots I can't wait to work with."

"Well, let me see."

"Okay." Bella reaches into her backpack that is resting on the floor between her legs and pulls out her camera to search for pictures to show Drip.

"See this one? I took it from the second floor."

"Oh, nice. How did that tree even get there?"

"Right? I don't know. And I still don't know how it's planted."

Bella shows Drip all the shots. He looks carefully, going back and forth several times to compare and contrast, to refine his observations. Bella appreciates his attention and positive comments.

"Wait, I got a really good shot with my phone. I'll show you." Bella reaches in the front pocket of her backpack, but her phone is not there. She looks in the side and main compartments but can't find it. She starts to pat herself down, feeling for the hard shape in her pockets. No phone.

"Oh, do not tell me you lost your phone in the haunted building. Did you drop it?"

"No, no, no, no, no, I couldn't have," Bella says, but as she thinks back, she knows that there were several moments between the two times the ghost told her to get out that she could have dropped it.

"Shit, I think I did. In the stairwell, the echo of my steps and the voice. Maybe I didn't hear my phone fall. I think the phone pocket of my backpack has been unzipped this whole time."

"Well, shit. You gotta get a new phone."

"I can't! Can't afford it, the pictures on it, my whole life. My phone is my personal assistant. I have to get it back."

"You can't go back into that building," Drip says with conviction and finality, "the ghost saved your ass once. . . ." He leaves the conclusion of this statement for her to conjure up.

"But. . . ."

"The ghost has your phone and has already ordered pizza on it. Let it go."

"If I go now, he'll give it back for some cash."

"He'll take your cash and your phone, Bella."

"Drip, I know you don't understand this," Bella is holding back tears, "but I have to go try to get my phone."

"All right, all right, all right, I'll go with you. Damn!"

"I really can't ask you to do that. This is not your fuckup or your problem."

"So, you think I am the kind of dude that would let you go in there by yourself with no phone or way to communicate?"

Drip has already started the car. He shakes his head, knowing he is going against his better judgment. Bella knows it's a ridiculous ask. But she is so grateful he is going with her because she knows she has to go right now.

She shows Drip the entry point to the building on 10th Street. They circle the block four times before they find a parking spot a short distance down the street. Someone is taking their time pulling out of the narrow space that barely fits Drip's rental car. By the time they get to the entrance of PS 64, the sun is very low behind the buildings, casting long shadows.

Bella approaches the place where the plywood has to be pried away from the frame, but she sees that it is already open.

She wonders if this is her fault. Did she fail to secure it in place in her haste to get away? Drip holds the board as she climbs in, and he follows her. This time the courtyard is full of people. It looks to be all men, either alone or in groups of two or three—about twenty in all. Nobody looks in their direction. It's as if no one wants to be seen. No one wants to make contact. Drip gives Bella an "I told you so" look.

"This was empty last time. I was *just* here! No one else was out here," Bella tries to explain herself again.

They walk through the crowd and go up the stairs to the building. Just as Bella reaches in the broken glass window to open the door as she'd done before, a man approaches the door from the other side.

"Can I help you?" the man says. He is heavyset, a mixture of muscle and fat. He is Bella's height, in his early twenties. His hair is cropped short, but he has a scraggly beard—spotty with bigger blank spots than hair spots. He is wearing black wool slacks and a black buttoned-down shirt. His heavy, spicy cologne assaults Bella's olfactories. She makes the effort not to overtly turn away. His big silver-and-gold watch is tight around his wrist. He has thick gold chains around his neck.

"This is not public property, yo. I think you musta got your addresses mixed up." His voice is clear, deep, and smooth. He has a Puerto Rican accent. This is not the voice of Bella's ghost. Drip slowly pulls Bella back and steps in front of her.

"Hey, man, we just came to get her phone," Drip says in a soft, soothing tone, "she was here earlier. She's a photographer, she was just trying to get a picture of a tree."

The man just stares at Drip and then at Bella, back at Drip and then again at Bella, like he can't believe their nerve.

"Get the fuck outta here, man. This is not the spot to be retrieving no lost property."

256

Drip steps back. He is towering over the man and wants to show deference. "Look, we only want to get the phone. That's it."

"Yo, yo, yo, that's Drip McAffrey," a voice says from behind Young-Man-in-Black. "Drip McAffrey!" The person still has not appeared.

"What, you a pro player or something?" Young-Man-in-Black says. Already his demeanor has softened.

"Brooklyn Nets, yo!" says the disembodied voice.

"Brooklyn Nets suck, yo," says Young-Man-in-Black. The other man appears. He is older, thicker, and dressed in a white T-shirt and black jeans.

"Right," Drips says, "I don't play for the Nets anymore."

"Yo, Drip," says the older man in the white T-shirt, "you here for something for that shoulder? I got something for that shoulder."

To Bella's amazement and relief, the intensity of the moment dissipates. Young-Man-in-Black opens the door wide. The Older-White-T-Shirt-Man has his black jeans rolled up to create thick cuffs and is sporting blue Converse All Stars. Bella wants to say that she has some just like that. She thinks this is her only in to this men's club of fandom and testosterone. But she knows better. She remains silent and just smiles. Drip does not turn down the offer, he just repeats their purpose. But before he can finish the explanation, Older-White-T-Shirt-Man is nodding his head yes.

"Get the phone for Drip here," he tells Young-Man-in-Black. Without a word, Young-Man-in-Black is off. He disappears into the darkness of the interior.

"So, you want something for that shoulder or not?" Older-White-T-Shirt-Man says.

"No, thank you, man. I'm good," Drip says and takes another step back. "My shoulder is all good and I'm about to play in Europe."

"Okay, all right," Older-White-T-Shirt-Man says. "This is good shit, though, but probably not the stuff you want to travel with."

Young-Man-in-Black appears at the door with Bella's phone. He hands it over to Drip. "We found that phone on this motherfucker in the stairwell. He been hiding out in here without permission, without us knowing. Wouldn't have found him without that bright-ass phone light. Yo, you use up your battery with the light so bright. You know that, right?"

"Yes, I know. Thank you so much!" Bella looks at the phone. It is still on, a new crack snaking its way across the screen.

"Well, Drip McAffrey. Good luck in Europe," Older-White-T-Shirt-Man says, "good luck with that shoulder. If you change your mind, you know where to find us."

"Thanks, man, seriously!" Drip offers Older-White-T-Shirt-Man his hand. They do a short dap, drawing each other close to the chest, almost a hug.

Bella backs down the stairs. Drip turns her around toward the exit, puts his arm around her shoulders, and propels her toward the opening. Bella has to run to keep up with Drip's long stride.

When they are in the car, Drip wastes no time pulling out and driving off. They ride in silence. Only when he is parked again in front of Bella's building does he take a deep breath in.

"Holy shit," Bella says.

Drip is still gripping the steering wheel. He begins to laugh, puts his forehead on the top of the steering wheel's arc. Bella adds her nervous laugh to his.

"You know, you the type to get a brotha killed!" Drip's laughs are loud until he muffles them by covering his face with his hands. He wipes off the little beads of sweat at his hairline.

"How often does that happen? Does your celebrity open every door, every time?"

Drip takes a moment to answer. "Yes, right up to the moment when it doesn't."

"And that's what's scary, right? You never know if this will be that moment."

"Exactly," Drip says. "Even with all of that, Bella, I don't make a habit of putting myself in danger like that. You need to be more careful with yourself. What if I hadn't driven by and picked you up? You would have discovered you lost your phone, and you would have gone back to that building by yourself." Drip pauses and waits for Bella's response. She has none. She knows he is right. She would have gone back to find her phone. But as she thinks about it now, it's as if she is considering the actions of another person, a different Bella. She can no longer imagine herself making that decision. Already she is no longer that naive woman.

"Yes, you would have," Drip continues scolding, "and if you had, that is what you would have found, a bunch of strung-out men outside and a bunch of predators on the inside. Seriously, the thought of you going in there by yourself is going to give me nightmares for a minute."

Drip is holding Bella's eyes with his pleading ones. She thinks he is so beautiful and vulnerable right now. She realizes that he was as scared as she was.

"I promise, I will not be so stupid again. But you know what, Drip? I live in New York City by myself. I make difficult safety decisions all the time."

"I know," he says. Bella's hand is resting on her thigh. Drip puts his hand on top of hers. "But going into that school was a stupid one, right? I swear, I wish I could move back here and protect you. But you have to be smarter. You've gotta be more careful."

This statement is unexpected. His scolding doesn't feel to Bella like his usual flirting. Though Drip's tone is more like a protective big brother, she is moved by his tenderness. It feels like sincere affection. Still, she wonders if he is expressing himself like this because he regrets his move to Italy.

"Is Milan not working out?" she asks.

"No, no, it's great. It's good."

"Because you sound like you are trying to move back. And I know that's not about me and my poor decision-making."

"No, I'm just saying. You're making me think you need me to stick around, like you need that level of care! Tripping over curbs and leaving your shit behind." Drip is laughing now.

"You do not want to stick around. I'm the type to get a brotha killed, you know?"

"I swear," Drip agrees. They both laugh.

"I don't need you to take care of me," Bella says, "I promise I will be more careful. No more abandoned buildings."

"I'm going to check up on you, believe me."

They give each other their best smiles. Drip closes his hand over Bella's, and she returns the gesture by interlacing her fingers with his. They both look down at their intertwined hands, as if they are sorting out their feelings and what is happening between them.

"Drip, I better get my groceries in the fridge," Bella says.

"Do you want me to help? I really only have time to help you take your bags up. I'm heading to the airport. I shouldn't even be in New York. My season has started and I gotta get back. Our games start this week."

"No, I'm good," she says. Drip has saved her from expressing the invitation to stay over that was on the tip of her tongue. She is relieved that he has forestalled it before it is spoken.

Bella pauses before she opens her door, and Drip seizes the moment to lean in for a kiss. Bella meets him halfway. She intends her kiss to be a light, friendly expression of gratitude.

But Drip pulls her closer, kissing her again. Bella pulls away from him. She doesn't want to stop, but she knows it's the right thing to do. She gently extricates her hand from his and looks down at her palms. He sits back in his seat. No one speaks, both hesitant to name this moment.

"Drip, thank you for saving me. Seriously, thank you for being willing to. . . ."

"I really wish I could stick around. I wish I could delay my flight."

"Me too," Bella says, and she means it.

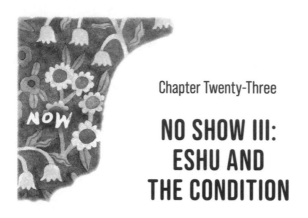

Chapter Twenty-Three

NO SHOW III: ESHU AND THE CONDITION

DECEMBER

Frank Herman is standing at the head of the conference table in a large meeting room at the Herman Gallery. Bella has taken her place to one side of Frank.

"There are a number of items to cover before we collect your signatures, Ms. Fontaine," Frank says to Bella.

Bella shares a reserved smile with Dorian, who is standing on the other side of the table. The conference room is a light and spacious rectangle on the second floor. It has floor-to-ceiling windows overlooking the street, and the white walls are the perfect backdrop for the art hanging there—mostly contemporary paintings and textiles. The door is set in a wall of glass that allows for views of the art displayed along the adjacent hallway.

Frank is tall and spidery—his lengthy legs and arms seem to belong to someone else's torso. He looks to be the older brother instead of the younger, because he is beginning to bald, and his three-piece suit suggests that this is what he is going for, the look of seniority. It's as if he is holding onto some childhood version of how a lawyer should look. His three-piece suit is from another era. It is gray plaid and loose fitting, even the vest. The lapels are too wide.

Bella notices an outsized David McGee painting on the wall behind Frank. More than notice, this large painting has all but reached out and hit her on the side of the head, demanding her attention. The Black man looming over them on that canvas has a devilish smile. He is set in a dark and moody backdrop—deep reds and black. He could be a court jester or a minstrel—his exaggerated smile, red-stained lips, white-gloved hands, blond cropped hair, and silly top hat. But he is wearing a nobleman's cloak and holding a king's staff. He is most definitely assuming the stance of authority. Perhaps he is some modern incarnation of Eshu, the African trickster god. This is who Bella decides he is, Eshu, because Eshu can be all these things—jester, minstrel, nobleman, and anything else that suits him. Bella also decides that this Eshu is a messenger from the artist to her. Eshu's smile is playful, but his eyes are not. He appears to be looking at Frank with a side glance.

Yes, Bella, Eshu is saying, *this is your beginning. This is how you get your art in important places, bought and beloved. You are living the dream.* Bella's back is to the glass wall and the hallway. She takes a deep breath and looks across the table again at Dorian, who is waiting for her to take her seat. He has always made a show of chivalry whenever they have been out together, opening doors and pulling out chairs for her. Not today. Today, he waits for her to pull out her own chair. This gives her pause, and in the span of one minute, the excitement of the occasion has morphed into anxiety. Dorian seems anxious too. He can't seem to stand still. And now Bella wonders if he is fidgety because of their doomed relationship or because there is something not good with her show.

"Is Ellen coming?" Bella asks, hoping for her support. The two men look at her and then each other, as if there may have been an oversight. Shouldn't someone have summoned Ellen?

"I am not expecting her," Frank finally says.

"Did she say she was coming?" Dorian asks Bella.

"No," Bella concedes, "I guess I just assumed."

"I see," says Frank, pulling out documents from two folders and laying them out before him. "I have two sets of documents we will discuss this morning, Ms. Fontaine."

"Please, call me Bella."

"Okay, Bella," Frank says, the corners of his mouth turning slightly upward too briefly to qualify as a smile, "I'd first like to handle the permissions. We will need to get signatures from Olivette Fontaine, Miriam James, and the young girl Amanda Armstead's parent or guardian for their likenesses in your works. This covers both you and the gallery for the exhibition and any reproductions and collateral product that might be produced for sale."

"We have the release from the little girl's grandparent that Bella attained when she first took the pictures. Her grandmothers are no longer living, so we can move on from this," Dorian says to Frank. Then to her: "My apologies, Bella." He says this with such confidence that it makes Bella's heart hurt. Even as distress overcomes her at this new wrinkle, she feels bad for Dorian.

"Actually. . . ." Frank says, "my understanding is that both grandmothers reside at 40140 Mary Ave in Los Angeles. Am I mistaken?"

Bella is trying to figure out how to explain her situation with her grandmothers in a way that they will understand, but all that comes out is, "How do you know that?"

"We like to be thorough," says Frank, "I hope we haven't made a terrible mistake. I understand your grandmothers are . . . were . . . well . . . are very dear to you."

"Wait, Bella, your grandmothers are still living?" Dorian is incredulous now. He shoots a look at Frank. His eyes are full of uncertainty and embarrassment.

"Yes," Bella says.

"You told me they were, were. . . ." Dorian is stammering, "you told me they had passed." Dorian sits back in his chair. He rubs his eyes with his fingers, then intertwines his hands on the conference table in front of him, composing himself.

"I cannot get their signatures," Bella says in her most decisive voice. "That is not possible. I have already shown these photographs in an international exhibition. They have already appeared in public, in newspapers, and there's been no problem. There won't be any problems now."

"We don't take those kinds of chances," Frank says. "You understand, we have been in this business for seventy-five years."

"Then we can take those photos out of the show," Bella says. She is desperate now. "There are still plenty of photos remaining for the show without them."

"There is no show without those photos," Ellen says from behind Bella. She has just come into the conference room. "We have already discussed this, Bella. Those photos are the highlight of the collection."

"I took those pictures some time ago," Bella says. "My grandmothers are no longer those people, and I can no longer get them to sign any releases." She is fighting tears. But she remembers that she must fight for her show.

"Without their permission," Frank says, "there is no show. If they are incapable, perhaps you can ask their representative, a conservator or. . . ."

"That is not what I am saying," Bella says.

Bella looks up to Dorian, who is standing now. She tries to elicit his help. He holds eye contact with her, folds his arms in front of himself, and nods his assent to Frank's demand. Bella turns and looks up to Ellen, who is standing beside her chair.

"Ellen, please," Bella says.

"You lied to us, Bella," Dorian says. "What did you expect?"

"Dorian," Ellen says. Her voice is calming, maternal. "Let us not make this bigger than it is."

"I didn't lie," Bella says. She has to take in gulps of air to suppress the emotion welling up in her throat.

"This engagement is not just about one showing, Bella," Ellen says. "We are agreeing to represent you, to promote your work and introduce you to the world. This is a partnership. This is why we have taken the time to get to know you and understand what your art means to you. For this to work, dear, we have certain things we must sew up legally."

There is a pause in the room as if everyone else is holding their breath. Bella feels Eshu's side-eye on her now, his minstrel smile. *Fucking trickster*, Bella thinks.

Buck up, Bella! Eshu says, *handle your business! Don't fuck it up.* Bella hates his ugly face now. She feels he is both mocking her and telling her the truth. Why did she think this would be easy?

"I understand. I'll get the signatures," Bella says.

"Good," Frank says, as he reaches across the table with the documents. The two brothers return to their seats. Ellen sits in the chair next to Bella.

"Let's continue," Ellen says. Bella is gripping the arms of her chair. Ellen puts her hand on top of Bella's and says, "Breathe."

Franks instructs Bella on where her grandmothers should sign and directs her to put the releases in a folder that he provides. Dorian is looking at Bella as if she is a new animal he must regard as dangerous. His mouth is set in a half-moon frown. Bella knows that Dorian thinks she lied to him. She wants to declare again that she really didn't. His eyes at half-mast tell Bella that he is done with her. Frank hands Bella the contract. He begins to go over some of the provisions that he says deserve special attention. Ellen is sitting erect in her chair, her full attention on Frank. Every now and then she will chime in with a tidbit of explanation.

Bella is trying to focus, but she can't. She returns Dorian's gaze. She mouths the words, "I'm sorry." She tries a smile of contrition. Dorian's stare remains unchanged. His eyes are glazed over. Bella realizes that he is not looking at her, he is looking through her. He is somewhere else. She coughs and clears her throat to get his attention. His eyes refocus. He is back, but he looks over at Frank.

"Would you like some water?" Frank says to Bella.

"I would love that." Bella pushes her chair away from the table and looks to Frank for directions to fetch water. This is an opportunity to pull herself together. But before she can stand, Frank says to Dorian, "Would you grab us some waters?"

Dorian gets up and leaves the room. Half-mast eyes, crescent-moon frown.

"Do you have any questions so far, Bella?" Ellen asks.

"No, ma'am."

Frank continues, "If you'll turn to page five. . . ."

Bella focuses her attention on the contract in front of her. With Dorian out of the room, she tries to hear Frank. Frank shifts and moves his chair slightly to the left. Bella notices a different view of the painting behind him. Now she can see that Eshu has a dead chicken hanging from a hook in his other hand. *Why a dead chicken*, she wonders. Her eyes move from the dead chicken to Eshu's smile—dead chicken, smile, dead chicken, smile. She suddenly gets it. The chicken is his offering.

This is the beginning of your dream, Bella, Eshu says, *but it will cost you.*

Bella decides right then that the only way to get her grand-mothers' signatures on the release is to forge them herself. She closes her eyes and expects to see her grandmothers' faces in her head, with some kind of admonishment, but she doesn't. Just blackness and silence. Maybe finally, she is free of them. She believes this is a good thing, but she has an unpleasant sensation in her stomach that feels like loneliness. Bella is free, but com-pletely alone.

"Lastly, Bella," says Frank, "if you'll go to the addendum, which is the very last page, you'll find delivery instructions, how long we will keep the works, and how the unsold remainders will be returned to you or stored by us."

Dorian backs through the glass door with waters on a small tray, turns and places the tray in the middle of the table. He returns to his seat. Ellen hands Bella a bottle of water.

When Dorian looks in Bella's direction, she thinks to apol-ogize again, but now she doesn't want him to think she is sorry for Frank's treatment of him as the water boy. She attempts an appreciative smile. The apology will have to wait. She tunes back in to Frank as he is explaining the signatory page.

"Okay," Frank pauses and takes what seems his first breath since he began, "if you do not have any questions, you'll please sign above your name and write in today's date."

Bella picks up the pen in front of her. It is fat and heavy, with Herman Gallery etched on the side in gold script.

"Can I keep the pen?" she asks as she signs.

"Of course," Frank says and laughs. Bella is happy to have broken through Frank's hard, joyless shell.

She sees that Ellen has already signed on behalf of the gal-lery. This somehow gives her comfort. She is so grateful for Ellen's support. Frank slides the papers away from her to Dorian, who signs as curator.

"This means we'll be working together to put things up, right?" she asks Dorian.

"Yes," Frank answers, "provision three of the addendum." He says this less for informational purposes and more to chastise Bella for not paying attention. He assembles the papers in the two folders—Bella's and the gallery's. Bella shakes Frank's hand. "Remember, this is all contingent on full execution of those releases."

Bella nods.

Frank says, "Welcome to the Herman Gallery family. We have scheduled your show for the Fourth of July. It was the only date available since Ellen wanted to move things up. We don't normally schedule on a summer holiday. But we will make it work."

"Thank you," Bella says to Frank, "thank you so much."

She turns to Ellen, and they hug for a very long time.

"I know this is business as usual for you," Bella says, "but this is the happiest day of my life."

"This is just the beginning," Ellen says and cups Bella's jaw with her hand.

Dorian makes his way around the table. He holds out his hand and struggles with his smile. Bella grabs him around the neck into a tight hug. She buries her face under his chin. Frank and Ellen leave the room quickly. They know she has some repairing to do.

"I am sorry, Dorian," Bella says in his ear. She comes away from him. His smile grows a small fraction, but his eyes don't change.

"I owe you my entire life. Right now, everything good about it is because of you."

Dorian holds her hand. His eyes soften and his smile broadens for just a moment.

"What is the deal with your grandmothers?" he asks.

"It's complicated," is all Bella offers.

"Well, maybe you'll feel more comfortable telling Ellen the truth there," he says.

Bella suspects that Ellen already knows at least part of the truth, but she doesn't say this.

Dorian takes a step back. His half-mast eyes and crescent-moon frown return. He grabs Bella's folder and hands it to her.

"Make sure you get those signatures. We have until next summer. That might seem like a long time, but it isn't." He walks over to the door and holds it open for her to leave. "Once those are signed, I will call you." When they are out in the hallway, Dorian points left.

"The exit is that way," he says as an answer to Bella's hesitation. He turns in the opposite direction.

"Dorian, can I please buy you a drink?"

"I've got a load of work today, Bella."

"How about tonight, after you finish work?"

Dorian pauses. He stands with his hands in his pockets. Bella walks up to him, puts her hand on his chest. "I want to celebrate, express my gratitude," she says in a hush and steps in a little closer.

"What if I tell you I have plans?" he says.

"I would say, surely you have time for a quick drink." She presses even closer, looking up at him with her best smile. He looks over her head, up and down the hall. Bella feels the muscles in his chest and shoulders relax as he breathes in and out loudly.

"You want to come by later? I have a meeting that should wrap up by ten."

"Okay, yes," Bella says. She takes a step back.

"See you at ten, then," Dorian says. He kisses her on the forehead.

They part ways in the hallway. Bella goes downstairs and finds Stephanie at the reception desk. She has a tray of champagne flutes.

"Congratulations, girl!" she shouts. Bella approaches her, kisses her cheek, and grabs a glass.

Ellen and Frank come from Ellen's office and join them. Stephanie passes out champagne to everyone, including some patrons who happen to be in the reception area.

"Here's to my friend and protégée, Bella Fontaine. To her future as a brilliant artist," Ellen says. "She is all signed up for her first show. Congratulations!"

"Bravo!" says Stephanie.

Frank holds up his glass and so do the strangers.

"Thank you so much, everyone! This is a dream come true for me. Thank you!" Bella says, holding up her glass.

"Where is our curator?" Frank asks.

Dorian appears. He takes a glass, holds it up. "Bottoms up!" he says. He drinks the champagne in one gulp, smiles at Bella, and then turns to his mother.

"Ellen, can I speak with you?"

Ellen kisses Bella on the cheek, puts her champagne down, and leaves with Dorian. Stephanie puts the tray on the reception counter. She wraps Bella in a tight hug.

"Thank you, Stephanie," Bella says.

"It's about time, sister."

"See you soon, Bella," Frank says and walks out of the front door and onto the street.

"He'd be cute if he didn't take himself so seriously, right?" Stephanie whispers.

"That old three-piece suit doesn't help," Bella says.

"I like three-piece suits, just not *that* one."

"Well, it suits him," Bella says between sips.

"At some point soon, huge-collared three-piece suits will be fully back in style, and he will be the visionary," Stephanie says.

"Here's to visionaries," Bella says and finishes her champagne.

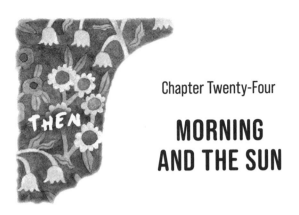

Chapter Twenty-Four

MORNING
AND THE SUN

I cannot find the mailbox key. It's usually hanging by a long string on a hook in our kitchen. In my father's household, I am the only one who checks the mail. Dad hates sorting through ads and promotions, and Bernard could not care less. So even if I had not been obsessing about the mail as I have been, checking it every day, I am most likely the person who has misplaced the key. I cannot remember where I put it.

I am sleep-deprived and still a little bit drunk. The birthday party gig I worked tonight lasted until four in the morning, and I was invited, along with the waitstaff and the deejay, to stay and finish off the booze after all the guests had left. This was the best part of the night, the impromptu after party offered by the hosts, Bob and Sarah Spenser, a fun-loving couple celebrating Sarah's fiftieth birthday. We were sitting around the fireplace in their living room while Bob tried his hand at mixing the evening's signature drink, dubbed the magical martini, and Sarah turned up the volume of the sound system, inviting us to dance to Sade. The waitstaff kicked off their shoes, and we all danced, martinis in hand. The Spensers seemed tireless. The party wound down only when the deejay said he had to go. I felt mellow, happy, and very adult, certain that the magical martinis were responsible. To top off the night, the Spensers gave me a very generous tip, three times the contract price. I belted out Sade's "Smooth Operator" my entire drive home in a state of unfamiliar euphoria.

Now I am exhausted, but I am feeling lucky, like I want to capitalize on tonight's good fortune. I want to check the mail to see if my Klineberg Photofest results have arrived. Did I win a spot at this prestigious international competition or not? I decide I will turn the whole house upside down to find the mailbox key, I am so sure the letter has come. But first, I need to pee. I go to our downstairs bathroom, a tiny closet-sized room located under our stairs, where you can almost sit on the toilet and wash your hands at the same time. I sit down and there is the mailbox key, right on the edge of the sink.

I go directly to the mailbox and find the envelope that I somehow knew would be there. I open it, read it, and at four thirty, I leave the house, get back into my car, and head to Gran's. It's still dark when I pull up to the curb. I retrieve the key from under the fake rock near the front steps and go inside. The house is silent, except for the distant whirring of Nan's ceiling fan. The entire house is softly lit by the light over the sink in the bathroom. Gran always uses that light as a night-light because the bathroom is in the middle of the house's central hallway.

I go first to Gran's room because she is easier to awaken. But she is not in her bed. It's all made up. Surely, she is not already in the garden. It's still dark outside. I don't look for her. I decide instead to try my chances with Nan. I am happy to see that she is where she should be—soundly sleeping in her bed. I stand over her for what seems a very long time because my eyes can't make sense of what I am seeing. I wait patiently for them to adjust to the darkness of the room. But the view does not change. I am seeing the outline of two sleeping figures in the bed. One person nestled in the arms of the other. Spooning. I close my eyes and count to five, then open them again. Now, I can see clearly. My two grandmothers are sleeping together. I back away from the bed and land in the wooden chair on a neatly stacked pile of laundry.

They are so peacefully asleep, perfectly still, except the slow rise and fall of their breath. They make two distinct low rumbles. I want to climb in the bed and take my rightful place. But as I sit here in the darkness and watch my grandmothers sleeping in this way, I realize that perhaps I am beyond sleeping in their beds with them—and not because I am too old, but because I am no longer needy or needed.

I am reminded of my twelve-year-old self, when I made a new friend at summer day camp. Lola was new to the United States from Nigeria. We had a great time together the whole summer. When camp ended and we discovered that Lola would start at my school, we were thrilled. I was happy to have a new friend with an exotic accent and different worldview. Lola was thrilled to have someone to teach her American ways. But Constance was not thrilled at all. Constance was my oldest friend. Every year, she spent the entire summer with her father in South Carolina, so we always had a dramatic reunion on the first day of school after a long summer apart. When the three of us showed up that first day, and Constance discovered that she had to share me with Lola, she was deeply unhappy. Lola was none too pleased, either. They immediately disliked each other.

I, of course, discussed my schoolyard travails with my grandmothers. It was always so wonderful to have their two different perspectives, often divergent, to help me sort out my childhood. But on this situation, they were in agreement.

"A threesome of friends can be difficult to navigate, Calsap," Gran had said when we discussed the matter as we walked the spiral to visit the Garden Goddess. When we got there, Gran dropped a rock for Constance, Lola, and me, asking the Garden Goddess to sort things out.

"Three's a crowd," Nan echoed just a few days later during our Sunday tea. She thought the matter serious enough to close the garden book on the table and make sure I got the message. "Female friendships can be messy sometimes, love," Nan had added, "and odd numbers are tricky, three is too hard."

Lola soon found a group of fellow Nigerian immigrants and left Constance and me in her dust, so the matter resolved itself. But my grandmothers' lessons stayed in the mental file I kept for such advice.

I decide that I will just leave and come back later. I stand up quietly and move toward the bedroom door. Then Gran coughs. Then again. Nan rubs Gran's arm. This stops me in my tracks, and I am just standing, hovering in the doorway. Gran coughs again. Nan sits up and reaches for the glass of water on the nightstand. The covers fall away, and I see that she is top-less, her bare breast swinging freely with her movements. She looks up and seems to look through me. She grabs the glass and turns to Gran. Gran props herself up on her elbows and takes it. She is naked too. She cradles her breasts with one hand and drinks. I consider running but remember that they aren't wear-ing their glasses, so I remain frozen in place, hoping I remain unseen. Gran coughs again. This is part of her usual morning. She sleeps with her mouth open and often wakes up with a dry and irritated throat. She always keeps water nearby. She now sits fully in the bed to finish the glass of water. And this is when she sees me.

"Bella, is that you?" She asks as she pulls the covers over her torso.

"Yes, ma'am," I say. Now Nan is fully awake too.

"What time is it?" Nan asks. She reaches for her glasses, puts them on, looks at the round white clock on the opposite wall.

"It's really early, Nan, I am so sorry for . . . to. . . ." I trail off. I have never apologized for being at Gran's no matter the hour. But this feels different.

"Is anything wrong?" Nan asks. She points to her robe hanging from the bedpost and I hand it to her. Gran grabs her robe from the post on her side of the bed. She is up and has moved around the bed to where I am.

"Are you all right, Calsap? You smell a little drunk."

"No, ma'am. Well, yes, ma'am, I am. But . . . I have some news."

"Oh, well, then, I'll put the kettle on," Gran says, heading to the kitchen. Nan shifts the covers to get up.

"No, no, don't get up," I say. I rub my face. I suddenly feel so tired.

"You have on your work clothes," Nan says, "you haven't been to bed, have you?"

"No, ma'am."

"Well, is it good news?"

"Yes," I say.

"Get in, dear," Nan says, pulling the covers down for me. "Tell us and then you can sleep."

"Yes, climb in," says Gran, returning to the room.

This invitation is too good to pass up. My grandmothers are behaving as if this situation is normal, and so, I do too. I want to lie down so badly. But I feel this is not the right thing to do.

"But three's a crowd," I say.

Nan laughs as I climb in.

"But we are not three, my sweet," Gran says. "We are one."

Nan kisses my forehead as I settle on her pillow.

"Have you been having nightmares again, Nanny?" I ask, deciding this is why Gran is sleeping with her in her bed.

"No, baby, not in ages," Nan says. She sounds so clear and so herself. So happy and so present.

The bed is still warm from them. I pull up the covers. My grandmothers are looking down on me. I fall asleep without telling my news.

When I wake up alone in Nan's bed, the curtains are open and the sun, filtered through an early fog, casts a low silver light on the room. I want to stay right where I am. My head hurts, and I am queasy but thankful I don't feel worse. I slowly kick off the covers to the edge of the bed and plant my feet on the floor. This effort feels like a herculean feat. I lie back flat on the bed and stay this way, half sitting, half lying down, long enough to fall asleep again. When I wake up, I slowly lift my torso to a sitting position. I don't want to rush this hangover. The house is quiet, and I know where everyone is. I am glad I do not have to contend with the smell of breakfast cooking. I find my way to the kitchen and make coffee.

I am sitting at the table when my grandmothers come in from the garden.

"No classes today?" Gran asks.

"Yes," I say.

"Well, then, you had better get a move on," Gran says. "Tell us your news, finish your coffee, and then be off."

"I won a spot in the Klineberg Photofest. I get to go to Toronto. I could win five thousand dollars."

"Well," says Nan, "well, then," she repeats as she sits in the chair beside me. "So, what does this mean?"

"How marvelous, Bella!" says Gran. "When do you go?"

"I go this fall and participate in an art show, with judges and money prizes. It's kind of a big deal."

"Will you be able to spend some time in Toronto?" Nan asks, "I hear it's a fantastic city."

"So, let's see then, by the fall you will have graduated. Since you will go as a college graduate," says Gran, "perhaps you can take some time to travel in Canada."

"I can't afford to travel. I've got too many great things going on here. My freelance work is picking up. I did a spread for the *Century City News*. I showed you that. And they said they would add me to their photographer list. My gigs are paying well. I shot the best party last night."

"Yes, a party," Nan says, "and they apparently paid you in booze."

"Yes, they did. But also in cash *and* with a hefty tip!"

"Did you drive here under the influence this morning, Calsap?" Gran asks.

I am blindsided by this question. The truth is, it never occurred to me that I was committing a crime this morning. I drove home and then to Gran's after consuming a good bit of beer and martinis.

"Yes, ma'am, I did, and I didn't even think about it. This was my first time drinking at a job."

"Oh, Bella," Gran says, "if you are not experienced with drinking, driving is the last thing you should have been doing."

"Well, we knew she was going to be doing these things in college." Nan comes to my defense.

"And this is why I wanted you to live on campus, where you can drink and then walk to your dorm and crash safely like a normal college student," Gran says. "This is different. She is driving around Los Angeles drunk," she says to Nan.

"A little bit drunk. I didn't drive far. I went home and then here."

"Why didn't your dad stop you from leaving the house?" Gran asks.

"It was four-thirty in the morning. He didn't see me," I say.

"Sweetie, please take care not to do that again," Nan says. "It is already risky for a young woman to be out alone at that hour. But driving around even a little bit tipsy is just asking for trouble."

"You're right, that was stupid of me. You see? Thank goodness you are so nearby to watch over me."

"If we were not nearby," Gran says, "you would not be endangering yourself to come to see us at all hours."

"I know, I just wanted to share my news." I hold my head as it pounds out a painful beat.

My Gran takes away my coffee and puts a cup of tea in its place.

"What is this?" I ask.

"Ginger and milk thistle tea," Gran says. "Apologize to your liver and drink up."

"What is that for?" Nan asks.

"For her hangover," Gran says.

"Thank you," I say, "will this make my headache go away?"

"Only if you keep up the liquids all day," Gran says.

"I will."

"Well, your Nan has some news of her own to share," says Gran.

"Yes," Nan says, shifting in her chair. "This is the right time, I suppose." She clears her throat and looks down at her hands. "La Lande du Breil has a graduate program." She looks up. Our eyes lock and we are all silent for a full minute. "They have a spot for you."

"What? I'm finally almost finished with school and able to spend more time here, and you want to send me away?"

As a high school graduate, I was accepted by ten colleges all over the country. Nan helped me look for schools with strong horticulture science majors. My plan was to be a horticulturist so that I could bring new ideas and knowledge back to my grandmothers' gardens. I had no intention of leaving Los Angeles for school. My dream was to take over the care of Nan's garden someday, and maybe we could return to our Sundays on the veranda. But Nan insisted that I apply to a list of prestigious schools. She'd said, whatever I wanted to be, I needed to go to the best program, and there were no schools in Los Angeles with a horticulture degree. I relented and agreed to apply to her entire list of schools as long as I could also apply to UCLA. I was accepted everywhere, except La Lande du Breil, the horticultural school in France that was Nan's first choice. Nan worked hard to conceal her disappointment. I worked equally hard not to show my relief. The French school did not want me, and I did not want it. To seal my college future, I maneuvered to miss the enrollment deadlines to all the other schools except UCLA.

Finally, Gran stepped in and called Nan off. "If Bella is so hellbent on staying home, then perhaps she should," she said one Sunday. "UCLA is a good school. She has plenty of time to launch herself out into the world."

After Nan delivers the news about La Lande du Breil, she busies herself with her breakfast, putting a plate of pastries on the table before returning to her seat. She does not meet my stare. I don't even ask her how she has pulled off this acceptance to La Lande du Breil without my participation.

"Is it so awful having me around? Haven't I been helpful?" I ask Nan.

Gran pulls out the chair next to Nan, sits, and says, "It is time for you to go, Bella."

"So, I am not needed here anymore?" I ask. My tears are rapid. "The two of you are sleeping together now? You're a couple, is that it?" It is an accusation.

Nan starts to speak, but Gran puts her hand on top of Nan's and Nan stops.

"Yes," Gran says. She squeezes Nan's hand and assumes that expression she reserves for delivering bad news and hard truths—sympathetic but resolute. "Three's a crowd," she says.

"But, but, but . . . we are one," I say. I am stammering now. I stand up so quickly that my chair falls backward and crashes to the floor.

"The world is a wondrous place, baby Bella," Nan says.

"Don't call me that!"

"Bella!" Gran says.

I run from the kitchen. I grab my keys from the breakfront by the front door and I leave.

"Bella!" Nan calls out.

"Let her go," I hear Gran say before I slam the door behind me.

When I get home, my father is waiting for me. I try to brush past him, but he grabs me in a hug that I do not want. I struggle to free myself.

"Dad, I can't talk right now," I say. But he is insistent.

"I really think we should." He leads me to the living room. Our living room is anything but. It is full of formal furniture we never sit in and old family pictures, mostly of Bernard and me, smiling into the lenses of cameras as if we are normal children with happy, normal parents. This room, so full of emptiness and broken promises, is the perfect place to have this conversation.

"I hear you won something important," my dad says.

"Yes. I'm going to go to Toronto, win the competition money. And then, I am going to move to New York."

"Oh! Is this a plan you have been formulating for a while or just fomented in your head on the way home from Gran's?"

"Does it matter? I am not wanted here, so it's as good a plan as any."

"Bella, don't be like that. Your grandmothers love. . . ."

I shake my head no. I want to tell my father that the two women who have been my entire life just confirmed for me that our three is now a crowd. But I cannot bring myself to say the words. I can only shake my head.

"Do you know what your Nan told me last week?" Dad gets up from his chair and moves next to me on the sofa. "I was there to check on them. I stayed for dinner. They seemed so happy. Your Nan was so like her old self. And I saw something different between them. We talked about the garden, of course, and had a really nice time. On my way out, your Nan walked me to my car. And she said to me: 'Your mother is a magical being. We are two old women who are beyond easy and convenient classification, and we are two people who need each other.' I said, 'I know, Miriam.' Then she said, 'Even we old people need to be touched and awakened, you know? And we do that for each other. This, too, is a part of healing and living.'"

Dad stands up, puts both hands on his forehead, and fans his fingers out over his head, like he is combing through a full ghost afro instead of his mostly bald head.

"Bella, she was so sharp and so alive. Her eyes were back to where they used to be. Clear. I wasn't prepared to hear that. But who are we to deny them this?"

He pauses for my response. And I want to tell him that they are not the ones who are being denied. I am. *I* am their number one person. *I* am their confidante. I want to tell him that I don't have anything if they have erased me from their lives. I want him to know that I was a part of healing Nan, too. But now they are both so willing to just throw me away. And so, yes, I can make plans and go win awards, but the only people I really care about no longer care about me. I am the third wheel. I want to tell him that when Gran said that we were one, I thought she was talking about the three of us, but she wasn't. She was only talking about the two of them, and that makes me nobody. But I cannot possibly tell him all this. He has no notion of my world with my grandmothers. He has no idea of all that I have lost. I have always just been a sideline to his life. I have always been a footnote to my mother's. How could he understand what my grandmothers mean to me? He can't. So, I nod my head yes, I understand. And I stand up.

"Can I go to my room now? I have to get ready for class," I say.

"Of course. Just give your grandmothers a little space, okay?"

"I will give them all the space they need." And I mean it. I vow to never go back to that house or my grandmothers again.

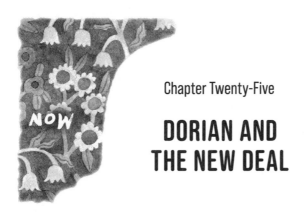

Chapter Twenty-Five

DORIAN AND THE NEW DEAL

DECEMBER

When Bella arrives at Dorian's apartment, the doorman is waiting for her.

"Ms. Fontaine?" he asks.

"Yes."

"Mr. Herman called to say that he is running a few minutes behind. He asked that I open the apartment for you. Can I help you with your bags?"

Bella hands over the two bags full of Dorian's favorite snacks—Marcona almonds, truffle chips, chocolate-covered caramels—and a bottle of pinot grigio that she could barely afford. She wants to let Dorian know that she appreciates him and all that he has done for her. She knows she has hurt him with her omissions about her grandmothers. Now that their carts are hitched together and they must be a team, she wants him to feel good about her again. Her show is on the books. She has representation. She wants to celebrate. And she wants to have celebratory sex tonight. She convinces herself that she wants Dorian.

The doorman unlocks Dorian's door and hands her the groceries. She steps inside, flips the light switch, thanks him for his willingness to bring her up. Bella closes the door and walks through the apartment turning on lights and making sure she is alone. She goes into Dorian's bedroom. His scent greets her at the door and escorts her throughout the space. She loves the smell he leaves behind—cologne, soap, an undertow of sweat. The bed is unmade. His dirty clothes drape on a chair and used towels on the exercise bike.

A pair of sneakers lie in a tumble in front of his bathroom door. She imagines Dorian kicking them off on the way to pee. In the bathroom, every item he used this morning is strewn across the stretch of dark gray granite. The sink still has a smudge of toothpaste in it. Bella has only been in this bathroom once before. She slept over and got dressed for a gig from her overnight bag. She felt then a little like she was in a hotel. But now, this entire space feels like Dorian inhabits every bit of it. It's lived in.

She briefly considers undressing and waiting for him in his bed. She has never done that kind of thing, but what if he arranged this whole late arrival, doorman-escort scenario to set it up? What if he wants her waiting naked under the covers? Bella knows this is not true. She wants to slide her dress off and slip into Dorian's unmade bed because she really wants this evening to end up here. But this is no longer the nature of their relationship, especially now, and it feels too manipulative after all that has happened today. She returns to the kitchen, opting to preserve her self-respect. She is unloading the food when she hears Dorian's keys jangling at the front door.

"Hey," he says walking into the kitchen.

"Hey, I brought some snacks."

"And I brought your favorite movie." He holds up a DVD of *The Godfather*.

"You remembered my favorite movie?"

"Of course," he says. "Leave the gun, take the cannoli!"

"And you know that I can't afford to stream," Bella says. "That is so super cool of you, Dorian." She is happy with this sign that Dorian is on board for forgiveness and maybe a night together. "Are you trying to buy my affection?"

"Are you trying to reach my heart through my stomach?" he retorts.

"Maybe," she says. "Honestly, I am so in the mood to watch *The Godfather* with you. Good call."

"Me too." Dorian opens the bag of truffle chips. "You know I can't resist these." He takes a chip and moves to the living room to start the movie.

"I'll put these in a bowl and bring the wine," Bella says.

She gathers the food and uncorks the wine. It takes her two trips to the coffee table. She sits next to Dorian, who is already on the sofa, the movie almost queued up. Her new DVD still sits on the table, as Dorian finds the movie on his smart television. She pours two glasses and hands him his. "Toast. We find ourselves in this awesome place, thanks to you. Thank you for finding me and liking my work and liking me."

"Cheers," Dorian says, "I *love* your work, but what makes you think that I still like you?"

"You told the doorman to let me into your man cave before you got here."

"I thought you might clean."

"Oh, fuck you," Bella says and punches him on the bicep. "Never say that to a Black woman, man!" She punches him again.

"You're right. I'm sorry. You know I'm kidding." He is laughing and defending himself.

"Do I, though?"

Dorian hugs Bella to halt the flurry of blows to his arm and shoulder. She stops and sits back into the embrace. She turns her face toward his, expecting a kiss.

He releases her and sits at an angle, creating space between them.

"Listen, Bella." He is serious now. "We can't go back to how we were. We have to be just friends."

"What does that mean, exactly?" Bella asks, taken by surprise.

"It means no sex."

"No making out?" she asks, letting her eyes express her disappointment.

"Yes, it means no making out. We are now in a business partnership. We have to work together. This needs to be mostly professional."

"It's a little late to be mostly professional," Bella says.

"I don't mean that. I mean not a couple. Not complicated. Herman Gallery represents you now."

"How is this different than before? Didn't we always expect to be here?"

"Yes," Dorian says. "But things are a little different for me now. I don't know if you know this but relegating me to curate your show is not the recognition I was wanting. It's my mother's way of keeping me down."

"But I thought it meant that you were in charge of the show."

"It does and I want to curate it. It's really not that." Dorian is struggling to be understood. "I found you. I was the first person to bring you to us. But you are not a one-time thing. Finding talent is what I am good at, and I want to be the person directing that part of the business. I should be directing the gallery by now. I should be the director."

"Who is currently director?"

"Ellen," Dorian says as if Bella should already know this.

"And you thought by now she would step down and make way for you. But she is stepping away more and more, isn't she?"

"She doesn't think I am ready, even though I have been covering the things she is forgetting and leaving undone. I am doing the work."

"But this is her life, Dorian. It's where she is the most herself. Her gardening and the community garden are her hobbies, they give her the balance that allows her to be her even better self at work. She needs purpose. This is where she believes she changes lives. Surely, you understand why she can't let go."

"I don't want her to disappear. I want her to take a lesser role. She really can leave the day-to-day to me."

"What does she think you need to do to be ready?" Bella already knows the answer because Ellen told her that she does not believe Dorian has a good business sense. But Bella wonders if Dorian is clear on how Ellen feels.

"She thinks I am only good at the art part of the business— finding and cultivating artists, curating their art. And I *am* good at that, and it's the most important part. The business part is management mostly. It's not hard."

"So, you will prove that you can do all the other stuff with this show. And that is why we can only be friends with benefits?" Bella asks, trying to slide in a new suggestion.

"It's why we can only be platonic friends."

Suddenly, Bella thinks she has figured out what Dorian is actually saying. She takes in a quick audible breath.

"You have another girlfriend, don't you? Have you found someone new, Dorian Herman?" Bella is more curious than jealous.

"No, Bella. Are you not listening? That is not what this is about. I am just focused on work now. Now is the time for me to take my rightful place. And I need you to help me, by being my friend and a committed artist."

Bella doesn't really understand why sex would not make their alliance even stronger, but she sees that Dorian is trying to be taken seriously by his family. She saw firsthand at her contract signing how his mother and brother dismiss him.

"We are going to team up to make our show the best thing since sliced bread?" she asks. Dorian nods.

"Then I'm in!" she says.

"Deal." Dorian picks up their glasses and hands Bella hers. "Cheers."

Bella meets his eyes. "Leave the gun, take the cannoli," she says.

Chapter Twenty-Six

DESTRUCTION
AND FORGIVENESS

DECEMBER

Bella is sitting cross-legged in front of Sima's plot. She has arrived early, the entire garden still christened by morning dew. She has come to meditate at the Goddess's feet before anyone else arrives, while the garden is quiet. Bella likes the early winter hours at La Plaza Cultural. The garden is closed to the public and fewer members are still coming regularly. All the plot gardens are sparse. The fall pumpkins, cabbage, endives are gone and the weeping willow is already naked.

Bella approaches Kali-ma. "Good morning, Goddess. I would like to express my gratitude—for the past." She places the first of three smooth stones she collected from the edge of the pond surrounding the Prima Lingua fountain. "For the present." She places a second stone in the middle spot. "And for the future." She places the last stone and then settles on the ground in front of Sima's plot. She takes a deep breath and tries to gather her thoughts about her art show and an upcoming gig she has for a neighboring community garden just a few blocks away that hired her to take promotion pictures for their upcoming lecture series.

In this moment, she feels that her life is bountiful and on track, and she is grateful.

"Thank you," she says out loud. And then she closes her eyes and tries to clear her mind by focusing on her breath. When she does this, she notices for the first time how noisy is the silence around her—the birds in the nearby trees are still boisterous. She can hear Stan's bees whizzing by, and the trickling of the fountain just around the bend. She wants to express gratitude for all these busy lives in the garden. She is so happy to be a part of their world.

"Thank you for letting me be a part," she says out loud. She takes another deep breath and smiles widely in appreciation.

Have you forgiven the destroyer yet, Bella? the Goddess says.

"I am not sure," Bella answers back.

Forgiveness is a form of gratitude. Did you know that? asks the Goddess. *When you acknowledge all the rights that have grown out of the wrongs, and the gifts that you thought were curses, you have opened up room in your heart for those who were responsible. That new room in your heart is forgiveness and gratitude—they are two sides of the same coin.*

Bella is trying to understand the Goddess's words. This is about her grandmothers. Perhaps it's about Bella's decision to forge their signatures on the consent forms for the Herman Galley. She feels certain her grandmothers wouldn't care. But the truth is, she is not sure she knows her grandmothers at all anymore. This is what gives her pause. Maybe the new version of Nan and Gran, the new and different people who chose each other over their granddaughter—maybe they would not be willing to sign the consents. Bella is deep in this contemplation when she hears footsteps approach. She opens her eyes.

Ellen has found her. She has surprised Bella with her early and unexpected arrival. Ellen usually comes in the afternoon.

Bella invites Ellen to sit. It takes her a long time to land in a sitting position and she complains about the stiffness in her legs as she attempts to cross them. Bella tries to explain who the Goddess is and why she is sitting before her. Now, Sima strolls up. Bella wonders, *Why has everyone decided to descend upon the community garden this morning?* She supposes everyone has the same idea as she did, to get an early start. They all know that days left to garden like this one, clear and relatively warm, are few before the winter fully sets in. Sima is wearing her usual tattered khaki shorts. Today, she is sporting blue Converse sneakers crusted with dirt.

"I see you like my plot," Sima says. Bella detects a thin thread of condescension in Sima's words, or is it just her imagination?

"Yes, I have become attached to your Goddess," she admits.

"Ah, yes, Kali-ma is hard to resist," Sima says and sits down beside Ellen. "Do you know her story?"

"A little bit," Bella says. "When I discovered her in your plot, I did a little more research."

Sima gives an approving smile. "I love her because, for me, she represents destruction for the purpose of new life."

Bella tries not to roll her eyes, but she is thinking, doesn't everyone know that she represents death and destruction? Does Sima really have to express things in a way that implies that her knowledge is special and the rest of us know nothing? Bella almost stands up and walks away. But she looks at the Goddess, who is sticking her tongue out at her. *Forgive the destroyer,* Kali-ma whispers. Bella takes a deep breath. And another.

Sima continues, "In the Hindu Trinity of male gods, there is a creator, Brahma. There is a preserver and sustainer god, Vishnu. And so there must be a destroyer. This is Shiva's role. The Goddess Kali or Kali-ma is the feminine deity who represents this same concept of death and destruction. She is not

Shiva in female form. Oh, no, in fact, the Goddess Kali is most often depicted standing on top of Shiva's prostrate body. Shiva is her husband. The story goes that Kali was charged with the task of killing a nasty demon . . . oh what is his name? Well, this was a tricky task because if you tried to kill this demon, every drop of his blood that hit the ground would spawn another demon. But not to worry, this badass goddess had a plan. When Kali-ma killed the demon, she drank every drop of his blood. Problem solved. But the demon blood made her drunk and crazy. She went into a rage. You know how angry drunks can be! And she killed every demon and bad thing in sight. She raged and raged upon them, killing and stomping their remains into the ground. The other gods got worried that the rage might start to damage other things, so they went to her husband, Shiva, and said, 'Do something about your wife.' And Shiva said, essentially, 'I tried, but she's in a state.' When the other gods insisted, Shiva decided that the only thing he could do was prostrate himself under her feet. When he did that, and Kali found herself stomping on her husband, the crazy spell was broken, and she calmed down."

"A woman after my own heart," Ellen says.

"Yes," Sima says, "she is fierce *and* efficient. We submit to her as the destroyer of our obstacles to enlightenment and those parts that no longer serve us. She will devour them completely, leaving no trace."

"I love that," Bella says, admitting that she is grateful for Sima's version of Kali's story.

"Me too," says Sima. "Are you the one who leaves the three stones?"

"Yes. They are offerings, three prayers, I guess."

"You guess?" Ellen says.

"They are three wishes or intentions. Yes, they are prayers," Bella says, feeling self-conscious.

"Lovely," says Sima.

Beth calls to Sima from the amphitheater. Beth's loud, raspy voice cuts through Bella's new appreciation for Sima before it can even begin to bloom.

"I am scheduled to work," Sima says. "I will leave you two with the Goddess." She stands from her squat. She joins Beth and they embrace. Something about the couple's embrace bothers Bella, makes her uncomfortable. Ellen notices Bella staring.

"They are my favorite people in the garden besides you and Geri," Ellen says, "but you don't seem to care for them, at all. I didn't figure you for homophobic, dear. That's not it, is it?"

"Of course not," Bella says, quickly turning her gaze back to the Goddess.

"Do you love Kali because she can destroy your past, Bella? Are you drawn to the Goddess, or are you drawn to those two lovely women on whose plot she resides? You seem conflicted, my dear."

"Dorian and I are no longer involved romantically," Bella blurts out, a clumsy, obvious attempt to redirect the conversation.

"Have you finished your prayers? Can we get up now?"

Bella obliges, even though she hasn't had enough time with Kali. She stands and offers Ellen help. Ellen grabs both arms and Bella pulls until Ellen is on her feet.

"So, what happened?" Ellen asks as they walk to her plot.

"Now that I am signed with the gallery, we thought we should be professional, not mix business with personal."

"Oh, Bella, that ship has sailed, honey. Our business *is* personal. We represent you now as an artist. We think of you as family. We will do for you as if you were our daughter. In a very real sense, our fates are tied."

"Well, then Dorian and I have decided to shift into a more family kind of business relationship, I guess."

"Do you think I have never slept with an artist? I have gained some of my best insights by doing so."

Bella stops and looks at Ellen. The woman who married into the Herman Gallery family is telling Bella that she cheated on her husband of sixty years in the name of art.

"Oh, don't look at me like that. My husband did too. It was the seventies," Ellen says. She sits on the bench across from her plot and pulls her knee pads out of her satchel. "I am just saying. I would prefer to hear that you are stepping away from the relationship to create more work. Now, *that* might be good news. Relationships take time and so does creation. We cannot sell what you have not created. What *are* you working on now, Bella? What's next?"

"I have several projects in the works," Bella says, choosing to move past the parts of Ellen that are disturbing to her. She is getting good at this. "As a matter of fact, I have a series of photos from the community gardens in this area, including, of course, this one. They focus on the planting cycle. I am using time-lapse photography to capture a number of plots at once. The footage is surprising. It looks a little like a competition—like the plots are racing with each other to the sky. Competition seems like a human concept imposed on the plants, right? But is it? Plants are competing for resources all the time, right? It's pretty cool."

Bella continues, "I also have a kind of *Secret Life of Plants* idea—I am comparing urban planned growth with wild growth in the city—exploring how plants subsist in obscure places here in Manhattan, how they are hidden in plain sight, out of our consciousness—*Where the Wild Things Are* in New York, so to speak. Those pictures will surprise you too. There is an abandoned school on Ninth Street. It's been closed for years. It has a tree growing out of a window on the fifth floor!"

"Interesting. Excellent. I look forward to seeing the results."

Ellen is leaning over her plot and pulling out what is left of her fall annuals. "If you and Dorian are cooling your heels because you want to focus on work, fine. Good. We need both of you to be productive. But if you are cooling your heels because this relationship is just not that hot, well, that's fine too. Just both of you be honest about it."

Bella kneels next to Ellen to help. But Ellen shoos her away. "Go work your own garden."

"Yes, ma'am." Bella grabs her backpack and decides that, with all this talk of productivity, she will take some pictures instead.

"By the way, Bella. Don't worry about your grandmothers and those releases. I will deal with Frank."

Ellen says this so matter-of-factly that Bella wants to ask her to repeat herself. This is the final piece to fall into place for her show. Ellen is telling Bella that there will be no obstacles. Bella will not have to face her grandmothers or forge their consents, as she had planned. Finally, Bella has certainty. Her show is, in fact, going to happen.

She tries to match Ellen's nonchalance with a silent nod and a measured smile. But she makes a note to thank the Goddess Kali-ma on her way out.

Chapter Twenty-Seven

EYE OF
THE HURRICANE

THE HERMAN GALLERY
Presents
A Collection of Works by
Bella Fontaine
July 4th—6:00 p.m. to 9:00 p.m.

Dorian

"You must be calm," Dorian says to Bella, "You must be confident and steady." They are standing in the Herman Gallery conference room. "This is the eye of the hurricane," he says, "the last two weeks have been a crazy flurry, and hopefully you will get a crazy flurry of interest and coverage starting tomorrow. But tonight is your moment to take a deep breath and shine. You get to take in everyone's reaction to your photos. Some will love the show, some will not. Some will be moved, and some just won't get it. But it's all okay because reaction, any reaction, is good. We want to cause a stir. You will win hearts and change minds. Tonight, you will create fans and patrons."

"Oh, Dorian, that was amazing!" Bella says, genuinely impressed. "Did you practice that speech too?"

Dorian and Bella have just rehearsed their show speeches. Dorian asked Bella to submit prepared remarks two weeks earlier for his review and approval. She has been practicing in her bathroom mirror and on the roof in front of her plants ever since Dorian turned her speech back to her with his comments. She nearly has it memorized. Today is the first time she has had a chance to hear what Dorian will say to introduce her and launch the show. He has memorized his short remarks too.

Bella feels like a different person, partially because Dorian treats her as if she is his new creation, and partially because she is wearing a new red dress that Dorian bought her for this occasion. The dress is fitted at the bodice and then flairs out from the waist. She is wearing black platform sandals that add two inches to her height. When he presented this dress to her two nights ago, she told him that she had already decided on what she would wear—her usual all black.

"Black is my comfort uniform."

"Everyone will be wearing black," he said. "We want you to stand out."

"But I am a photographer, my job is to be invisible. That's why photography suits me. Isn't it better for my art to stand out and not me? What if I just wear red lipstick."

"Just red lipstick? And nothing else? That would be something!"

"You know what I mean. Is it customary to dress the artists you represent?"

"We do everything necessary for you to be successful," he'd said. "I am curator of this show, and you are a part of it. You trust me, right?"

"Oh, so I can't be your girlfriend because you want me to be your creation?" Bella says in her best flirtatious voice. She has enjoyed these weeks hounding Dorian about being his girlfriend, testing his resolve to be professional.

This game—Bella acting like a lustful artist and Dorian, the disinterested professional, has given them a way to channel their tensions and provided an alternative focus when things get adversarial between them. The sexual tension has been building and it has added a playfulness to their hard work. Dorian's favorite refrain, "Please Bella, let's be professional," to her favorite new taunt, "I don't have to be professional, I'm the artist," has allowed Dorian to try on the role of the alpha male, while permitting Bella to play out her tempestuous artist persona.

The truth is, with all of Dorian's efforts to prepare Bella and set her show up, the two have never been more of a couple. He has taken Bella to every photo gallery exhibit in the New York tri-state area. They've visited the MET, MOMA, The Whitney, and the Guggenheim. They spent two afternoons at the Studio Museum in Harlem, took the train twice to the Brooklyn Museum. They've viewed dozens of videos of artists' television and podcast interviews. They've listened to past recordings of radio spots. They've read magazine features and interviews in print together over coffee, lunch, and late-night dinners. Once they turned their attention to the details of Bella's exhibition pieces, they spent days making the final cut for which would be included, composing the invitation list, and taking promotional pictures. They've argued about photo titles and descriptions and wall space.

They've told each other their innermost fears, which turn out to be identical—they are afraid the show will fail. And since they both agree that failure is not an option, they agreed above all else, they would trust each other.

So, Bella is wearing the red dress and the red lipstick. She has her speech in hand when she and Dorian descend the stairs

EYE OF THE HURRICANE

to the first-floor galleries. When they reach the central gallery where her work is displayed, she enters and takes in her photographs. This is the first time she has seen all the lighting and room features finalized. Bella pretends that she is a guest seeing everything for the first time, and she is immediately enchanted by the totality of the space. Her photos have been enlarged and reframed. They are mounted in what is essentially a black box studio, the walls, ceiling, and floors all painted black. This allows the subjects to appear as if they are floating in a void. The *Little Girl in Landscape* photos are in color. The *Home* series—the pictures of her grandmothers—is in black and white. The audio of her poem, *An Ancient Girl*, is already playing. It has all come together exactly as it should, but far beyond her imagining. It's like magic, she thinks, *Dorian and I have made magic.*

The previous night, when all the photos were unwrapped from the framers in their new sizes and then mounted, she looked at them, actually looked at them, for the first time since her move to New York. Even as she and Dorian debated and argued over what to include, she hadn't looked at them in the way she did last night, mounted on the wall and big enough to face Bella down eye-to-eye.

She approached the first photo. It is of Gran. Bella met Gran's insistent gaze. At first, approaching the photo felt like an act of bravery. Gran, larger-than-life, lit by the overhead spotlights so that every detail was heightened, emboldened. But the closer she got, the more it felt like a homecoming, just as it was intended. Gran's face is the map of Bella's childhood—every freckle and mole, every sparse eyelash, every crease at the edge of her smile. Her gentle eyes, the kind that comes from knowing all the answers before you even ask the question. She is looking into the camera with an expression Bella recognized. She is proud of her granddaughter. It is a look that says, I know you.

301

When Bella took the pictures for a college class final project, she spent one entire day photographing Gran in the garden. It turned out to be a perfect mid-fall day—clear sky, orange Southern California sun overhead. It was a workday for Gran. She had planned to spend hours in the garden clearing summer and fall away and preparing for winter. Bella combined those pictures with photos she'd taken of Nan one Sunday when she was still in high school. It didn't take a full day to shoot Nan in her garden. She was not the shy subject that Gran was. This picture of Gran, the one that is Bella's favorite, was taken after hours of shooting once Gran had gotten comfortable with the camera. It is a close-up shot right in that moment when she no longer just sees an intrusive camera, but instead, the person behind it. Gran's expression is a look of recognition and unconditional affection. Bella chose ten photos from that shoot for her project submission.

The last picture of this set with Gran was taken after she had cleared the vegetable beds. She and Bella had already harvested pumpkins and Gran had two flats of cabbages to plant. She was wearing old Levi overalls, which she only wore on heavy labor days. In the photo, she has the hoe in one gloved hand and, in the other, a small late-forming pumpkin that she holds up by the vines. Her face is smudged with dirt, and much of her gray hair has come out of the barrette and frames her face like a white halo. Her cheeks are flush, her eyes playful. She is teasing the camera now, holding the hoe and the pumpkin out to the side in a victory pose. She is sticking out her tongue.

Bella stood transfixed before this last picture of Gran. At first, she focused on her tongue, and then the pumpkin, and then Gran's worn boots, the rounded toes peeking out from under the hem of her overalls, which are too long and drape generously on the ground. Bella noticed behind her, just out of focus, is the cleared vegetable bed and a pile of dead leaves and roots. Gran looks exactly like Kali-ma, satisfied with her destruction, weapon in one hand, severed head in the other.

Even today, as Bella stands before the photo again, she is astonished that years ago, long before Gran and Nan banished their granddaughter, Gran knew who she was and what her task would be. And as always, she was right.

"Everything okay?" Dorian asks. He has walked up close behind Bella.

"Yes. Just trying to see everything with new eyes."

"And? What do you see?" He puts his hands on her shoulders and closes in behind her. Bella doesn't want to share what she now knows about her goddess grandmother.

"I am seeing that you want me to be your girlfriend," Bella says, sure to make him back away. But he doesn't.

"I do want you to be my girlfriend," he whispers in her ear. "Just not yet."

"Just not yet?" Bella repeats. "Who says that, Dorian?" She is laughing, shaking her head. "Why are we playing this charade? For whose benefit? Ellen's?" She turns to face him, feigns seriousness. "You know your mother loves me more than she loves you, right? You would do better to hitch yourself up to this wagon, sir. I am the rising star."

"That you are," Dorian says.

"Recognize," Bella says, and she walks a few steps away to put some distance between them.

Dorian looks at her, fully willing to play along, but then something behind her catches his eye. He turns on his heels and calls for Edwin, the maintenance person in charge of operations tonight. He directs Edwin to clean off one of the spotlights shining on the photo of Gran, where Dorian has spotted a cobweb. Edwin runs to get a ladder to complete this last-minute task before guests arrive.

Bella sees that her teasing has had the desired effect. Dorian gets a self-esteem boost whenever they play this game. Bella's petitions to be his girlfriend always seem to give him a testosterone hit that makes him shift into the master-of-the-universe version of himself. And this is the version Bella likes the most. He is confident and commanding. He stands up to his mother's demands. He can dismiss his brother's arrogance. For the short time that he feels in charge of himself and his surroundings, he is Bella's hero. The game is fun and satisfying for Bella, and she is certain that if they were actually a couple, the sex would be epic too. But she also knows that she is not good at sustaining this way of building him up. If they were together, once the "why can't I be your girlfriend?" theme is no longer useful, Bella wouldn't have another play to bring forth Dorian at his best.

Ellen

Ellen finds Bella still standing alone in front of the last photo of Gran. She wraps her arms around Bella's waist.

"Are you seeing what I am seeing?" Ellen asks and waits in silence for Bella's answer.

"Yes."

"I learned about the Goddess Kali-ma just last fall from you and two wonderful old ladies at La Plaza Cultural," Ellen says, "and now, here she is. Was this your intention, your vision, when you took the picture?

"No."

"So, do you consider this a sign?"

"When I first sat before Kali-ma in Sima's plot, the Goddess told me to forgive the destroyer," Bella tells Ellen, "and last night when we were finishing up, I was putting the stones in front of the photos, and I finally understood. I was dumbfounded, but then I remembered this is how things are with my grandmothers. Forgive the destroyer, forgive the destroyer. I get it, Gran! I understand now, so I have already forgiven the destroyer."

"Have you?" Ellen asks, sounding surprised, approving.

"Yes, I want to express my gratitude to my grandmothers for sending me away. And I will as soon as I am able."

Ellen exhales deeply and holds out her arms as if this is the news she has been waiting for. "I am so happy to hear that. Very good! Your own forgiveness will save you, you know, Bella, dear. That is how forgiveness works." She grabs Bella's shoulders and turns her so that they are face-to-face.

"So now, the press is here, waiting to visit with you," Ellen says. Bella smiles her practiced smile, and Ellen points toward the front of the galley.

"Take three deep breaths, dear. You must be confident and steady. This is the eye of the hurricane. The days leading up to now, you and Dorian have worked tirelessly, heroically. I am so proud of you both. Hopefully, you also have a flurry of activity starting tomorrow, due to lots of interest and coverage. Hopefully. But today is your day to be calm and centered—and to shine. Enjoy every reaction to your work. Some will love the show, some will not. Some will be moved and some just won't understand. But it's all okay because reaction, any reaction, is good. We want to cause a stir. You will win hearts and change minds. Tonight, you will create fans and patrons."

Bella feels for a moment like she is caught in a déjà vu. *Oh, Dorian*, she thinks. She should have known that he stole his pep talk from his mother. Bella is disappointed, but also impressed that Dorian has learned so well from this master. She follows Ellen's instructions and takes three loud inhalations.

"How do I look?" she asks Ellen, pressing her lips together to even out her lipstick.

"You look stunning. Like a work of art, yourself." Ellen heads to the front of the gallery and Bella follows her lead. But then Bella remembers she has something to tell Ellen. She grabs her arm and Ellen turns to her.

"I finished *for colored girls*," Bella says, referring to the first edition copy Ellen gifted her over Sunday tea.

"Oh? And? What did you get?" Ellen asks.

"I loved it. The language, the voices. The narratives felt old and brand-new. There were scenes that I could not relate to. But other ones that fit me perfectly, like my own clothes. It felt like Ntozake Shange was offering belonging and understanding. I don't know, validation. I felt like the reference to the rainbow, all the women in different colors, was a symbol of self-beauty, in all the variations and complexities of Black womanhood. I felt like she was saying to me, you are perfect even with all your stuff. It felt like an ancestor saying to me, you belong right when and where you are." Bella shrugs. "That's what I got."

"Well," Ellen says, taking in a quick breath and nodding, as if to sort all the thoughts Bella has offered her. "That's beautiful, Bella. Of course, I did not know what you would find. I just suspected that you would find something important. And my goodness, you have. Promise me we will take this up next Sunday, once the dust from tonight has settled, yes? Promise?"

"Yes," Bella says, remembering for the first time that there will be a tomorrow after this climactic day. She is having a hard time imagining what tomorrow will look like, but she appreciates Ellen's reference to their future together.

"Now take that belonging that Ms. Shange has reminded you of and apply it to this moment, Bella, dear. And remember, if you find yourself having difficulty with any of it, I am here," Ellen says and gives Bella's shoulders a reassuring squeeze.

When you are a part of a Herman Gallery event, you must

always remember that no matter the artist or author, no matter the celebrity or guest, Ellen Herman must always be the sun of this orbit. Bella learned this from being Ellen's frequent companion and through her photography work with the gallery. When you are clear about this fact and surrender yourself to Ellen, all will go smoothly. Bella is hoping that Dorian remembers this, too, and allows Ellen to do what she does best.

Tonight, Ellen is dressed to shine. She is wearing a sequined black-and-gray blouse over black silk slacks. Her outfit somehow sets off her salt-and-pepper hair, and the lighting catches the sequins, adding a sparkle as she makes her way across the gallery. Her slim figure creates the illusion that Ellen is taller than her actual height. But really, it is her personality that commands the room. She is the ultimate hostess. She seems to know each person and where to direct them in the show. She ushers Bella through the pictures and short interviews. Bella repeats the answers that she and Dorian rehearsed for the questions that Dorian had, rightly, predicted. She was not prepared for the final interviewer, a forty-something, short, thin man wearing a beret.

"Ms. Fontaine, we understand that you have already secured your first sale, congratulations! And from such a famous New Yorker. Is Drip McAffrey a friend or is he a new fan?"

Bella looks to Dorian in surprise.

"Drip? Is he here?" she asks.

Dorian steps forward and addresses the reporter. "Yes, Drip McAffrey is a friend and a patron of Ms. Fontaine's. He has purchased two photos, *The Garden Goddess at Dawn* and *Me and the Goddess*. McAffrey and Bella met when she did a photo shoot of him right before he left for Milan, Italy. As you may know, he is also an artist represented by the Herman Gallery. They have a mutual admiration for each other's work." Dorian looks now to Bella for endorsement.

"Yes, we are," is all Bella can muster. She is close to tears and looking around for Drip.

"We understand that he paid twice the asking price for the pieces," the interviewer says.

"Yes," Dorian says, "he wanted no competition. He is unable to be here tonight, unable to leave Italy. So, he wanted to secure his purchases and express his support of Bella."

"Twice the price?" Bella says out loud. Dorian grabs Bella's arm from behind and pulls her closer into his side. He is trying to reign her in. She turns her attention back to the reporters.

"So, you are a fan of his work, as well," the reporter says, "does that mean that you have commissioned a famous McAffrey tattoo? Perhaps, you two are more than friends and colleagues?"

Bella blushes and is not sure why. "No, we are only friends. I do not yet have one of his tattoos, but I think they are the most beautiful I have ever seen. He is a kind person and an enormous talent."

"Yes, we will be showing his work next May at the end of his second season with Olimpia Milano."

"Ah, May," the interviewer says, "we will look forward to that."

"Yes," Bella says, "I know it will be extraordinary." She looks to Dorian to see if there is something else she should say. Dorian nods in agreement.

"So please be sure to see the full show. Start in the first gallery and please enjoy!" Dorian ends the interviews and ushers Bella away from the group and says, "Good work."

"Why didn't you tell me about Drip?"

"I was going to surprise you during my remarks. I guess Ellen wanted to give the reporters a heads-up, sometimes they don't stay long enough to hear our program."

"Twice the price, Dorian? Why didn't we give him the friends and family discount?"

"He didn't want the friends and family, Bella," Dorian says, laughing a condescending laugh. "Drip loves you, you know? He wanted to be your first and he, as is his way, wanted to go big." Dorian has stated facts but in a kind of question, as if he wants to know for himself if there is more between Bella and Drip.

"You know Drip and I have never . . . we aren't. . . ." Bella has a hard time getting it out.

"I know," Dorian says.

"You already asked Drip, didn't you?"

"Of course, I did!"

"Of course, you did," Bella says as she and Dorian watch Ellen approach from the crowd.

Geri

"Our dirty friends have arrived," Ellen says, giggling at her gardener joke as she and Bella walk over to greet a large contingent from the community garden. Ellen welcomes the group and escorts them in. Geri hangs back with Bella.

"Excuse me, where is the photographer for this gig?" Geri says, pretending to look around, "I need to make sure she is on the case."

"The photographer is a man, and he is not your concern, miss," Bella says as Geri delivers a bear hug, careful not to smear Bella's makeup.

"Holy shit, you look super hot!" Geri says. "And yeah, it's my concern. This night has to be perfect, and rumor has it the best photographer is busy doing something else."

"Yes, she is busy doing things she is uncomfortable doing. She'd rather be taking pictures."

"Mommi, this is so awesome! I told you that when this moment came and you got all famous, I was going to have your back. Well, I am here for you, mama! I am so proud of you and so happy to be your friend."

"Thank you, partner. And I hope you are with me because seeing you reminds me—tomorrow after I hang up this fancy red dress, we have a retirement party gig at the Jewish Community Center."

"I know, I know, I'm there!"

"Okay, just confirming, 'cuz so far this little shindig hasn't paid *any* of my bills."

Ellen makes her way back to Geri and Bella. She hugs Geri and thanks her for coming and bringing their community garden friends.

"Bella, ten minutes and counting, we will start the program. Dorian will gather your family."

"Okay, I will be right there," Bella tells Ellen.

"Seriously, though," Geri is determined to make her point, "bask in this gloriousness, Bels."

"I know, I am, just as soon as I finish this speech, I will be able to bask."

"Whoa, who the hell is that? He has got to be your brother. He looks just like you."

"Yes, that is my big brother, Bernard," Bella says.

"Wait, did you ever tell me you had a brother, Bels? C'mon! Holding out on me?"

"I probably didn't," Bella confesses, "I'm sorry. But he hates gardens, and I hate sports, so we have pretty much dismissed each other for our entire lives."

"Well, he is here for you tonight, though, right?"

"Yes." Bella realizes Geri is right. Bernard did not have to come. This is not likely his scene. But he did, and Bella is grateful. Bella also sees for the first time that Geri is right about how much she and Bernard look like each other, and she wonders how much of it is genetics and how much is just that they wear the same cosmic childhood scars.

Bernard

Bernard is the first of Bella's family to arrive. He is alone and looking dapper in a black suit, white shirt, and no tie. Bella has already asked Stephanie to be in charge of him tonight, to which she happily obliged.

As Bernard approaches, Geri is called to help one of the older community garden patrons find the bathroom. Bella promises Geri an introduction when she comes back.

"Hi, Bernard," Bella says. She kisses both of his cheeks, a gesture that is new to them. She wants to show her appreciation for his presence and timeliness. "You are very early by Fontaine standards."

Bernard's sarcasm is already primed. "Yes, I see all of the white people are here, which means the rest of us will be here shortly." Bella suspects he stopped off for a few drinks on his way here.

"You know Mom and Dad flew here together," Bernard says. "Amy is meeting Dad at his hotel."

"What do you mean?" Bella says, sure she misheard Bernard.

"Dad let it slip that he was flying down to LA from Portland to accompany Mom on the flight."

"But Mr. Blackshear is coming with Mom, and plus, she no longer needs a support animal to fly."

"Yeah, fishy, right? Unless I'm crazy, I'd swear there is something going on between them," Bernard says.

"Well, that's easy. You're crazy."

"We'll see." Then Bernard changes the subject. "I have come with my press pass, so I expect to be given the same deference as my media colleagues."

"By all means. But you may be opting for a lesser status than brother of the artist," Bella says, "because your dear sister, you know, the artist, has arranged your own private docent." Bella points to Stephanie, who is already making her way over. "You remember Stephanie, don't you?"

"Oh, yeah, okay then, fuck the press," Bernard whispers. He puts his press pass in his jacket pocket.

Stephanie arrives and Bernard greets her, "Hey, Stephanie!"

"Hey, Bernard. Let me take you through the show." Stephanie grabs Bernard's arm.

"Later," he says to Bella.

"Don't go too far, Bernard, they want family upfront for the presentation," Bella says.

"I will deliver him back in plenty of time," Stephanie says, shifting to her professional air even though she is not officially working tonight.

David

When Bella sees her father, he and Amy are standing in front of the last picture, *Little Girl in Landscape*. It is a photo of a small girl standing in front of the Garden Goddess, her hands joined in prayer, tips of her fingers pointed to the sky. The frame angle is a close-in aerial shot. Bella used a ladder to take the picture so that the viewer has the perspective of the ancestors looking down on the girl from heaven.

"The little girl in the photos, who is she?" David asks, after he and Bella greet, hug, and kiss each other. "She looks like ten-year-old you."

"She's Amanda, Mr. Armstead's granddaughter, Gran's next-door neighbor," Bella says. Originally, Bella intended the girl in the picture to represent her. But Bella now thinks maybe she is Nan too. Little Amanda agreed to the photos one Sunday when her family joined Gran, Nan, and Bella in the garden for dinner. In the picture, she is wearing a pale yellow church dress.

"Why are there three boulders placed in front of all the pictures?" David asks.

"Stop asking so many questions and just take it all in, David. Jesus!" Amy says. She has deemed herself the art show expert. Bella sees that Amy is clearly still the boss of her father. She dismisses Bernard's news about her parents.

"Is that true, Bella? Am I not supposed to ask questions?" David asks his daughter, feeling out of place in the gallery setting.

"You are the father of the artist," Eddi says, walking up to join the group. "You can ask whatever you want."

Eddi has come upon them through the crowd like an apparition. She has Mr. Blackshear in tow. He looks dapper in a navy-blue suit.

"Hello, Eddi. Hello, Mr. Blackshear," David says, a little too formally. Bella shakes Mr. Blackshear's hand and hugs her mother. She thanks Mr. Blackshear for coming. David kisses Eddi on the cheek. Bella registers the softening of Eddi's stance and the slight brush of David's cheek against her mother's. Bella also catches how Eddi looks down and David briefly closes his eyes. It is a split second of intimacy so subtle that Bella would have missed it if she wasn't looking for it. She now believes that her brother was telling the truth.

"Amy, this is my mother, Eddi Fontaine and a dear family friend, Herbert Blackshear," Bella says.

Amy smiles and shakes their hands. She is uncomfortable already. She has to compete with the presence of Eddi Fontaine, who is not just her boyfriend's ex-wife and the mother of the artist, but a celebrity in her own right. Bella wonders if Amy knows the rest of it. Amy stands a little more erect. She is wearing a tight-fitting orange cocktail dress and matching high platform shoes. The orange dress highlights her tan and her blond hair. The bun at the crown of her head, with cascading curly tendrils, looks a little like an octopus has perched on top of her head. Even with her platform shoes, Amy somehow looks smaller than she is. And Eddi looks Amazonian standing next to her. Bernard's words come back to Bella—*how is the teenager?* In the black high-heeled boots her mother is wearing, Eddi is tall enough to face David head-to-head, eye-to-eye.

Bella marvels at how her mother has become a much more solid version of herself. She has gained muscle to her frame. She was already tall with broad shoulders, large breasts, and long legs. She is deeply tanned, and her arms and legs are toned and defined. It strikes Bella that her mother looks like she works outdoors. What has she been doing that has brought about this transformation? Eddi has let her shoulder-length hair go completely gray. She is wearing it straight, and it looks silky in a stylish bob cut. She is wearing a black one-piece jumpsuit over the boots, with a long green floral scarf draping her shoulders.

Amy is not trying to stand anywhere near this imposing figure. She seems to be looking around for a way to escape. Dorian picks up on this from across the room and makes his way over to the group. He says to Amy, Eddi, and Mr. Blackshear, "We have not met. I am Dorian Herman."

"The Dorian who discovered Bella and made all this happen?" Eddi asks. "So nice to finally meet you."

"Thank you, Ms. Fontaine. It is a pleasure to meet you," Dorian says to Eddi with a slight bow. He turns to Amy and then Mr. Blackshear. "Would you like to join me for a drink? I see your hands are empty."

"I could use a refreshment," says Mr. Blackshear. Bella notices that Mr. Blackshear checks in with her mother, who signals with a nod that she is fine.

Mr. Blackshear and Amy follow Dorian to the bar. Bella is so impressed with and proud of Dorian. *He is actually* doing *Ellen,* Bella thinks, *only his own smooth, confident version.*

Bella turns to her parents. "They want us upfront, but what is going on with you two?"

"What do you mean?" David asks.

"Don't play innocent with me." Bella takes an authoritative tone that surprises them both. "I am an adult and so is Bernard, and we are not stupid or blind."

"Your mother and I . . . your mother and I are. . . ." David can't form his words. But his quick attempt at an admission surprises Bella even as she demands it.

"We are rediscovering each other, Bella," Eddi says. "We have lost so much time."

"What about Amy?" Bella asks, reigning in her incredulity.

"I'm going to tell her as soon as we get back home."

"What are you telling her exactly, that you and Mom are back together? You live in different states, for chrissakes!"

"Don't worry about the details of our lives, Bella, honey," Eddi says. "Just be happy for us."

Bella closes her eyes and takes in a breath. She relaxes her shoulders back and down in an exaggerated motion. She shakes her head and smiles at her parents. They are both grinning, looking at each other in short awkward turns. David touches Eddi's hand gently. They lean into each other. *They are like children,* Bella thinks. So different from the people of her childhood who had such little levity or affection. Bella decides there is nothing left to do but to lighten up.

"I *am* happy for you, Mom," Bella says, looking from one to the other. "Jesus, it must be the yoga," Bella imitates her father, who turns a deep shade of red.

Chapter Twenty-Eight

ANCIENT GIRL

Eddi

Bella and her parents make their way to the presentation podium in the corner of the gallery. Bernard and Stephanie are already waiting. Ellen is standing at the microphone, her sons at her side.

"Good evening, friends. Welcome to the Herman Gallery," Ellen says and then waits for the crowd to quiet down.

"I am Ellen Herman. You may know that our family's gallery has been a part of this neighborhood and Manhattan's art community for seventy-five years. My late husband's family built this business primarily on a tradition of finding and promoting diverse emerging artists. And now my sons are taking up the mantle and bringing our family's passion into the twenty-first century. In the truest sense, the exhibit you have come to see tonight is possible because of the discovery and effort of my youngest son, Dorian." Dorian steps up to Ellen's left. The crowd claps.

"Before he speaks, I want to acknowledge a celebrity in our midst. Someone who has dominated the art and horticulture news in recent months for her spectacular exhibit in Los

Angeles. She also happens to be the mother of our featured artist tonight. Please help me welcome Eddi Fontaine."

Ellen holds her hand out to Eddi, offering her the podium. Bella doesn't expect her mother to step behind it, but she does.

"Old friends and new ones, thank you for this amazing New York welcome." Eddi's voice is like silk, smooth and soothing. The microphone loves her. She takes a long, deep breath. She does not have to wait for the crowd to quiet down; she is pausing for effect. In the silence, people move closer to the podium. She looks around at the walls and then to her right, directly at Bella.

"They say that artistic genius comes from terrible childhoods. Most specifically, childhoods with terrible mothers." Eddi turns to the crowd. "What you are witnessing before you here tonight, ladies and gentlemen, is inside the head of my beautiful and brilliant daughter, Bella—what was her childhood, saved by her grandmothers and their gardens."

Bernard moves closer to Bella and whispers in her ear, "There she is in all her glory. Somehow, this is about her again?"

"Shhh, she just called me beautiful and brilliant."

"You are so thirsty! Why are you rewarding her for speaking the obvious?"

"Bernard!" Bella says. She wants Bernard to park his anger for one minute, while she revels in her mother's transformation.

But Bernard continues, "I never took you for being so needy. But then, you did kill off your grandmothers, so. . . ."

Bella punches Bernard in the shoulder. She moves away from him and focuses on her mother's words. Eddi has been through a metamorphosis in the year and a half since she and Bella almost died on the roof. She is a polished package. She is dressed impeccably. She has muscles and bronze skin. Her makeup is soft but precise. Bella wonders if Eddi has someone representing her and telling her what to wear and to say. But more than her appearance, she seems to have shed all her phobias. This is the first time Bella is witnessing her mother speak in public. She would never have imagined her mother so confident and composed. Eddi is captivating. Bella looks out at the crowd, her eyes fighting the spotlight, to see if her mother is having the same effect on others as she is having on her.

Bella spots Dr. Bradford Ferguson near the entrance. He is standing next to a woman Bella does not know. The woman looks a little older than Bella. She is shorter, with a rounder, softer shape. Her skin is the color of caramel latte. She is wearing a conservative suit and cornrows snake up her scalp to a woven bun at the crown of her head. She has a kind face, in a no-nonsense kind of way. Bradford and this woman's positioning suggests that they came together. Their shoulders are touching, and they are slightly turned inward, toward each other. Ellen must have invited Bradford. And now, with his date, he gets to see Bella's entire life unfold before him. Thinking about how her show will be seen through Bradford's eyes is unsettling for Bella. But the good doctor is also seeing Ellen in her element and Bella knows it will be meaningful for him. He will know that Ellen is getting better. Bella tells herself that this is why she is glad he is here.

"My work is about the redemptive power of claiming our own little piece of the natural world, our gardens, and specifically about coming to terms with tragedy among beauty. What is life, after all, but tragedy among beauty and beauty among tragedy? Life and death happen in an eternal loop and at the same time, dependent on one another to move things forward," Eddi says and then pauses.

Bella turns to Bernard. "What is she talking about? Has she done something to Nan's garden?" Bernard meets her eyes. He gently grabs her bicep with his free hand, takes in a quick breath.

"Yes," he whispers, "it's not Nan's garden anymore, Bella. But it's amazing. You have to see it. Sorry to be the one to tell you."

Bella closes her eyes. She takes a very deep breath in. She looks at her mother, this new wonder before her, so strong and sure, and in this moment, she knows her mother is this new person because of the garden. *Forgive the destroyer.*

"How many of you here have been saved by a garden," Eddi continues, looking around the room. The community gardeners raise their hands and nod, their chatter beginning to swell. Bella looks at Ellen, who is raising her hand too. For a moment Bella believes Eddi is reading her mind.

"As I thought," Eddi says, taking back control of the room. "Unexpectedly, I was, too, and so was Bella. And many of us have created beautiful things directly out of our pain and our suffering. Yours may be your garden. Yours may be a painting. A song. A photograph." Eddi shifts her attention and her body toward Bella again. "Thank you, my darling Bella, for being your perfect self and for turning your lived experience into this—for sharing your beauty and your talent with all of us. I will boldly speak for all the adults in your past when I say, we are sorry for our part in all that you have endured and . . . you're welcome." The audience rewards Eddi with muted laughter.

"Thank you all and enjoy tonight." Eddi backs away from the microphone.

The room is now filled to capacity and the crowd's applause is a roar of cheers and chatter.

"Damn, she is good, I have to admit," Bernard says, "how did she get so fucking smooth?"

"Bernard, you have to forgive the destroyer," Bella says. Bernard looks at his sister for a long moment before he says,

"Which one?"

Blessed Miri and Kali-Ma

Eddi leaves the podium and makes her way to Bella. They hug and then her mother stands next to her and takes her hand. Bella is calmed by this. She wants her mother to transfer her composure and self-assurance onto her. Ellen returns to the microphone.

"Thank you, Eddi. They say talent runs in families, which seems a little unfair to the rest of us." Ellen pauses to laugh at her self-deprecating observation and the cooperative crowd chuckles along with her. She continues, "I am deeply thankful for the talent and commitment in my own family. Particularly, my son Dorian, who has curated this exhibition. I am so very proud to introduce him, so that he can speak to you about what you are experiencing tonight. But before I hand you over to him, I want to announce that, effective immediately, I will be stepping aside as Director of Herman Gallery. Dorian will be stepping up and into this role. He has been working tirelessly to prove himself and has shown us all that he is more than committed and capable to take on this new and important role. I present to you our new gallery director, Dorian Herman." Ellen turns to her left where Dorian is standing. They embrace. Dorian is smiling, but he is not surprised. Clearly, Ellen has already told him, and they've kept it a secret until now. Bella is a little sad and disappointed that neither of them, her two closest confidants, thought she should be let in on the announcement before now.

"Thank you, Mom. Thank you, all. My entire life has led up to this opportunity and now that it is here, my only desire is to be worthy of your trust going forward." Dorian is speaking to his mother. He turns to Bella and motions for her to join him. "About our wonderful show tonight."

Bella puts on her biggest surprise smile for Dorian and Ellen, who is standing on the other side of the podium. She blows Ellen a kiss. Dorian turns back to the microphone.

"*Ancient Girl* is actually a combination of two series of photos taken by Bella Fontaine. The first series, *Girl in Landscape*, was taken in her spare time while Bella was in high school, and the second, *Home*, was a school assignment while she studied photography at UCLA. Bella's work came to my attention when the *Home* series won first prize at the prestigious Klineberg Photofest, where it was shown in Toronto. Bella used the Klineberg prize money to move to New York to pursue a career in art and photography. For those of you here from her hometown of Los Angeles and those of you who know Bella from the East Village Community Gardens, you already know that she is as talented with a trowel and hoe as she is with a camera. She learned all that she knows about the plant world from her grandmothers because she grew up in their two magnificent gardens. She first intended to study horticulture, but instead focused her studies on photography. I must say, as a fan and a patron and her art dealer, I am so grateful to her and whatever circumstances led her to that decision."

Dorian turns and looks directly into Bella's eyes. They are standing very close, too close for a professional relationship. But they are too enraptured in the moment to know this. Dorian smiles at her. And the spotlights make his perfectly straight teeth gleam. She loves him in this moment. But then, she loves everyone in this room who showed up and filled the space and are spending time with her photographs, her work. Her heart is full. And the smile she returns to him is her whole face. Dorian, in turn, thinks Bella is her most beautiful in this moment, and he forces himself to turn back to the crowd, briefly looking down at his notes to get back on track.

"Before I turn things over to our artist, I also want to announce the first sale of the evening. The first sale of a first collection is a monumental moment for both artist and gallery, and for Bella it comes from a very special person. Drip McAffrey, formerly of the Brooklyn Nets, has purchased two of Bella's works on display tonight. He, unfortunately, could not be here. As you may know, he now lives in Italy, where he plays professional basketball for Milan. He has been a fan of Bella's from the very first time they met. And, Bella," Dorian addresses Bella by leaning into the microphone without looking at her this time, "Drip sends his love and a hearty good luck tonight. So, congratulations, you are officially an artist in demand!"

The audience swells in applause. Bella is light-headed and cannot catch her breath. She feels she needs a moment to take in all that has happened. Drip. Her first sale. Dorian's promotion. Her mother. It's all too much. But there is no way to stop this glorious train for her to gather herself. Dorian turns to Bella and holds out his hand.

"I present to you, Bella Fontaine," he says.

Now Bella is sweating in her armpits, and she cannot remember her memorized speech. She is comforted that Dorian placed a copy of her speech on the podium earlier this evening. She had hoped she'd be able to start her remarks without looking down at the paper. But she cannot even remember how to begin. When she takes over the podium, she does not see the speech. There are no papers at all. Dorian must have inadvertently taken Bella's speech when he picked up his. She looks over at him and he is having a quiet celebratory conversation with his mother and brother. Bella cannot get his attention.

Bella's mind is racing—what are the first words? How do I begin? Then Nan pops into her head and reminds her with her church lady wisdom, "Always start with a thank you."

"Yes, dear," Bella hears Gran's voice, "thank everyone first and the rest will come."

Bella thinks of the heroic job her mother just performed at this microphone and she decides she must at least try to follow suit.

Three deep breaths.

This is the eye of the hurricane.

Dorian.

"Thank you, Dorian, and congratulations. . . ." Bella stalls by looking over at Dorian and Ellen. And now the words come, "You were born to do this work and I feel so very fortunate to be a part of this new transition for the Herman family." Now what? The lights shining on the podium make it difficult to see the faces in the crowd. Bella looks out to where she knows Bradford is standing, but she only sees the outline of his frame. She is grateful for this. But it's no use, she cannot remember what she planned to say. Just as Dorian had warned her, she is too filled with emotion and excitement. There have been so many surprises and so many wonderful people. The words have escaped through the top of her head. Amy's octopus.

Then beyond the blur of the crowd, Bella sees the giant photographs of Gran and Nan. And they are smiling back at her from their frames. She closes her eyes for a second and imagines that only the three of them are here—Gran, Nan, and herself. She opens her eyes and decides to just tell the truth.

"I have led some of you to believe that my grandmothers are no longer living. But they are." Bella's words render the room silent. The room is so quiet, she hears a toilet flush in a distant bathroom down the side hall between galleries.

"I believed that the women in those photographs, the ones who raised me and taught me everything I know about love and life and God and nature, had changed and no longer loved me. So, they became dead to me. Several people in this room, knowingly and unknowingly, helped me realize that my grandmothers made the ultimate sacrifice for me. They knew, in all their wisdom, that they had to destroy the garden that was our lives together, so that I could cultivate my own. They knew they had to cut me loose. Otherwise, I would never have left home. I would never have gotten here. And here is exactly where I am supposed to be." Bella pauses to give the lump in her throat time to dissipate. She swallows hard, but it isn't moving.

"I wish they were here tonight so that I could say that I understand now, and so that I could thank them for everything. Everything. All that I am is because of them." Bella looks to her left at Dorian. "Thank you, Dorian, for finding me and working so hard to make this exhibition what it is." Bella looks beyond Dorian for Ellen, but she is not where she was.

"I want to thank Ellen Herman, too, for taking up a void in my soul and helping me come back to myself, but I am not seeing her. . . ." As Bella says this, the lights in the gallery go up and the crowd begins to part. There is Ellen coming toward her from the rear, arm in arm with Miriam James on one side and Olivette Fontaine on the other. The crowd widens into a circle around the three women. They begin to clap. Ellen points her clapping hands at Bella.

Bella is frozen in place. The sight of her grandmothers in the flesh overloads her brain and her heart. And she wants nothing more than to hear their real voices in her ears. Bella runs to them. Gran is bouncing in her place as if she wants to run to meet her granddaughter. They embrace and the crowd erupts again in applause and cheers.

"Calsap," Gran says.

"Angel," Nan says.

"I'm sorry," Bella says.

"No," says Nan, "Olivette is sorry. And so am I."

"We were wrong," Gran says, "what we did. The way we did it was not right."

"It was how it had to be done," Bella says.

"We have missed you so much," Nan says, "Your absence almost . . . it almost. . . ."

"Killed us," Gran says.

"We almost killed each other," Nan says.

Bella's family surrounds them and shields them from the onlooking crowd.

"Okay, Ladies, pull yourselves together," David says, "the show must go on."

"This *is* the show," Bernard says.

Stephanie

Stephanie has taken the trays of champagne from the caterers and assumed her favorite role, circulating the room, passing out the flutes for the traditional Herman Gallery toast. She is supposed to be off duty, but only she can do this job properly. Bernard is hovering on the edges watching Stephanie work the crowd. Bella watches him maneuver by maintaining his distance so that he can receive Stephanie's last glass of champagne. He wants her to end up with him. But he has some competition. Teonna and Lala are standing at a distance. They are watching Bernard watch Stephanie. They are both on board for facilitating this match up. Bella wonders if they are tracking Bradford, too, and what they think of Bradford's date.

Bernard is taking it all in. He is a good reporter, Bella concludes. She is glad he has found his calling. After he escorted his sister back to the podium, extricating her from their grandmothers' embrace, he retreated to his holding spot on the periphery. He knows that Stephanie's friends are surveilling him and he turns to catch Bella watching him, too, over her shoulder. He makes his way over to where Bella is standing. She has just clinked glasses with a group from the community garden and a couple who are regular gallery patrons, the gentleman a childhood friend of Frank's.

This is now Bella's job, to meet and greet every single guest and make a connection. Dorian is on the opposite side of the room. He is circulating too. Bella knows from their rehearsals that Dorian is purposefully asking guests if they have met the artist. And if they haven't, he either ushers them over to Bella for an introduction or sends them to her with a specific inquiry or comment. Bernard reaches Bella as Ellen begins her toast. Everyone raises their glasses again and Ellen says words of gratitude and well-wishes. She expresses her hopes and aspirations. She asks everyone for a coming together of intention, that Bella, this new talent, continue to be fruitful and productive. Her toast first sounds like a prayer and then a blessing.

Stephanie reaches Bernard just in time to hand him a flute. She tells him she will be right back and then takes two glasses to her girlfriends. Bernard holds his drink up in the direction of Stephanie, Lala, and Teonna and then downs his champagne in one bottoms-up motion. He looks back at them and they do the same. Bernard turns his attention back to Bella. Her crowd has moved on.

"The prodigal daughter returns," Bernard says. "Look at your grandmothers. Are they actually signing autographs, as if they have done something special here?" He shakes his head and laughs a good-natured laugh. "They are so *extra!*"

Now Bella laughs at his use of her word for Beth and Sima, who happen to be standing in the group of elders surrounding her grandmothers. Only right now does Bella realize how much the two women are like her grandmothers. They have found their tribe of gardening groupies. Some of them are holding their programs out to Gran and Nan, who are writing on them.

Bella can't tell if they are autographing, as Bernard suggests, or handing out gardening tips. You never know with these garden-obsessed folk. Bernard would not understand.

"So, Bella," Bernard moves in close so she can hear his whisper, "are you a lesbian, too?"

"No, Bernard. There are at least two men in this room right now that I'd like to sleep with. Well, actually, one I've been trying to sleep with, and the other I want to marry."

"Oh, fun, let me guess." He looks around, delighted to play this game.

Dorian walks over to Bella with Celine Thompson-Green. She is on the arm of a man who appears to be twice her age and three times her size. His shirt tails barely cover his stomach, and he is mostly bald with a long oily ponytail that falls at the nape of his neck, isolated and lonely in that sea of flesh.

"Bella, you know Celine Thompson-Green, and this is Sammy Russo. Celine is a longtime friend of the gallery and one of our best clients," Dorian says, more for Mrs. Thompson-Green's benefit than Bella's.

"So, the wedding photographer makes the big time," Celine says, smiling and pulling Bella in for a hug.

"Hello, Mrs. Thompson-Green," Bella says, "How are Allysia and Darryl?"

"They are good. Alli doesn't call her mother nearly enough, but that's how it goes." Mrs. Thompson-Green is fanning her hand in the air as if to dismiss a servant.

"You are a talented young woman, your wedding pictures were a-maz-ing," Sammy Russo draws out the word. "And these here tonight are stunning."

"You stole my word, stunning, Sammy," Mrs. Thompson-Green says. "I said stunning, dear, because they are."

"Celine is interested in *Gardens Take Time*," Dorian says.

"Yes, Bella," she says, "I want it. Even though I already have your work on my walls, I must have that one."

"That makes me so happy, Mrs. Thompson-Green," Bella says, "thank you."

"Please call me Celine. You have a bright future, Ms. Fontaine," Mrs. Thompson-Green says to Bella, "I knew you were special when I first saw your wedding work. We are running to another event," she turns to Dorian, "we'll talk next week."

"Thank you so much, ma'am," Bella says.

"Ugh, please, call me Celine!"

"I deeply appreciate your support and your patronage, Celine," Bella says, as she and Dorian have rehearsed. She hugs Celine again, more tightly this time.

"Keep up the good work, kid." Sammy Russo extends his hand and Bella remembers to exert a firm grip.

Dorian escorts the couple to the front doors of the gallery. Bernard closes in.

"Dorian. You want to marry Dorian," he says, "because he deserves it. And the two of you are practically married already. And you want to fuck . . . let's see . . . that guy over there." Bernard tips his head toward a young man who is standing with Geri near the bar. He is one of the young hipster members of La Plaza de Cultural. He looks like he came straight from the garden. He is wearing dirty black jeans ripped at the knee and the crotch and a gray stretched-out T-shirt that used to be black. He is sporting ancient red Air Jordans. His man-bun is perched on the very top of his head, with the sides of his head shaven clean. His long beard needs a trim.

"Really, Bernard? Okay, you are so, so wrong about that guy. And you are wrong about Dorian. He's the boss now. I've just been trying to sleep with him."

"Ah! Okay, then," Bernard resumes his search, "I am guessing you want to fuck . . . him." He points his champagne glass toward Dr. Bradford Ferguson. "That guy is almost too good-looking, though, right?"

As if on cue, Bradford turns and looks at them just as they are both admiring him. He smiles and heads in their direction. His date is mingling among the elder gardeners, waiting in line to speak with Bella's grandmothers. He is making his way through the crowd alone.

"Do you see those fucking dimples?" Bella says to Bernard, trying not to move her lips. As much as Bella is enjoying this banter with her brother, she is uncomfortable in this moment as she tries to minimize how she is feeling about Bradford. She has missed him. She came to realize some time ago that it was she, not Bradford, who might very well be the asshole between them.

"Dimples, Jesus, I might want to fuck him, too," Bernard says.

"Marry," Bella says, "he's the one I want to marry."

Bradford

"Congratulations, Bella," Bradford says.

"Thank you, Dr. Ferguson."

"What's up? I'm Brad," Bradford says to Bernard.

"Hey, man. Bernard. I am Bella's brother," Bernard says as they do an abbreviated dap–handshake combination.

"Yes, I see the resemblance. I already admire you, Bernard. You had to grow up with Bella. I imagine she was a tough sibling. She can be hard on a brotha."

"Yeah, the worst," Bernard says, enjoying himself. "You must not garden, then."

"No, not yet," Bradford says.

"You better get on that, Dude." They both laugh and do some more dapping.

"Of course," Bella says, "two peas in a pod. I am happy for you two to meet. You have a lot in common, two old men having been raised by two old men. Brad, just as I spent my childhood with my grandmothers, Bernard, here, spent his with his grandfather, Addison Fontaine."

"Was he not your grandfather, as well?" Bradford asks, confused by Bella's reference to her grandfather as belonging only to Bernard.

"Yes," she says, embarrassed. "We just sort of divided our grandparents in that way. Granddad Addison, quite literally, belonged to Bernard."

"He is no longer living. He *actually* died though," Bernard says. They both laugh at Bella's expense.

"Brad is a geriatric specialist, Bernard. He takes care of Ellen." Bernard shakes his head. He is impressed or at least pretending to be.

"Speaking of Ellen, Bella, I brought someone I'd love for you to meet," Bradford says, turning toward the elders where his date is still mingling. "Dr. Kathryn Bennett, over there, is a researcher. She is doing some groundbreaking work on dementia and behavioral interventions. When we got some of Ellen's recent test results back, I was so impressed with her numbers, I called Kathryn."

Stephanie appears at Bernard's side and loops her arm through his. "Sorry to interrupt, but can I borrow Bernard?"

Bella is certain the girls sent Stephanie over to intervene and clear the way for her to fix things with Brad. Once Stephanie and Bernard are gone, Bella has her chance.

"Brad, I owe you an apology," she says.

"No, you don't. Didn't you hear what I just said? You were right, I was being a, what did you call me again? A pompous, condescending, close-minded prick."

Bella cringes as he says the words. "That was uncalled for, and it proves that I was more of all those things than you."

"Are you always so competitive?"

"No, I promise. Tell me about your researcher friend again."

"Yes, Kathryn. She wants to study Ellen and all the things Ellen is doing to stave off her progression. How amazing was her speech tonight. Seemed like it was totally unscripted. Ellen is a marvel."

"Yes, she is," Bella says, "have you met the other marvels in the room? I see Kathryn has."

"I have not met your grandmothers yet. I was hoping you would introduce us."

"Of course, that would be my pleasure." She takes his arm and as she ushers him over to the group, she says, "I thought Kathryn was your date. I thought about scratching her eyes out."

"You did not," Bradford says.

"I did." Bella pulls his arm closer to her and meets his eyes. Maybe she could be a part of Dr. Ferguson's world. Maybe they could be together. Bella remembers that she is wearing a new red dress and red lipstick. This is by far the most dressed up Bradford has ever seen her. The realization gives her a boost of confidence. He has seen her at her worst and yet, here he is. She meets his eyes again and holds them as long as he lets her.

"I am pretty possessive, you know, Doctor. Your researcher friend got lucky, this time."

"You are something else, Bella Fontaine. You are *some-thing* else."

Chapter Twenty-Nine

THE ROOF

JULY 4TH

Bella's garden seems to know that it will compete with fireworks tonight. Each plant engages the strings of illuminated bulbs in a dance—the tilt and sway of their leaves and blossoms refracting and reflecting the light. It is spectacle—movement, color, and song—wind chimes in the gentle breeze.

Bella hands out sparklers and Bradford follows behind her with a lighter gun, setting everyone's sparklers ablaze. The Empire State Building is all lit up too—red, white, and blue. The sky is clear of clouds, and all that is left of the sun is the thinnest orange sliver along the horizon. Everyone plays with their sparklers like children—making circles and spelling out words. Gran has one in each hand, and she begins what looks like a folk dance. This reminds Bella to turn on the music—she connects her phone to the small portable speakers she brought up from her apartment. She chooses her Stevie Wonder playlist since he is Nan's favorite. And now everyone is dancing and waving their sparklers like wands to Stevie's classic, "Do I Do." As soon as anyone's sparklers peter out, Bradford hands out and relights replacements.

Bella's grandmothers sit down in the chairs near the azaleas to recover from their revelry. Bella pulls up a chair and wedges it between them. She just wants to take them in. She breathes in their scents—Gran's earthy smell, bergamot and lavender, and Nan's Estée Lauder. She takes one of their hands in each of hers.

Nan kisses the back of Bella's hand at the knuckles. "I have never seen anything this beautiful, Bella, including your young man . . . what is his name, Bradley?"

"It's Bradford, Nanny, but he is not my young man. He is just a friend."

"Yes, he told me to call him Brad. I remember now," Nan says. "He is lovely, apparently inside and out. So why is he not *your* young man?"

"Well, I think I am going to work on that. I think he's a keeper too."

"This *is* a little slice of heaven," says Gran. "How have you gotten everything to bloom at once?"

"Planning and a little luck, I imagine," Nan answers for Bella.

"Yes, planning and a little luck," Bella repeats. Hearing one of Nan's favorite sayings in her own voice, and not just in her head, makes Bella smile. Gran notices.

"What is it, Calsap?" Gran asks.

"I have missed you," Bella says. "I have not been a whole person without the two of you."

"Ah, but look around you, dear," Nan says. "You are beyond perfectly complete. None of us really are whole all the time. We work our entire lives to be. And let's be honest, whole is not necessary. We do with what we have and it's almost always enough. But look at all of this, your art show, your friends, your garden. . . ."

Gran chimes in, "This is a whole lot!"

Bella obediently looks around her roof. Dorian and Ellen are sitting at the table that was her gift, talking to Amy and David. Bernard and Eddi are standing at the roof's ledge looking at the skyline, her arm looped through his. Bella sees little-boy-Bernard succumbing to the spell their mother is casting upon him, and she is glad. Brad approaches her and her grandmothers with offerings of wine. He serves them and then quickly takes his leave. Bella is grateful that Brad has taken on the role of host, leaving her this moment with her grandmothers.

"Eddi tells me that this roof used to be a desolate place," says Nan. "A place you wanted to escape from . . . and now look at it. You have made it a sanctuary, dear."

"Well, you taught me well, Grandmothers."

"I suppose we did," Gran says, "New York suits you, Calsap."

"Yes, I think it does. It was dicey at first, but I am beginning to feel like I belong."

"Now that you are settled," Nan begins and then pauses, "I know I have no right to ask, but will you come to visit us? Will you come home some time, if we send you a ticket?"

"Yes, ma'am, I will," Bella says, "I have not yet been to see the Famous One's garden exhibit," she tips her head in her mother's direction, "and I would love to see what you are planting in yours. Has the garden been taken over by roses and hydrangeas yet?"

Nan gasps as if Bella has wounded her.

"No, dear," Gran says. "But the rhododendrons have not been the same and I have a theory that it is because they miss their sister."

"Then I will visit soon, I promise."

"With that promise, I think I am ready to call it a night," Nan says.

"Yes, I thought I conquered that mountain of stairs, but I fear it has conquered me," says Gran.

Now that the sun has fully set, the grandmothers recruit David and Eddi to help them one flight down, insisting that the party continue while they rest in Bella's apartment. Eddi and David take hold of their respective mother's arm and disappear through the door. Something about the fall of night and the summer's evening breeze draw kindred souls to each other. As the boom of fireworks begins to sound and showers of brilliant colors explode overhead, Bernard and Stephanie snuggle together on the garden bench, their faces turned up to the sky. Mr. Blackshear and Ellen cease their intense conversation at the table to find the source of the explosions. And to Bella's surprise, Dorian and Amy stand together, close together, at the roof's edge. They are deep in conversation, huddled face-to-face against the city skyline with fireworks shooting in every direction behind them. Bella pulls out her phone and takes the picture.

She and Bradford join Ellen and Mr. Blackshear at the table. Bradford sits at Mr. Blackshear's side and Bella pulls her chair in close to Ellen.

"Who is that young woman with Dorian?" Ellen asks.

"That's Amy, a friend of my father's. She is a kind woman. Likes to garden," Bella says.

"Does she?" Ellen asks.

"Yes. Her name is Amy Weiss. I met her at the gallery," says Mr. Blackshear. His mind, as always, a steel trap. "We had a nice long chat. Charming girl. She lives in Portland but is considering transferring. She says her accounting firm wants to promote her to the East Coast."

"She is an accountant?" Ellen asks. "And she could be Jewish. Weiss, Weiss. There's a chance she could be German, but. . . ." Ellen seems to be thinking out loud.

Mr. Blackshear fills her in. "Jewish . . . I asked her at the gallery, curious about her surname."

"Yes, that's right! She's an accountant," Bella says, remembering her conversation with Bernard. And suddenly Bella sees the lightbulb that is hovering over Ellen's head.

"There you go, Jewish accountant!" Bella says.

"There you go," Ellen repeats, "there you go!"

THE END

ACKNOWLEDGMENTS

Thank you does not seem an adequate sentiment for all of the help with this story and the development of this book.

I am so grateful to these characters for refusing to be quieted in my head. So different from my own experiences as a grand-daughter, daughter and mother, Bella, Olivette, Miriam, and Eddi refused to be denied and I am thankful for that and them.

A special thank you to the women in my family. My two grandmothers, Clemmie and Mary, were so intentional in their unique ways of cultivating the fertile garden that was my child-hood. My mother, Toni, and daughter, Jennifer, toiled in the multiple readings of the drafts of this book. Thank you for your time and patience, honesty, and encouragement. I simply could not have finished without your generational perspectives.

The late Michael Denneny once said that the editor's read-ing of a manuscript may very well be the only perfect reading of a book. I am forever grateful for his hand in the editing of this book and his generosity and care with this fragile first try. I take comfort in knowing that he is now with his friends, lovers, and the multitude of authors he championed who left this plane much too early before him.

Finally, deep gratitude to Anne Durette, for her sharp eye and careful, ruthless work to get this book where it needed to be.

ABOUT THE AUTHOR

 Gina L. Carroll is the author of *A Story That Matters: A Gratifying Way to Write About Your Life* and editor of *Stories Are Medicine: Writing to Heal, An Anthology.* A self-professed story wrangler, Gina founded StoryHouse Texas, a creative space dedicated to cultivating and amplifying the diversity of vision and voice in story. *The Grandest Garden* is her debut novel. She currently lives in Houston, Texas.

To learn more about Gina, visit www.ginacarroll.com.

SELECTED TITLES FROM SPARKPRESS

SparkPress is an independent boutique publisher delivering high-quality, entertaining, and engaging content that enhances readers' lives, with a special focus on female-driven work.
www.gosparkpress.com

A Story That Matters: A Gratifying Approach to Writing About Your Life, Gina Carroll. $16.95, 9-781-943006-12-0. With each chapter focusing on stories from the seminal periods of a lifetime—motherhood, childhood, relationships, work, and spirit—*A Story That Matters* provides the tools and motivation to craft and complete the stories of your life.

Child Bride: A Novel, Jennifer Smith Turner, $16.95, 978-1-68463-038-7. The coming-of-age journey of a young girl from the South who joins the African American great migration to the North—and finds her way through challenges and unforeseen obstacles to womanhood.

Seventh Flag: A Novel, Sid Balman, Jr. $16.95, 978-1-68463-014-1. A sweeping work of historical fiction, *Seventh Flag* is a Micheneresque parable that traces the arc of radicalization in modern Western Civilization—reaffirming what it means to be an American in a dangerously divided nation.

The Cast: A Novel, Amy Blumenfeld. $16.95, 978-1-943006-72-4. Twenty-five years after a group of ninth graders produces a *Saturday Night Live-*style videotape to cheer up their cancer-stricken friend, they reunite to celebrate her good health—but the happy holiday card facades quickly crumble and give way to an unforgettable three days filled with moral dilemmas and life-altering choices.

Trouble the Water: A Novel, Jacqueline Friedland. $16.95, 978-1-943006-54-0. When a young woman travels from a British factory town to South Carolina in the 1840s, she becomes involved with a vigilante abolitionist and the Underground Railroad while trying to navigate the complexities of Charleston high society and falling in love.

Just Like February: A Novel, Deborah Batterman. $16.95, 978-1-943006-48-9. Rachel Cohen loves her Uncle Jake more than anything. When she learns he's gay, she keeps it under wraps, and when he gets sick, she doesn't even tell her best friends—until she realizes that secrecy does more harm than good.